SAY HI 4 ME

(WHEN GRAVITY WAVES)

ISBN: 978-0-9995419-5-1
Library of Congress Control Number: 2019913110

Cover Artwork and Design: Raghu Consbruck
www.eighteyes.com

Published in the United States by Inword Publishers
Interior Design: Bhakti-rasa
www.inwordpublishers.com

For more information please contact:
Amy Tychell
www.mysyfytychell.com
www.facebook.com/ATychell
Genre: Science Fiction | Post-apocalyptic Survival |Humor

SAY HI 4 ME

(WHEN GRAVITY WAVES)

AMY TYCHELL

INWORD
PUBLISHERS

Prologue

Despite his antennae, George hadn't realized he was an alien on an unknown planet when he lifted his youngest daughter onto his knee. He thought he belonged. As much as anyone did.

The last faint pink shimmers of sunlight were entirely overwhelmed by the silvers of the rising moons at this rotation. His family cells were warm and well lit, the whole hive-like complex ventilated. Breathing and alive. His daughter tugged at his whiskers painfully.

"No Char, be gentle with Daddy." He pulled her arms down. She giggled and reached for his antennae. He'd been tickling the back of her neck. This was penance.

"Uh-oh," she gasped breathlessly. She had one antenna firmly in hand.

He couldn't understand how pudgy babies managed such skilled, rapid strategic assaults. A grown man, imperiled by the phantasm of a toddler's miraculously multiplying limbs.

"Placid! Placid!" he called, tears searing his eyes as he pried sensitive body parts from Charlotte's merciless grip. Placid strode into the room shaking her finger at Charlotte.

"No Chary, let Daddy go. You don't want to hurt Daddy."

The deep yellow eyes of the squat monster who'd so recently laughed sadistically at his tears and protestations widened with shock, though her grip didn't relax one iota. "No hurt Daddy?"

Placid reached toward their daughter and began to peel George's antenna from Char's fingers. Then she lifted Charlotte into her arms. George wiped his eyes and smiled at them, smoothing his antennae into his hair where they'd be less enticing.

"When you tickle her with them you make them too tempting, George." She smiled back at him.

His tickling skill had rewarded the two of them with the plump demanding bodies running around torturing everyone. He winked at Placid catching the meaning in her smile.

"Some things we save just for Mommy." It had been a nice, long Winter, but he would be glad to head out into the mountains again in the coming weeks. The thin slabs of translucent muscovite George sought, faceted the interior walls of the Deep Mountain Lab and hive compound. A superior material for wall construction, propagating light from any source.

He loved the hunt for the glowing mineral veins in the mountains. His lonely work. He didn't love as much the countless hours, the many returns of the moons, his work

2

required far away from the Lab, his family, their community. But once each cycle Winter snows kept him home. Playtime. When he energetically made up to his family the time he spent afield.

Now Spring warmed the mountain trails he strode. George's eyes half-heartedly traced the languid tongues of muscovite glimmering in the wetness as he tracked along the creek. His attention otherwise compelled by an alien hum.

He'd returned as soon as snowmelt permitted travel. Just before Winter there'd sounded a roar he'd sooner forget. Here, in the deep mountain terrain he mined, the roar still echoed in his mind. A roar sufficient to bring the snows down the slope if the snows had been there. And a brief twinkling of layers of floating light. Sinking down into the valley.

That roaring, ferocious vibration bruised the roots of his antennae. He touched them tenderly now. At the time, before Winter, he'd been too frightened to investigate. What could he do against such a specter? He ran home, his fear obliterating his excitement over all the rich veins of muscovite he'd discovered. He denied his experience, ashamed of his fear. He told no one, not even Placid. He returned now because his denial poked and prodded him all Winter.

There wasn't any roaring. Here, surely the same valley, where he'd stared at those very snow-tipped needle-peaks, the pain of the roaring vibration bringing him to his knees. Instead, this day he heard mild thrumming, a persistent drone.

Braced for strength, George bent his head to the forearm holding his staff. Before Winter, he had run from some other-worldly challenge to his knowing. He pushed himself to come back. He didn't want any confirmation. But in this return, he faced something even more sinister. The specter had taken root. In its insistent drone, he heard change coming to his home.

1

MOONRISE—NO CLOVER

The descendants of Earth's refugees depended on harbored Earth culture and science. These, the only treasures apart from their lives, the refugees secured in their twenty-first century exodus. Now their descendants traded Old Earth quips like baseball cards.

On Planet 101, a lone moon rose with the sun. Or the planet dipped. At least it didn't make an excited little wiggle. That happened before—no one enjoyed it. Other moons hung in the wings waiting to make an entrance.

Like these unknown worlds, Planet 101 among them, Phoebe didn't understand she was an alien. Wholly forgivable.

Because she was human. And the entire concept was alien to human beings.

"Have a nice life." Rancid-tempered, Ms. Garrett leaned out of her cabin catching Phoebe's eye. Phoebe hurried down the hallway, clenching her jaw. She shrugged her duffle further up her shoulder in reply. Swept away by shipmates and their stingy goodbyes. The airlock hung open. And so she left. One, two, and then down onto that last woven metal step cutting a cookie in the mud. She was shaking. The ship, formerly her ship, loomed behind her like a lost moon.

Human civilization had been a wonderful thing, if you believed the film clips. Her grandfather, a refugee from Earth, claimed most were made up. 'Movies he called them. But to her generation, with Earth and human history so fantastically remote from their experience, everything was regarded as a fabrication, all records of Earth were unbelievable. And none could prove otherwise. Earth was gone.

Phoebe pushed through the mud. In her mind, she whirred along in an electric car, where the great leaves didn't slap her.

It was a hundred miles to Jay's boat, or a few thousand steps. Whatever. It was still morning when she got there. This day that opened so cruelly dragged through the hourglass like wet sand.

Phoebe was muscled and tall, a little sweaty and sticky from squelching through sucking mud. Some of the foliage slicked her going by. Repulsive. Like wet tongues. The leaves slapped her with drips of glucose, proving the limits of imagination's protection.

She swung herself aboard with ease. But the boat bobbed and she stumbled into the cockpit, grasping and crouching like an old woman. The mud on her booties stank. Green-gray stains trailed her onboard. It was the organic age.

The tongue of the Great Toad had rolled Phoebe up and swallowed her. She'd given up on proper caring gods. Look around. The muscles in her jaw ached. She kept trying to break a smile. Like lifting weights with her mouth. Grounded. On a lame planet that wiggled itself lost. Oh, her smile was definitely broken.

The age of industry, the digital age, the space age, those were fabrications from Earth's past. Apart from human pretensions, Earth history offered nothing. As useless as taking a device camping. You could look up how to start a fire if you could get a signal.

Real advances in genetic science were swept up with the Earth refugees in their exodus. Lucky. Now on the two planets Phoebe knew for sure the refugees claimed, the descendants lived off genetic mods. Hijacking planetary organisms for materials, enslaving them for manufacturing.

Whoopee! They had water, air, mud, plants and whatever tech they salvaged from their ships. The advanced race pretensions they brought with them from Earth wore thin in the primitive refugee settlements on new planets, three generations on.

They didn't have roads, scissors, needles, looms, paper or psychiatrists. For an advanced race throwback like her, travel in space, leaving the new-settled planet behind meant—Ta Da —pretension perpetuity. She'd been exceptionally prescient, selecting to attend Space Academy as a third-gen child. When her virgin flight took off above her home planet, she would

7

have been happy if they never touched down on another. But they didn't depart from her home planet, the Third, to suit her. Phoebe, just another galaxy-hungry junior Space Cadet.

Like everyone else, Phoebe was a grandchild of aging Earth refugees from a digital culture, a culture that claimed cities, streets, mass transportation and choices. They shipped out from Earth with the supposed video proof. Not that her generation believed. She tasted the bitter reality. The great human exodus from Earth barely scraped a primitive existence from dirty planets. Like wild dogs.

Maybe this was all there was. Air to breathe, water to drink, soil to grow food. Mud. Maybe every planet would be mud. Hell, Earth was named after mud. Maybe Phoebe didn't feel like she belonged on muddy planets because she was AI. Hmm, she liked this fantasy better than her whirring electric car. She wanted to crawl back in the machine where she belonged.

Blasphemous, Phoebe suspected. A free-willed human wishing she was AI. But what did the Great Toad care? In reality, she knew she wanted a life she could be proud to claim. During the ship's brief lift-off she'd felt incredible. Soaring through space with the stars streaming like tears, felt orgasmically alive. The thunder of entering Planet 101's atmosphere with vibrations that shook her to the core with terror, wet her with lust. She laughed to recall Old Earth had vibrators too. Hers was way bigger.

Announcing his joy at her arrival, the guy on the boat next door went below and let out a fart so loud she could feel it reverberate in her hull. "Oh Great Toad," she intoned, leaning her head on the forearm she braced to the velocitor mast. Jay's FLY, the craft he'd loaned her, rocked in the shallows as the head next door pumped most of the river through its bowels. It sounded like a celebration. Her blessings grew.

Cai's eye view ...

Cai knew that Jay felt sorry for the new kid. He flushed the head again with gusto. He'd had high hopes for the officers on that ship from the Third too. Not sex hopes like Jay. Colleagues. Now they were all stuck here together on Planet 101. No one much cared anymore about vain aspirations for mutually advancing science, empire-building, or interplanetary travel. Every dream squashed by the instrument crash on 101. A planetary blip, orbit loss, solar storm, gravitational wave— didn't matter. Whether refugee, or new settler descendant, human aspirations were getting their comeuppance. A humbling.

Cai listened to her clatter aboard. It would be amusing watching her adjust. He had watched her waddle through the mud. Even from a distance her disdain and resentment palpable. Nice-looking kid. Tall as he was, thin, earned an officer position, must have considerable competence to be chosen for a virgin mission from the Third. Jay admired her, but that was likely sex. Cai tucked his smirk into his cheek and went up to meet her. He hoped his fart cacophony mortified her. This could be fun.

Phoebe checks out Cai …

The old guy's name was Mordecai. Cai, Jay called him. The retired head of bio-engineering and science on Planet 101 emerged on deck through his hatch. His head wholly populated. Wiry tufts of hair wandered around like shaggy grey bees swarming a hive. Third-generation scientist descending from one of those who'd come in to Planet 101 from Earth. The same wave of refugee ships that settled on her planet, the Third, but his grandparents sent by another Earth continent. The populations on 101 and the Third now suspected fleets from each Earth continent somehow managed to select different destination planets. According to Phoebe's grandfather, no one on Earth agreed on much.

Phoebe was a third-generation kid too, but her grandfather had been in his dotage when he'd fathered her mother. Cai was more than twice her age. His toilet activity likely represented a victory. She should applaud.

He passed his hand over his head tenderly. Phoebe hoped he'd bumped it during his fart levitation. Her imagination started to run. In her mind's eye he doffed a silly tin helmet, and she drove a car that whirred.

Phoebe pulled hard at the cord to rev up her two-cycle mind. Lawn mowers ranked high among the many things from Earth she couldn't believe in. Wallpaper was on the list too. All his grey hair got her thinking of lawnmowers. Without a ship to fly, her mind didn't know what to do anymore. Fly her mind.

"We should share recipes." She forced a laugh, hefting her loaded market bag up in explanation.

"Yeah, like how to prepare a snail that looks like camel dung."

10

Her eyes widened. "Does it look like camel dung before or after it's prepared?"

"Why? Do you want the recipe?"

Did the world brighten for a second? Light breaking through his crusts. What was this guy's thing with dung anyway? She remembered to be grateful for toilets. Earth got those right.

Cai winced, pinched by his own hard ass ...

Something about her sass just broke his damn heart. She could be his grandkid. Probably trained her whole mean life for space travel on the Third and now she was stuck here in Mudsville, 101. He couldn't imagine how hard it would be to crash like she must've crashed. He watched his own dreams deflate slowly across a lifetime, patched a million times. She'd hit the proverbial wall.

Hoo-boy, now she had Jay and his fish farm to look forward to. After flying across a galaxy just once. He shook his head. That was like sliding down a razor into a bowl of iodine. He fondled his whiskers. They'd found iodine here. He could make bombs with iodine. He let his mind trip over potentials. A few switches flipped got the siphons going and the MIDGE headed down river. He needed to feed Smudge.

2

PHOEBE ON THE FLY

Her stuff stowed, Phoebe sat in FLY's cockpit squinting at her shrunken destiny.

The *formerly her ship*,
Earth ship,
very large,
very, very, very, large Earth ship.
Not her ship.
Not large enough.

Yeah. So with decades of increasingly hysterical warnings, humanity somehow still only had weeks to evacuate Earth. Typical. Axis destabilization commenced Earth's final act. Eighty years ago. Each departing ship held fewer than 1,000 people. Too little. Too late. Phoebe reviewed the terse and pithy version, just like her grandmother used to make it.

At the end of the twenty-first century, scientists witnessed the ice melt shift the Earth's center of gravity with their eyes popping blood vessels like they were pulling Gs. Pointy heads with bloodshot eyes. Oh do please wonder what they see. They grabbed the first seats on any available spacecraft. Left behind, the meek inherited the Earth.

Nearly every country on Earth had something space-worthy. Private or public. What they had, slung off. Following probe-dropped breadcrumbs through wormholes. Probes— robot space cadets. Breadcrumbs—data on human habitable planets.

Idle plans for sometime/maybe planetary settlement had been dandled fondly for decades. When Earth began to topple into oblivion, shit just got real. No need to tell that to the bleeding-eyed scientists. Peeing their pants as they watched the ice-melt make the shift.

Evacuating Earth ships, the refugee exodus peppered a new galaxy like snot from a sneeze. All aboard? Ha! Not even a fraction. Looked like any other exodus. Chaos, death, shambles. Where'd they go? Cockpit jockeys and hangar hard-ons. Greybeards, scientists, and a bored-shitless billionaire or two. Now *that* was the operative question. With Earth gone, they sure weren't coming back.

Roughly a hundred ships from each of six continents got away. On Phoebe's home planet, the Third, just the contingent from Eastern Europe landed. Eighty Earth-years later, most of those old Third ships housed schools, hospitals and research labs for the raw settlements. Like hermit crabs, they brought their key institutional structures along.

Thirty of the Third ships were exempted from ground duty and refurbished to attempt modest space exploration. Down to twenty-nine explorers, since her ship SARAH got grounded on her maiden voyage to the newly destabilized 101. Maybe the other twenty-nine found planets settled by the other continents. Because only North American descendants were here on 101.

At least the contingent that settled on the Third had space travel ambitions. On the 101, American refugee descendants were totally disinterested in connecting with other continents' refugees. The former Americans had one clear mission. They wanted a world they could own.

Billions of people and, sadly, not all of the vain ambitions, were left behind. Nature's payback to the deniers. She favored few.

The chaotic departure meant destination planets chosen on the fly. The disorganized ships were barely able to communicate within their own fleets. None could comm vessels from other continents.

The ships had labs, stores, power, computing capability, and a prospectus of forty-odd habitable destination planets. Those aboard were young. A few families. They all carried vast data archives. Human history, culture and sitcoms. No books.

Despite all the vids she'd seen of people reading, Phoebe found it hard to believe that words ever stayed fixed to a page. She added folding paper books to her lawnmower list.

In a lucky coincidence, as the Earth heated so CRISPR tech got crispier. Good thing too. Among the many insults of climate change, the ships were forced to depart without capable scouts and campfire girls. No one camped outside in the heat as the twenty-first century waned. But CRISPR gene editing and reprogramming became a stitch in time. Djinn-tech. Gene-ies. The magic of the organic age.

Jay's little craft, the FLY, rocked in brown river water. Her neighbor, Cai, had personally bio-engineered both hulls from bug cement, the only two in this settlement. His MIDGE, at over thirty feet in length, was twice as big as FLY. MIDGE, so deftly mocking. Reduced her favorite verb FLY to an insect. Like Phoebe and her weevilled ambitions.

GM insect-cement turned out to be a great building material. Especially with undeveloped planets and non-existent manufacturing. The GM cement provided an endless supply of waterproof gunk manufactured from the human waste stream by CRISPR-rigged insects.

None of the Earth refugee ships on either the Third or the 101, brought much in the way of settlement supplies. But both planets now supporting human life were well-equipped with microorganisms to doctor and plenty of biomass. Hence Cai's pride in dung she supposed, looking leerily into the river.

The organic era, the twenty-first century on Earth, was an auspicious boon to refugee settlers. A last great gift from Earth's last great gasp. Agro-mining, using plants to extract metals. Bio-engineering using microorganisms' products and systems for raw materials and manufacture. So easy to re-program even bugs themselves did it. The nineteenth century, nature-derived, pharmaceutical cornucopia swollen in the twenty-first by gene-tinkering. An infinite capacity for discovery, invention, augmentation, sustainability and adaptation. Far beyond the confines of distillation and extraction. Just slice, splice, hijack, reprogram and use.

At least for the Third and the 101, ships' digital archives meant each succeeding refugee generation got their Old Earth intro from ship data. Videos, documents, research papers and Wikipedia. In the hardscrabble camps on their raw, new planets of refuge, they tucked into the ship's tiny package of culture from Old Earth. Vicariously, without a single coin to spend. They bought the t-shirts, drank the Kool-Aid. Wore that culture like a toddler clomping around in Grandma's high-heeled shoes. Phoebe added stilettos to her list of Earth's best sucker-punches.

She'd been lucky to be born to the Third with its sights still stuck on space. Of the thirty ships from the Third on their maiden voyage, her ship found an Earth refugee settlement at their first stop. Mission accomplished. Then the 101, the useless tit, got nudged out of orbit or something. They'd been had, tricked. The 101 suckered them in.

And why not? The Thirders just wholesale delivered the 101 another ship full of tech. The 101's nav-destroying planetary disruptions meant her Thirder ship, SARAH, would never leave. Phoebe knew the descendants on 101 hadn't caused the problem. But she enjoyed conspiracy theorizing. Not like the Americans held the patent.

So SARAH's officers lost their vocation. No ship. No fly. Phoebe was hustled off to make a new life for herself. For the 101, if the planet survived, their ship brought a useful bounty. For Phoebe, a maiden voyage became a little slide down the good-time razor of life.

This first day for the rest of her life, Phoebe played house on the FLY. She stowed her stuff and made her bed. The little craft was clean. Timber frame, smooth walls, water tanks, galley, some kind of siphon propulsion. Batteries, eating agromined metal, powered lights, cooking, simple pumps in the head and sinks. Two bunks in the cabin. Banquette seating, fixed table. Plenty of soft bedding, silk harvested from the larvae they farmed here, knit into products by GM spiders, wasps, moths. Some GM chitin polymers used for countertops, tarps, other stuff she didn't recognize. Deck was surfaced with a natural latex epoxy. Odd mix of crude, rustic and slick.

Phoebe didn't plan on voyaging anywhere with the FLY. Here for a couple of weeks of Old Earth time. Just an interlude. Like vacations back in the Earth days when careers were a thing—an artificial moment sandwiched between dreams, reality and death. This was the best it could be for the rest of her life. A small tight cell on FLY, mud-free.

Phoebe's generation tired of hearing the Third would never live up to Earth. Who'd want to? Wackoville. On Earth they laid yarn paintings on their floors. Rolls of colored paper were pasted on the inside of the dwellings. Boxes they called home. Gift boxes with wrapping paper outside-in. They brought clumps of dirty soil inside with stuff still growing in it and littered their domiciles with carved sticks and stones. Sculpture, vases, *objets d'art*. Distributed by the millions from robots at warehouses. More boxes. A culture of things. Foil, bags, tiles, hair clips, fake flowers, guns, thousands of different screws.

Phoebe liked the electric cars that whirred along. They'd be useful here. Clean, whirring boxes above the dirt. She liked imagining Earth when it was run by apes. And that early Mayan Queen who raised the dragons. Not any of it meant anything anymore. A yesterday with no relation to their tomorrow.

Every single thing Earth enumerated. Enumerated humans stacked in boxes a mile high, moved the numbers around every day after drinking their hot drugs in the morning. Then they'd return to their cell-block homes and remove a stack of colored sacks and climb into beds in their outside-in gift-box dwellings.

Earthers had so many boxes. They worked in them, lived in them, ate food from them, shipped in them, rode in them, flew in them. A culture of enumerated boxes. Recycled. Even so, they made a separate continent full of waste they floated in the sea. No ships departed from that continent.

Box people, coders and programmers became gene tinkerers. The refugees undaunted by the new organisms on both the Third and the 101. New boxes to open. Dauntless after heat-shattering a planet, sinking it below a plastic continent.

Fleeing their past through a wormhole. Leaving a whole lot of nothing to the meek.

On 101 Phoebe found plenty of meat for her conspiracy sandwich. She heard the first-gen scientists, the ones who'd touched and tasted the real Earth, were troubled by unexpected similarities between Earth and 101. Not something scientists on the Third mentioned. As though Planet 101 had been seeded by Earth, the first-gens said. Not just a lucky plenty in basic resources. Plenty of coincidences too.

The trees and other flora generated metal-rich latex, nickel, cobalt, lithium. Wild fields of grains were genetically linked to Earth-derived wheat and corn. Wasps with enervating venoms similar to those first-gens knew from medical science on Earth. Possibly the ships accidentally brought the wasps along. But there was too much of Earth's pharmacopeia on Planet 101. Evidence of God, claimed some. Phoebe saw the ghostly meek. Watching.

Stuck on 101, with her dreams of space lost to a backwater future farming fish with Jay, Phoebe craved a beacon, like a known landmark in the sky. Jay was fine as a lust-buddy, but Phoebe wanted a galaxy for living. Just one omen that would set SARAH free. Three generations removed from the rats who fled the sunken ship called Earth, Phoebe still had the flee in her bonnet. At night she scoured the sky for anything remotely recognizable, a bearing SARAH could use to navigate off this haunted, muddy shore. Jesus Toad. Poke some pins in a cobweb.

3

Look what he hauled in

"Oh lubbamudbuddy, Smudge!"

Phoebe saw MIDGE roll in and dock as the sun was thinking about slinking away. Fussbudgie. Amused to see Cai exclaim over a slug of mud on his deck.

"You're being a fussbudgie. It's just muck," she called, watching him try to wash the sludge pile off his deck with a pail of muddier water.

"It's fussbudget I think." He said grimly, trying to get the sludge to fuss-budge along.

"Don't be silly. It's a bird. Nothing to do with balancing numbers."

Cai froze, rattled his head. Looked askance and then back down at his slick of mud. An important game was afoot. "His name is Smudge. He won't like you calling him muck. Be careful."

Cai stalked the lumpy splatter. Don Quixote came to mind. She'd only read the Wiki. Unlike lawnmowers and high heels, fighting enemies made sense. Mud was the real enemy here. Phoebe, entertained, paralleled Cai on the FLY's deck. She needed more beer. It went so damn good with his crazy.

The mud splatter opened its eyes right at her. "Fuck you" fluoresced across its bulge.

"Whoa!" Phoebe flew backwards. "What the hell is that thing?" She fell to her knees. It was an animal. Slick, mottled, skin. Made of mud. Oh Great Toad, what did you put in the beer?

"Smudge is an octopus, don't call him a thing. He's really beautiful. And cut your freakin' noise down." Cai talked to her over his back while he stroked Smudge, calming him. Smudge wrapped arms around Cai with obvious affection.

"What the hell is an octopus doing on 101?" They had animals on the Third. She was so focused on her space studies she barely knew what the animals were until she put a fork in them. They definitely didn't have octopus. She wanted to do a happy dance. Why a cursing octopus made her life worth living she had no idea. Awesome beer.

"Hush your noise, woman. You think you're the only one asking that question? Everyone has questions. But Mr. Fuck

You here is sentient. I don't want anyone persecuting him because they're scared of what's here."

She cringed, a little guilty, looking around. The guy was nuts. There wasn't anyone listening. And Holy Crap! He had an octopus! Smirking happily she tried to muster up. "I guess. If you call 'fuck you' sentient. Why'd you name him Smudge?" She was ready to go with Mr. Fuck You.

"For the love and forgiveness of a dark childhood." Cai said. Enigmatic. Slitting his eyes sideways. "I'm gonna get him back in his tank. I have to entice him using his stuffy. You might want to put on that helmet." His eyebrows lifting as she stepped into his cockpit. Accepting her curiosity. He got it. Smudge clearly hypnotized him too. He indicated the tin helmet in invitation as she came aboard.

"His stuffy?" She donned the helmet, musing. He must be drinking the same beer. "To learn self-love through the love and forgiveness of another being?" Hell, guy had a cursing octopus. She was willing to go the distance. But drugs, for the first time in her life she wanted drugs. No way was beer strong enough.

"Yeah. Where do you think religion came from?" Smudge had oozed into the cabin and was now waving eager arms at a sort of skin-covered bladder Cai held. Cai opened the port to a tank and pointed with the bladder. "We need a god because we can't forgive ourselves."

"Suit yourself. I've accepted the Toad God. He just swallows and doesn't ask any questions."

"Doesn't sound like a girl's god."

"Ha ha," she said. "Long tongue though. What about you?"

"I don't need a god. I have Smudge to love."

"A 'fuck you' god works for me too. What about forgiveness?"

"He's really naughty. Forgiving him is a major occupation." Smudge fluoresced a happy face, then the tongue on it stuck out. He slithered into the tank and took his bladder stuffy with him.

"Why the tin helmet?" It wasn't the first time she worried about insanitation in this cabin. Still, too cool. She wasn't leaving until she got some answers.

"You've heard I led most of the genetic engineering and science we use in this settlement?"

"Jay mentioned you'd developed the cement for the housing and his boat. But you're retired right?" Jay also mentioned you were crazy and prickly but I'd be safe next door, she thought, not worried about telepathy with the tin helmet.

"Not important. Point is, I come from a line of scientists. My granddad worked microwave weaponry on Earth before we fled. In fact, that's his helmet. Supposed to be a gag. I met Smudge because he used that stuffy of his to zap me. I think of it trademarked with a capital 'T'." He watched her sink to the banquette. "You want a beer?"

Phoebe nodded. Definitely. She definitely, definitely, wanted a beer. And then another one. Smudge splashed and she saw him flash a smiley face on his skin. She wondered if he'd get a beer too. Cai uncorked a chitin-polymer bottle and poured frothy brew into a couple of earthenware cups. She was reeling from the microwave input. "How come I get to wear the tin helmet?" It was all she could manage.

23

"Mostly he plays with the thing. The sTuffy's a microwave transmitter. I only get random hits. But he can aim it when he's pissed. He doesn't have a lot of patience when you're slow to catch on."

"How long did it take you to 'catch on'?" Phoebe barely knew where to start but staying clear of anything that might annoy Smudge was the better part of valor at this point.

"Smudge and I have been friends for years now. He's why I retired."

"How long do they live? And don't they like salt water?"

She was more curious than frightened. Even though she was pretty sure he didn't mean the octopus was the one with a dark childhood. And whose childhood is so dark they need to remember it with love and forgiveness? She shuddered. There were depths to this abyss. No wonder he had to flush so hard. But the beer was great.

"My best guess is that someone's tinkered with them. For both the lifespan and the fresh water at the very least. On Earth, they lived at max five years."

"But your ships didn't bring them, did they? Weren't Americans the weirdos?"

"Our ships definitely didn't bring them. And the sTuffy tech is organic and really old, practically fossilized. Not Earth tech." He took a big swallow. The froth mossed his upper lip.

"This is really insanitary y'know?"

"It's perfectly clean."

"C'mon, only the insanitary put tin helmets on. They're famous."

"I'm beginning to see a trend with the budgie. You're like a walking, talking, glitchwich."

"Whatever." She wasn't paying attention. She wanted to ask why he let the damn octopus mess around with a weapon, but she feared getting zapped. Even though her worldview had just slipped sideways a few hundred degrees, she leapt beyond insanitation worries, instantly more at home. Science, programming, engineering—these were her métier, the proud province of Space Cadets. Hell, this was better than the camel dung convo. Plus beer!

"The sTuffy seems to have been dormant for a long time, maybe centuries of Earth time. Same sort of interval we can posit for the domestic-to-wild of many of the flora species here." He took her cup and poured them both another beer. His home brew did him credit. Her brain was already in outer space.

"Smudge just flashed an emoji. He said 'fuck you.' Emojis are back a few, but they're hardly fossilized. Catch me up." Phoebe rocked her head back and forth. Her new absorption strategy. Smudge mimicked her in the tank.

"Yeah, that's my doing. Once I saw him messing with electricity and microwaves, I loaned out a portable device from the lab ship to see what he'd do. He connected with it, that's for sure. Downloaded a bunch of stuff. He likes vids, comics, graphics. He'll spell words, but he mostly uses the emojis to interact. We've been playing with this stuff for a few years. I think the sTuffy might have been a sort of portable comms unit, and perhaps a weapon too, for the same beings who seeded this planet with so many Earth species."

"Beings? What? Centuries ago? If they brought Earth stuff here, you're saying they were on Earth. Whoa. You think they're still here? Cuz if they brought octopuses generations ago and left, how could Smudge learn to play with their tech?" Had her mind ever raced so fast? Toadswallop. She'd been trumped by an octopus.

"Nah, all the seeded flora is wild now. Would've been cultivated if they were here. I figure they abandoned their settlement or agro-experiment, whatever, when they realized the 101 was so unstable. Only thing that makes sense. 101's a great planet in most ways."

"Huh." She said, feeling the air above her head for sparks. "Where's a mirror?"

He ignored her. But she wasn't trying to make it easy for him. "As far as Smudge goes, Earth data doesn't give me anything about how cephalopods pass information from generation to generation. So I can't tell you why he enjoys the thing or how he figured it out. He was sure happy with that device though. Helped us find our way with each other."

Cool. Microwave relationship counseling. "When you say you retired because of Smudge, you meant something bigger didn't you?" She glanced toward the tank nervously, hoping Smudge wouldn't take offense. Nope. Oh yeah, worry about offending an octopus. Didn't see that in her cards.

Ohhh—cards. Stiff paper cards that told the future. Named after a vegetable. Taro cards. Ha. Tack fortune-telling vegetable cards onto her lawnmower list. She drank some more, trying to stop her tongue from licking the inside of the cup. It was all this talk of tentacles.

26

"Yeah. He led me to too many questions. Way too uncomfortable for the rest of the science crew. I still get to putter around with equipment and data, but I don't have to explain what I'm up to anymore."

"People can be real ass-triches." She did her best slinky Mata Hari. "Look what happened to Earth."

"I think you mean ostriches."

"Nah. Ass-trich is better. They put their butts in the air when they stick their heads in the sand."

Cai laughed.

"I should go. First night in the new bunk. Plus, I'm reeling. And I don't think it's the beer." She handed him the helmet and her cup.

He watched her pull herself out and followed her into the cockpit. "You probably feel like you've been et by a coyote and shat off a cliff."

"I'm calling you Dr. Doolittle."

"I can take it. Budgie, octopus, coyote, eagle, aliens."

"Wait, what eagle? I missed eagle." She looked up into the night sky.

"You have yellow eagle eyes." He said this while his eyebrows took a couple a high dives.

"So? Smudge has yellow eyes too."

"I noticed. But I bet you see better with yours."

"If you say so. Right now all I see is my bunk calling me."

"I hear mine too." He smirked. Listen," he paused, shading his words with his hand, "you might want to stay aware, even dressed tonight. Smudge doesn't usually climb up on MIDGE when others are around. He's nervous about something. He wants to stay close."

"Is this like a cat and the earthquake thing?"

"Maybe. Just add cat to the rest. I didn't see him when the planet blipped out last time. Might not mean anything. He's just nervous. Might be you. Might be something else. "

"Well. That's not ominous at all. Crap."

"Good idea."

She laughed and stepped down below on the FLY. Barely flicked on a light when a couple of loud reverberating, fake-farts echoed from the MIDGE. She wheeled around sputtering. Stuck her head out the hatch. "I hope that was Smudge farting?"

"Yeah," Cai said laughing out loud. "He does it with his siphon."

"And this morning? Was that him too?"

"Yeah. He was welcoming you."

Cai was enjoying this. Waaay too much. "What about all that pumping like you just laid the world's biggest brownie, Dr. Doo-Doo?"

"Nah. That was real." He laughed, waved, and ducked below.

4

FLY HURLED

FLY hurled Phoebe violently out of sleep. Something hit the hull hard and heaved her over. She flew out of her bunk. Arms flailing. Bedding tangling her limbs. The wall leapt up to bash her hip. She yelped. What wall? Mean and sharp. She tried to stand. Down. Where's down? The side of her bunk was over her head. The hull bucked like a gyro. Blankets and sheets cobbled her feet. She'd just been waking when she hit. What? Black licked up all the light. The FLY heaved down again. Angry slap. Phoebe fell face-first into the side of the bunk. Banged her chin. Crap. She needed to get out of here. If FLY swamped, she'd be trapped.

She forced herself up. Grabbed bulkheads, countertops, rails. Dragging herself out of the cabin. Splashed through a slurry of water in the galley and hauled herself into the cockpit. Her hair thankfully braided before bed. Clothes on. Yay Smudge.

Wind punched her hard in the face. Water-laden. Heavy with dirt and debris. Ugly. She squinted. Her eyes stinging against needles of rain, wind, darkness. Vicious probes to her wet-laced lashes. Her cheek skin rippled. Grey specters of water danced across the darkness. Sheeting. Sharp, loud, slaps swatted the FLY. The noise sheered her ears. Screaming wind wrangled her off her balance. She couldn't find her feet. Forced down. Whining, whipping wind. Pushing. Pulling at her. Yanking, flailing, her limbs, her skin. Her braid belted her stinging eyes like a stick. She held on. Hull bouncing. Airborne. Smack. Roll. FLY almost swamped.

Move by Braille. Taking hours to barely cross a few steps of deck. Find something. Ropes, rails, mast—whatever she could read with her hands. Push body into the wind. Seeing nothing. Squeezed eyes, pressed shut. The wind beating her eyelids, roaring mean, prickly, sharp bitter. Pry them open, they hated her will. Fought her like she was laying them out for a whipping. Water jets needle eyes, face. Breath sucked away.

Feeling her way. Can't see anything. Hearing overwhelmed by the pressure of air and wind and sound. Hull vibrating. Banging. Rich, sloppy, sodden slaps on body and FLY. Fingernails breaking as she scraped by feel for handholds out of the cockpit. At least an hour to get this far. Felt like a lifetime. Minutes stretched to breaking with agony pounding at her every sense. Hands stiff. Bloodless. So hard to move. Even lying down, crawling. Wind flattened her back. Smacked her butt with stinging debris. Hull flew. Legs airborne. Up, up, nearly away, then banged flat down hard on the deck.

Phoebe slithered, her head low. Her chin throbbed and she could feel her bruised hip burn when she muscled through to the foredeck. She wanted to get somewhere. Somewhere she could see. The wind howled. Sucked her hearing right out of her brain.

Splashes near on the water, sounded like a monster's boots in a puddle. Each boot came down larger than a ship. Phoebe ducked. Debris hit the deck hard, tearing at her back as it passed. She got pummeled. She crawled. First around the mast, gripping deck rails she dragged herself flat to the gunwales running hard with water. Her feet flew up behind her as FLY dropped off a huge crest of wave. Airborne with the heaves in the wind. Waves. Mountainous rolling mud waves. FLY nose upright. Climbing a wave. Vertical. Phoebe slid back. Hands breaking at her hold. Her fingers locking in white spasms. She hoped to god she could hold on. Where was land? The MIDGE? Cai? How many hours of the fury had she endured?

Where was FLY? The dock? Muddy waves rolled over the bow, choking her. She needed to see. Filth dripped from her hair. No one cared. How to understand what to do? What this is? Define, analyze, strategy, fight back. Fight what? Someone playing with a micro gravity inducer on a whole freaking river? A gyro? Not possible. The aliens Cai said were long-gone? Could they rouse a whole river?

Something flew across the deck. Cartwheeling. A tree limb? Banged Phoebe's shoulder. Mud-loaded stiff, she couldn't duck away. Again, her body rose up in the air. Levitating. Phoebe saved from the deep, dark drink only by the white-knuckled grip she had on one rail. The mud sprayed off her, the deck, the river, as she smacked down again. WHAM down on the deck. Her arms wrenching out of sockets. Hips screaming. Air punched out of her lungs.

Phoebe gasping for breath. Did Smudge detonate something? Transmitter? Fucking Americans. Weapons? This was no good out here. Muddy water slopped from her chin. Face down, flat on the deck, she felt giants walk her spine. They grabbed the FLY, tried to heave her over. Mud-gut monstrosities rose from the water. Battle joined. She had to get off the deck. Even swamped she'd be better below. She couldn't see the banks to the river. No dock. No escape. Nothing but mountains of oily black seething water. No Cai or MIDGE. Could she see nothing because there was only nothing left?

But then a whisper of movement so fine it caught her eye. Her dock line? Yes. Humming taut out in front. Taut to what? No way she was still tied up at dock. Miles of muddy water heaved around her. Great swelling wet mountains of the stuff. So what held her like a bucking steer on a rope? Fucking rope-a-dope.

If she could only crawl a little bit further, she might see. SMACK! Really cool. Foul-stinking aliens. Her hipbones.

Fashioned black and blue, with the pointy bits cudgeled off. She never noticed them before. Phoebe had to rev up her brain. Beating her body blue against the deck on her hipbones preferable to sailing off windborne into the night. Oh yay. Point. The dock was out in front. She ducked her head to wipe her eyes on her arm. A dock. The dock. Hanging for dear life onto FLY. The dock tipping vertical into the brown river waves. Shitski. Land was long gone.

But. Unbelievable. Cai was out there. Shocked, frozen, Phoebe watched as he rode the edge of the dock using her dockline to secure himself like a rock climber on a castle wall of water. Guy was bleeding nuts. Dr. Freaking Doo-Doo.

"Drop your anchor" he screamed. Then again, "Drop your anchor!"

She couldn't unravel why. Paralyzed with helplessness. Spasmed fingers, stiff, bruised limbs, breathless, numb. A whole troop of Refuseniks. Catatonic. Again penetrated by Cai's desperate scream. Galvanic. Phoebe groveled forward. Unsteady. Shaking. Released the anchor clip and let the rode pound out to meet Cai on the wall of mud-water. He still manically balanced on the vertical section of dock. He cut her dock line with his great sword. Fine. She had no clue what weapon he used. Borrowed something from the butt-brained monsters' battles. The wind milled her punishment. Whacking cruelly like a teacher with a stick. Useless, she knew she should go back.

Cai's wild cut released him from the wall. He flew back like a banshee in the dark sky. Slugs of rain, lightning. The screaming torrent of a river thickened to porridge submerged

33

her bow. Phoebe lay swamped, clutching FLY under the glut. Her shoulders fully engulfed. Her legs floating in inches of sludge. The bucking FLY still so animated.

The giants hurled logs at her little craft. Battering the FLY without mercy. Logs that pitchpoled and sank and banged up underneath the hull. She saw them. Lancing up, up. Lightning flashed a mud wall nearly upon them. Cai was gone. Fisting her hands, Phoebe willed Cai back. Tears spurted from her eyes. A mud-water monster studded with mobile rocks strode toward her. Sifting victims. Murderous. Her glimpses of Cai obliterated. Gone.

Phoebe sobbed into her armpit. Bullied by muddy water. Gagging through her tight, scratched throat. The FLY bucked and heaved under her. Creaking with strain. Phoebe wanted to cower. Cover her head with her arms. She couldn't unpeel her fingers. Somehow, she managed to snake back. The deck slicked. Blood of Titans. Mud blood. This agony of her last hours coiling to strike her name from the lists.

Everything, every single move or action felt meager. Hollow. A mean, weak, vain effort. The planet, the river, her life joined in toying with her. Winding her spirit. Spinning her like a top. Spooled like dried-up threads of life shriveling an old woman. Teasing, hurting, taking. Phoebe wanted to fight back. But how? HOW?

Her brain couldn't even drivel in peace. Still teary, sniveling, Phoebe was brutally assaulted by a huge, wet, clammy mass. A patent energy that flung her back. Now she had neither sight nor breath. She couldn't free herself. Faceless,

34

enveloped, Phoebe scrambled. Feeling for the mast. Panicking, she needed to freaking breathe.

Phoebe barely peeled her head clear of the sucking plaster, when she was flung down on the deck by the force of an arm like a log.

Cai screamed. "It's Smudge! It's Smudge! He's trying to help you. Stay down!"

Phoebe only faintly heard him over the roar of the water and storm. But then she saw him. Pulling himself to the MIDGE. Hikey-butt of a Toad! He'd tied the MIDGE to the FLY. He was here. He'd rafted them together with a cable through the gunwales.

Round and round. Like a top their storm circus spun. Her head dizzy. Phoebe tried to give in to the press of Smudge's body and arms. She kept her head low and shifted her face to breathe. She found she could hold the mast. A great, horned, branch crashed the heaving bow and pinwheeled toward them. Smudge pushed her out of the way flattening them both.

Phoebe gathered Smudge into her body. There was nothing she could do here for Cai, she slobbered and grizzled her bitten tongue swallowing the lumps in her throat. Sliding her butt back toward the cockpit, she understood why Cai wanted her cut free of the dock. The dock was a weapon against their vulnerable hulls. But riding the anchor, if it worked, might put them at this thing. Face this thing bow-forward into the swell. Better than athwartship.

Smudge's wet weight a comfort. Rafting the boats was smart. Even now, several hours into this thing, Cai had made them less lethal to each other. Gave them more options. A last sob squeaked out. She giggled. She thought she felt a rumble against her chest. Did Smudge need to be in a tank to fart? Even through all of this, Cai, funny how she knew him now. Anchor. Spirit.

FLY's stern did tuck in behind the bow. The anchor must have snagged something. A pounding drew her attention. Good. Cai liberating his own anchor. The dock long gone. There was nothing left around them. Nothing she recognized. Only howling, lashing rain and mud wave mountains, sheeting lightning and airborne debris. A typhoon of wind. A rage of muddy river. FLY bounced and banged and jerked and corkscrewed into the air.

"I'll stay low Smudge, but let me see if I can help Cai." She tried to disentangle herself. Lifting an arm only to be encircled by another. Bleeping annoying. Plus she was sure he copped a feel.

Phoebe gave up on the arms and started pushing at his great head. "Did you just cop a feel?" Smudge fluoresced a happy face with a lecherous tongue hanging out. "C'mon Smudge let me help him." There was no way she was going below. It was safer. Sure. Like a coffin is safer. They were going to die. Fine. Bring it. But she wasn't going to be buried alive down there. It just ached too much. Too many hours. Too much holding on. Too many buffets and slaps and clunks of debris. Too many insults to body, spirit, mind. She had no tears left. Little gasping breaths of air to swallow before they were snatched away. She let Smudge embrace her, sinking to the sole of the cockpit.

The winds whipped overhead. THWACK and another great branch bounced across the deck. Leaves and small twigs

36

swirled in the air. Lightning crackled above. Smudge pulled her hand free of the mast. Phoebe could hear Cai shifting and see him ducking as he jumped from his boat to hers on the rollicking hulls. Insane. She saw his anchor line pull out in front. She and Smudge slid back helplessly into FLY's cockpit. She didn't know how to help.

Cai came back to them screaming above the roar of the storm. "Let's all get on MIDGE." Strands of sopping wet hair veined his face, neck and shoulders like a necrotic disease.

Cai took Smudge into his arms. The winds roared overhead and Phoebe clung to the rollicking hull with braced feet and stiff fingers. They both leapt onto MIDGE. Smudge slithered himself through the hatch into the open port on his tank.

Cai joined her in the cockpit. "We have to stay up here. I'm sorry. I might need your help."

"I'm not much good." Her throat tight, she scraped out her words. She could see her heart sitting on her chest. Pumping. Burning. Who wore it on a sleeve anymore?

Phoebe and Cai clung to handholds and watched the wall of muddy water cascade toward them. They kept their heads low, eyes open. Both were crouching and ducking as branches flung themselves around. Leaves didn't feel so pliant whipping skin at 60-plus knots. Space ships were much safer. Like coffins and water tanks. Electric cars. Whirr-Whirr. Much more removed from the raging elements. Death definitely safer.

"Do you have a tarp? Should we cover ourselves with a tarp?" She asked.

"Great idea."

Cai moved to help her. Each holding on with one hand, using their free hand to lift the bench cover and tug out a tarp. Surprisingly heavy. Wind didn't agree. Already grabbing it. Tearing at it with vicious puffy wind-hands.

The tarp was strung all around the outside perimeter with tie-downs. They stretched it over their backs and used their hands to anchor it under their knees and feet. A miracle. Deny the wind the weapon. They peeked out the opening in front. Peering at wave after wave of violence heading toward them. Somehow Phoebe felt grateful. Sheltered. Not alone. An orchestra of whipping leaves, twirling small branches. The wild sheets of a rain ballet. Staged across thick, sluicing bow waves.

The storm raged. Too many hours now. At least seven, maybe more. Day could break soon. Maybe it already had. Phoebe's hands were frozen to the rail. Her thumbs snagged the tarp clips. Terror feeling the evil trying to deliver them from her grip.

Phoebe observed dying takes forever. Just endure. Assault after assault. Fighting from the trenches. Their hulls jerked and rose and tipped and bumped and banged. The noise blew out her ears. It was quieter under the tarp but no less frightening. Even with the covers pulled up the monster still lurked under the bed. Just kill me already. Stupid nature, back to rob her of another world. Phoebe bent her head not caring if Cai saw her tears. Just hiding anyway.

Hull ballet. Violent sick-thick sea. A shrieking cacophony. With a lecherous cursing octopus contaminating their water tank. Why bother crying?

38

The tarp rippled angrily overhead yanking at them. Phoebe feared she wouldn't be able to hold much longer. Her fingers white-clamped like frozen metal cleats. With no life left in them. Her guts churned. Microbursts of defeat and adrenaline flew along her cells nearly visible, they were so insistent.

Her brain congealed, dull. She peered out the tarp, watching what was washing over the bow. Rolling to them. An over-friendly tank. Miraculously, she and Cai woke up in time to rise in unison still holding the tarp. Utterly engulfed. Phoebe's arms now threatening to tear off as the wind flailed and the wave tugged. Thrusting an ugly, gritty, tongue into their mouths and licking hungrily at their eyes. Gasping together they wrestled the lunging, freed, wind-embodied tarp.

If this was dying, why did it have to be so hard?

Her nose ran free trying to clear her air passages. Finally they had the tarp tucked under assorted stray limbs she no longer felt. She'd lost count. Couldn't recall how many parts she had anymore.

Phoebe tried to wipe off her face on her shoulder. Scared to aspirate mud. She could hear Cai sputtering too.

"Get down, wait a sec, just get down low. Hold the tarp down." He was pushing at her. She had no fight left. Battle-weary, confused, defensive. She crouched again, finding the bench beneath her butt. She tucked some tarp under her leg and pulled the other end down over her head.

"Get on the floor. Can you hold the tarp? I'll get something to wipe our faces." Could she let go was more the question. Was he moving by feel? Phoebe lowered herself further. The heavy tarp collapsing in reluctant swells and billows under her drenched muddy body. Her eyes stung even though she squeezed them shut. Her mouth tasted grainy and foul. Her face dripped. Mucous, mud, tears, drool. Who knew? Who cared? She no longer tasted her tongue's gore. Her hair glued in weighted clumps to her forehead, cheeks and chin. Her braid had a hard-on.

Phoebe could hear Cai thump down below. Then he was tugging at the tarp at her head. He passed her a wet cloth and gripped the tarp himself, sinking underneath it with her. She could free her hand to wipe her face free of muck. But they were still being pelted with debris. She blew her nose. Mud. Marbled serum. The cockpit was filling with mud. Cai dogged the hatch to the galley. He passed her a bottle of water. Came up. Locking them out here with the poor protection of the tarp. What could they do to help themselves out here? Nothing until the storm ended and the burst-dam, bomb swell that carried them winnowed out into what? A forest? A mountain? Deep in her heart she saw the story her Taro card spelled. This would never end.

"Rinse and spit. Then drink."

She did, grateful to drink. Still tasting the dirt. Or maybe Smudge cooties. Ewww! Too tired to care. Phoebe passed the bottle to Cai. He rinsed and drank too.

Huddled underneath the tarp, passing a bottle like rummies, she knew the intense comfort of brief respite. Desperation squeezed her, clawed her and tore at her will. But she lived. Fear nagging and whining as loud as the storm. She was not alone. "Smudge is a lech," she said. Her voice husky and strained. "He copped a feel."

"Huh. Sorry about that. He downloaded some porn on that device. Did he flash you the leering emoji?" But Phoebe didn't answer. Passed out, or asleep. The tarp tugged at his fingers. Another swell of water and mud slithered across their heads, some of it dripping in. He weighted the tarp with a slump of leaden limbs.

5

PHOEBE WOKE FIGHTING

She'd never give in. Like those old rodeo vids, she was the steer bucking the cowboy. Hooved that pizzle-posted cowboy. Oops. Not dreaming. When'd she drift off? Both she and Cai slumped like the dead in the muddy cockpit. Must've got him good with her hooves. Jolting awake, her head snapped on her spine with a recoil like a whip. Mega-hurts. She massaged her neck with crippled fingers.

The smothering tarp lay collapsed around them. Gasping, she yanked it free of their heads. Cai blinking, groggy with exhaustion, limply helping her push the tarp away. His face dull, immobile, shell-shocked. Rubbing his tummy where her hooves had obviously impressed him.

Phoebe waggled her bobblehead on the stick of her cemented braid. Was her hearing gone? Or was there no sound? A faint plastic crinkle of tarp. A wet slither. Odd watery light. A persistent, echoing nothingness laying heavy on them. Like post-explosion deafness. Thug aliens. The latest up in her blame parade.

Her head felt blown-up like a big empty balloon. She waggled it back and forth. Hot pain scorched her neck where she'd ricocheted her head on her spine on waking. She was glad the cowboy was dead cuz the steer didn't have any buck left. Udderly bedraggled. Udder, cow. Get it? No reply from her two-cycle.

Phoebe's limbs were caked with grey sludge. Branches and twigs like a giant's dump of pick-up sticks littered MIDGE's deck. Below the debris, rivulets of water traced canals through the gunge. Did she hear tinkling drips? Slumped like a Mr. Potato gone rotten, she was one with the earth. Again.

Sticky crusts cracked across her eyelids. She brought her still-bloodless locked fingers up to rub her eyes. So much dirt on everything. Futile trying to uncrust her eyes. The smell of dirt, the grainy feel, the mucous-moist, oily, grime. Poop. She whirred in her little car, tidying her mind. Great Toad in his heaven. Her engines stuttered. Udder, rudder, stutter.

"Jesus Cai. Where are we?" Phoebe whispered. The MIDGE had . . . ? Who the hell knew what? They were suspended at a lopsided tilt in the quiet, deepening grey.

43

"Somewhere else." Cai muttered kicking open the hatch and levering himself into the galley. "I think we might have ricocheted right off the planet. Maybe a sort of momentum-tether, gravity bomb. We're alive. Already beyond me. I don't have any answers at all." He sounded stunned, depressed. Grim, no grin-bear, Dr. Doo-Doo.

Finding everything curious here, on the dark side of the looking glass, Phoebe wobbled her bobble, watching Cai swing into the cabin. Oh, MIDGE is hanging sideways, heeled on the rock. Natch, she nodded wobbly-bobbly. Still breathing. Only the Shadow knows why Cai thinks we're off-planet. Not gonna ask. Hanging here in the rock like an ornament. Cai grim, as though being serious will help. She leaned into the soft-upholstered interior of her imaginary little electric car. Whirr-Whirr. Her face a puffy sphere of dirt-dusted, crusty dough. Oh yeah, bruised and blobby. Yay.

"Get in here Phoebe. We'll pretend it's safer." Yup. Crawling under the covers always keeps the monsters away.

"Good idea." Her finger lifted at him limply. Going all earnest on him. Something about the spirit being willing. She blew a snot nostril-bubble. Watched the bubble blossom from the leeward corner of her eye. Not really. How big could it get? Blowing carefully, she let it swell. Oh Phoebe, you sly vixen. The rest of her wasn't moving. Waterlogged Sponge Bob. "Remember that coyote shit?" she said, waiting for her bubble to burst.

He leaned back in his off-center galley, nodding. Gave her a grim-bear smile. Her heart, still humping around on her chest, drooled like a baby.

44

Once her screaming muscles deigned to move, she followed him in by feel. At least the boat, the water and the skies weren't in motion anymore. Oh yeah. No water. She crawled into his banquette cushions. How'd she know-no water? She knew cuz? Sideways. MIDGE. May she rest in peace. Whirr-Whirr.

"MIDGE the mudball ship. Viscous toad spit. *A* LaGrange effect. Or tether-bola-ed by the long toad tongue. Sure. Line 'em up, Bartender. I'll take 'em all." Voice impossibly cracked. Her bruises were counting themselves. Aloud. She could see a shadow of Cai handing her a cup. "Water?" she croaked.

Cai was on his knees. Tricky to maneuver inside a heeled boat. She was impressed with his stowage. Just the salon cushions had shifted. They were piled usefully around her. Only a few noticeably wet. She sipped the water, sure she was drinking octo-pee. It didn't matter. That was desperation for you.

"How long was I out?"

"I gave up paying attention because I'd lost my mind."

"Jesus Cai, how to float your boat."

"When we sailed down the side of a cliff in my new reality. Sounds like a song. Snagged by a bubble, or the gravity of the planet that nudged 101 out of orbit, or a rift, a tunnel. *A Lagrange*, as you said. Hell, maybe even Heaven."

"Am I drinking octo-pee?"

"Fine," he said, "okay, not Heaven. Thing is, I don't think we're on 101 anymore."

"Didn't this happen to that girl from Kansas with the yappy dog?" She furrowed her brow. Like corduroy only crusty.

45

Corduroy should be on her list. Why'd they need cloth with fuzz rows? She could hear Cai's grim-bear snicker. Crawling around on his knees. Didn't matter. They were where they were. They could breathe. They were alive. So far, the only monster was the lech with a weapons-grade sTuffy peeing in their drinking water. She drank up.

"Let's eat, and reconnoiter Oz when we're done."

"I'll eat what you've got." Like the bartender gave her a choice. He hadn't lined up her toxic cocktails either. Hadn't stopped her from drinking every one. Gulp-gulp. Her voice rang, water cleansed of strangling sand. "Can we see anything out there? Should we wait for daylight? Was that really gravity displacement back there?" She hated to ask the poor old bear. How could anyone know? Oh Cai, such trials with Phoebe.

Cai passed her a bread stuffed with cured fish and fungi. "I'm not sure we can count on daylight, or anything else anymore. The velocitor's toast. The batteries won't last forever. I think we should check stuff out while I still have a charge in my gauntlet. Maybe there's nothing to see."

He didn't give her any grease to slick up her two-cycle. Not much on the sandwich either. Her mouth chewed like a Pinocchio puppet. "Let's take some food and water, and your big knife would be good. I can't believe I'm willing to move my body. But no way I'm sleeping either. Too much like game over, Rover. What about Smudge and his sTuffy?" Something about leaving MIDGE felt urgent. Maybe the old teetering in the dark business.

"He'll do as he pleases. He should have water, but he can always hang out here for a bit. He's the only one who can activate his sTuffy, so it isn't any use to us. If he wants to come, I'm not stopping him. He's more skilled at survival than we are."

Still chewing, Cai stuck his knife in a pack with water and food. He handed Phoebe a duffle with a corked water softy and some other rudimentary supplies he kept in his 'go' locker. "There are some clothes in my cabin. Why don't you clean up and get changed? Drink all the octo-pee you want. Smudge has his own tank."

Dragging herself off the lopsided banquette Phoebe accompanied her bruises to the head in his cabin. Flakes and clumps of caked slime thunked from her body as she stripped and bio-toweled herself. Her braid drummed her back like a log. Unbraided and pounded with a fresh gummy bio-brush, the mud fell free. 101 had better bio-erasers than the Third. No doubt due to Cai. They should pack some spares and a medkit.

Phoebe's cleansed hair floated like a black satin wave. The citrus scents in the cleansers swelled her sinuses. Stung her nose in a nice way. Brought tears to her eyes. Clean didn't help her get past WTF. Have to add that corner to the monopoly board. She gulped against a wad of apprehension. Damn sandwich wouldn't go down. They needed to get out of here before the panda-moanian monster ate all of them alive.

Cai's floor vacuum pulled her debris piles away, whining resentfully. Once every inch of head and body was bio-erased and buffed clean, she put on a fresh stretchsilk uni that didn't even sag much on her frame. Felt so damn good. She slithered the soft silk around her polished skin. Her lips parted. Like life in all its raw horror was sensual, erotic. Something she needed

47

to open herself to. Tender, like that tender-woman song. She ground the lumps of terror with her heel. Puffy dough-girl was clean, Momma.

She'd run her bra through the bio cleanser and stuck a fresh liner in the uni crotch. Ready to batter up. What was that? Making pancakes? She choked a laugh at fear. Snarling in the corner of the head baring long sharp teeth.

Cai must've looked at his hydrometer. That's how he knew they'd . . . ? What? Switched planets in a roiling mud bomb? Perfect. You couldn't make this shit up. She gulped a breath or two of citrus-scented air. Two-cycle firing again. Full power.

"You saw a new read on the hydrometer right?" Time for him to take a turn in his cabin.

"Yeah. You've lost a few pounds. Atmosphere has more oxygen too."

He considered the little bag of GM fungi hanging over the sink. Looked so proud of his personal air-qual canary he snapped his suspenders. A fine figurative. The fungi bloomed blue. Bet it never did that before. "We came out ahead."

"I need a planetary sobriety meter." Phoebe smashed her puffy clean face into her hands. "I'm melting! I'm melting!"

Cai laughed. Yay! Mission accomplished. "Call it the coyote turd effect. Lemme get cleaned up and we'll go find us a wizard." For a new lightweight, he was movin' kinda slow.

Phoebe lay on the cushions to wait. Smudge dragged himself out of the tank and blanketed her wetly. Copping a feel again and giving her a few hickeys with his suckers. Phoebe wrapped her arms around him, grateful. She didn't mind his damp. She'd take any comfort she could find. Could she wander into someone else's mind? Maybe that's what happened on the 101 when she stepped aboard Cai's ship. This whole insanitary thing. What was this effervescence bubbling inside battering her old wannabe-battle-hardened rigor? Her elastic spirit stretched so thin. Like wire anymore.

Cai led them out on deck. Turned on his gauntlet flashlight when they both crawled through the hatch. Smudge loped behind them, grasping his sTuffy. Three grey shadows moving against a greater grey shadow relief.

Phoebe lifted her head and looked around at the thudding quiet. FLY was gone. She saw a ragged-toothed scallop on MIDGE where FLY once rafted. Could've been her. Gone. She heard her own heart. A misty, foggy world inside and outside her head. Grey. Not much of anything to see or hear. No slap of water on the hull. Her heartbeat was the loudest thing. Maybe her heart pounded larger in her chest. Less gravity, more oxygen. Leaning MIDGE no safe harbor anymore.

Loud hearts on a boat. Phoebe and Grim-Bear. Shouldn't a boat creak and ding, rattle and splash? Even in quiet water. But they weren't in water anymore. So the boat stopped complaining. Foundered with a list.

She'd read about that. Dam breaks, river overruns and boats end up pinioned in the orange groves. Except theirs warped out in an outer space particu-lobe. Slung across the sky on a boat with an octopus. She sure got her money's worth with the Great Toad. She tried to breathe, shut her eyes. So hard to balance when the deck refused to lie down like a good girl.

Cai watched her. She knew he saw her calculate like a child in the classroom with her tongue gripped in concentration between her teeth.

"We appear to be grounded sideways in a black cave. How'd that happen?" She waved her arm gesticulating helplessly at the audience. Her eyes adjusted. She saw love-struck hairy beetles on Cai's forehead masquerading as eyebrows. He regarded her with pursed lips. Like he was trying not to laugh. The nerve.

"Sorry," she said squatting on the tipsy deck. Taking another breath or two for fun.

His elbow rested on his knee. Cai sat in the cockpit letting her find her way. He seemed content to wait. MIDGE wasn't going anywhere anymore. At least she'd better not.

"Whaddaya waiting for?" she asked.

"I'm waiting for Go Do."

"Isn't that supposed to be God-oh?"

"I'm gonna be waiting a while, aren't I?"

She laughed. She watched him idly cant light around them. He wore the lighting gauntlet on his forearm. The MIDGE was wedged into a rock crevasse with the stern hanging over a precipice. The light revealed some black rocky walls behind them, above them, in front of them. No rocky bottom beneath the stern. Just a bunch of nothingness she'd pretend she didn't see. Not like Cai let the light linger. Smudge slithered rapidly off the bow.

"I guess we're going that way." Phoebe pointed at Smudge. She felt a little buoyant. Lesser gravity. Aha, she could feel it now. Yeah. They were just a couple of matter of factors going for a walk in the park with terror leashed between them like a dog. Hippity-hop to the barbershop. Jesus. What the hell was a barbershop? "Did you check the air?"

"Yup. All good. Elevated oxygen though. Bugs might be bigger here. This could be worse, right? Let's explore, see if we can find water." She forged ahead. Dim light. Yet she didn't need his flashlight. And that was the other thing. She wondered if he'd noticed. He strode up alongside her.

"Have you ever played tennis at night?" he asked, his old self finally catching up. Sucked in by her assertive stride no doubt. Let's play the change in planet as a walk in the park. They weren't dead yet.

"What's tennis?"

"A sport with small balls."

"At night? Sure."

"Did you notice how well you could see?"

"No better than the other guy. But I gotta tell ya, he wasn't looking at his balls."

Cai moaned. "Tennis is a sport, not sex."

"Look, according to you guys, everything played with balls in the night is a sport."

"Not small fuzzy balls."

"Depends on the guy."

"I'm not gonna win this am I?"

"Nah," she snickered. "You might want to take up tennis. You're on about my eyes again, aren't you? You think I can see better."

"Yup."

"You're saying they're GM."

"I think so."

"But yellow eyes go way back in my family, even on Earth my gran says."

"Yeah. Maybe as far back as a fossilized ganglia microwave transmitter."

"Wow."

"I'm just guessing, but Smudge's alien buddies were GM-ing, I'm pretty sure. I mean we're all GM-ed, but only recently at our own hand." He took her arm as they fake-sauntered into the rocky cavern. The two of them still feeling the pull of MIDGE's shadow. Smudge galloped ahead. "And I feel like I know these alien GMers were on Earth before they hit 101 because of the octopodes we've got and some coincidental flora, et cetera."

"So you think they messed with humans when they were on Earth picking up octopussies? By the way, does this matter anymore?"

"Apparently with no ill effects. Look at you. . . . It might matter."

"Uhm. Thank you? But maybe there are other effects. Like cancer. GMers look at cancer tumors like they're cell mutation-incubators. When did cancer show up on Earth?"

"That's an interesting idea. I'm also thinking there are special edits all of us might carry."

"Do you think I might have other adds, like being super-smart or something?"

"Not that I've noticed."

She could see him grin. "Big bugs eh? I'm gonna sic 'em on you."

He laughed, letting her pull in front. "We should try and keep up with Smudge. He'll go for water."

"Look," she said pointing up. They could barely see enough in this dark, misty cave to follow Smudge. But there seemed to be filaments up ahead hanging down like a passel of dingleberries from the butt of a hairy giant. No signs of life yet.

He shone his light where she pointed. "That looks like a bunch of dingleberries hanging down from the butt of a hairy giant."

"Will you stop reading my mind?" she protested.

"Is it my fault you have a dirty mind?"

"How would you know?"

"I'm the one reading it aren't I?" he laughed.

"What's my mind saying now?"

"I dunno. Something dirty?"

"Boy, I sure hope you can run fast for an old guy."

Now some of the dingleberries were swinging back and forth above them, a few loose ones rolling contentedly on the fissure floor. Smudge was making like Tarzan. Phoebe wondered whether Tarzan visited Oz. She hoped Smudge hadn't seen the porno version.

"Looks like root fibers and dirt," Cai said, fingering the ones he could reach.

"Yay. More dirt."

"See? That's where your mind always goes."

Phoebe found herself worrying about the dingleberries.

"These are pretty big dingleberries. With my luck we're gonna run into giant dung beetles or something."

"With the size of these dingleberries, that'd be some dung beetle."

"Those aren't dingleberries and you know it."

"Yes, I know it. Hey, before we get eaten by dung beetles . . ." he paused.

"You're gonna say something sappy aren't you? Ditzballs. Didja know they used to have these folded pieces of colored paper with sappy sayings on them they'd give to each other, like for birthdays and stuff? People would sit around all day and make that shit up." Phoebe added sappy cards to her lawnmower list. Then she remembered the bubblegum she meant to add when she blew a bubble from her nostril. Choice. "So what were you gonna say?"

"You couldn't make *this shit* up. But it beats the hell out of life on a fish farm, doesn't it?"

"Sadly, you're right. Fecking insanitary." She moved aside fast. Smudge was swinging the dingleberries. How could this be fun? Little bubbles were popping in her. Must be the elevated oxygen. Like sunshine, 'cept from a person. Psychosynthesis. Only maybe not with a psycho.

Despite his upbeat tone, grim-bear seemed a little sober. His face a literal map of squints and creases. She zoned out with her cool new eyes. They were her same old eyes but they felt cool and new. Oxygenated. Mesmerized by the way his agile brows embarked on an independent journey mining the crevasses of his forehead like little hairy grey beetles. She almost expected little hair-hands to appear with flashlights and lunch pails. He looked sideways at her.

"If you are sure you are finished . . . ?"

She didn't realize she'd stopped to stare. "Oh yeah, yeah. Let's explore, pack a lunch, y'know," chagrined he'd caught her in the act.

"Watchya doin?" he asked, waiting for her to move.

Unbeknownst to her greater person, her lesser person was still transfixed. Only because she just now noticed that somehow he had managed to make his lanky grey hair look like he flayed one of those Earth llamas with a jet engine. Hmm, maybe they weren't llamas. Were llamas the ones that prayed? Did four-footed animals pray? Maybe she was thinking of Buddhas. Nuh-uh. Those guys were bald.

She kept her pause mellow, no sense in warning him. "I think I want to insult you in a way that respects my intelligence."

"Bingo," he said.

"You're right, it shouldn't be that hard."

"Wait. Did you just insult me?"

"Nuh-uh. You did that all by yourself."

"I did? Wow. Tough crowd."

They'd been walking for a while. His light patterning rumples of black rock, dust, stringy fibers, occasional slicks of wet. Something had cracked a path through the rock. Water hopefully. It was nice to feel steady rock beneath her feet. She felt completely unafraid. Like fear got exfoliated with all the other fouling. Like she could never be afraid again. Like fear was wrong. A thief. Hope-stealer. Exorcized that motherfucker.

"Are we there yet?" Phoebe smirked at Cai. They could hear Smudge click the hanging rocks together. He must have found a higher trail that gave him easy reach. She hoped he'd zap any giant bugs with his sTuffy.

"How long should we follow this fissure?"

"Until we're tired and hungry. Then we'll eat, rest and head back. I'd really like to find out if there's a there out there though."

"What if there isn't?"

"I can't believe there isn't. The plant fibers make the case for water and light."

"Why go back after food and rest then?"

"Because then we know we're talking about a long haul. So we head out better prepared."

Somehow he managed to get out in front of her.

"Hey Phoebe?"

"Yeah?"

"Have you ever heard of a revolving door?"

"Don't think so . . ." How'd he come up with this stuff?

"You go through a door and it comes around full circle, swoosh behind you again."

"It comes up behind me and hits me in the butt? I don't see why I'd go through a door that hits me in the behind."

"It's a door, not a popularity contest. It won't hit you on the butt unless you're too slow."

"I thought it was a door. Now you're telling me it has opinions? It's gonna hit me in the butt if it thinks I'm slow?"

"It *was* just a door. Now it's a door with the right idea."

"You saying I'm slow?"

"No. That was the door."

By this time she moved close enough to swat him. She made the attempt. He ducked just in time. "You sure have a roundabout way of making your point."

"Our form of bingo. And before you say it, no, not the aboriginal dog. I got you up here didn't I?"

"Fine." How'd he know she was wondering about the dog? "What's up?"

"Look at that water." He indicated the wet staining the rock and dirt alongside Smudge's newly strung dingleberry railing. Guess he wasn't just clicking his balls.

"You've been following it? Good idea," she said, looking ahead to see if she could anticipate his point. She couldn't see much. More water for sure, tracing along the rock like a pathway. She sniffed, couldn't smell anything useful.

"Okay, I give up."

He smiled. He knew she'd give up. "It's getting wetter."

"Source!" They both said it at once. Triumphant.

Nice little juice-jolt. They not only had a path in their black rock forest. They had a destination. She charged off, faster and stronger than he.

6

THE GREAT WORLD SWAP

The great world swap, Cai thought. Unbelievable. Hell, what a miracle. Lower gravity, higher oxygen, absolute trust, still alive. Kindred, especially in the ribbing. This, the second real friendship he'd known. Now he got to play the wise mentor. He got to watch the leapfrogging younger, better, version of himself. Immensely satisfying. A family that fit. Love with actual understanding. All the loyalty. None of the shit.

She was all of what? Twenty-nine? Just launching. Damned if he'd let anything get in her way. He licked his finger and gave himself a point in the air. Found her a new planet hadn't he? He laughed to himself. She'd piss all over his taking the credit.

"Cai?" she called, excited. "C'mere quick!"

"Whatcha got?" He asked, but then he saw it, the water was coming out in a stream and kind of spilling down on the surrounding material leaching into the pathway they'd been following. They could see a greater gleaming darkness higher, like saturated soil or maybe even a dark cleft in the rock. Just a few body lengths ahead of them.

In seconds, they were right up to the source of the darkness and the source of the little stream. A cleft. A nice, person-sized, black hole.

"That looks like a giant's asshole."

"Nice image," she said. "Gives us somewhere to go." They didn't have many choices. Into the giant's asshole, or not. "At least it's a big asshole."

"Never heard that as a term of approbation before."

Phoebe laughed. "I'm gonna go first, okay?"

"Be my guest," he said holding out his arm.

She pulled herself into the cleft. They thought they were wandering blindly before—inside was a whole new world of basic black.

"Shit," she cursed, then moments later, "I wish I was a bat."

"Why? You wanna hit a ball?"

"No. I want to hit two of them. And I will if you don't stop giving me a hard time." He heard her cursing some more. Something about fracking psychosynthesis. His brain was gonna rattle right out his ear at this rate. Her glitchwiches constituted elder abuse. He pulled their gear in on his shoulders and noticed he was standing more upright. Closed eyes felt better. Saved him from the particles she was hailing down on him.

59

"Hey Phoebe?"

"Y'know it's starting to worry me when you say that? Anyway, yeah?"

"I've decided what we are."

"I'm not gonna like it am I?"

"You worry too much." She didn't worry about anything near as he could figure.

"Fine. What are we?"

"We're woom-mates."

"What's that? Some sort of fancy womb-bat? Wasn't that one of those floor robots that all the cats rode around on?" Fucking cats had electric cars.

"Give me a second. I think I just sucked in some helium."

He was squeaking. Welp. Better not find helium. She'd want some helium.

"Honestly woman. You should come with a manual."

He still sounded a little high-pitched.

"Woom-mates . . . ? You were sayin'?"

"Yeah. We more or less just died, right?"

"Okay. You're the one sucking helium. So?"

"So now we're making our way through this interminable, dank, dark, cavern."

"Yeah, and?"

"And it's like leaving the womb, right?"

"If my mom looked like this inside I think I'd go back down the other hole. But okay. I get it. We're wombmates. Once we get outta here there's no going back, y'know."

"There's never any going back, Woomie."

"That's gonna get old fast, Woom-bat." He knew she heard

him snickering. He smiled. He began to do some sort of hopping gyration. A dance? Yeah. The fucking Woom-bah.

☾ Phoebe-Woomie

This sure felt like a giant's asshole. It stunk. It was moist, even slick in some places. Unpleasant fluids and solids dropped on her naked skin, her face, her hands. He better deeply regret letting her go first.

The smell should worry Cai. They'd had a breathable atmosphere, but she was definitely smelling unfriendly gasses here. Not helium. Not old man payback either.

"Hey Phoebe-Woomie," he said. The cave they were traversing contained the sound nicely, he didn't have to yell. "Hold up for a minute."

"Okay. Feels like it is opening up a bit just up here. Oh crap!"

He scrambled forward, smells forgotten, until he slammed into her back.

"Are you okay?" he whispered, resting his hand lightly on her shoulder. Protective.

What stopped her? She let him see the light ahead of her. It almost looked like ship lights or flashlights. He wiggled around beside her to get a better view. Their cleft opened out like a crack in the side of a cavern. He doused his gauntlet. Evidently very much a cavern. With floating illumination.

Not a huge cavern, maybe the size of six to ten of their boat hulls sandwiched together. Three across, two-plus high. The stream still threaded a path through the center of the cavern bowled at the bottom. Water runnels down along the sides. They had gravity. They were standing upright. Nothing was floating around them. Except the damn lights. Their gear lay obediently beside Cai.

Light, sight, gravity, atmosphere, and worrisome gas. Phoebe's two-cycle skipped, trying to catch up. The lights and the smell of gas were scary. What could make those? Why here? Were there beings here?

Nothing happened. No movements. No sound. No one leaped out at them while they peeked and whispered.

"What are those lights?" she asked "Do you see anything?" She didn't see anything.

"I don't know. They look like floating bubbles to me. I think it means gas, one way or another. I smell gas too."

"Well, at your age I certainly trust you on the gas front. Someone had to make them right?"

"Maybe not. Look, the sizes are random."

The sizes were random. Some were very large, maybe a third the size of MIDGE's hull. Some were small, like mini-orbs, like lit gourds or mushrooms floating in the air. Some small ones floated near. She reached out toward one.

"No!" he said, grabbing her arm and pulling it back. "They might have explosive or poisonous gas in them. Careful. Let's just sit here for a minute and get our bearings."

They sat on the lip of their cleft, the stream flowing discreetly between them. Seemed safe enough to take a break. Good time for food and water anyway.

"Why'd you want to hold up back there?" Her eyes darted around the space trying to make sense of where they were, watching intently for threats.

He sniffed the air pointedly, "you smell that?"

"Yeah, it smells pretty bad."

"It was worse back there. I think the gas in those bubbles might not be good for us."

"So what do we do? Go back?"

"These bubbles seem to contain it. They might be selectively capturing the gas."

She twisted on her butt taking in the whole 360. "Wait a second," she said shaking her head. "Hold that thought," signing STOP with her hand. "Look, how much more toadswallop do we have to take?" Of course someone was pumping gas into bubbles. They'd been catapulted into a breathable absence of everything and within hours of arriving somewhere that might actually support logic, not to mention rational thought, food, water and a bush to take a piss behind, they were going to be roasted by gas-bubbling natives. Well, technically, there were no bushes yet.

"You mean making the air less poisonous AND providing light? There really is a sentient life form behind this isn't there?"

"Might just be coincidence. Natural battery plus some kind of energy- trapping organism. Happens."

Phoebe deflated, relieved. She wasn't going to be captured by gas-snatching natives. Just electrified microorganisms in explosive gas. What could go wrong? "So back or forward?"

Steady again, she pulled at a sack of food, her stomach pecking. They'd been traveling colon-corridor for more than a couple of hours. They were safe enough. She smelled a faint tinge of gas but it didn't burn her nostrils. It was restful to actually sit and have everything behave. No mud either. Her life was shoed like a centipede. All the little laced-up shoes dangled in her mind. Waiting for the next one to drop. Speaking of cool, primitive, tech: lacing was pretty up there. Like the wheel and siphon power. Worth starting a new list.

The gas-bubble lights, fewer than twenty, continued to bob around the cavern. Cai winced every time one got too close to a sharp rock face. The bubbles nudged the walls and ceiling of the cavern without popping. Big relief. Maybe they could get from their cleft across the cavern to where the welling stream threaded out. Hopefully, there was an out. In their lifetime.

"A natural battery is pretty cool, if that's what it is. Useful microorganisms make life worth living." Cai got up and wandered back a ways for a quiet piddle.

She waited. All the little shoes tapping.

"I want to keep going. You ready? Duck those bubbles okay? Let's follow the stream," he said.

He reached down and stuck his hand in the water and sniffed at it. Touched a few droplets to his tongue. Didn't wince. The stream led to another cleft. Larger, with bubbles of lit gas clustered up high above in the ceiling, lighting their way. Convenient.

They were slowing down. Pace less breathless. Up and down, sometimes along small waterfalls. The rock was wetter. But there were root fibers to grab. Comfortable ambient temp. They were nearly silent. Heavy breaths, sighs and the usual creaks and groans from Cai.

As they walked their stride elongated. They were no longer able to zig-zag across the little stream. Phoebe led, duffle tied across her back, sweat trickling down slick between her cheeks.

They stopped looking up at the orbs. The stream deepened enough to be a concern. No burble or churn—must have worn a channel smooth. They couldn't see the bottom. A slip might cause a sprain, a fracture. Not something they could afford. Cai limped. Did he hurt himself in the storm?

Phoebe noticed light seeped all around them. Who turned on the light? Pulling up short, she saw daylight shining in at them. Hardly breathing, blinking, she saw red foliage, maybe trees. Sun must be red here. Here. There's a here.

Red sun. Not unheard of, weird anyway. Cai wasn't wrong. Fear grabbed the bile brush and painted her throat. She hadn't wanted to believe in a here and now. Just trippin' along a trail with Cai in the grey, fey light had been enough. Not sure she was brave enough for a whole new world, she forced herself to breathe. They'd made it so far.

Red. The sudden extreme light was almost as blinding as the dark. Cai stumbled forward, moving Phoebe aside so he could see ahead too. The brilliant red was almost too much. An assault on their senses. Great painterly strokes of red, black, brown, yellow and white. Hard to think in these colors. Foliage, growing stuff. Dusty red soil with red-striped white grass tufts. Cai sniffed. Apparently satisfied, he drew a deep breath.

Floating gas spheres, nearly invisible outside in the red sun, limned pink. Turquoise blue sky shone on water now glacial teal bubbling beside them. Like owls they blinked and gripped each other, neither displaying any ability to process what they saw. Barely daring to breathe. Beyond the red foliage, trees broad-leafed and white-flowered, Phoebe saw small clouds of dust rising. A stampede of animals?

Not animals. But voices? Faraway voices. Loud. Not words she could recognize, but voices, human voices? And laughter. Or were those mere echoes in her brain.

Her hands didn't know what to do. Clenching Cai. Squeezing her face like she was her own grandmother. Her legs gave up. She fell to her knees. Gulping air. Smudge splashed in the deep pool behind them. Cai folded down on the ground beside her. Both somehow sobbing, shoulders shaking. Hushed. At this moment finally acknowledging the barely leashed terror dogging them all through the storm, through the caves, every step of their way. They crawled back into the cleft.

"I don't think this planet is red-dy for you." Cai said. Grin contorting his teared cheeks.

Phoebe moaned, tipping her wet cheeks into her hands. "Oh that's really bad. You're punny."

Smudge showed no fear. He was squeezing his sTuffy with one of his arms, tugging at Cai with another. Cai turned to look. A little ways from their cleft, below them and over a few feet, there appeared to be a structure. Translucent, mineral, perhaps. Pinked by the sunlight, geometric, like a large megasaurus honeycomb, broken free. Human scale hive. Mostly obscured by carnelian red brush. A crystal structure? Manufactured? Smudge squeezed his sTuffy. Phoebe and Cai watched as symbols lit up across the structure. Streaming up and down on the gleaming translucent vertical and horizontal shelves and slabs. Smudge laid his sTuffy aside. The lights stopped. Smudge slithered into the deep wide stream. His arm reached back, dragging his sTuffy in with him. His skin marbled in peacock camo. Nuff said.

Over there. Voices, or echoes of her untouched hope. Over here, something their eight-legged weapons specialist could activate. And everything was red. At least the octo-pisser went camo.

Jay's getaway. The FLY renamed, GONEAWAYFORGOOD. Maybe the Great Toad saw that coming. The thing about Jay—he'd probably be happy for her. Guess she's a space traveler after all. She rubbed her cheeks. Feeling the tear-streaks parting the red dust. She shut her eyes. Tomorrow. If a tomorrow happened she might lift her lids. Terror settled between them again. Down boy. Down.

7

Maria lands on the red world

The human-like figure walking a mountain trail near their cloaked ship was the same being Maria saw when first they landed. She could ask NEW CLEO to verify, but she didn't feel any need. A clothed bipedal form picked his way high above the red-smeared timberline. That Fall, as Maria named their landing season. Before soft pink snows frosted the pretty red world. The computer registered him. The signature of a man.

At their arrival then, his head twisted toward their bellowing. A visually cloaked ship was still audible. He looked and looked and then he wandered away. Months of Earth time drifted by. And now as the snow melts like watered blood, he has returned.

Maria ducked her head mulishly between her shoulders. She wore an old space-walk helmet and a spaghetti of tubes and cords hung down her back like a pony tail. Through the dusty platform screen she could see fleshy coral fronds of plants and the stubble of broken brush and grasses. Beyond the melted circle below their ship, islands of pink snow. Strawberry ice cream. A cinnamon stick or two.

Davis, stuck with Kendak, regarded her from a safe distance ...

"What happens to a fish out of water when you find water again?" Kendak indicated he wanted to move into the officer's station to sit. But he'd have to forfeit his safe distance from Maria.

"There are very likely fish in that water. But she's a fish from a goldfish bowl, Kendak. I'm not sure she'll belong in any world." Davis perked up, although at ninety-plus the perky part was likely hard to spot. He watched the stream slither turquoise through the blushing landscape sparkling in the red sun. "I never thought I'd fish again."

"The devil only knows what that water would hold Davis," Kendak spidered himself to the officers deck using the web of handholds. His brown-spotted skin and scalp so pale, his few remaining wisps of gossamer hair were invisible.

Davis galloped behind him in his brain. His body, unimpressed, assumed the safe pace of a sloth. At least he still had his own great white mane. Too long, too thick. His hands crippled. That fishing rod, and all the denizens of that deep stream, the stuff of dreams.

69

Maria flashed a glare ...

Looking toward them as they entered her fishbowl. Resentful. They would only see the cabin lights reflect off her face shield. She wanted to ask the computer about the man, but not in the presence of Davis and Kendak.

Every day this Winter, hidden safely in NEW CLEO, Maria wandered the corridors and looked out upon the red world. Venturing outside just a little. Playing with Josie, taking samples, exploring. Thinking. When the winds didn't howl at her and the snow was thin.

Linda dead. Kendak and Davis dying the slow deaths of the aged. God, they were taking forever. Soon. Just she, her marsupial-creature Josie, and NEW CLEO. But outside, if she chose, there were others.

A society, CLEO, the ship's computer told her. Life measured in doses, her retort. Events, milestones. Alien human drama. Like acts from a script on the vids. Linda, Kendak, and Davis understood their lives that way. Maria's was punctuated differently.

Maria lived perpetually out of step. Would a bigger, populated, parade of events minimize or exaggerate her disconnection? Add some comedy to her private tragedy like Josie did. Give her a sense of living. Born literally spaced. Maria needed the ground. That icy, wet, dirty red thing out there with stuff growing all over it. That living.

Months prior, when they broke atmosphere, Kendak tried to make her see the wisdom of the decision The Three had made, ignoring Maria's protests. *First time you've ever seen land with life Maria. Do you want to reach out and touch it?* Kendak asked as he limbered himself down. Entry to atmosphere after all these decades hit hard on his old bones.

☾ Maria remembered that day

Maria clutched the beaten, worn, pilot-seat cushion. One of the only seats with a view. Over-used, though the pilot never sat there or anywhere else. CLEO, piloted, flew, resourced, cared-for, medicated, mended, entertained, taught and otherwise handled most everything. Her best friend, her partner, her teacher, but never her confidante. Computers kept no secrets, she knew too well. Secrets could kill.

Nearly thirty Earth-she'd-never-seen-years, marked her lifetime. Now she entered planetary atmosphere for the first time. Seventy-plus years in for the ship, and for The Three. Maria was conceived and born on this ship. As were her parents. Now The Three alone remained. In the stead of parents, grandparents, community and family. Sharing the ship and their lies with her. The meager, sorry leftovers from a thousand Earth refugees. Four people and a ship full of lies.

They landed here for her. Because The Three were dying. Finally. They promised. If NEW CLEO listened to her they wouldn't land, at least not here. What would the passing of command look like she wondered? What was the key? She had searched for an over-ride so many times. But though the ship comforted her and counseled her, NEW CLEO did not obey. Penetrating an atmosphere? Someone commanded. Would

71

they tell her when they died? Could they? Would landing kill them? Finally.

Maria pulled her shoulders in and flapped her hands repulsed. "It just seems so filthy." All that rumpled red messiness. Blooded.

"Yes, Space is comparatively sterile." Davis agreed with her.

In a nutshell. Life crawls, contaminates, spreads like disease. But she knew Davis craved it. He answered for Maria. "I want to touch it again. Don't you Kendak? Has CLEO defined any of the life forms yet?" He sounds impatient to get out there. He doesn't have much time.

The Three could barely walk, barely talk. They clutched their worn fabric seats too. Everyone was alert. Linda nodded her head spasmodically. Kendak occasionally looked her way with concern but then leaned into the descent. As though he willed the ship forward. He smiled at Maria. Maria grinned back like they were great buddies. She'd gotten slick since Joseph's murder. Big she-Cheshire, tonguing resentment against her teeth.

Joseph erred. Curious. Like a cat. Maria wished she had a cat. Cats don't tell. They don't have lips to lie. They couldn't kiss either. She'd never known the touch of lips on her lips.

Joseph, her twin, died many Earth years ago. God, it felt recent. His death always felt too near. She still turned every corner expecting to see him. Like he'd only gotten lost.

He wouldn't recognize her. She was a woman now. An adult with breasts and long legs and long blonde hair. He was blonde. He was her twin. Her twin brother, but when she

72

turned the corner and saw him he looked so small. So skinny and freckled and funny. She reached to touch her cheeks as though to feel her own freckles like swiss dots on the pale. His hair stood light and fluffy, electrified. His ears poked out to the sides. In med bay CLEO could correct many medical problems but there was nothing wrong with his ears. They said. Kendak, Linda and Davis. Nothing that murder couldn't fix.

"Computer's still filtering. Breathable, as we knew. Plenty of life forms. Lots of respiration. Even that water has stuff respirating." Maria tapped keys to advance the scroll of the screen at her station. Like she didn't remember Joseph. Like she was simply present with them. Descending. Joseph, the ghost, cross-legged on the floor at her feet.

"How much damage can we sustain landing?" Davis? One of them asked. Not that it mattered to them. After this they'd never go anywhere again. But they needed to be sure they were as defensible as possible inside the ship until they determined whether they could safely disembark. Why? The ship would kill them with age as would any planet.

"Not hull breaches. One of the thruster ports seems like it's clogged or broken. Maybe we hit something on that asteroid when we fueled. CLEO should've told us though. Not fun to have it foul our landing. Get ready." Kendak was scrolling inputs at his station too.

The Three had raised her. She and Joseph newborns in incubators when a gas leak took the lives of everyone onboard. Kendak, Linda and Davis were repairing something. Taking a convenient spacewalk outside the ship. A terrible gas accident took all the lives on the ship except theirs. Two infants incubating. Three opinionated space-walkers. All further postulation terminated.

Maria found little data on the gassed, the dead. The Earth refugees seemingly recorded almost nothing of their lives on board or before boarding. Their bravest act leaving Earth. No diaries, no journals, no passwords, no access, no legacy data ghosts. Her parents were dead. So were her grandparents. Kendak, Linda and Davis didn't know if she and Joseph were related to others aboard. But she wasn't to worry. She had a new family now.

Joseph died when he got too curious. Maria knew. The Three claimed he opened an airlock and trapped himself accidentally. At twelve. Yesterday. Nearly twenty Earth years ago. Accidents happened. Of course, Maria knew that. They were taught to be careful.

Joseph, playing detective, was trying to figure out how everyone, several hundred similarly careful people, managed to die in just the time required for the repair that saved the lives of Kendak, Davis, and Linda and two babies incubating. Her family now. All the family she and Joseph ever knew. If these were her family why did she care about the others? Those that were lost to her.

The only continent on this planet was rich with life, Davis noted, surprised. That's why they landed here. Funny in all these decades to have only encountered a single chunk of dirt solid with lifeforms. Like a hunk of leftover meatloaf in a vast ocean of gravy. One way or another it was the end of the line for them. But not for Maria. They said they hoped it would be a new beginning for her. They'd wanted a rich, diverse, fecund planet. Not an isolated continent-island in a vast, chemically-suspect sea. This red continent was the best they could do.

Had they avoided planets that might have held other human refugees? People that might reignite Joseph's investigation? Maria believed it had always been too late for questions. The ship nudged her into the present. They'd breached atmosphere.

They'd traveled for seventy years to complete an exodus from Earth that should have taken no more than a year. NEW CLEO took the wrong wormhole. All their bearings lost. A decade too many passed. Wisely, the Earth refugees agreed to restrict their population on board, fearing dwindling resources. Hope in plenty, they blindly searched for somewhere, anywhere, safe for human life.

Kendak, Linda and Davis were too old to show triumph as they dropped at last to this new Earth. They only wanted to breathe real air and to die on real soil. They wanted to feel the warmth of sunshine and know the taste of fresh water and rain. For that, they held out. They squandered a lifetime they told her. Many, she concurred.

Maria was grateful they let her live. She was even grateful they'd let her have a brother. She would deny curiosity to stay alive and earn a NEW CLEO without them. She dulled herself with the drugs CLEO, acting psychologist, prescribed many years ago when Maria was helpless with grief over Joseph. CLEO taught Maria to grieve helplessly. An act that bought her the oblivion she needed to survive her time with The Three. Her family.

Davis was fed up with space. Claimed he had been for decades. He wanted to feel the wind again on his skin. As though he remembered what that felt like. He craved the warmth of the sun. Not, he assured her, the same as roasting in front of a heater vent. He glorified swimming, doused entirely, water drenching his hair. Davis wanted to fish as he had as a boy, on Earth. He looked hungrily at the stream they saw shimmering a thread through the vast red forest. Like sprays of giant red roses, cinnamon hearts and valentines. Davis looked aghast at seeing a forest. Maybe it was all the red.

Maria watched Davis laugh and clap his hands. "Look, I see trees, I see mountains! CLEO, project our landing site please." He was always so polite with the computer. Like she would ignore him if he swore. A hologram lit up to display a flat plain in a river valley with billowing apple-peel trees covering the surrounding slopes. A burnished meadow with low grasses and brush. All painted in flesh, raw beef, vermillion, brick, carnation, roses, tomatoes, and chestnuts. Salivation. A cornucopia.

Kendak and Linda rose out of their seats. Each quivering soul trying to comprehend the view through the cloud cover as it correlated with the computer projection. The Three creaked with excitement. Maria stiffened.

"Are those buildings? Or what are they?" Linda exclaimed, pointing at a bundle of mounds with some sort of grid pattern transecting them. The mounds miles from their proposed landing site. In their vicinity the tree canopy was too dense to reveal any comparable mounds. The arousal drove them all back to scan monitors.

"CLEO can you detect any metal signatures, manufacture, or gas emissions?" Davis croaked at the computer. He didn't often speak, preferring to type in his questions. But his hands were so arthritic he couldn't comfortably type. Linda even had to help him pull up his pants. Kendak did too sometimes. Reluctantly. Davis never asked Maria for help. She was prickly with all of them. The Three, her family.

Davis told her he believed she had never recovered from the death of Joseph. *'Your childhood was not normal,'* shaking his head. *Our lives aren't normal. What is normal? I am ready to die. But Lord, I am so grateful for land. My journey will end at last. You, Maria will finally know planetary gravity, an atmosphere. You will touch living things, things the ship can't provide. You will understand rain, and earth, and water. Air in your lungs tasting of plants and dust, growth and decay. Fertile ground.* Maria tired of his endless refrain.

But Maria's face was strained, just like The Three. All the smiles forced. They belted in again. Readying. All hands gripped seats, or knees, or seat belts. All feet pressed firmly on the cabin sole. They had to remember to breathe. Tears leaked from Linda's creased old eyes.

The uncomfortable jolts eased as the ship slowed dramatically. None of them were used to hearing the engines thrust and whine. Drifting much of the way for fear of wasting power: years and years, with countless fears. This was the moment to use everything they had. The slow-down a fresh discomfort. They'd landed on asteroids to refuel. No previous landing required they penetrate atmosphere.

Tears rolled down Maria's face. She hated this. Soon she would walk on a life-filled planet containing CLEO's corpse. Soon she would be alone. A ship's corpse to talk with. She would never leave. She couldn't refuel the ship by herself. She couldn't handle all the systems. She wasn't even sure CLEO would respond to her when the others were dead. They were landing a giant coffin. NEW CLEO. Such a clever name for a coffin.

She pretended to smile as the tears flowed. Even though they only saw a reflection of her face. She knew engines and systems and communications. She knew how to read star maps and find water-bearing asteroids for fuel. She knew how to open an airlock. She knew how to die. And the worth of all the stuff she knew would die with her.

Fighting gravity, CLEO propelled slowly downward. Floating onto the plain. Details sketched themselves throughout the trees now billowing back from CLEO's turbulence. Despite herself Maria stood and pressed more closely to the screen. Trees, twisting in the wind. Large red leaves turning and prancing for attention. Jeweled water blinking and sparkling in sunshine. Strange. Much disorder. A clutter of color.

Beautiful. Messy. Maria did feel nearly compelled to touch. So, so, different from the flat dimensions of trees in vids. All these were thick with shadows, lines, depth, texture, movement. Lush. Swollen.

Maria wanted to land. Land. What a concept. She itched to run. When had she ever felt the need to run? When had she ever seen a plain of candy grass unfettered by hallways and corridors and locked rooms with room to dance and play and run? When had she ever known water she could splash in with her whole body? She could almost see the great prisms of droplets quivering in the sun. When had she ever thought that there could be a promise fulfilled in the land that space alone could not answer? Space was empty of life. Space was untouchable. Unreachable. Unknowable. This was carnal. Pulsing warm and wet. Feel it. Spasms of sharp pain shattered in her heaving breast. She hunched away from them. They wouldn't be permitted to witness her hunger.

8

IN ALL THE RED, RED WORLD, WHERE'S SMUDGE?

They must've slept. Phoebe yawned and stretched. Peering through the red foliage embellishing the cleft. Must be Spring. New grass pushed through the dry, rumpled remains of the old. On 101 in Spring, the old dead grass stayed fluffy and tall. More challenging there to see the fresh green shoots against the dross. Winter here had pressed the old grass to the ground. Phoebe looked out and up, beyond the forests. Far away she saw sun-kissed, pink-nippled peaks. Odd, she thought, blinking at the weighty unreality of it all. Snow.

She still heard the yelling voices. But they were fading. She and Cai hovered between sleep, dreams, and titty-tops, vulgar pink. This world and that. Fighting impulses.

"What are they?" She nodded her head toward the sounds. "They sound hostile. How come Smudge can turn on those crystals with his sTuffy?" Phoebe muttered sideways into Cai's sticky hair. "How'd your hair get so sticky? You looked like a blow job before."

"I don't think that's what you mean. Anyway, I napped against a web." He looked calmer, lighter, more present. A nap and trivia does the trick for grim-bear.

"I might want to go back to bed. And helium. Let's go back to MIDGE and start over." Phoebe narrowed her eyes at Cai. "I think I'm inside your mind."

"How do you figure that?" He looked concerned.

"Well, I know I'm outta my mind and I am not a horny octopus."

Silence.

"How come you're not saying anything?"

"If you're in my mind and I answer, then I'm talking to myself."

"Fine. Pretend I'm not in your mind and answer me."

"Where you hear hostile, I hear human," he whispered. Of the three tracks she'd offered, that's his pick.

"Isn't that the same thing?" She grinned. Fears and tears were gone.

"You're the alien. You'd know. Why don't we go chase them down?" He asked, waking up fully, daring her.

"Good idea. What could go wrong?"

"Fine. I'll go chase them. You come and rescue me if it goes bad." He began to untie his pack. He apparently saw no point in taking any supplies.

"You boggle my mind."

"Mere reading is for lesser beings."

"Pick up your pack. Let's be smart and get some proper rest somewhere in those trees. Approaching a group of maybe hostile beings can't be sound strategy. We know they're here. They don't know we are. But by the way, where is here and why are there humans on it?"

"Excellent questions. I'll look them up right now." His eyebrows were hopping when she spoke. Like she surprised him. Push-ups, high jumps, mining, the antics of his eyebrows a never-ending drama. Comic relief for all the vulgarity.

"Great. While you're at it, look up that ship's console Smudge activated."

He looked back at her, his brows taking cover in his sticky blow job. "Aha, you think it's from a ship too?"

Smirking, she tapped her head with her finger. "Alien super-power," she said.

Dust hung above the forest branches, marking the crowd of bodies moving away. Walking dammit. No levitating cars. Still, pink fairy droppings, an antique ship's console, and so far, no giant dung beetles. Chalk it up, Toto. Phoebe plucked a new blade of candy-striped grass and chewed the stem. She wasn't sure about candy. Something sucky and sweet. Not her thing. Logged candy canes on her lawnmower list.

"I see what you mean about Woomies." Phoebe sucked the sweet inner core she hoped wasn't a worm, from her grass chewy.

"I give up. What do I mean about Woomies?"

"Cuz this here," she said waving her chewy at all the pink and red fleshy growing things, "s'like vulva valley." Phoebe slatted her eyes and sniggered.

Cai moaned some more. "I was thinking fairyland myself."

"Whatever strokes your boat."

"It's not a boat."

"La la la la, I don't want to hear any more about it. Bad enough we're in vulva land."

Cai floofed her away with both hands and leaned over the pool to consult Smudge. "Hey Smudge, we're going to find a place to hole up. We'll come back here to check in. You OK?" He just had to say hole up.

Smudge fluoresced a happy face and held up a couple of arms gripping some big wiggling bug things. Bugs equaled food for Smudge. Big bugs, big food. Maybe they were crustaceans. Same diff. Phoebe wasn't planning on a swim.

"We can track the natives after we figure out a base camp. That crystal ship console looks as decrepit as Smudge's sTuffy. Won't be flying out anytime soon." Cai spoke like a Senior Space Explorer. Where'd he dig up the script?

"Buk-buk-buk. Bwark! Buk-buk-buk." The stack of brick-colored bushes rustled ominously next to Phoebe. She shrank back toward Cai, bumping him with her hip. She pointed.

"The bush speaks," she whispered.

Cai cocked his head and they both watched stunned, as a black and white-spotted, feathered creature hiccupped out of the brush. "Buk-buk." The creature pecked the blush-powdered ground with a yellow beak and scratched intently with tweetie-bird-yellow claws.

"HA!" Cai yelped and then covered his mouth with his hand. The tweetie ignored him. "That's a chicken."

"Here be chickens," Phoebe intoned, eyes glittering. She was thrilled. She'd never seen a chicken.

"That's unexpected."

"Really? You expected dragons?" Phoebe wanted to giggle.

"Maybe. Just not chickens." Cai was sober. He looked back at their cave, their past, hungrily.

"Can we just go back to the cave?" Phoebe's giggles soured. Naps, nipples, vulvas, chickens, dead ships and hostile natives would unnerve anyone eventually.

"That's what I'm thinking."

"Because I feel like this whole future thing is gonna kidnap us."

"Yeah, I read you. Give a moose a muffin . . ."

"Hey. I've heard that before and I always wondered . . ."

"Forget I mentioned it," Cai said, sounding terrified. He acted like she'd mangle his moose-muffin. Grind his tender childhood memories into PHOEBLIVION. Hey! That was gonna be the name of her new ship. Cai was such an inspiration.

"Basically, if you open the curtain to Future, she's gonna slap you with a pair of jet skates and shoot you skyborne." He always talked over all her best thinking.

"Is that my future or your future you're talkin' about? Cuz the jet skates are mine. I own the jet skates." Frack the cats' lame electric robot cars, Phoebe was going for jet skates. She did a Woombah dance. Or maybe the funky chicken.

84

". . . but even if you don't step toward the open curtain," Cai went on as usual, like he hadn't heard her, ignoring her dance. "Future's already found a way to wrap her long, cold, arms around you and vault you away." Cai was looking at the chicken unhappily.

"Jesus, Cai. You make the future sound like Death."

"The future is death, little girl."

"Oh Goody, now you're channeling Granny the Wolf from Little Red Riding Hood. I'm going for the jet skates. The moose can have all my goodies. The wolf can take the moose. Isn't that the Farmer in the Dell? Damn. He had chickens too."

Maybe Cai shouldn't have offered up the muffin. He looked back fondly at the cave. "I guess we're going then."

"Yup. Try to keep up. I've got my skates on."

The chicken crowed. Ear-scalding. Crap. That could get old. Phoebe's mouth watered for some reason. Pavlovian. Like most refugee descendants, she'd come to associate the word 'chicken' with anything that ever tasted good. With that racket, no wonder they ended up on a platter.

The atmosphere was drier than 101. Spicy. Might be all the red chili dust. Yum. Chili-chicken. But the foliage was similar to the deciduous flora Phoebe recognized from the Third. In red it all looked weird. Small red leaves, big red leaves, fleshy fronds, mahogany trunks. Dense variegated clumps of grasses, bushes, and trees. No large webs or flying insects she noticed. Powdery pink and terracotta earth. Near the cleft, the new grasses were striped red, white and brown. Plenty of flower buds, white, green, red, brown, some open, bright with red, blue and purple pollen. The air smelled flowery, sweet and

85

pungent. Like Spring was already ripping along. Seeing the faraway colored specks of pollen, Phoebe tipped her head in wonder. Oh yeah. Eagle eyes.

Cover enough. A distracted Phoebe ended up trailing Cai, both hugging low to the ground. They left the chicken scrounging. Cai's butt hung so low—looked like he was put-puttering pink farts in the powdery dust. Clouds, blushing for him, lifted as Phoebe and Cai crouched, bush bundle to cluster, heading for the deeper forest shadows. Lesser gravity even affecting how particulate gathered, rose and hung.

In the forest cover Cai picked up a stick, Phoebe wondered if his leg was just sore or actually wounded. She followed him as he bent under a watermelon red, broad-leafed plant. Yum. Food theme. Phoebe licked her dry lips. She'd never tasted watermelon. In her mind a juicy red perfume explosion of sweet flower succulence.

Cai snapped his stick to a good length and peeled the bark. Predictable. A strange comfort, but she'd take it. They'd ridden the shadow of doom for what? The whole night lost to dam break. Being comatose took a few more hours. More than half a day to transit the cave. A dreamless sleep. She shook her head.

And where were they now? Alive in vulva valley. Breathing air. Feet on the ground. Plant life, water life. Jesus-Toad. A chicken. Looking for base camp with Captain Grim-bear.

It is what it is. An inexorable directive to live gave her the freedom of a moth in a lava flow. Let go and let God? They used to say that. Before they saw the leftovers served up to the meek. Don't think so. Jet skates and choices, the only point in having free will.

Strap 'em on. Just living's not enough. Choose. Seize life, star hooker. Not waddling a path in someone else's mud anymore. Skate the tongue of the super toad. Rock the woombah. Fire up the old will like a Gatling. Clenched jaw and gritted teeth, mowin' 'em down.

No one ever has your back. Phoebe felt Future's long, icy fingers tracing designs up her spine.

9

GEORGE TRACKS THE DAMN SHIP

George tread the mountain path so soon after snow the thaw still marked a line. He'd have to fight the melt. Fit his mood. He shrugged and shook his hair back over his shoulders. Stabbed the ground with his stick. Barely kept his balance on the slippery rock. Their society was cracked like a hen's egg, leaking their lives into the thin red soil of their small continent. Infuriating stupidity. He slammed the stick so hard into the rocky ground the slapback nearly broke his face. Their societal fissures, like the cracks lacing the mountain rock all around him, had grown.

For tens of generations, George's people, the only people on this small, red continent, eked out an existence. Labbites, Shorn, and Longhairs, threaded through all, the genes of the Reapers combined by chance and happenstance, with human genes the Reapers harvested on Earth. One crashed Reaper ship here, with a whole shipload of harvested genetic material. The twelve Reaper shipmates had to combine their own genes with the similar genes of humans, to generate a new life form. A population diverse enough and large enough to survive. They survived. Barely. George would be lucky if his own babes completed their turn.

And now a ship has come. George glared at the gloaming mist. Oh, he knew it was a ship. He'd seen the layered lights break in the sky. Before Winter, he heard the roar of engines. In the valley he stalked to this Spring morning, so determined, he heard the alien hum. He saw the melted circle in the snow. He nearly touched the strange distortions in the mists and the contorted whorls of dust. He remembered when the ship came down before the Winter snows. When George had run, disbelieving, afraid. Ashamed.

Now this alien ship added to his troubled toll. Not a Reaper ship as he had hoped. This thing wasn't at all like the one the ancestors crashed here twenty-odd generations back. George was certain a Reaper ship would light up the broken remains of their ship's consoles, activate their old transmitters, even after all these cycles of time. He watched his broken pieces of console. All across the Winter. Nothing. This was an alien threat. Unknowable. Joining the party with the others gathered around him like a storm.

With each generation the Reaper genes were further thinned. The population of over 100,000, grew unsustainably. The Continent insufficient territory. They broke apart. Those who were physically marked with Reaper characteristics, were shunted aside. Like George, Labbites with the capabilities to manage Reaper science and Labs. The scientists, with triple-lensed yellow eyes, antennae, and sensate whiskers. Maintaining the look they'd used to camouflage their antennae on Earth, they wore their hair long.

The Longhairs identified with the Reapers, though multi-generations along, they lacked the physical characteristics. Their long hair served as a proxy. They became the nomadic protectorate of Labs and Labbites.

The Shorn were disgusted with their Reaper ancestry. Ensuring all in their clan marked themselves separate. Now shorn of hair, brows rumpled in a dim genetic vestige of antennae, the Shorn fought the Longhairs for territorial supremacy. Becoming well established in towns and the single city.

Then calamity struck. Two full cycles of seasons without sun. The planet withered. Food couldn't grow. Populations of every species declined to a fraction. Predator and prey. Some species extinguished entirely.

As George toiled across his mountain trail, his people were eight generations past the calamity. A handful of Labbites, a mere thousand souls. Shorn and Longhair populations each thirty times as large. Food still felt scarce. The territory hadn't gotten any bigger. Shorn and Longhair vied for supremacy in endless wars, a bitter means to keep the population sustainable. They survived.

And now a ship.

George's boots were damp. He'd followed quite a circuitous pathway beyond the circle melt of the ship. Not running away this time. More like counting his troubles. Losing track of his steps and the turns of the glass. Hereabouts the little mountain valley forests were riddled with shelter mounds he'd built, or his ancestors built, in the centuries each mined the rock and earth. Not exactly secret shelters. Yet, he was surprised to see lights glowing pink against snow smears on the rocky ground ahead. He rolled his shoulders, shifting the tension to his rigid jaw and churning gut. Not at all anxious to speak to anyone.

"George. Well met." Eric stepped out of the pink mist. The path narrowed by bare-limbed brush just breaking Spring buds. Eric planted himself in George's way. Big, cloaked in felted copper-hued fibers, the beautiful cloak marbled with tones of red-earth and blush, now dewed. His queue of long blonde-grey hair hung across his shoulder. The full lips usually bared teeth in a friendly grin. Not now. No getting around him either.

George stopped. He stacked his hands on his walking stick, tracing the rough burrs with a single thumb. "Eric," he said with a nod. Two ruffled predators, one yellow-eyed, both staunch, they faced each other, nearly touched. Cloaks down their backs like folded wings. George asked the begged question, "Why are you here?" George could see through the open door to the shelter. Eric had claimed a bunk. Well, so. There was another.

"I seen something. Something that shouldn't be." Eric said. He stepped aside to let George pass. Give him some time to put down his things.

George cast his eyes downward. His foot led him forward into the shelter. He slung his pack on the free bunk. Charlotte's chortles rang in his brain obliviating his prayers, his denial. His back to Eric, he stilled.

"The broke Reaper consoles that I always be fixin', ya recall?"

Eric spoke to George's back. Maybe he read George's antipathy. George's brow puckered. This? This was an unexpected sally. George swung on his heel, opening his face. All the shades and shadows gone, he shone like a flower to the sun. He drew in a new breath. "Yes. The consoles, I remember. And what?" he swallowed, confused, "what did you need to tell me?"

"Aye, they lit up, George. A whole bunch of signal lights. All in a row. Lighting up the whole console in regular sequences. Even the broke off bits. Come with me. I'll show ya. What does it mean?"

"A minute, Eric. When? When did you see this?"

"This morn, this very morn. I've come lookin' for ya. I heard you were on the trails near here. I've been running the whole mountain lookin' to speak with ya. What does it mean?"

"Wait, Eric. Not before the snows this Winter? You only saw the lights just now?"

"Nay, never. I woulda run to ya if I'd seen it before. Ya know me, George." Eric's hands drew up palms outward, in front of his chest. A head taller than George, he towered over him. His thick, ruddy, brow vee-ed, his dark eyes frightened. A giant among the Longhairs. To George, a child. "Have they come back for all our people? The Reaper kin? D'yer think they come back for us?"

George grasped Eric's broad forearm with both hands. Squeezed his fingers pressing the cloth sleeve against Eric's flesh. He could feel the warm power of the man. "Peace, Eric. I am not sure what this means. I agree something has happened. But tell me more about the time before the snows. Were you watching the consoles always?"

"Aye, always. They are with me at me home. I'm lookin' at 'em with every pass of the moons. I plink 'em. I try things. Everything I can think of to turn 'em on. Nothin'. Nothin', no lights, no signals, no hums. Never for all these cycles passed. But I think they're alive. They move, they respond. But I don't get what they respond to. No sense in it. And never whole runs of lights all in a row. Never so clear. Til this morn. Til just before I came to tell ya this morn. But you're asking like you know something. What does this tell ya?"

George smiled, a little wry. "Nothing simple, Eric."

10

PHOEBE

She and Cai wandered the red forest in a lesser light. Cast by moons perhaps. The red sun not reflecting pink on every shining thing. Clear enough. Phoebe carted a big blue egg she'd found. They were searching for a secure hollow, or a sheltered nest of soft branches, when they came upon a large mound.

Phoebe cradled the egg in the crook of her arm as she ran her hand across the surface of the mound. "Feels like an organic cement or something. This was made."

Cai hurried to stalk the circumference of the thing. "Here Phoebe," he called, not shy. The alien voices had departed some time ago, "there's a door." Thing's probably cookie dough, Phoebe thought. There'll be a witch inside for sure.

Cai, ridiculously incautious, pushed at a wooden door. Phoebe saw him slide his hand across the dark interior wall. Light blossomed inside the hovel. A large room with two bunks, a table, a small stone box, and some other chunky things at the back. The witch hung in the shadows, invisible. Phoebe entered with Cai. She rushed to shut the door. Lock out the bad, the watching. The flap-brained chicken.

"Wow. I feel like Goldilocks." Phoebe put her egg down on a counter at the back of the room. Laid her duffle on a bunk. Stroked the puffy mattress. Maybe leather, skin? Straw fill? Soft enough. Smelled good. Big enough. Sketched the size of the beings. Not baby bears.

Cai was kneeling, rubbing the front of the stone box.

"What's that?"

"Might be a stove, friction-activated, like the light." Cai withdrew his fingers, stung. "Yup, gets hot fast." Excited, he stood pointing at feeding ports where the stove also leached heat. "Look, look," back at the counter indicating a deep stone bowl. Cai pumped the wall lever and water streamed off a vee-notched thing. He stuck his head into the stream and drank. "If we can't drink the water here, we're dead anyway."

"We found base camp, Captain. Let's cook my egg." Phoebe hopping, ready to crack her egg on the hot stone stove. Cai swung over quick with a hammered metal pan. He pulled out their bread then twisted around to toss his pack against the door. That'll keep the monsters out, grim-bear. She tore hunks of bread for each of them.

"Is that supposed to be filled with snot?" Phoebe let Cai crack the egg and dump the innards in the pan. Egg substances

95

bubbled. A big orange tumor rolled around the middle. Phoebe wanted to play with the pretty blue shell but the pieces dripped with mucous. Earth might have oversold the egg.

Cai used his stick to slide the hot pan onto the table. They sat side by side on a bunk and chewed hot egg-dipped bread. Phoebe moaned. "You sure only fried egg snot tastes this good?" All sorts of possibilities opening up.

"S'not snot, Woomie."

Cai's brows were poised, ready to pounce. Phoebe slung a heaping glob of molten orange yolk into her mouth. It's like he brought his own hairy shills along to applaud his lines.

She stuck out an orange tongue. "Mattresses, bunks, stove, pans, sink. Do you think they might be Earth refugees?"

"Could be. But that crystal console isn't Old Earth tech. So I dunno. This shelter makes me feel better. At least we aren't camping in an alien hive dripping with webs and carcasses." Cai mopped up the last of the egg. Phoebe was finished.

"Makes ya wonder, all this stuff, y'know? We can do the pots and pans, the streets and bunks and markets. But it's raw luck that brought us chicken lickens, in these cool, porcelain eggshells. We're never gonna be lucky enough to see a seahorse, cuddle a kitten, get splashed by a dolphin. Most of the really cool stuff is gone for good." Self-determined. Hah! More like selfish-determined.

"Hey Cai," she called, migrating toward what looked to be a closet in the back. "What's this hole in the floor?"

A foot-high ring of stone with a deep hole in the center hung against the back wall of the closet. There was a lever on the wall. Cai rose to her summons.

"I think that's a head." Cai knelt and sniffed the hole. "Doesn't smell, might use a heat technology like the stove." He pumped the lever, water poured out of the wall at waist height and streamed into a separate drain. "This must be for washing hands and bodies. It's warm." He wiped his hand on his uni. "I keep thinking we are on the trail of those gene-manipulating aliens. Y'kno? Smudge's sTuffy and that antique console. And I gotta think the chicken ain't just luck."

"Until we get a better handle on these mattress-using toilet-building, Gene-ies, let's use the bushes. For all we know that's another oven or something. Fried egg juice's one thing. Boiled excrement I can live without. I'm done. I'm going to bed." Phoebe hurtled onto a bunk. Shot through with stimulating discoveries, she sat bolt upright, pulling one of their thin blankets over her head. Sleep would be impossible, she thought, as she slumped like warmed wax.

The red sun pinked the morning when Phoebe stepped out their base camp door. Rested and at peace. She'd found some little clay jars of dirty salt and herbs. One jar held a brown, tacky, sweet substance. Honey, Cai said. Not unlike the glucose crystals sprinkling the leaves on 101. She added some to tea. Worked okay, stuck to everything though. She wanted another egg, with salt this time. But the yelling alien voices had returned. An egg hunt could wait.

Steeled to face a cruel Future, they chewed some cured fish from MIDGE and shouldered their packs. Left base camp and crept toward the raucous gathering. Muckabuckingduck, the selfish-determined had no call to worry about a mere tussle with Future's minions.

Tall, grassy foliage fell over the stream banks. Parting the grass, Cai thumped a message to Smudge using a couple of rocks under the water. Voices and raised arms came from a clearing almost visible, opening up beyond an avenue cut by the stream. No treetops evident in a space well-bracketed by bleeding forests of red.

Cai probed the ground in front of him with his stick. He pushed heavy, arching blush fronds from his face. Oozing forward in the dense cover, silent, parallel to the stream bed, following the voices. He sighed heavily. Fairy vulva land and candy-striped grass. Rose-colored brush erupted beneath chestnut-red trees.

Phoebe swaggering forward, dragged at her other, clingy self, hankering after their base camp or the cave. Better yet MIDGE. Turn the dial back. Start the sequence over. She'd had run-ins with Future before. The lying, scheming temptress. She could see that cold, white finger beckon. Sick. That's what they meant by *ill-fated*.

So freakin' vulnerable here. Every hope crawled with risk. Voices, laughter, meant a sentient social species. Opportunity? Choice? Threat? But what options did they have? Stuck at the table, now they faced Future, dealing out the cards.

The volume of the voices, still excited, diminished. Phoebe saw naked arms waving at all the angels in the sky. There weren't any angels. She wished she could draw comfort from the familiar human-like squeals and laughter.

Nearly close enough to see the beings, distinguish words, she heard the sound tamped down. The excitement smothered. A single sonorous voice called. A call to prayer?

Wouldn't describe any of the Earth refugee populations she'd heard of. Phoebe swayed like a cobra rising from a basket, poking Cai on the shoulder to get his attention. She saw his shoulders quiver with a silent laugh. Then he bowed and shook his head.

Phoebe held a hand to her throat. She pretended she had a translator implant. Cai watched her interested.

"We defy. We win. Today's the day for victory," loud cheers. Phoebe translated and Cai pushed closer.

"The Shorn will triumph as we always do," quoted Cai, his fingers pressed to his neck too.

Phoebe rocked back on her heels; her brows mobilized like gun turrets. He'd caught her out. "You don't have a translator," she sputtered.

"Neither do you. Bet we find octopodes here. They're speaking English but they sure don't sound like refugees."

Phoebe wasn't ready for aliens. Especially English-speaking aliens with antique ships that wouldn't fly. The world constricting like the snake charmed from the basket.

Well covered by forest, Phoebe overlooked a clearing where the streambanks widened, breaking open the stream with its jeweled water shimmering turquoise in the sun. Cai's face and pale-clad body sliced with shadows, like cracked panes of lake-ice pinked at sunset. An Earth painting came to mind. Snow here on the peaks. A pretty pink icing on Future's uncut cake.

Cai knelt. Checking the ground carefully, give him a magnifying glass and a butterfly net so he could science away his angst over aliens. Shadows sliced across him like knives.

That's Cai. Always calling for trouble. Trouble panted back, eager to run.

In view, forty or so giant grasshoppers milled about in the clearing, speaking English softly in groups. Grasshoppers in togas. Sure. Phoebe covered her eyes. She clutched at Cai, scratching him with her own grasshopper limbs.

Someone was on a platform. Jiminy Cricket. With a top hat and an umbrella. Jesus Toad. Two more for her lawnmower list. Sure, humanity could bring lawnmowers back. But, duh? Not Jiminy Cricket or grasshoppers, with or without top hats. Not vanilla orchids, or fish shaped like stars.

Phoebe pinched a glance from her squeezed eyes. Blinked the grasshoppers away. She and Cai rigid together, with three monkey-sight, -hearing, -sound. Numbed dumb. She watched the 'aliens were people too,' the self-determinators out there, with her bravely squinted eyes.

"Those alien Gene-ies aren't showing a lotta respect for species integrity."

"You mean the rumpled blue brows. You're right. They look like modified humans. Sorta. Mostly." Cai threaded his fingers through his whiskers.

"I think alien Gene-ies are colonists. They colonize species rather than worlds. Like taking over a people from the inside out. This biology thing with genes you've got going Cai, it's a whole other way to wage war."

"I like how you're wrapping my gene work in with the aliens. But we're always being manipulated biologically.

Doesn't matter whether it's Nature, God, aliens or any other GM'ers. Biology isn't destiny for humanity. Our self-determination sets us apart from other species."

"More like selfish determination. And how do we know other species aren't self-determined? They wouldn't know how to tell us if they were. Even for a lot of humanity, just not having a voice lets biology define your destiny. Look at we walking womb-ded for example. Because of Earth-men's selfish determination, it took the whole of human history before women finally got a real voice to argue for their self-realization. Now we are stuck out here on primitive planets being pressured back into incubating humanity's new future."

"True and profound Woomie, but I gotta think that most gene-mods reduce the destiny quotient for biological determinism. You are right, those with a voice are favored, or those who successfully claim they speak for species-survival. But if you look out at those beings you see a species where gender seems hardly visible, and complexions are uniform. Like they don't use physical characteristics to differentiate. Maybe colonization from the inside out has distributed diversity within and across the species. Maybe helping broaden access to voice self-determination, to freedom."

Phoebe's head tipped from side to side, "Sure, that's one possibility. But in unconsented mucking around, maybe the power of the individual to affect the whole is lost or squashed. Well, whatever. Our presence will certainly put those ideas to the test. For falling within a largely common gene pool, we look pretty different, so will they embrace our differences or reject us? And if these aliens are so advanced, how come they seem so primitive? No tech, really ancient uniforms, and even though we understand the language, they're not knocking my socks off with their insights."

"That's what you get stepping outside your cave, Plato. Just us, against them. Them's *others*. It's a whole new world, Woomie."

Unlike grasshoppers, the aliens wore clothes. Beneath old-fashioned togas, some kind of light-colored, sleeved shift. Except the tall guy, the Jiminy Cricket, on the stage. His under-shift was dark violet. All the toga robes in dark colors sashed across a single shoulder over their shifts. Their hair short curly or shorn. Jiminy wore a deep purple toga with a brooch sparkling at his shoulder.

Some had foot coverings, sandals or boots, and some feet were bare. No horns or claws. They had feet, toes, hands, fingers, heads and faces. Shorn like sheep, free of fur or hair. Their complexions looked washed-out, brown, sugar-cookie, beige, but with skin, not scales or feathers. Weird bumps like shriveled tumors marred their foreheads. Blue-marked brows. No evident tech. No sTuffies. They looked bred. Their differences from Phoebe and Cai dropped down like a translucent barrier, rendering the alien-humans into undifferentiated shadows. *Unlike*. Uniform. Other. A non-people, people.

Phoebe puffed up feeling like a mud-chicken staving off attack. She wanted to convince herself that better than giant grasshoppers, alien almost-humans shouldn't pose a threat. Just folks. The talk-eat-piss-relatable folks. Sure. Like she'd *just* been transplanted to another planet by a gravity bomb. *Justs* a menace. Dragged off like carrion all the fear ya shoulda felt.

Tall, lanky, 'folks.' Phoebe tried to make them remind her of any young adult from 101 or the Third. Maybe she and Cai could pass with a few mods to their gear. Add a toga sash, sheer their hair and paint their brows. Could use some of that blue pollen she saw in the flowers as face paint. Did they bring a depilator in the med kit? Phoebe looked into the distance beyond the clearing. Trying to see beyond her reluctance for the next step. Maybe they could just skip it and take a pass on this encounter. Get back on MIDGE. Hop aboard another la grange bubble-ride somewhere else.

Always plot the endgame first. Helps when the crotch drops out of the middle. The red velvet mound under her hands felt tumescent. Thrusting forward, feeding off Future's energy. Great. Phoebe just sitting here on some hidden, massive, dragon's dick. Didn't matter. As Cai said, Future's death anyhow. Rolled up, lurking inside all the proffered 'justs.'

Look away. Far-away. Mountains and foothills spiked red and brown and rosy-fingered into the sky. Floating things that looked like hot gas bubbles with platforms stood guard over the valleys. A watery red sun bounced a blushing light. More gas bubbles hung nearby. Dusted like sugar-pink balloons shining prisms where dust didn't cling.

"What should we do?" She leaned toward Cai as he joined her on the warm mound. Poor grim-bear. His best-bud was a lecherous octopus. Surely he could handle a humanlike alien or two.

"If we can stick with them where we can hear, we might be able to figure out how to make our next move."

"Were you guys hostile when we arrived?"

She'd never thought about how her ship's arrival affected his people on 101. On the Third they'd suffered such a shortage of settlers. They hungered for others of their kind. Their whole society wanted to connect, to trade, to learn, to share resources. To bring back Earth, probably. That sense of a whole people, a society, a culture, a purpose, a direction. Not a meagre, bitter, aimless, remain.

The Third's ship officers, even Phoebe's Space Academy instructors, never entertained the idea of hostiles they might encounter when they proposed searching for planets settled by other Earth refugees. But a strange ship landing had to be threatening to anyone occupying the ground. Any planet's sentient occupants would be unnerved by spaceship arrivals with the means to determine an unknown agenda.

These beings were definitively not Earth refugee descendants. Way to move Smudge. Would she and Cai otherwise have wrapped their brains around a potential encounter with aliens? Especially lumpy-hairless-blue-browed, English-speaking, Earth-wise aliens? Without their discussion of Smudge and his ancient, console-activating sTuffy? This whole self-determining thing demanded a wisdom genetic mods had yet to deliver.

Thank the Great Toad she was hanging with a scientist like Cai. Cuz for all its lacks science sure made hay when the ground got yanked out beneath your feet. Stuff exploded in your face just like the hypothesis said it would. Fun in theory, but better to have someone along who'd faced the gory, terrifying reality a time or two.

"Not really." Cai said, breathing calmly with wide open

eyes. Taking his time to suss out the aliens. "We saw you coming. As soon as you broke atmosphere we had a good feel for your ship. We knew you were an Earth ship. And I think we reckoned we had the numbers."

"So, because we didn't pose any real threat you didn't feel hostile?"

"Well that, and you were bringing resources we lacked. People and tech. We had everything else. Why? Did you expect hostility?"

"Not at all. Naive now that I think about it. We never covered defense in our training. We only thought about nav and landing. We didn't even drill our plans past first arrival. Funny. All I think about since. I never want to be anywhere I can't leave again."

"Oops," he said. " You might need to refurbish MIDGE a little."

"If there's any other ship here, you know I'm piloting. I'll be flying those gas bubbles out on my jet skates." To date, her version of space travel seemed pretty highfalutin. Run really fast and get stuck in the mud. Future—racking up her score.

Phoebe stood. Hell, 'follow beings' worked as a plan as far as she was concerned. By the seat of her pants like always. Jokers, Aces, they were gripped in Future's icy hands. Fire up the damn jet skates. Phoebe looked back at the mound. Could've sworn it flexed.

The crowd left the open area, walking a road, or a wide, well-worn path. Likely heading away from the gathering to return to homes or a village. The path led away from the stream. As the open spaces were left behind, Phoebe and Cai moved closer to the road with the crowd, back far enough to maintain their foliage cover.

"You think they would win?" One tall being said to one whose shorn scalp glinted. Maybe silver. Phoebe named them Tall and Silver. Jiminy the leader, long gone.

"No chance. They're not prepared at all." Silver answered.

Phoebe looked around for a fuzzy ball or two, or some other sports equipment.

"Are they human Cai?" Phoebe whispered.

"If it quacks like a duck . . ."

"Yeah, quack me up, Woomie. But seriously, are they?"

"I'm a geneticist. I think in percentages. To me they look like they are mostly made up of human genes."

"That's what they said about those apes we descended from. And those guys were packing some heat." She thought back to the vids she'd seen about the apes. "Even if these aliens have mostly human genes, they might want to wipe us out. Biology doesn't opt them out of their selfish-determination remember."

☾ Bye-bye Cai

Cai hung his head, resting his chin on his chest. Her profundity warring with her perverted insistence that humanity descended from *The Planet of the Apes*. He shut his eyes, shook the ole rattle. He wondered how many more shakes his brain could handle. He pushed some strands of pink vulva aside and kept pace with the crowd.

"Hey Woomie?" Phoebe pinched his shoulder.

"Oww," he mouthed, feeling his eyebrows raging at her.

"I'm going back a ways behind some bushes, K? Don't leave without me."

She dropped her duffle at his feet. Must've been a couple hours since they'd left base camp. Time enough to get hungry, eat, water a few bushes. Cai looked up at the sky wondering about the passage of light and time. He hacked a few times, covering his mouth to keep the sound from carrying. Phoebe coughing too as she strode away. No coughs amongst the aliens. Maybe some kind of evolved filtration capacity. The air hung with particulate. Lesser gravity. Cai toyed with devising a breather of sorts. Something simple they could employ to protect their lungs. Could he devise something quickly enough to let them approach the aliens without giving themselves away?

On 101 they timed their days to cycles of sleep, punctuated by meals and hunger, pacing according to Earth times, human body times, using the ships' clocks to help them regulate. The sun on 101 shadowed on rhythms that didn't work for human bodies. And then the planet warped out of whack. So, their internal clocks sharpened even more. Worked here too. He figured they'd slept for twelve-plus hours Earth time. They needn't rush.

Sat down. He took his own pack off too. The crowd on the road splintered into little groups of two and three. They weren't moving fast, constantly stopping to chat, argue, and regroup. But Phoebe was taking the world's longest pee.

Cai began to worry. Just like Phoebe to get swallowed by

vulva valley. He could already hum the tune. He stood again and rocked on his feet. The wound on his leg bothered him. He'd cleaned it on MIDGE. Maybe new microbes and all demanded a bit more care. Too late now. Phoebe had her skates on.

After counting his billionth heartbeat, and twice that in eyeblinks, Cai craved something other than nerves to accurately measure passage of time. So much for his brief absence of terror.

On the anxiety clock, Phoebe left forty-eight hours ago to 'water the bush' and possibly 'fertilize the soil.' Alone in the bush near the frolicking, laughing, talking, bouncing, hopping, worrisome, enemy/ally, alien game-goers.

Cai's gut chewed.

What if she'd been bitten by something? What if she'd been swallowed by a sinkhole, or worse, snagged by a giant spider? Privy-privacy was one thing, but they knew nothing of the dangers here. She could be exploded by gas, attacked by a chicken-dragon, squashed by a giant bug. His patience thinned to a mere approximation. Never mind, he couldn't wait a second more.

Phoebe's privacy forfeit, Cai stood and cautiously circled in the direction she'd taken. As though they noticed him move, the lively groupings on the road stilled. Cai ducked instinctively. A shadow pulsed through the center of the groupings, splitting them to the roadside, intensifying with sound and motion from the back of the dispersed crowd to the front. The timbre of voices shifted from chatty and gleeful, to threatening, raucous, deep, and angry.

Cai looked up, expecting to see a predator overhead. A

drone, a craft, a threat bearing down on the aroused crowd. What alarmed them now?

Something moved up the center of the road from the backmost clusters of aliens. They mobilized around it, meeting it, attacking it. And now the volume of protest rose. The aliens, or something else, called, screamed and howled. Angry repetitions. What did they chant?

A phrase echoed from the furthermost quarter, passed like a ball, from group to group. 'Long hair,' Cai heard distinctly. The chant picked up and repeated, flapping. A burr on cracked machine belt. "Long hair, long hair, long hair!"

The beast moving through the center resolved itself into a many-limbed, shorn-headed scramble, pulling and pushing and hauling and beating the whipping, long black hair of Phoebe. Still attached to her head, Cai saw, scarcely relieved.

"Cai! Cai! Cai!" she screamed for him, punching every limb that pulled at her, clawed at her. Some individuals poked at her from the sidelines, reaching in with long arms and rigid, jabbing fingers, 'long hair, long hair.' He could hear her curse as she fought back. Cai, bursting to jump in and slash them with his machete, his elbows, gouge eyes with his fingers, break chins and bloody noses with his fists.

Cai stayed down, white-knuckling a branch till it bled red sap. An anchor against his own impatient fury. Phoebe's only hope was his restraint. He had to follow and gauge. Find their best chance. He'd never resented his own maturity before. He tasted copper from his tooth-pierced cheek.

11

ALL THEIR TROUBLES AND NOW A SHIP

Nothing is ever simple. Both Eric and George laughed in taut surrender. Eric relaxed at least one whisker. Knowing he was about to enjoy George's humor about the way.

"I'm going to show you the way, Eric."

"Ain't it the truth. And I sure thank you. It isn't hard to go astray, to be lost." Eric replied, smirking at the familiar refrain of the litany, despite his anxiety.

> *"Making things hard is always a mistake. For the truth is always simple. That's why there is the expression, 'the simple truth.'"*

George continued, finding reciting a comfort too.

*"First you must go about things the simple way.
Faith, belief, not thinking. Thinking is not a
virtue. Our world is littered with traps. Attempts
to make you think, ways to trick you out of simply
having faith in the truths you are told. The truths
we agree upon. Curiosity, and open-mindedness,
will lead you away from the simple truth.
Whoever found any peace with a questioning
mind?"*

Eric nodded his head, still smiling.

*"Arithmetic is a grave danger. So it is with words
of more than one syllable. Thoughts that involve
multiplication, statistics or division are dangers
incarnate. When these are used you have a sure
sign the simple truth has been forsaken. Even
children are wise to the dangers of numbers. We
need to learn from their protests. They know the
way.*

*The labs and the scientists aim to complicate. For
one reason only: to obscure the simple truth.
Faith. Belief. Our known, simple, truths. Here we
find the answers to every question.*

*You have heard the claims. Science claims to
search for real answers. But that's because real
answers are the only real threat to faith. Scientists*

don't seek real answers. Instead, they seek to threaten our simple truth, our faith. They seek to beguile you with their complications. But you, you among the believers, you need never go wrong. Simply keep your faith in the simple truth. And look away from the devil who clouds the clear water."

Eric clapped his hands. "So good you say it, friend. And more going on than I reckoned, I ken."

"What?" George tipped his head back in feigned surprise. "You mean more going on apart from our perpetual wars, our unsustainable surplus of people and the attacks on diversity and minorities in our society?"

"No, and the attacks on learning, medicine and the Labs too, George."

"I include the attacks on Labbites in the campaign to disgrace diversity and science."

"Ain't ya Labbits now?"

"I'm trying to resist Kertof's dictates. He isn't my leader. And he surely hasn't my respect." George sat on his bunk and brought his pack between his knees to open it. He noted that Eric had a kettle boiling on the little stove.

"Kertof says ya bleed like Labbits. His war song this cycle. 'They breed like rabbits and bleed like Labbits. They seek not the simple truth.'"

"Ha-ha. Very funny man. If it weren't for the breeding of the rabbits and chickens the Reapers brought, there'd be little food for any of us since the calamity." George pulled a cloth packet from his pack. The History Keepers had told of ungulates domesticated on the Continent by the Reapers. They once provided milk, butter, cheese and meat. But neither ungulates nor History Keepers had survived the calamity.

The one large shelter room contained the bunks, a small stove, a very tidy kitchen with a stone sink and taps and some shelves. Eric deftly shifted a tiny wooden table between them. He placed cups and the teapot he'd just topped with boiling water from the little stone stove, on its polished surface. A door at the back of the mound led to a simple toilet and cleansing room.

George unwrapped a knotted loaf and tore off two chunks of bread. One for each of them. He had several generous pats of special Labbite-cultured cheese, layered between coral-tinged fern leaves, peeled clean for each bread knot. Eric poured steaming tea, sweetly fragrant with flowers, into the two cups. They ate. Unhurried.

Finally, George brushed crumbs from his mouth and whiskers. His antennae steepled above his head. Eric stared, looking fascinated by George's Labbite features, as many were.

George felt his wiry grey hair falling round his face like large, soft, flower-petal ears. George's face had more moving parts than Eric of the Longhairs.

Labbite faces differed from most faces on the Continent. Labbites were the only group so distinguished anymore. They possessed the only known sensate whiskers and the only three-lensed yellow eyes. Eyes critical to surgeries and gene manipulation. The Shorn, and the Longhairs, like Eric, had rudimentary vestiges of whiskers or antennae. Sensate ridges on their foreheads or temples. In many cases, not even sensate. A physical testament to the decline of their society.

They'd fissured along physiognomy, much like the mountain rock. Broken and divided socially by minimal physical distinctions. The strange physical differences had become rare, marginal characteristics because of the innate recessiveness of Reaper genes. Those who manifested them were called Labbites.

The Continent's settlers, once a desperate accidental society, had broken into three physically distinct quarreling subcultures. The gene-marked, separated from those less marked. Making pariahs of the Reaper-blessed. Now the scientists, as Reaper-marked Labbites, were relegated to the fringe. A disgraced minority. Shunting aside any access to the boons from their Reaper genes.

Genetically, the three groups descended from the same cluster of ancestors. A single Reaper ship brim-full of human eggs and sperm and other assorted genetic harvests had crashed on the Red Continent twenty-plus generations ago. The Reaper ship was navigated by, at most, only a dozen individuals from the very advanced Reapers.

History Keeper lore told them Reapers were a bipedal, human-like, sentient, space-traveling life-form, bent on harvesting genes throughout the galaxies to foster radical mutations and achieve maximum genetic diversity within their species and settlement colonies. The whole of their technology was vested in genetic manipulation and expanding organic creativity. Organisms the font of their communications, life support, transportation, education, politics, technology, social change, material infrastructure, energy production, galaxy exploration—an orchestrated culturing of genetic harvests. Every species that evolved could be made to evolve to order. All could be recoded to serve Reaper-species aims.

Faced with no hope of escape and a severely circumscribed Reaper gene pool in the crash, the twelve survivors used their own DNA to form embryos in combination with the fertile human matter they'd gathered on their foray to Earth. Within a century of Earth time, before their own natural demise on this very Continent they'd crashed, they'd produced multiple genetically diverse generations, resulting in a surviving population of a few thousand Reaper-human individuals.

Albeit a population genetically more human than Reaper, their progeny nonetheless. Bequeathed what limited human language and culture Reapers had collected, experienced, or stole, seeded with as much Reaper technology and science as they could muster from within the remaining capacity of their crippled ship.

Could any have foreseen the political ramifications of this human-Reaper merge thirty generations on?

"Nothing is simple. Surely that is our legacy. I will frighten you more, Eric. Because I believe there are two ships. The only logical conclusion, given your observations and my own." George sipped some tea.

"Ya saw the run of the lights on the broke Reaper ship console parts too? When? And ya didn't tell me? But why not tell me of that, George? Ya saw somethin' of the Reapers, aye? They're coming?"

"No, Eric. I've seen a ship. Arriving before Winter, a ship that hasn't triggered the consoles. One that still hides itself now, half a cycle later, above a singularly revealing circle of melted snow. One that evidences nothing of Reaper technology. You, alone, have given me the input on the consoles, telling of this new arrival of a ship sympathetic with Reaper technology. I can only surmise the Reaper ship has just arrived. This day. When you saw the activation of the console with this rise of the sun."

Eric jumped up, nearly knocking the table over. George held his tea aloft and gripped the teetering table with both feet and his spare hand. Eric held his arms crossed over his head as he hopped up and down.

His face crumpled in empathy, George waited. Nothing was ever simple. No wonder anyone with a brain abandoned the creed.

George understood how hard it was for Eric to wrap his words around his thoughts. Their wars, the disintegration of their peoples, the marginalization of his tribe, the Labbites, had denied many smart folk like Eric the ability to articulate the depth of their thought, their caustic wit.

"Eric, I will not call a meeting. We have seen how our people handle complexities of this sort. You and I must contain this knowledge between ourselves. Perhaps until whoever landed here makes themselves known to us. There is a war going on with our peoples. We must not advantage or disadvantage one side or the other until we know what it is these aliens will ask of us. Or, perhaps, take from us. Or how they will interfere. Can you do this with me my friend? Can you become a Watcher with me? I may find help with other Labbites, but we cannot speak of this amongst the warring Longhair and Shorn."

George regarded the child-giant-man standing above him in such distress. He is so young. Despite this early silver in his hair. He is so frail. Despite his powerful musculature and size. He is kind. He finds such great delight in learning. He is so full of promise, he makes me remember my own sweet babes at shelter in my home.

Eric began to speak, hesitant. "I know what you're saying, George. Not a small thing, this. And I'm so full of questions. I wanna know too. But I understand ya. I knew it when I came to speak with you. This is the opening of a new way. A way not all of us will cross. Only some can know." Eric sank onto his bunk and curled his great bulk. Fetal. What would come?

12

CAI SUFFERS PHOEBE'S CAPTURE

Cai had never really faced up to the inadequacy and helplessness of mature restraint. Nothing quite like the pleasure of getting a full frontal. Somehow, he had to stay with the crowd holding Phoebe, but at the same time get ahead to see if he could anticipate an opportunity to get her free. Shouldn't be hard. It was a damn road. It went somewhere. Her captors followed it.

Like a bug on a pin Cai tortured himself over leaving Phoebe. But there was nothing he could do. Yet. He stuffed his rage, a monster, into the callus of his soul. Accepting his real mission. Not angst. Rescue.

Moving rapidly, Cai kept to cover. But cover above meant a littered ground. Pretty much everything got in his way. A confederacy of branches, limbs and roots tripped him. Slapped him in the face. Snagged the packs and his uni. His caution eased as he moved further from the road. Streaking ahead, near enough to see the cleavage in the trees that defined the road and predicted the crowd's direction.

Cai ran. He thrashed through the forest, his eyes open, his arms and stick sheltering his face. Both packs bounced against his back. He no longer felt his wounded leg as Phoebe's distant cries 'Cai!,' pierced him like a hot needle. He knew about heartstrings now. Cruel lacerating wires.

Cai almost missed the moment the forest leapt away. The sky opened and he snatched a thin trunk, barely stopping himself from sending noisy debris over the edge of a vast chasm. He'd come to a rock-sided canyon. He saw the road come out and pick its way like a delicate spinster, down the steep, rocky slope between endless slides of scree and huge boulders. A powder pink path that formed the only visible line of descent in the riot of red rock cliffs.

Well, wily coyote. Really dangerous and no cover. How could he stay covert to follow or head off Phoebe's captors? Cai, ducked down deep in the bushes, heard the approach of the clawing crowd-beast tearing at Phoebe. Her call was rasping, but still made her presence known, moving, mostly upright. Relief poured across him like acid scoring an open sore.

Then the entire drama boomed in audible frenzy. Phoebe swung out of a cage of limbs getting away just at the cusp of the slope. She dove for the steep, scree-lined rockface. Suicide. There was no footing on the dangerous cliff. Cai toothed his hand. Typical insane Phoebe. He bit the edge of his palm hard, needing the pain. And then Phoebe was free. Skating, surfing, gliding down the avalanche of scree like she'd been born to do it. Clawing handholds from thin air. The angry screaming mob froze in hung clouds of dust from thundering rock at the precipice.

Phoebe's arms flailed for balance but she held strong and managed to raise each leg in some kind of crazy tandem can-can with the rock. The rockface moved like so many greased ball bearings, sliding and gliding, speed-steady. Astounded, Cai almost rose above his cover. His jaw fell open and tears blurred his eyes.

The crowd was as ballistic as the rock slope. Some tried to follow her, but stumbled and tripped and collapsed in heaps on moving rock. She was twenty yards ahead of them now and widening the distance with ease. He watched her loft her arm up in the air like a mast, like a boat near pitchpoling down the side of a vast wave. Dwarfed by the slope hanging above her and rippling down below her thrusting legs. She looked like an ant on a mobilized red sand dune. The slope was liquid, rumbling, alive.

Thirty-odd of the alien-humans chose to run down the safety of the road, well-clear of the moving avalanche of rock. Cai clenched his hands, his body taut. Phoebe's only escape now was down the slope. The road goes down the slope and then runs alongside the cliff base. Unless she finds cover down there, she has no hope. Jesus, Phoebe. He thought he heard her yell "Whee!"

"Whee!" she called, again and again. Dammit, he wanted to laugh. He could throttle her. She made her mad escape look fun. Rode that damn rock like a wave. She must have been bruised if not gouged or wounded by that kicking, punching, capture. But didn't look it. She looked like Surfer Girl making waves in vulva valley.

☾ In red-blinded fury

Phoebe just went for it. When she saw the rocky cliff face something in her broke, snapped, clicked into place. She knew this rockface. She owned it. Her demon inside sprung her free of her captors. The field of stones called to her like gems to a dragon. She'd read about flying high on a scree slope, well buck a quacking duck. What was there to lose? Devil take her. To whistle down this slope like a bottle rocket was beyond living. What was she saving herself for anyway? Future's asked for this dance.

Before she cracked open the fortune cookie, her body was soaring in full-blown flight. Out of the starter cage. Her feet stuck to the rolling rock, balancing like she was nailed on. She felt herself engage with vulva land. *Baby woncha rock me onna Space Cruise?*

Whoopee. Rock-run. A great, heaving, giant-gliding, sliding, downward-pelting run. Rocks capitulated. They romped underneath her with rumbling, throaty laughter. Monster-skating all stars. She a cruising conveyor over the ricketing, rolling roar. A bubbling froth of rock. Slick-witch. No hands, no stick. Craziest, wildest, zaniest, most insanely fun momentum ever. Pitching, wheeling, lurching, a rock-wave surfer.

Her arms wind-milled, her butt clenched. Nothing to cling to but her guts. Lift a foot, skate down with the other. Ten yards a step. Who's counting? Red sun winking. Feel the wind. Then place her foot, lift the other and glide again. Her mind vacated. Cough capture, not butt-bare,, clawing, punching chucking quackers, burning sun, hot breathless air, Cai (he so better be watching) filed away for later, Baby. She strode, she rode, she pumped her legs, she tilted, she flew. So noisy. Rubbling, smacking, cracking. She, intensely focused, moving, pitching, hoping, choosing, winning, grinning, toppling, floating, so incredible, so fast. Exhilerfuckerating.

She felt like a river, sparkling in the red sun, bubbling, free-spitting cold-cheeked, white-frothed—a live thing borne by rollicking knuckles of rock. Rock it-rocket. Rocks threw her, cavorted with her, chuckled under her, laughed with her, played with her, bounced her, punched off her calves. More living than she had ever known. So fast. So intense, time slowed for her. Gave her the chance of knowing. Tasting life.

She could see everything, feel everything, hear everything. The noises of insects. Whoa, there were insects? How had she missed them? The buzz of the people screaming at her, arguing and chasing her down the road. The pounding of her heart like great drums of war. Her wheezing, pumping lungs. She tasted the dry pink fairy sprinkles. She heard the moan and creak of the rock. The knuckled chuckles and groans and rumbling joy. Her mouth open. Her teeth bared in a crazy grin. Careful now, don't sever the dry tongue pointing like a puppy tail between her open lips. Never let this end. Stars glittered in her eyes, like a galaxy, like life had found her out and concentrated itself upon her, upon only these moments, only this being in all of space and all of time.

Then with as much shock as when he had taken her, the demon who fucked her this hard, down this whole great ride, this unfathomable moment of joy, evaporated. Came. Went.

And there she was stepping off the rock escalation like a fallen woman. Washed out, breathless, torn of clothes, wet with sweat, dripping. Exaltation sucked out like the ghost of a last breath.

Spent. She was the shell, the wreck that was left. Jilted. Tears of joy still rolled unbidden down her blush-grained, snotty cheeks. Taking a sobbing breath, she tried to gather herself, looking helplessly around for a there to hide her wanton self. To retreat, to recover. To hold herself and remember this one brief life she lived. She pushed herself to think. Maybe she *could* get away. Phoebe, shaking, forced herself to move, to try to run to freedom. But sobs and tears came like they belonged to an innocent. She stumbled into a ragged run toward the road.

The captors were coming, she could hear them yelling. Maybe she could get free. Maybe without breath, with soggy muscles like milk-soaked bread, with tears burning her eyes, clouding her vision, with thirst raking at her throat, dry, raw. Maybe she was the engine that could. Klutzy, awkward, blinded, and sobbing, she jogged, or jagged or just lifted her legs in some wilted motion. Somehow propelled forward.

The road, the away, the where, the hiding, the escape called. Too much nowhere, too little to get there. Not near enough energy, or knowing, or will, or limbs that worked, or anything else to make it.

They closed on her even as she bumbled from them. She was netted by their grasping arms, their tripping legs, their yelling cacophony. Her tears came harder. Tears for Cai, for her seconds of fleeting life now fled, for her demon lover. Her virgin innocence sundered. Then the hands were crawling all over her. They were plastered into her with the screams and spittle and shouts and punches and laughter and glee, like vicious muscled ants, bites and grabs and pulls and pushes. And she gave into them. In defeat, not in triumph the way she had yielded to her demon.

She let herself hang, strung among them utterly at their will. She heard them chanting over and over "long hair, long hair." And she wanted to protest, "I'm not a cow," her head lolling, she whispered "I'm not a cow."

Her brain blank, empty. Sounds merged together in an angry hum. Her eyes, mouth, face, caked with tears, mucous, dirt and spit. She had no care left. Her feet went forward when pushed. She didn't resist. She let them take her dull mind to wherever they took their cows. Did the people who hated the cows shoot them like they did the horses?

She had nothing but fog, dim awareness, stone streets, rough hive buildings in pink stucco, stacked like logs, windows clear, brilliant prisms, strewn like eyes across a corrugated beast. Hardly large enough to see out, she murmured to herself in her bubble of nothingness. Metal, or mirrors reflecting the crowd now joined by hundreds, if that wasn't reflection or the exaggeration of her weary mind. Holding sticks or pikes, metal-tipped. There were young, old, short, tall, sick, limping, missing limbs, faces buggered. All clothed the same, pastel shift with a sash robe over one shoulder, short curly hair or shorn, biscuit skin, dark or yellow eyes, lean-fleshed. Mean.

Tired and weak and thirsty, she let herself be pushed along. She licked her dry, chapped, dusty lips and brought crumbs into her mouth. Stuck there like dry bread, choking her. She had nothing. Hardly breath, not even will.

The last thought she had when she left the world was why hadn't she known? Why hadn't she known that to contest with passion as a gladiator with a beast, as a man with extreme sport, as a woman with a demon lover, as a fight to death, why hadn't she known that that's how men lived? Just like the vids. They burned through life event to event, from sex act to sport, to fight, to war, because that was where life pulsed. Not held safe. Erupting. The storm not the shelter. Unlike womb-man, woman. A function, more like shelter than storm.

Look at the rewards. How did mere love compare to actually living? To actually fighting through each moment with a punch so assertive it could pass through a dimension? From mere breathing, to feeling the harsh breath of death brush along a cheek? How had she not known men fanned the combustion, the great flames of human spirit, the crashing inferno of will, self-determination and passion in so-called sport? Men exalted in life. Women bore it. In wombs, where cherished coals of another's life were kindled.

Did womb-bearing pressure still carry that price? Did womb-bear chemistry stifle women's pulse of life, bank her coals to harbor, to shelter, to protect from life's storm? How had she not felt compelled to kindle her own fire? Sneaky culture. Spawn-hungry, the new planet settlements offered their last remaining walking incubators the mere guise of freedom. Culture still infiltrated, still induced a gendered destiny to tamp the fires.

Now Phoebe understood the raving craving of men. The feared denial of billowing flame. She understood how romantic love might pale next to the sweaty, profound, deep, lost passion of sex. On that rock she rode life balls-to-the-fiery-wall. She ran her dry tongue softly across her parted lips.

She was so thirsty. Then she fainted.

Slivered awareness. Light breaks sketched in shadows. Hands grabbed at her, lifted her on shoulders high. A captor. Gentle hands. She glimpsed a face. One kind, tender face. A giant holding back the cruel crowd from trampling her. He lifted her. His name was Brattoch.

☾ En-Phoebled

Cai held his head in his hands and groaned. At least she had managed to cover her ass. He knew that must have been how they caught her. But he could imagine her wheeing

126

through her flight down the rock with her ass bare. Because that was Phoebe. She knew how to put surviving first.

At the very least she was alive. She'd pulled the crowd down the road away from him. She had snagged their attention, freed him from the risk of discovery. He could see the road wind down and through the center of the valley. A large basin of water sparkled. The stream turned river, a turquoise pink-silvered thread. The slopes were entirely rocky on both sides of the chasm. There was some cover in the huge boulders but these would be tricky to navigate. They were scattered amongst broad low channels of scree.

Cai saw her scree surf ending in recapture. Too few places for her to hide. He had to catch up somehow. He picked his way across the forested ridge of the chasm until he was at the road. There was no one on it as far as he could see. Those at the bottom were chasing down the road to intercept Phoebe. He noted big boulders that would give him cover. For most of the way he could run.

Cai ran. Downhill. If he hadn't been so filled with terror for Phoebe, it might have felt easy, good. His heart pounding, lungs bellowing, legs pumping, arms keeping the beat, he ran, dodged lumps and bumps and sags in the dirt road. The sound of voices intensifying. He would come upon them soon. Trying to reel in his pace, he scanned for cover. And then an arm in the air, a shout, so close he could almost see the spit spray. Oh crap. They were right there. He smartly tucked himself behind a MIDGE-sized boulder, and held still, sweating in the shadow, breathing heavily, silent as possible, while he listened. They were near.

Yells. Screams. Softer orders batted back and forth. Feet pounding. Aliens falling, tripping, running. Cai heard Phoebe, husky-voiced, yelling "no, no, Cai NO! Cai Cai."

Cai squeezed himself into the rock. His face and body scraped, pinched and scored. He craved pain. Pain to dull his agony. Would he could just be brain. Crisp, cool, clean thoughts. His wire-shredded heart leaked. He had to find a way to get Phoebe free. His sweat evaporated, chilling him. Tears burned his eyes. A bitter laugh lanced through him. At Phoebe, triumphant, riding that mountain slide with fearless abandon. She scared the piss out of him. He'd "whee" her when he caught up.

13

THE GROUND RUSHED TO MEET THE SHIP

With a misfire in the power of a thruster, the ship collapsed on its airfoil and dropped hard to the ground. Tipping, laden, heavy. The sounds of metal crumpling and screaming rips. Alarms klaxoned, reverberating throughout the cabin. The rocking tilt unhooked or unbolted Linda's chair. Linda, still buckled in, crashed around the cabin. Rolling, smashing instruments, hands, her leg crushed, screaming cries. Kendak, Davis, stunned immobile. Linda careened out of control. Linda's foot caught on a steel brace under the console. Her lower leg threatened to tear off with the chair's vagrant momentum.

Maria, foolishly standing as they landed, loosely banged around the room like a ball in an Old Earth lottery machine. A bounce on her head, a bash into a bulkhead. A near collision with Linda's rampant chair. Maria's empty seat belts whipped their metal hooks like steel beads. Stinging Maria's cheek as she flew by. Her nose spurted blood. She tucked her head to her chest and curled into herself, as the ship finally rocked to a standstill. Linda screaming in unbearable agony. Strapped in, Kendak and Davis were wounded by flying objects they couldn't duck. The awkward landing burning seatbelt rashes onto their chests and thighs.

Maria's nose bled so badly into her chest she almost choked. The top of her head was bruised and tender. The ship rested. Beeping, howling and screeching from various alerts and alarms serenaded the cabin, shrilling painfully against raw nerves.

"CLEO, cut sound to alarms!" Davis croaked. Maria saw his hands wander tenderly across his chest as though he probed for breaks. He released his buckles. The alarms silenced. "Cut power to any systems at risk." Davis commanded. CLEO obeyed soundlessly. Maria unrolled herself to tend to Linda. Dizzy, she found herself wondering anew whether Davis's written commands held CLEO's key. Davis demurred when she requested a key to CLEO's navigation. He'd said she had enough on her plate just keeping an eye on all the other systems she single-handed these days.

Linda lay on the floor crying, her crushed leg bleeding, raw shards of bone torn through the fabric of her pants.

"Oh God, Linda!" Maria, head-spinning, rushed to unstrap the broken bundle of old woman, tenderly freeing her to lay flat, careful of the shattered leg.

Pinching her own bleeding nose, suppressing her groans, Maria scrambled to fetch the med kit. Linda was truly suffering. Despite the tilted deck, Maria was soon back, stabbing Linda's shoulder with a pain-killing syringe. Step two, unwrap a chemical pack for the leg. They'd have to take Linda's leg off below the knee. They simply had no way to repair damage this grievous. Shutting her ears to Linda's cries, Maria smothered Linda's leg in the chem pack. Her confidence in the numbing agents justified as Linda sighed. At least the chems stopped the gasped sobs. Her head flopped to the side, her face and jaw slack. Maria covered her tenderly with a chem-warmed blanket. She was stable for now.

"Open ventilation," ordered Davis as he watched Maria tend Linda. Maria tasted the freshness in the air. Her mouth gaped. Air so sweet and moist. Maria tipped her head back pinching the gauze on her nostrils. None of them would be stepping outside anytime soon. Hell, The Three resorted to walkers even shipboard. Linda might not walk at all ever again. Not quite the arrival they hoped for. Another entry for the log they didn't keep.

The spherical NEW CLEO tipped forward, off-kilter in landing. CLEO's wounds touched Maria more than Linda's. But NEW CLEO raised Maria. Told her stories, dug up funny cartoons for her, handled the twins' education, gave Maria guidance and instruction. Shared years of comfort, laughter, learning and play. Linda became relevant when, as part of The

Three, she told Maria and Joseph the tale of the deaths. When Linda's words filled the corridors of CLEO with ghosts and mystery. The news broke the twins from their cocoon. Aroused Joseph's curiosity. The news led to his death.

The screen Maria looked through before they landed now faced the ground. Daylight, dirt, and some broken, burned shards of fiery bush showed, but not much else. Maria walked the canted floor to Davis and Kendak.

"Linda's leg looks bad." Davis whispered.

"It is bad. We'll have to take it off. There's no way we can repair it without a surgeon, maybe even if we had one." Maria whispered back, her speech thick and nasal. "Are you guys okay? I saw you feeling your ribs."

"Yeah, I'm fine, chest is burned from the straps. Ribs are bruised maybe. Not likely broken. Chafe on my thighs too. Can you make it to sick bay? Is there any way we can cause the ship to roll more upright?" Davis handling the conversation. Kendak nodding along.

"I think so, but I don't want to move us until we stabilize Linda. I'll bring the surgical stuff in here. We should act promptly to minimize the trauma. Her limb is useless. We have to take care of this now." The surgical unit could bite off the leg and cauterize the vessels and nerves. It would pack the wound and administer antibiotics, painkillers and all the other protectives. God knows what microbial contamination they faced. At least CLEO's air filtration capacity was stratospheric. They survived on used air. *Fresh* filtered air was a godsend.

Davis and Kendak could just damn well stay put in the tipped cabin while Maria put together the surgery unit. When she came back, she rolled Linda onto the stretcher and strapped her in. The chem pack and trouser leg stripped off, Maria doused Linda's butchered flesh with sanitizer. She clamped the surgical unit on. Tubes and wires led back to the med cart, where Maria programed the unit for surgery.

Kendak and Davis observed. Linda out for the count. After whirring and flexing for around ten minutes, the unit unclamped. Maria pulled it away. The gory mess of Linda's calf and foot neatly gel-packed, compressed and sealed. Maria heaved the whole bundle into the waste cycler. Linda breathing steady, dead to the world. Davis and Kendak crawled to the stretcher and helped Maria strap Linda in as tightly as possible. They ratcheted her firmly in place and then returned to strap into their own seats.

Maria reached for the ship stabilizer controls and toggled them active. Her wads of scabbed nose gauze long gone. "CLEO, push the North stabilizers to right the ship and hold steady on East and West, prepare to receive on South. Maria held herself taut against the bulkhead with the hand rails there. Safe enough. CLEO didn't need to alter position much and her hydraulics were smooth. With a groan and a squeal, the motors began the push into the South jacks. Maria barely felt a thing.

But Linda now hung comatose from the bulkhead. Maria trotted over joining Davis. A slow release of the ratchets, laid Linda's stretcher horizontal. Stable on the cabin sole. Maria brought the med cart over to activate treatment and monitor Linda's vitals. Linda coped, but the vitals showed trauma took a toll.

Kendak and Davis creaked to the viz screen. Like kids, with their noses pressed to the glass. Maria took Linda off to medbay. She wanted to clean herself up, eat, rest. She wouldn't be curious. Not with them.

"Aww! Crap, you're kidding me." Maria much rested, vented as she returned to the main cabin. She scrolled the system checks. Hammered the keyboard with a series of queries. "Something is trying to access our stores-bay vent. It's chewing the valve insulators." Maria stood, poking various camera feeds, twisting and wriggling on her feet in distress. Kendak puckered his brow. Objecting to her? Curious?

REPULSE. Repulse this insult to CLEO. This is an attack by an alien. Ewww! Taking damage from an asteroid was one thing. Even a clumsy landing forgiven. But spewing saliva? Chewing on CLEO? Yelch. Way too much like the lice that crawled all over Maria ever since CLEO told her about the blood-sucking insects. Maria was nauseated.

"Kendak, can you see it on camera?" Davis asked, calm and neutral.

Kendak had taken up the cause. Maria saw him file through their weapons systems, not seeming very revolted. No weapon she knew of could pry off an animal chewing the hull. Kendak sent a few of his scans to her as they both searched for camera feed from the vicinity of the stores bay port.

"Here, I've got it!" Maria trumpeted. She linked Kendak and Davis's screens into her feed. The image wasn't clear. The camera needed lube and grinding. Lenses scored after decades of travel. A grainy shape moved into view.

"That's an animal?" Maria asked peering intently at the screen. "Huh. Kinda reminds me of a giant squirrel. Impressive paws though, almost like hands. Like a koala, or a primate. Slubbering spit, thing is really trying to chew its way in. How do they know how to do that? What does it want, I wonder? Can't smell any food can it? Isn't the ship still hot from entry?"

As though Kendak and Davis would know. How could they know what scent signatures their ship emanated? Frozen packaged waste was blasted out. No residues. CLEO's skin had to be clear of whatever might attract that thing. Especially after a hot entry.

"We've got something it wants," Davis smiled, as though intrigued by the busy creature. "Hell, we respire. The whole ship breathes. Maybe it reads us like the computer reads this planet. What does CLEO say?"

"Warm-blooded, hemoglobin, respiration, lungs internal, mammal, fur-covered. Very hard teeth and claws. Opposable thumbs, hands on four limbs. Possibly flies or glides, depending on gravity. Weighs about two kilos. Marsupial. Has parasites. Ewww!" Maria read the stream aloud though the men could see it on their monitors.

"Cool. Sort of a miniature kangaroo-koala-squirrel. Life lives on life, Maria." Davis sounded pompous. Hell, so what if she was a woman of thirty and she squirmed like a teenager over a few bugs? He'd actually met bugs before. He lived with bugs on Earth. Maria shivered with disgust.

"Dizz-gusting! Those things are sucking its blood."

"The stuff we eat comes from things that were alive. We are groomed by parasitic microorganisms. They are inside us, helping to digest our food and externally, they eat our waste and clothe us. We wear their byproducts for God's sake, Maria. And we suffer because their populations are dwindling. We'll need to do some blood sucking of our own here." Davis paused, "You in particular, if you want to survive."

Then he tried a different tack. "Damn thing's really kinda cute. Maybe it's just curious. Computer says it's a she, by the way. Doesn't detect any venom sacs either. You might have to get out there and scare it off, Maria. Unless you want it to come in here. Might be looking for a place to nest."

She always knew they'd find a way to push her out there. The aliens weren't supposed to chime in.

Daylight still blazed, Linda's systems read stable. Maria didn't have any excuse to stay inside. Kendak and Davis scrolled and typed, pretending to ignore her.

The Three were frail. Fact. She wasn't. While they deeply cherished planetary life forms, Maria cherished the damn ship. The Three would use her love of CLEO to drive her outside. Force her to interact with the stupid planet. By making her want to stop that little mutt of a creature from contaminating Maria's perfect CLEO world.

"Fine." Maria pulled on a helmet and went to the locker to suit up.

"You shouldn't need a helmet out there, might get in your way." Kendak didn't get it. She knew he'd go out in a heartbeat if he was her age.

"I want the comms," she said, pausing, as good as they were at jibes, "CLEO keeps Joseph with me." They never enjoyed hearing her bring up her dead twin's name.

She exited the main airlock close to where the miserable thing was chewing. It didn't feel like space walking at all. The suit dragged her down. Her gloves made her hands clumsy mitts.

A red-red world stole Maria's breath. To stand here, steps from broken tufts of valentine red grass, softened the ice queen's shard in her heart. Kneeling, she toggled off the comms. No, they weren't allowed to witness. She pulled off her gloves, leaned forward, touched the soil and grass with her tremulous hand. The animal forgotten. The ominous skittering easy to ignore. Maria's lower body clung like a separate being, attached to the ship. Her upper self reached. A blossoming heart-melt inside her made her want to strip bare and let her whole skin feel.

First drop the helmet. Let it roll a little. Now her head was absolutely free. Strands of her hair floated across her face. Her nostrils flared. The air tickled her nose. Flushing the toxins, the Joseph-ghosts, the eavesdropping old men, she cast out her breath. Then the gloves. Clipped together she flung them atop her stilled helmet. Standing on the narrow step, Maria peeled her suit off like the littlest Mermaid's tail and ventured out onto land. The liner her only clothing. Her fingers, her face, bare. *Ave* Maria. Plucked, exposed, to touch, to know. Borne finally free of CLEO's womb.

A toddler. Unbalanced. New damp yielding surfaces with unyielding gravity tried to plant her in the soil. Shaky raw breaths drawn into shattering lungs. The soft scalp of the world accepted her thin-booted toe as she parted little tufts of flowery-red grass. Long, slender blades spilled over her feet.

Maria flapped her arms in a stilted, crippled ballet. Pink fairy dust motes danced with her in the soft breeze. Bittersweet Joseph-tears welled. Blink and the tears twinkle like stars. Her jaw dropped in awe. So much to take in. A swollen gulp of air. She could run. Run forever free.

An echoing poem of life's gifts tattooed itself invisibly on her skin, her eyes, her heart, her soul. Maria looked back at the ship. Startled, she saw the animal gripping high on the curve of hull, rising in challenge. Maria shook her head and abruptly stepped back. Locked eyes with the alien's opposing pair. Black, deep, unblinking wet wells. A shiny quivering nose, a chittering protest emerged from the cat-sized, mahogany-red, fur bundle.

Maria succumbed in a trance to the creepy-critter. I'll call you Josie. New-found muscles tugged her mouth, linked to her new-warm heart. Maria smiled. Josie, for Joseph, who is gone.

Maria barely managed to scale the laddered depressions up to the stores port. New-gravity weight hung from her like ballast. Josie watched Maria approach. Curious. As though she recognized Maria posed little threat.

Maria wheezed with unfamiliar air. Her tentative tongue probing the air's taste, curled. How could air taste this good? Fresh. Clean, a washed and shining scent. Maria's hands clutched sweaty on the holds. The air heavy on her back and shoulders.

She wanted to slide back down to the giving ground. Where she would lie with her hair strewn across a brush of red grass and feel the earth pulse living into her soul. Her foot skidded, missed the rung. She clenched hard with weak muscles. A shadow floated overhead. Predator? Was she prey? Maria shrank against the hull. Josie cocked her head, not running. No sign of fear.

Crapper wrapper. Jesus what a drama. All this feeling, this creature-reaching. Excitement bubbled in Maria's core. She heaved breaths of air so moist she felt like she could drown.

Five more rungs up to Josie's coveted vent. But Maria was overcome with nausea. She had to forfeit. Maybe food could help tempt Josie to leave the vent alone. Limp, Maria slid, bumping rung depressions all the way down to the ground. Leaning against the ship to catch her breath. Slow, dizzy. Barely managing to hold her stomach down, she gathered her things and headed in. Her brain at least renewed with a plan for torturing Kendak and Davis. Cheshire smile style. Maria's turn. They pushed her out here. Time to bait the bears.

With her gear stuffed back in the entry locker Maria strode into the main cabin hiding her roiling gut. Kendak and Davis looked ready to pounce.

"Well? Didja like it? The real world?" Davis talked through the bread in his mouth, finishing up a sandwich. One eye flicking toward his monitor, likely keeping tabs on Linda.

"Made me kinda sick. It's okay. Smell's nice. I saw the creature." She sat in the pilot chair and pulled up the feed tracking Josie and the stores vent. "There. You can see it," she announced, sneaking a glance at Davis and Kendak to catch them if they bit.

Maria ran the vid on the big monitor. Josie looked at the camera quizzically. Probably saw the indicator light. She stood up on her hind legs.

"God! Look at the hands it's got for feet!" Kendak shouted, rapt. Josie's little feet-hands were gripping some of the raised rivets on their hull. Her front paw-hands fisted, like she wanted to punch out the camera or something.

Maria smiled to herself, go devil-girl. "Maybe I should try to kill it?" Maria gave them a little frisson.

"You don't really think you need to kill it do you?" Kendak looked aghast Maria would even consider such a thing. He was ready to defend little Josie, a creature who posed no danger to them.

"Maybe we could butcher it and eat it?" Maria said, hiding her satisfaction. Childish, torturing them like this. But the forgiveness welling inside her battled with her Joseph-ghosts. Just a slash or two more for them, in final remembrance. A little granite marker chipped from her soul.

Davis acted completely flummoxed. Aha. They could stand to suffer some repercussions from sending her out. Why should she be expected to relate to an animal? Unlike The Three, she'd never encountered a wild beast. They should have predicted her reaction. Davis gave little impression he'd considered what this planetary arrival might mean to Maria. "Just see what it does," he said, sounding alarmed. Maria watched him neatly avoid Kendak's eye.

Maria turned off her monitor. "Later. I need to eat and get some sleep. You guys should rest too. How's Linda?"

140

"Not as well as I'd hoped. Her system isn't handling the trauma well. Still out, but her blood pressure is too high. I'm not sure what we should do." Kendak scrolled as he spoke. Neither of them looked her in the eye.

"Let the CLEO handle it. She probably just needs time." Maria waltzed away.

The Three were napping when she snuck out of CLEO again. This time she didn't bother with a suit. The camera feed showed Josie still out there. Half a day she'd spent so far, tormenting their hull, said CLEO. Maria felt the pocket full of granola she carried in hopes of pacifying Josie. A big adventure. Fun. A word that hadn't occurred to her in decades. Her very first chance to make a friend.

Convulsive, Maria hunched up her shoulders when wind tickled her skin as she opened the airlock. The tickling scared her. Odd. When had she last been tickled? Joseph? He would love this. Meeting a creature. They once dreamed about the animals they might someday know.

She and Joseph built many worlds together. Real in every salient way. But not real like this. Nothing had ever been real like this. Maria felt guilty just like CLEO said she would. CLEO therapy taught her names for all her feelings. Not something The Three could teach her. On Earth they hadn't learned to parent. Their own parents raised them through devices too. Each of them, including Maria and Joseph, related best that way.

Kissed by fresh air, tickled by wind, touching living things with her hands and feet. This chance to court a creature friend. Maria had no idea how to interact with a living world,

141

living beings. She wasn't programmed to do this. She was out of her element. And worse, to land on a world, to live on a world, betrayed Joseph by giving Maria experiences he would never know.

The wind played with her hair. Maria relaxed her hunch a little and dug the granola out of her pocket. Where was Josie? Maria stood in the shadow of the ship, her feet learning the tiny tripping hillocks beneath her feet. She studied the hull.

There. Just above the airlock. Josie must've seen Maria emerge. The creature sat back on her hind paws and stared, shiny black eyes unblinking. Maria smiled, unsettled by the exciting tugs she felt inside. She crouched to the ground. Josie cocked her head, interested.

Maria held her hand forward, palm open. The wind breathing warm on her shoulders, licking her bare neck. Josie retracted. Startled or curious? Maria froze. Josie put her front paws down and scampered toward the ladder holds. Shooting quick glances at Maria's granola handout like she recognized the granola as food. Could she? Maria steadied, feeling the pull of her muscles fighting gravity. Hard to move in gravity, but harder to stay still. Maria grinned, almost laughed aloud when Josie turned and climbed down, bottom first. Using the ladder like a pro.

On the ground Josie pivoted and faced Maria, mere feet from Maria's outstretched hand. Josie's wet nose wiggled. Her black eyes blinked. In a flash Josie darted over and grabbed the treat from Maria's hand. Then rapidly scampered a dozen yards away. Using both hands she mashed the granola into her mouth. Maria saw the sharp little white teeth. She heard the crunch of Josie chewing. Josie cocked her head. She wanted more.

Maria watched as Josie ran to the base of the ship where the stabilizers had footed. Josie began to excavate soil and debris. Holding something in her paw, Josie turned and considered Maria again. Maria hurriedly filled her hand with granola and held it out. Josie approached slowly this time. Stop-start. Hump-hump. Wiggle-groom. A little dance. Finally within reach, Josie pinched the crumbs of granola with her soft fuzzy fingers and dropped a payment into Maria's hand with her other paw. Josie scurried away to eat, stuffing her cheeks while gazing curiously at Maria. Not as far this time, Josie chewed.

Moving very slowly Maria lifted her hand to see the gift. Damn! Looked like Josie found a clip neatly plied free of their ship. Maybe from the fouled stabilizer? Well, wouldn't do them much good anymore.

Hmm. More than granola interested her new friend. Like she thought in terms of exchange and barter. An economy. Radical. Excited, Maria held her hand toward Josie, thumb and forefinger generously offering to return the clip. Josie came forward, tentative, still chewing. She ignored the clip, pulling instead at the wire port bracelet Maria wore on her wrist. Maria startled, snatched back her hand. Josie flipped away, well out of reach, obviously frightened.

"Okay, okay. I'm sorry." Maria spoke softly, repentant. "I'm calling you Josie. After my brother, Joseph." Maria felt her eyes tear. She could see him darting through the brush, playing hide and seek with Josie. Far beyond their wildest dreams. Did

143

animals understand words? Dogs did in the vids she'd watched. So did parrots, horses, cats, primates, dolphins and the octopus. CLEO gave her studies of Earth, including animal behavior. Animals could be taught to understand human conversation. They emoted. Better than a computer? A desperate craving she didn't understand burned in her chest.

Her mind struggled, overwhelmed. Interspecies comms was magic, rivaling what she had with CLEO. CLEO was programmed to respond to her. An animal, an alien life form, could choose. Even more remarkable, Maria could influence that choice simply by being someone the animal would choose. Or not. Shocking. Moving. At once so meaningful, Maria wanted to cry. Why? Why did this thought choke her up? Josie might choose to love her.

How did feelings become an impulse to reciprocate? Because a need erupted. She wanted to give Josie something. Josie had already given her a hard-won clip. Theft or salvage. Maria couldn't give Josie the bracelet because that linked her comms throughout the ship. Maria didn't wear jewelry. She had some The Three said came from her grandparents. Like they even knew. The jewelry came from someone. Didn't matter. It wasn't the right thing for Josie.

She had tabs on her suit. Hundreds of those on board. Her hands wandered her clothing. Found a tab she could probably work free.

"Hey Josie, you can have this and the clip." She held both out. Josie watched her with interest. Then she scurried forward, stopping abruptly just short of Maria's outstretched hand. She waited. Maria admired her caution. She gave herself just enough room to be clear of Maria's grasp should things go sideways again.

Josie crouched low looking up under Maria's hand to see what she'd been gifted. Then she slowly stretched out her paw holding her own palm up. Maria carefully let the tab and clip drop into the open paw. Josie pulled her arm back and then hopped a yard away to consider her booty. She sniffed at them both, and tucked them into a pouch on her abdomen.

Maria gasped, astonished. "You have pockets in your fur!" Josie scurried away, startled again. Then she romped and bounced happily racing under Maria. Off-balance, Maria tumbled over and laughed. But Josie had scampered up the ladder and was well out of reach. Taunting Maria. Playful. Staggering, Maria realized she no longer remembered how to play. But she wanted to remember. She wanted to play.

Winter is coming to the planet, CLEO said. Ironic. Just as Maria began to thaw.

14

GEORGE

After the very sobering meeting with Eric, George the Labbite geologist continued his long plod somewhere. A direction frustratingly uncertain. The receded snows exposed his favorite stream as a mere trickle, not yet swollen with melted snow. This he could follow. A less treacherous pathway through soggy earth, crumbled rock and dense forest. Misgivings weighed on his every part.

The nearest transmitter or ship's console remains had to be his first destination. Knoll Tain Lab. Nearby. Other Labbites must've noticed the console parts or devices signaling. Kertof, too, had a Reaper device and George feared this was the kind of thing he'd attend to.

A bright green-black chicken ran out of the brush at his feet. Buc-buccing loudly, then screeching, irate. Who knows what startled the creature? They rarely flew. Change was coming. All the months of denial had only given George less time to prepare his people. Now they had two ships to contend with, and Kertof had begun yet another War.

George stopped at the verge of Knoll Tain's Lab. He braced his pack between his calves so it wouldn't wet in the damp earth. Ungloved, he pulled out the ties in his braids shaking his antennae free. He'd just picked up a timid hint of the red velvet fungi network in the newly revealed base of a tree. His antennae would deliver a small impulse. He let them know he'd arrived.

A Labbite didn't need to knock. A stream of Knoll Tain Labbites filed out of the main Lab entrance. Squinting at him in the bright sun. Wiping at their tearing eyes. Their gazes shifting to macroscopic, at least those blessed with inner lenses, that could view microscopically. These were the gene editors, his people's last surviving surgeons. Apparently, his arrival was marshaling the most stellar of their troops. George knew they'd sussed out his mission. They were on alert. As he suspected, the activation Eric witnessed on the console meant those who had consoles or devices knew about the ships.

Maybe because the Labbites were so deeply buried in individual pursuits they hankered for consensus, for hive-like groupthink. Or maybe that hunger was caused by the politics of 'difference' that isolated them from their Shorn and Longhair relatives.

The Reapers had been so bent upon genetic diversity, they so embraced 'difference' as an attribute critical to the survival of the species as a whole, George wondered how their mixed progeny managed to make 'difference' such an offense, such a threat.

Labbites struggled to accept that *Homo sapiens*, their dominant relatives, unlike their hive-minded Reaper relatives, used 'difference' to allocate status, and behavioral rules and roles. To stratify—and codify—rights, responsibilities and power. Behavior in support of the structured rules and roles established trust in tribes made up of choosers. Those who weren't programmed to follow a species-map. The breaking and rebuilding of trust was a critical building process in the evolution of Homo sapiens society. Whereas the gene coding for hive-minded species attributed primacy to the value of hive betterment. Did social-trust building and social contracting, or programmed hive social behavior, work better as an evolutionary strategy for species success?

Reapers were soundly in the hive camp. For them, advantageous characteristics were equally distributed because each improved individual advantaged the whole. They didn't understand how individual physical advantages could be used to differentiate, to stratify, to divide, to shun, to oppress, to compete and to war. They didn't believe that war winnowed out the weak or that it bettered the whole to focus on strength as the single best attribute.

George was partial to his Reaper characteristics. He liked his whiskers, antennae and yellow eyes. Antennae might disturb lovers and friends not so endowed. He kept them braided in his hair except when he was alone or when he needed them. Some of the minerals he sought had signatures he could detect if his antennae were free. He often sensed atmospheric signals he wasn't able to interpret meaningfully. Maybe the pure Reapers were more capable. If they had come back, perhaps he would soon find out.

"Well met, George." Moriah spoke, as the first in line to greet him.

"Moriah, Justice, Herald, I am happy to see you." George knew he didn't look happy. If pressed, he could remember the names of the ten or so other Labbites gathering at Knoll Tain's threshold, but he had too much on his mind. Even if the others had already seen the devices signal the arrival of a ship, George wanted to have a quiet meeting with just the leadership. He suspected that he alone had discovered the landing site of the non-Reaper ship. Caution was warranted.

George nodded at individuals filing out, and clasped forearms, as they did with him. "Could I speak with you three?" George asked, certain that everyone knew whom he referenced.

"Yes, of course. Come in. We'll take refreshment in my quarters." Moriah led George in through the double doors and down the long hallways. Large flakes of translucent muscovite, lit from behind, laced the walls and ceiling. Moriah's quarters were deep in the cavern, separate from other living quarters and working labs. Herald and Justice followed George. The other Labbites returned to their own concerns. Trust evident everywhere. A stark contrast to the anxiety and whispers George encountered in his interactions with Longhair groups or Shorn.

Moriah opened her quarters and indicated pallet seating for them. She bustled to the stove adding a hot kettle of water to a waiting carafe of tea. The three men served themselves tea and sat sipping until Moriah joined them.

"You have seen or heard about the activated consoles and devices this past day." George stated without preliminary. Three grave grey heads nodded, antennae steepled. "That might suggest a Reaper ship or other sympathetic technology has arrived on our Continent." More patient nods. "But before this Reaper signal, in fact, before the Winter snows, I saw and heard an alien ship break atmosphere and land."

Three hands set aside cups, and three heads leaned toward him, not quite so patient anymore. "Two days ago, I returned to that ship's landing site and I heard it hum, alive with machinery. Hidden from my eyes, it casts a melted circle in the snow. Very large. I fear a hold of a thousand beings or more.

"After seeing the melted circle and hearing the evidence of a ship, I had a chance meeting with Eric Longhair. And he told me of the Reaper console's activation. The console pieces he plays with activated a signal sequence. This is something none of us have ever witnessed. Nor did our History Keepers ever reference such a thing. But I know that the alien ship did not activate our Reaper devices. I watched my own set of console instruments for the whole of this Winter just in case the arrival I had seen activated them."

"We had felt hope at the Reaper device activation. Perhaps because that makes this alien event seem acceptable, familiar. If they are linked to the devices of our ancestors, we are hopeful to see them. But what you say about the unsignaled arrival before Winter, and the alien nature of the hidden ship, casts shade upon my hope." Justice's strained voice faded. He was very old.

"So, there are two ships, or there is an alien ship with something capable of activating Reaper devices. Perhaps a Reaper arrives in a mission within the alien ship. I see reason for cautious optimism yet. We know there is little here on our Continent to invite invasion. Our Reaper ancestors didn't choose to land here. They crashed. The likelihood is still strong that rescuing us, or otherwise aiding us, is the attraction."

There was no other Labbite quite as analytical or as succinct as Moriah. George nodded in agreement with her counsel. "I suspect you know that Kertof theorizes Reapers are from the same stock as the Wasp Queen. That our ancestor's ship landed to "plant" meat crops as the harvested food crops for the large Wasps here. And we have truly functioned as a crop for the Wasp drones. Our wars supply a regular meaty culling for them. They couldn't ask for a better meat crop. We even butcher ourselves." George hated to give voice to Kertof's theory, but the game-changing arrival of ships meant a reckoning with the truth one way or another.

Herald laughed. "Kertof has a sort of brilliance for a stupid man. But say he is correct, wouldn't an alien ship promise us, this 'meat crop,' some hope of escape? Thus, we may conclude, even Kertof's theory suggests we might regard this alien ship arrival as a reason for hope. For change, escape, wisdom, or at the very least, for unity. Any of which we can well use.

At a minimum, any threat offers a divided society a chance for unity. We desperately need unity. I suggest we use the ship or ships to seek unity regardless of that ship's agenda. Because the ship's agenda is not something we can manage for, or know. Now that they have landed us an opportunity, let's use them to heal the divisions between us."

"You three are reliably brilliant in your counsel. I am so grateful I have come to you." George felt a great weight lift off as these three capable people joined him, sharing his burden. "Speaking of unity, Eric has gone off to battle the Shorn alongside his fellow Longhairs in the latest war in the killing fields. With these ships here it occurred to me, less elegantly than you have stated, that we could all stand to have the Shorn and Longhair not kill each other while we sort through our threats. I told him I had an idea that you might be able to help me deliver a pause of sorts to the fields. A little bit of deviltry that could upend Kertof's war for a cycle or two."

George realized that their brief tea party had already miraculously defined their overarching aims. They were only left to devise their strategy and tactics. George hadn't trusted Labbite wisdom enough. His tribe's scientific discipline made critical the precise definition of the problem. Because a clearly defined problem was more likely to deliver a solution just as clear. He worked with them heartened by the vigorous intellectual exchange. For the first time in nearly a full cycle he felt hope.

15

CAI ON PHOEBE'S TRAIL

Finally at the base of the rockslide, Cai clung to the riverside foliage cover making his way to the edge of the city where the aliens had taken Phoebe. Soon he would be unable to hide. He had to prepare his disguise.

Cai unpacked the med kit. He dunked his head in the river and then massaged his scalp with depilator. All his hair had to go. A whiskered long hair no more. Using the blunt side of his machete and the depilator, he removed his facial hair in stages, careful to keep the chemical from his eyes. Filled with urgency, he was past any ability to calculate the passage of time. Too long. That's all.

His scalp was clear of hair. Likely far too pink. The shorn aliens didn't have pink faces or scalps. He needed dyeing. He broke some berries, too green. Finally he settled on some black pollen that stained everything, even his palms. He rubbed his head. Cleaned his stained hands with a bio-eraser Phoebe had wisely packed. He found some bright blue pollen in a white flower to smear on his bare brow. He ignored the ache in his leg. His crazy run couldn't touch Phoebe's athleticism.

Cai cut one of the blankets with his knife until it could hang diagonally across his shoulder like one of the toga sashes the captors wore. A small stick through a couple of knife holes knit the ends together. He uni trousered his legs, but he could devise no alternative. He made himself dirty—at least somewhat similar to those who pounded the dust in the clearing. The dust that made both him and Phoebe hack raw. Did her cough expose her? With lesser gravity, the dust hung in the air.

He stashed his machete under the sash and drank his fill of water. Forcing himself to eat the food they'd packed. His gut was eating itself inside out with worry over Phoebe. No nutrition to be found there at all.

He felt bad for teasing her about her yellow-eyed alien genes. No way that kid was in any way like her captors. Her rock surf demonstrated a spirit from a whole other dimension. The aliens couldn't match her. Not beyond a few clumsy steps. They didn't have her will, her guts, her courage. Phoebe personified their missing edge.

No dusk fell. No shadows in the streets, no cover. But he couldn't wait. The audible excitement over her passage was his only lead. He took a few moments to hide their gear. Like it mattered. He marked his way with subtle nicks in the trees and then hung within cover to gain enough wit to mimic passersby.

Every snatch of conversation seemed to include a reference to the 'long hair.' He rubbed his bare scalp to reassure himself. Phoebe better still recognize him. He'd find her. He and Phoebe were both a little taller and leaner than many of these folk. Why hadn't the elevated oxygen given the aliens greater size? They were clearly bred. Uniform in their skin color and overall appearance.

He watched their gait and rhythm. Aha, some individuals wandered alone. He could get by striding by himself. He took a shuddering breath, like Phoebe with the rock, he told himself. Just go for it. The cold, icy arms of Future pulled him into a tango.

Shaking himself into bravery. A frightened old Cai playing the young buck. Zap 'em with his farts if they got close enough to grab or claw him. Walking with calm purpose, dodging lingerers, he closed on the hubbub chasing Phoebe. Denser crowds. Groupings became cliques, then companies, like multiplying cells. Cai stalked through them all.

Streets and alleys paved with stone blocks and cobbles, someone had too much time. More laborers than occupations. Paved streets to carry more than foot traffic. Carts to haul rocks and supplies? Stucco-wrapped, stacked tubular buildings lined every passage. The aliens had taken hives as homes.

The conversations spoke of enemies. The Long Hairs. In capitals. A sober, serious talk of winning. He and Phoebe witnessed a political rally. Not sport.

Phoebe didn't lack balls. Cai was surprised she could walk.

Rode it like she stole it. Her spirit igniting him. Even with a stubborn infection on his leg, he stepped higher, faster. Following the quieted clamor of the crowd.

He overheard the anger. Not much laughter except in scorn for Phoebe. "We got them. We got the Longhair." Would anyone object to the capture of that magnificent woman streaming down the rock like a Goddess? Didn't think so. Nothing like envy to bring out the scorn. Aliens didn't know from shit.

Ignoring differences, Cai listened for sympathy. Allies. There. A soft face. He looked into the face, searching. The eyes, her eyes? Shifting away, wary. Careful. Cai looked for other loners. Kept moving. Looking without looking, seeing without showing himself. Every eye seemed hard. Few smiles. Menace, war, fear, competition, tainted every conversation.

A cancer in Vulva Valley. Forget allies. Could he head Phoebe's captors off? The streets crowded with people. Mean. Wooden hand carts piled with wares wove among the throngs. Large stone wheels leaned against buildings. Wheels too cumbersome to use, standing in place like décor. Other parallel avenues appeared when he looked across the grid of narrow alleys. Thinner crowds on those. Worth hazarding.

He got up as close as he could to the foremost Phoebe-trailers, then turned into an alley hoping to find a way to get out in front. Maybe he could catch a glimmer of her captors' destination. Cai vibrated with terror over losing Phoebe's trail.

The alley was shadowed. A narrow passage between stuccoed stacks. Paved in flesh-toned stone. Baked, glazed terracotta-colored tiles on the doorsteps. No bug-eye windows filled with spies. In his alley, just the ruffled stucco lines of some version of insect cement. Cai ran his fingers along the walls. How impenetrable? Could he break her out of such a building? They had a will, he and Phoebe, an edge against these aliens.

Scratching sounded behind him in the alley. Feigning calm, Cai looked back, apparently unconcerned. Just a shorn alien wandering behind him, scratching the stucco walls with a whisk. Cai kept his pace unhurried, matched to the alien's. At the corner Cai turned up a street that paralleled the street taken by Phoebe's captors.

He barely heard the 'Long Hair' chants at this remove. Cai was not alone. Small groups shared the street. Broadly-spaced, exchanging news with words sheltered by their hands.

He could make up some time. Cai picked up his pace. Unlike the alleys, the street side of the buildings contained more windows and doors. The buildings hives or stables. He'd never thought of human occupation that way before. So little to distinguish one dwelling from another. But unlike his planet 101, or Phoebe's planet the Third, this place was a city, populated by multiple buildings. And the streets were really paved. The loss of Earth hit him then. Centuries of infra-structure gone. The there they thought they might make there. Never to be known. Too many lifetimes beyond their reach.

Why such unrelenting uniformity in clothing, in color, in street, and building, and skin and hair? Being different must be nearly sinful here. Phoebe would fit right in. Not. She was difference incarnate.

Before Cai had a chance to lose himself in thoughts of

157

Phoebe, he was pushed hard from behind, forced to stumble forward. An electric jolt of contact. He tried to resist the push, to stop himself using the rough walls to gain purchase. No joy. A door opened beneath his scrabbling fingers. He was pushed into a cavity. His feet felt a wooden floor. He lost his sight in the dark. Hands behind him shoved him in. The door shut out the street. Cai's eyes adjusted. Lights came on. He saw three of the shorn aliens surrounding him. He wheeled around to punch his way out.

"Stop it! We won't hurt you. Settle down," said the alien blocking the door, thrusting back at Cai. But with pacifying gestures. Cai's brain struggled to bridge the schism of the familiar language from obviously alien beings. His enemies.

"I've got to get out of here. I've got to go. What do you want? Please let me go!" Cai wheeled frustrated and desperate. Appealing in every way he could. He needed to track Phoebe. They'd cause him to lose her. What was wrong with these people? Couldn't a stranger walk down their streets unmolested?

"Settle down. We know you are with the Longhair. We know where she's being taken. We can help you. Just settle down." A woman spoke this time. A voice of honey coming from this dark, closed prison cell.

Cai had no alternative. At least they understood the reason for his agitation. He gave up for the moment. He had to listen to them. They were too many. Even if he could escape, he realized his disguise didn't give him cover. He needed more information. Maybe he could use their help. He had been hoping for allies. He had no other choice. Future always tormented him like this—with sluice gates that robbed him of choice. There was always only one way forward.

"Okay. I give up. Please just tell me how imprisoning me here can help."

"Sit. Please sit." The woman again, the unaccented female voice. As his eyes adjusted to the dim interior light, he saw pallet seating in a room. He felt soiled. How long since he had known even the vague approximation of civilization? He felt his every scruffy animal vestige.

The woman apparently agreed. She passed him a wet cloth. The others entered the room and sat. Two men, one woman. Wearing the shifts, the sashes, the shorn heads, all decked out in the biscuit skin. He rubbed his face and neck and head with the rag and then cleaned his hands as best he could. The rag had a sweet fragrance but left no film. Surely only scented water. He barely restrained his raging impatience. Drowning in his own impotence. Aged.

"Thank you." Cai passed her the soiled cloth.

"You are welcome. Would you like some water or tea?" She indicated a large tray with ceramic cups and a ceramic bottle he assumed had water. Further examples of labor-intensive crafting. Like ancient Earth culture. But there was advanced technology in that ancient ship console. Technology in the lights in this room. In how they got here. What had driven them backwards? Religion? Like they'd taken the Inquisition with them in the material they'd swept from Earth? The religious cults on Old Earth had objections to women's hair, he remembered. He feared so much for Phoebe. Burning at the stake, stoned to death, a parade of women victims stormed his mind.

"Both please," he said, desperately thirsty. He guzzled the bottle she handed him. The cool water from the dewy bottle tasted like heaven. He gulped, feeling water trace its way from his mouth to his stomach like a cool healing balm. He wiped his mouth with the back of his hand and accepted a tepid bowl of tea. Also delicious. Sweet and flowery. He resented every bitter mouthful.

"Thank you. But I really can't afford to wait here with you over tea." The civilized ritual oppressed him. Colonized by a teacup. "I need to help my friend."

"Ah good. She is your friend. That is better for us." The woman was in charge. The men just nodded from the sidelines.

"She is relatively safe for the time being. She will be taken to our prisons and held there until our Lord Kertof and the judges have time to question her. She is valuable to them. They think her a spy and they will want information from her. Or they may want to trade her to her kind."

"Her kind? She doesn't have any kind. We don't have any kind here," Cai spit out. Indignant. Phoebe's uniqueness was obvious.

"Ah yes. She is a Long Hair, no?" the woman asked.

"She has long hair. I had long hair too until I rid myself of it. So what? She didn't come from my planet either. To be precise, she's not even my kind."

The lumpy brow of the woman's otherwise smooth countenance, furrowed and rippled. "I don't understand this 'other planet.' What is a planet?"

The two men had risen and were hopping foot-to-foot.

"They came on a ship, Taletha! It is as we told you, there are others on a ship. There are other places, we can get a ship now. The stars we see. Others live on those stars. Perhaps Reapers? Our Reaper ancestors came from somewhere on a ship. Maybe these two grew out of their antennae too!" The men were clutching at each other while the elder of them postulated his argument.

Cai wanted to put his head in his hands or crawl into a hole as he witnessed this absolutely critical conversation slide off the face of their shared understanding like surreal time slid off a clock. The talk of ships delivered a dangerous careening detour. Nor did Cai want to think too hard on beings generated from antennae.

"We need to get Phoebe out first." Cai was vehement. He had to reestablish the importance of his mission. "That is more urgent, at least urgent to me. I need my friend freed." He cast around for an idea that would get them back on the rails. "Phoebe knows ships."

Three faces riveted to his own. The men bouncing excitedly. The woman trying to preserve calm with gestures and her molten voice.

"Sig and Dern, peace, peace, please. This other is correct, we must concentrate on liberating his Longhair friend before the magistrates give her their attentions. We will only have the time before the light silvers. There is much to do. Talk of ships and planets and even of our war and our rebellion must wait until we have leisure."

The men were easy to placate. Like normal men. Because

161

A, a heroic rescue was action and action was always good. And B, because they clearly believed Phoebe would fly them to the stars on a ship. Like waving smoked fish under Smudge's nose. At least something, some impulse they had that he could work in his favor. He felt hopeful at her words. Maybe he didn't have to worry about Phoebe being stoned, or burned alive at the stake.

Cai skipped over the alarming pieces of the speech. War? What war? "What is your plan, Ma'am? Might we work together as allies?"

"I am sorry. I forget my manners. You must call me Taletha, or Leetha for short. Everyone does. These two are my nephews Sig and Dern, as you heard." Sig was the one who had whisked the wall behind him in the alley and who had pushed him through the door. Dern was smaller than Sig. Shorter and more wiry, leaner than Sig. He looked younger. There was a slight silver sheen to Sig's head that indicated some age.

Cai studied Taletha more closely. He could see swirls of silver in the short coils on her head. Though her calm assurance and velvet voice already suggested maturity to him. 'Down boy,' he thought to himself. Not now.

"Come into my eating room," Leetha said. "I will provide some food and drink and we can begin our planning. Dern, you should go up to the palace and see if any of our friends can be persuaded to be a part of the watch detail for the Long Hair spy." Dern nodded and rose to leave. "Come back as soon as you know whether we can put someone in place." He assented with a murmur and left the room.

"Ma'am, Taletha, I mean," Cai addressed her as he rose and followed her to the other room. Do you have somewhere that I can clean up?" He indicated his scruffiness.

"Of course. If you can wait to eat, I am sure Sig can find some things for you to wear. You can shower and I have sanitary facilities. Sig will show you now." Sig came forward and led Cai through the interior to another large room with a stone floor, benches, an evident toilet with a pump handle and a floor depression with a hole in the center and a handle on the wall. Lights came on automatically as they entered.

"Remove your clothing. You will dry yourself with those," Sig said, indicating a stack of folded cloth. "You use the shower to wash yourself, and soap too," he pointed to some waxy chunks of material. "I'll get you some clothing." He turned, about to leave Cai alone in the mysterious room.

"Wait. Can you show me what this shower thing is?" Cai pointed to the depression in the floor.

"Yes, no trouble. You pump this and warm water will sprinkle down on your body and go out through that hole. The soap will make lather with water and take all your dirt off. You know the toilet, yes?" he seemed reluctant to give instruction.

"Yes. Thank you," Cai said as Sig swiftly turned away and shut the door. The toilet was wondrous. He sat, thinking fondly of MIDGE and Smudge. Then he pumped and a powerful punch of water shot across his ass and down into the ceramic bowl where it disappeared. Best used naked, obviously. Pre-shower.

Cai stood with water dripping down his legs, and stepped

into the stone depression. With a few pumps he was wet, lathered, rinsed and blessedly cleaned. The shower beat microbe cleaning, for sure. The door opened and an arm reached in, dropping a wad of clothing on the floor. Modest. Gratifyingly human. Cai put on a clean, pale blue shift and his old boots and carried the leathery burgundy sash thing into the dining room. He felt twenty years younger. He wished he could see himself.

Taletha's eyes shone with approval as he entered. A woman always makes the best mirror. He wondered when his sense of them as aliens departed. Taletha helped him brooch the sash to his shoulder. She waved him to a seat. Sig and Dern were already eating. A steaming pile of flatbread centered the table and a bowl of stew with a ceramic spoon sat at his place. Maybe he would taste real chicken for the first time.

"Dern is already back from the palace. He learned Brattoch is guarding your friend. You said her name is Phoebe?"

He nodded, his mouth full. He had no idea whether this was chicken but the combination of rich warmth, spicy flavors, and all their kindness in the face of his desperation, felt overwhelming. He ducked his head as his eyes stung with tears. Bowed to the chicken god. Better than mud chickens any day.

"We are remarkably lucky. Brattoch is one of us and he may be the best of us. We have all hated that he worked for the palace, but now it turns out that he was right. He ends up being where we need him. Freedom be praised."

Taletha raised her cup of beer and the others matched her.

"Freedom be praised." They echoed. Okay, fine, Cai thought. Religious nuts, just as he feared. At least they were religious nuts on his side. He didn't have to rescue Phoebe by himself. They praised freedom. Yup. He did too. Yay. Cai raised his cup smiling. Let's get this party on.

The attractive Taletha's proposed rescue of Phoebe couldn't be as simple as she claimed. How was it that all these shorn opened their doors and helped their supposed enemy? Why did these two young men simply accept his claims about himself and Phoebe? Why did they so readily embrace his desire to rescue Phoebe? And what the hell was the problem with Long Hair?

Cai stayed quiet, listening to Sig and Dern obsess over the space ship they'd seen. Before the Winter snows apparently. They asked how he and Phoebe stayed hidden for so many cycles of sleep.

Cai didn't have to explain because Taletha dismissed the ship and curtailed that discussion. She told Cai of their rebellion. They were among the shorn rebels who were disgusted by their leader Kertof's use of territorial encroachment as a pretext for war with the more nomadic long hairs. Taletha recounted a brief history of the ancestor ship that had crashed here on the Continent. Apparently the population descended from these Reaper ancestors. The Reapers created a surviving tribe by combining elements from other life forms they encountered. Cai asked Taletha whether the Reapers had known Earth and human beings. Taletha claimed only the History Keepers could tell of such a thing. But none of these History Keepers had survived a calamitous absence of sun. A sort of ice age that had decimated crops and lives, even rendering some life forms extinct.

Cai was desperately curious about their history, ancestry and their way of life. Planet 101, and Phoebe's home planet, the Third, farmed bugs and microorganisms for shelter, fuel, clothing and so on. But these people appeared to use bug leavings. He'd seen little evidence they'd controlled the bugs, bred the bugs, or programmed the bugs.

They weren't Earth refugee descendants. But they were certainly human bred. They made no reference to Earth. Not people, technology, history, or culture. Yet they had walls that lit up as though programmed and the food and tea had been cooked or heated on very curious stoves. They had toilets, streets, prisons, palaces, plumbing, wars, and chickens. They were clearly more advanced in settlement than 101. They had organized more labor, more structures, more societal divisions. But they lived primitively. With territorial wars, and little advanced technology.

Get a grip, Cai. They spoke an Earth language. They agreed to help him rescue Phoebe. And they knew of a recent landing of a space ship. Win-win. He reeled his wandering mind back to the fish he was actually trying to catch. His only real concern was sticking with these people long enough to get Phoebe. The rest they'd figure out later. That ship console Smudge found must be associated with their Reaper heritage. He could hardly wait to tell Phoebe another ship had recently appeared. Maybe they could pack up the jet skates and hitch a proper ride. Drink up folks, party's over. Time to head for the sky.

16

THE SHIP'S CREW WINNOWED

The flashing red light in the corridor meant imminent death. Kendak moved as fast as he could to the hallway monitor. "What is it?" he asked CLEO, still trying to catch his breath.

"Linda is in cardiac arrest. Imminent demise. Imminent demise." The warning beacon sounded repeatedly, keeping time with the flashing red light. Kendak hobbled to sickbay, not that he could do much once there. The corridor angled steeply upward. A detour to the elevator would be no faster. What to do? What to do? He wracked his brain. Imminence, immediacy, hurry, not in the wheelhouse of the aged.

Davis was already in sickbay when Kendak arrived. Looking dark and sober, he nodded his head between Kendak and the monitor. Kendak closed his eyes, noting the flatlines.

"Healing the leg was too much stress for her system?" Kendak queried, breathless. Maybe it was something else, like the air. They'd come here to die in any event. All except Maria. Didn't stop the fears dive-bombing him like impatient gnats.

"Where's Maria?" Kendak wasn't sure why Davis should know. "Did you tell her?" One brief glance at death was plenty. Bring on the distractions.

"Maria's gone." Davis tended to Linda's body. With tender patience unhooking, unplugging. Unlatching her from life.

Their contingent reduced by a full third. They expected death here. Why surprised? "She's gone?" Kendak was horrified. He scanned the sickbay for another body. Surely they would have notified him? "CLEO is Maria dead too?" he asked, panicked.

"No, Kendak, only Linda died. Maria ran out after that animal." Davis tenderly lifted Linda's arms to her chest and placed one of her hands over the other. The body was still supple, still warm.

Kendak tried to focus. His mind moored on useless things. Maria ran away? And Linda dead. Still puzzled, he found he'd rather wonder about Maria than acknowledge Linda gone.

They talked about Maria as an eternal adolescent. Her behavior was so alien. Even now, Davis's words reminded him of his mother discussing his sister running after boys. When had he last thought of his mother? There weren't any boys here, were there? Surely Davis or Linda would let him know. Kendak considered the whole of the room slowly. Searching for some clue to remind him of what he was supposed to do next.

"Animal?" his voice finally articulating at least one of the

168

thoughts darting like minnows under his limp mooring. When had he last thought about minnows? His voice rasped. He'd moved too fast to get here. And Linda already dead.

Davis huffed impatient, "CLEO update Kendak on Maria's marsupial." Davis attempted to unfold a body bag. Not many bags left. Davis's arthritic hands pathetic, clumsy with the folds in the papery fabric. Like the clawed toes of an old, grey bird.

"A marsupial genetically separate from common Earth species penetrated the ship through a newly-opened maintenance access portal. Maria left the ship to contain the animal and repair the portal. The animal absconded with portal hardware and Maria is seeking to retrieve it. Maria departed NEW CLEO at 1500 hours Earth time."

Kendak remembered the creature now. Named Josie, Maria said. In the week or so they'd been on the planet, the creature had become overly familiar with their ship and Maria. Just like a damn boy. Sniffing around for Maria under CLEO's skirts.

"Should we try to reach her to tell her about Linda?" Would Maria care? Kendak wondered if Maria cared about any of them. They related through devices anyway. At a certain point it didn't matter who or what was on the other end. Pro forma to inform her though. Not that he could recollect what the term meant. But he snagged the darting minnow anyway. At his age he took what he got.

"I'd rather she adapts to this world while she can. CLEO anticipates winter storms. She'll have little enough chance to romp around out there before we are all cooped up in the ship

169

again. There is nothing anyone can do for Linda now." Davis described Maria as he would a child. 'A chance to romp' and 'cooped up in the ship.'

Kendak supposed Maria finding an animal to befriend might help her adapt physically and psychologically. She would need to shift her bonds from the dying to the living now, as though she'd notice. Did bowl-bound goldfish even form bonds? Shift was not the right verb. Acquire? Establish? Better.

CLEO had informed them that a sentient lifeform with some human DNA populated this planet. Maria had found hair for analysis on one of her forays. Partly human equaled truly alien. Not the Earth refugees they hoped for. But how had human DNA found its way into other sentient lifeforms beyond Earth? Not worth any speculation. They'd never know.

Kendak, Linda and Davis discussed *ad nauseam* how Maria might safely gain access to the alien population. With Linda dead, and Kendak and Davis to follow any day now, that sentient lifeform was Maria's only chance for society. But they hadn't come up with anything yet, and Maria showed no interest in the idea at all.

Kendak, like Davis, soon found himself not at all concerned about Maria's marsupial absconding with portal hardware. If only Maria would chase as far as she needed to go.

☾ Brattoch smitten

Brattoch made himself scarce when medics arrived to clean up the Longhair woman. He lingered nearby. Clinging to her by the threads of the invisible web she had used to snare him. He had never encountered anyone like her. For her he would switch his allegiance to the Longhairs. Forget the rebels. Watching that woman fly down the rock macerated his brain and exploded his testicles. She amazed and horrified in one swift move. She stopped his breath.

He wanted it, her, something. He ran his tongue wet around his mouth, salivating. When he carried her, she crumpled into his chest like a boneless infant. That a being of such magnificence and strength could collapse so completely, reduce to such a fragile bundle, broke him. He knew he must've pushed others away trying to reach her, hold her, protect her. Trying to kindle her spirit against his skin. Everyone always gave way to him because of his size. He held his breath. Would she give way?

As he swung her up into his arms her silken hair fell across his forearms and curled against his neck. He was torn between brushing the shimmering hair away and burying his face in her. To wake her with nudges and tenderness. Bent over her, his muscles arching around her, encapsulating her. He simply wanted to fuse with her.

Such a confusing, molten chasm he must traverse. What did he know of her other than her ride across the rippling, liquid, eternity of the great rock wall? But what more could you ever need expressed in a woman, even across a lifetime? In that miracle of living, she lived a lifetime beyond his ken.

The medics left. He looked into her cell. He had dismissed the others. No one really cared. The war was on. They were looking for a fight, a brawl, a battle. Everyone knew they would head to killing fields soon, probably when the moons rose. None expected interrogating the spy would provide anything but worthless delay. The Shorn bought themselves the element of surprise by capturing her. But surprise was frail, hard to hold. The palace buzzed with battle lust. Brattoch reasoned they could hardly afford to bring her for questioning, or even take the time to feed her.

So clean and white, she lay silent on the pallet, sleeping. Peaceful in a simple blue shift with feet bare and strands of long damp hair clinging to the bedding. He would feed her. His shift had ended, but he would stay on. Still ensnared, still so deeply compelled by her, by the need to touch her and know her warmth again.

Brattoch sighed and locked the cell door. He removed the chalk stick from the hanger and carefully wrote Nottakow on the slate at the door. Her name was so desperately important to her. He would honor her name.

The palace, wrapped around the caves and prison quarters, was composed of a labyrinth of passages. A literal hive, reclaimed, their History Keepers said, from the Wasp Queen who had once dominated their Continent. The Reapers, his ancestors, had somehow ended wasp dominion and reworked their leavings and hives to suit their own life form.

The halls were stone-floored or laid with polished wood. The encased organisms that lit the walls responded just as brightly to new occupants. Ramps, passages, and steps suited the limbs of Reaper progeny. The great meeting rooms, eating rooms, the plumbing, cleansing, light, ventilation now suited their needs. Sometimes uncanny, sometimes discomfiting, these similarities between the wasps and his people.

Brattoch made his way toward the soldier's mess. To make himself present, visible to his fellows. To eat with them and join their battle talk. Encouraging distraction, allowing their memory of Nottakow to fade. And all the while, he thought of how he would find a way to reach the rebels and enlist their aid in freeing her.

The hallways were long spiraling affairs. He had taken thousands of steps to cover the distance between the cells and the mess.

Soldiers and guards littered the surrounding hallways. Soldiering meant plenty of gossip within little enclaves, jockeying for status that wouldn't matter a whit once the pikes of war truncated their worthless lives.

Brattoch managed to pass unmolested. He was surprised to see Dern enter at the back of the giant mess hall. Wonderful. He hardly dared hope he would find such a direct means to get a message to the rebels. Dern caught his eye and strode forward unbidden. Brattoch stepped back into a vacant entryway to afford them a little privacy.

"Well met, Brattoch," Dern reached to clasp Brattoch's forearm.

"And you, Dern. What has brought you to me in such a hurry? Did you feel that I had need of you, as I do?" Such coincidences often made him wonder if atrophied antennae still possessed the power to link like-minded.

"The Longhair spy is not a Longhair, Brattoch." Dern spoke hurriedly, without preamble. "She has come from a ship. With others of her kind. We must rescue her before Kertof discovers her true identity. We, the rebels I mean, have her partner at Taletha's." Dern whispered, spitting in his excitement.

Brattoch snatched Dern's arms gripping hard enough to elicit a wince. "What do you mean? I cannot understand. Tell me slowly. We have time. I know where she is. I took charge of her myself. So already we are ahead. I cannot absorb this ship, this not a Longhair, this partner she has . . . ." Brattoch paused, really feeling desperate about her posited partnership. "A Longhair man is her partner you say?" Brattoch looked past Dern's shoulder to see if their furious whispering attracted any attention.

"Yes, a man, but he says he is her friend, and he is not a Longhair, he is from a ship. He speaks true. He has no brow bulges and his eyes . . ." Dern stopped himself as though he could barely bring himself to complete the description. "His eyes are blue, blue as the pollen upon our brows. This is how even Taletha accepted his story of the ship must be true. He has no antennae. But he speaks our tongue. And his clothing is very odd. I cannot stay. I must go back to Taletha's and bring the rescue forward. I am sure Uncle will involve himself. Could you go back to her cell and be prepared for us, keep the way clear and prevent any from Kertof reaching her? I must return immediately."

Dern tugged his arms from Brattoch's impassioned grip waylaying the million questions Brattoch would ask. Brattoch a trusted leader. He'd be expected to accept this dump of world-shattering information.

Brattoch let Dern go. He pinched his lips together and looked to the mess hall mindful of his bodily needs. Water, food, a snatch of rumors, then a hasty, very secretive, remove. Sneak back to Nottakow and defend her until? The stuff of dreams for him from the first moment he saw her. And now his vision broadened. He would take her hand and together they'd step beyond the Continent to walk across the stars.

17

BUT KERTOF HAS PLANS

Kertof dismissed the dull penetrating buzz of his people with a hand swatting at so many flies. A veritable rabble roused in the streets outside of his quarters. Bees in a hive. The Reapers had bequeathed them stacked dwellings, fashioned to mirror the efficient hives of insects. And he, their Queen—he smirked, rueful—ruled here, protected at the very heart of the society. He rubbed his shorn head, distracted. His ministers stood nearby awaiting his orders.

"What's the status on the Longhair prisoner? Are all the commands ready to march? We must seize the advantage Beezee. We must march soon if we are to take them by surprise." Kertof noticed his brother snapping his heels to attention. Stars only knew where his mind had been.

"The prisoner has been cleaned, fed, and medicated Kert. Her only real mission must have been to warn them of our attack. We've pre-empted that action, so we hold her until we return here from the conquest. Everyone is ready to battle. You can hear them in the streets." Beezee gestured toward the open window. A layer of powder sparkled on the shiny wooden floorboards.

Kertof nodded out the window. The assemblage raised arms to coming triumph. The whole process bored and wearied Kertof. War and pretense. Every handful of cycles the Longhairs and the Shorn fought to winnow the population down. The survival of the best. Their little game. A fight to the death.

"Keep a one-person guard on her while we are gone. Do you have some fellows we can trust? Ones we won't miss in our attack of course? Kertof swirled as he spoke, animated, assured, pretending his excitement was barely contained. His affectation. He waved the bulk of the advisors from his presence. Detestable cretins. Only Beezee remained. A lesser cretin. His brother.

The Shorn had the advantage. He knew it. And that ship. The real reason for his galvanic energy. A ship for certain. Atmospheric penetration was hard to overlook. Not a gigantic gas bubble as some other witnesses attested. Kertof encouraged their delusion. Now with Spring melting the Winter snows, now with the excuse of war, Kertof could locate and enlist that ship in his designs for leadership over the entire Continent.

Kertof was confident a ship had landed. Gas bubbles exploded in the sky when they collided with whatever contained the atmosphere. But with the ship he'd seen layered lights. Gas bubbles didn't float down, nor were they lit in concentric rows. Gas floated up, dammit. This thing had regular rings of punctuating light, aimed itself at the ground, and was steadily driven down. Under control. He would swear. He prayed the Labbits were ignorant of the event. If new resources or opportunities had arrived in his environs, Kertof intended to appropriate them.

"What if the Longhairs have that ship in their control when we conquer them?" Beezee asked, cheeks puffed, full of himself.

Kertof hated Beezee reading his mind. He laughed in scorn. "Well I doubt they'd be able to control it, whatever it is."

Beezee smirked at Kertof's image of hapless Longhairs.

Kertof went on. "More likely that thing will control them. Another reason to push forward I believe. Whatever came in on that ship whether Reaper, alien, ally, bug or simply some rogue technology, cannot be allowed to gain the advantage. We must seize the moment."

"Are we sure we can? A ship represents technology unlike any we have ever seen before. We've never even seen an intact ship. There are so few of us, even among the Labbits, with Reaper proclivity. How could we hope to overwhelm such advanced technology?"

Kertof hazarded a glance at the chip of ship console he kept on a shelf in his main office. His steward claimed the chip lit up earlier, while Kertof was busy inspiring his people in the

178

field. Before the Winter, when that ship came down, his chip of console hadn't activated. The stupid people he worked with were always jumping at shadows. He had hoped regular wars would have rid him of the dullards. Was there a single brain anywhere among them that would help him seek the ship?

Kertof wanted to skewer Beezee with the ceremonial pike hanging on the wall. But Kertof assumed he wasn't the first leader resenting questions from his followers that he couldn't address. Somehow Beezee unerringly wallowed in them.

Kertof gripped his certainty that he'd dominate the aliens with the sheer force of his will. After all, he'd single-handedly excised the Labbits from society proper, despite their supposed Reaper advantages.

"Consider the very advanced technology we live with Beezee. Are we not further along than the technology remains we have discovered in some of those derelict piles from the crashed ship?"

"We live in old hives, Kertof! Reaper ships were bio-organic technology, with grown wires, lighting, switches and fuels and capabilities we know nothing about anymore. So, in a word, NO."

"Consider it, Beezee. If a bug can grow housing material that we can use, is that not advanced technology? If bugs or fungi grow our clothing and we can harness them to serve our needs, doesn't that seem advanced?"

"Hardly. We took what the Reapers appropriated for us. We haven't advanced. We've lost ground. No antennae in all the Shorn. No more third-eye lenses except among the Labbits. Remember? The ones you exiled. The ones responsible for our medicine, hospitals, education, history, and whatever technology we still manipulate from the Reapers bequest. What about weapons, Kertof? When we fight the Longhairs with our pikes and spears, we might kill a few. We direct the explosion of a gas bubble and kill a few more. We kill a few of theirs, they kill a few of ours and we call it a day for a few cycles. But that ship will be a whole new game. A ship that can travel the stars and land safely on our Continent could wipe us all out."

Buzz, buzz, buzz, Kertof endured Beezee's relentless drone. To discuss this on the eve of a triumphant battle. He sniffed disparaging Beezee. Not giving him any inkling his comments had any merit.

"Because our Continent is the only land mass, an island in a hostile sea, we have been living in the shadow of a potential enemy since our population growth became unsustainable. The point is potential. The gas bubbles are always a potential threat to us all. Lack of food, resources, and no chance of rescue or escape, forces us to limit our growth. Of course each group sees itself as the most worthy. The calamity taught us war is the optimum way to ensure the best of us survive. We've dealt with potential threats for our entire existence.

Space has given us a ship before. The Reaper ship brought our ancestors here. It crashed here and amounted to nothing. We have a real enemy. A misguided population threatening our claim to limited resources. Our real enemy is the reality that we don't have enough to share across all of the people with an ancestral claim to this land. Increased border conflicts always brings us to this pass. We have two choices and two choices only: eliminate the Longhairs or push them back and reduce their territory. And, of course, we must seize whatever resources they have denied us. Including any atmospheric anomalies like this thing we discuss."

Kertof turned back toward Beezee, his eyes fiery. Some of the advisors had wandered back in during Kertof's diatribe. They nodded, a few murmured 'hear-hear.' Beezee caught Kertof's eye and raised one brow, conceding to leave off mentioning the ship for the time being.

"Let us organize our attack and plan to leave as the light of the sun ends. I will be outside shortly. Beezee do you have a moment to confer on the disposition of the forward flanks?" Beezee came forward and they retired to Kertof's private chambers as the others again filed out of the room. Everyone had much to do. Bodies needed to be counted. Ranks readied for sacrifice.

"What about the rebels?" Beezee asked as Kertof seated himself. Upholstered pallet seating glittering with embossed metallic paste work, encircled the space. A large table centered the room. Open wood shutters revealed tall windows funneling breezes throughout. Shelves displaying artifacts and other precious items claimed any available wall space. Translucent panels enclosed flickering lights that steadied, flooding the room with light, if a hand warmed their surfaces.

"I have someone watching them. I believe they will try to free the Longhair prisoner." Kertof arranged his robes in his lap, setting his stone cup of tepid tea on a small table at his side. "I am arranging for them all to be neatly dispatched together far from here. Frankly, we cannot afford them anymore. They are too much of a distraction and they fragment the support we have in our base. Especially now, with this damn ship, I need everybody behind us. Our only hope is sticking together with purpose. These individual directions be damned!"

"You are afraid of the ship." Beezee said, surprised.

"Yes, I am afraid of the damn ship. And I am afraid of the damn Wasp Queen. And I am afraid of the damn gas bubbles. I am afraid that the Longhairs will be overtaken or worse, appropriated by whatever operates that ship."

"But the Wasp Queen? Surely you don't think we have to fear the bugs? How absolutely revolting!"

"Beezee, I know I said we control the bug technology, but have you ever actually considered that they might control us? Maybe we are neatly farming ourselves in little rows like planted seeds for the bugs. We think we stepped into this good thing. I am sure seeds in their fertile soil beds think the same. All a little bit too neat. And you are right, our weapons probably count for naught compared to what must be out there. Including the venom of a very large wasp. I often wonder if the Reapers merely brought us here as a meat crop for the drones. Do any of us really know what the Reapers were? Maybe they gathered us and planted us. After all, they were Reapers. Maybe they are genetically linked to the wasps."

"But if we are farmed, why would the bugs allow us to kill each other off?" Kertof was proud to see Beezee unnerved.

"Ever heard of weeding? Maybe we are just getting rid of the weeds for them. You know they eat corpses. Maybe the war is their regular buffet. Just think, we conveniently butcher their meat for them."

Beezee was sickened. "Shouldn't we join with the 'weeds' then, rather than fight others of our kind? Wouldn't we be stronger together?"

"That's the problem with weeds. They won't join a chorus of happy harmony. We have no hope of organizing them. They'd just fragment us even more. Diversity would make us stronger provided the joiners think the same way we do."

"The Reapers believed genetic diversity was salvation. Clearly, you don't harbor their illusions. I suppose I should ensure rebel sympathizers guard the prisoner. Make things easier for your people, yes?"

"Thank you, Beezee. I am going to cross that particular distraction off my list. Let's start the march in a few turns of the glass. I'll see you then." As Beezee went off, Kertof wondered again about the Reapers. Yes, they reaped genetic diversity for the survival of their species. They sacrificed so much in species-integrity on that altar. So what species-survival did they ensure?

18

KERTOF'S SPY

Uncle never liked Taletha, sister of his wife Vera. For that matter, he didn't much like Vera but she was useful. Hot meals, warm bed, cover story—a wife provided all. Especially when she asked for little. Vera had learned very early to ask for nothing.

He whisked the front door. It was their signal. He was a friendly ally of the rebel group after all.

"Quick Uncle, come in," Letha waved at him beside the open door.

"What is it? Letha, what is wrong?" He entered pulling the door shut behind him. As though anyone other than he watched her dwelling. "Has something happened?"

"We have a Longhair, wounded, he is sleeping. But he says he has a ship. It can't be true, Uncle, can it? There is no ship."

He could hear the hopefulness in her voice. His job was to help the rebels rescue the Longhair so he could get rid of rebels and spy in one move. He knew they had a game afoot but he had not suspected they had another Longhair spy. Must be a partner. The ship story was utter nonsense. But this turn of events might actually work in Uncle's favor.

"Many people hold to the vision of the ship that Sig and Dern go on about," he said, dismissing Letha's fears. "Do we care about a ship? Does a ship matter? We rebels simply wish to end these pointless wars with the Longhairs. We want only to make a change that lets us choose a different way." Uncle gestured magnanimously.

He saw Taletha barely concealed her revulsion. He knew she hated him calling her Letha. He told Vera 'Letha' sounded like 'Lisa' with a lisp. Letha always acted like everything about him repulsed her. But the rebels didn't choose their affiliates. They couldn't afford to be selective. Besides, selectivity was just the kind of intolerance they protested. He enjoyed watching her swallow her disgust. She succeeded. She forced herself to be civil to him.

"True, a ship doesn't matter. The Longhair claims he is not a Longhair though. But neither is he a Labbite. Why should we rebels help him if he does not affiliate with the Longhairs?"

"Of course he jumps on this claim to be from an imaginary ship, especially if Sig and Dern provided him with that convenient bit of gossip. Let me guess, they told him about the ship before he'd barely spoken, yes? Before you even told him you were rebels against Kertof's war?"

Taletha considered, "Yes, I believe so. But he does discuss strange things like devices to read with, and machines that make pictures. He doesn't sound right. He seems very ignorant of our ways for a Longhair spy. I don't understand why the ship idea offered him an out. What did he need an out for? We were bent on helping him as a Longhair."

Uncle had long believed the ship a child's fantasy. Neither Sig nor Dern were children, mature adults more like, but they perpetuated so many silly notions. Uncle was comfortable dismissing these phantasms that cluttered the mind. Life was simple: make your way easy and amusing. Toying with the rebels was amusing. Getting rid of them in a 'rescue gone wrong' with the spy would be amusing. Pleasing Kertof would continue to make his life comfortable and easy. He'd stumbled upon the perfect occupation.

"Don't you remember those old ones in our village, Letha? They would tell us they kept the word of the History Keepers. They would try to tell us about, what was it? Technology? And science? And machines? And so on. They had so many strange words. And all they did was try to pass on these strange words to every new generation. The best thing about our wars is getting rid of that kind of uselessness. Such delusions drawn in meaningless words, words of fantasy, to pass from generation to generation, shames all our people."

He had to be a little careful or Taletha might wonder just how much of a rebel sympathizer he actually was. Vera told him Taletha thought he showed up for the food, but contributed

186

little. And she complained to Vera that he liked to lord over them all with his philosophizing, even when his ideas conflicted with theirs.

"Let's discuss this some other time. Now we should plan a rescue, no? The sooner we send both of these Longhairs back to their homes, the safer you will be. Luckily, our rescue action will remove us all from the battlefield. Kertof will begin to march on the Longhair ranks at first moonrise. Let's act fast and take advantage of the confusion in the streets." Satisfied, Uncle stroked his chin.

Taletha asserted herself. No doubt regretting letting him take charge. "Can you get word to those at the palace? Can we ensure we have assistance where the prisoner is held?"

"I would like to meet your Longhair guest before I go, Letha." He started to move toward the dining room but Taletha cut him off and directed him toward the ramps to sleeping quarters.

"He is sleeping right now. Wounded, remember? I want to ensure he is able to run with us if necessary. We need him. Otherwise why would his partner trust us? Here, I will show you."

Uncle was happy. She jumped to his bidding while he dismissed her concerns.

She indicated the Longhair asleep on a pallet. Uncle found him unremarkable. An aged man with clearly new-shorn hair. An immediate testament to his lies about not being a Longhair. Only a Longhair could have a scalp that pink. Uncle noted the wound on the leg. Ugly. Torn. But clean, no spreading red swelling to suggest infection. Still, better this

Longhair was somewhat diminished when Uncle finished him. In the caves with the others, as Uncle planned, at the end.

Uncle led the way back to the entry, "Tell Sig and Dern to bring him up to the guard barracks. I will meet them. I will notify Brattock and arrange for our passage through the tunnels in company with the released spy. At moonrise, when the march begins. You will join us too, Letha?" He started for the door.

"The cave tunnels lead nowhere near the mountains, Uncle. How will you get them back to Longhair territory?"

"They found their way here, Letha, I will help them get beyond the palace guards. Then they can go their way and hopefully we won't have to meet them on the killing fields anytime soon. We can only do what we can do. They are dangerous to us here and dangerous to themselves."

Finally rid of Uncle ...

Taletha shut the door behind him firmly. She knew Sig and Dern would not be willing to let the Longhairs run off after they secured the release of the woman spy. Taletha had been disinclined to believe the boys about the ship until she'd heard Cai speak and had gazed into strange blue eyes. He brought the History Keepers to her mind.

When she was younger, she and her friends tried to recite all the words they remembered from the ancestors. Solar, laser, space, genetics, magnetism, botany, culturing, calendars, pets, astronomy, cephalopods, ungulates, clocks, years, centuries, and so on. So many of those forgotten words now recalled to her tongue.

Where did they come from? The words? The Reapers? Uncle's impatient dismissal of the ship persuaded Taletha. She would join this rescue. She would help them return to their ship. A ship was the only explanation. Cai brought new words here. Words that reminded her of what the Reaper ancestors brought here. Words weren't phantasms. Words held meaning, promise. What was there for her here among the Shorn? Her warring society was stupid and ugly. Versions of Uncle and her helpless sisters. Even a phantasm of a ship held greater promise.

Returned from their errands, Sig and Dern assembled supplies on the dining table. Sig looked upwards where they could hear a restless Cai stumble around.

"Uncle was here," Taletha announced.

Dern rolled his eyes. "I suppose we have to enlist his help."

"However we feel about him, he is on our side." Taletha asserted reluctantly.

"Is he?" Sig didn't even try to soften his tone. "Did you tell him about the ship?"

"Yes."

"He thought it was nonsense, didn't he?" Dern chipped in, more than willing to denounce the man who claimed to be his stepfather. Married to his mother yes, but no kind of father, or husband for that matter. "Did you have to feed him?"

Taletha sniggered. "No, he left without eating this time. He will notify Brattoch about our plan. He will meet us at moonrise. When they march. Plenty of cover in the confusion. He wants to take us all out through the tunnels."

"Whoa, the tunnels? They don't lead anywhere near the mountains. Nowhere near Longhair territory or where we saw the ship come down. I thought he didn't want us exposed to the dangers of the caves. Why is it only now convenient for us to retreat there, especially when they lead away from where we want to go? And when the march would give us such easy cover? I smell something foul, Taletha."

"I couldn't refuse his help, Dern. He is the best informed about all the ways to get the Longhair out. He knows all the guards and he knows the caves under the palace. Who else do we have? Brattoch alone is not enough. We don't have time to argue anyway. Uncle has made himself a part of this whether we like it or not. We must take this opportunity and look for a way to improve on it when our circumstances are better. He doesn't care about the ship. We'll find a way to ditch him."

"He knows a little too much for a metal harvester, that's what I think." Sig chimed in. Cai limped into the room. He didn't look healthy.

"Trouble in the ranks?" Cai looked hard at Taletha. "Did you drug me?"

"Yes. I gave you a light dose to help you sleep. I cleaned your wound. You must've noticed?" Taletha only now realizing he might resent being drugged. He came from some other place in the stars. She was unsettled by the notion.

"Another of our group has been by. His name is Uncle. He knows where your friend is. He will help us get her out. He knows the caves and tunnels leading out of the city. He has helped us before. We don't like him, as you heard. He doesn't treat my mother properly. But he doesn't believe in your ship, so we think we can get rid of him once your partner is free."

Taletha was impressed with Dern's summary. "I am sorry I drugged you without telling you. That was wrong of me. But would you have let me?"

"No. But better my wound is clean. I am sure I couldn't have slept otherwise. Thank you, Taletha. Thank you for being honest too. We are not the same kind. We will make mistakes with each other." Cai smiled at her. "When do we leave?"

19

BRATTOCH'S RESOLVE

Brattoch headed toward the vacated corridor, willing his feet not to hurry overmuch. He waved 'later' to Jared. So intent, he almost neglected to stop at the kitchens to pick up Nottakow's rations.

He shrugged away the onslaught of disturbing news—ships, partners, rebel escape and not-a-Longhair, harkening back to a memory of Sig and Dern claiming they had seen a ship drop from the sky and land in the mountains. In the first season. Well before the Winter snows. Though he dismissed the notion at the time, Brat trusted Sig and Dern.

But a ship, and the rescue of a ship's crew, demanded a whole other kind of faith. He shook his head in disbelief. Like dream-sharing. Like this Nottakow woman. He rapidly transited the corridors. A dream made live had crumpled in his arms. His innards roiled. Whether or not she was a Longhair spy or a dream-ship's crew, her imprisonment outraged him. He would free her. Soon, with the confusion over the coming battle.

Nottakow's cell ...

Phoebe drifted awake, nerves tingling pleasantly, wanting to stretch like a cat. Instead, she stilled herself, eyes shut, listening, counting through the litany of waking like taking readings on a Geiger. All limbs present, no pain, utterly clean, so incredibly relaxed, almost a bother waking up the rest of her cellular family. No nerves, no muscles, no bones interested at all in facing guards, prison, torture, and threats of death.

She teased a few more cells awake. Gladiate a chicken. She'd like to be glad-she-ate a chicken. Made sense. All that action in the arena. She felt all the BIG hungers. Brain cells joined the two-cycle, firing full-on.

There was someone in the room with her. She could hear him breathing. A he, she knew. How? Dunno. She flexed her bare toes. Yup, naked. 'Cept for a thin shift she could feel on her shoulders. A thin cover too, top to bottom. Her nudie toes waving out from the end of the cover, in the wind. Some of the shoes from her self-centerpede cluttering up the floor.

Comfortable. Alone on a soft bed in a cell. Except not alone. The not-alone part buzzed irritably on her Geiger.

"Hello?" she whispered, faking-timid as she tried to sit up, only managing to lift her head with shoulders balanced on her elbows. Playing timid an unfamiliar gambit. Maybe they'd pit her against a lesser chicken.

The big man, the kindly giant she remembered from before, watched her from the corner of the cell where he was sitting on the floor.

"I won't hurt you," he said, voice low. Staying seated, he looked all earnest and such. Like grim-bear. Only without the furry eyebrows.

"I remember you. You carried me. I was trying to tell you people I am not a cow." She did remember him. Wicked helpless slotting into place. Oh you vixen, Phoebe. Make that first move. Wicked helpless 'n sexy, although the latter more her than strategy.

"Yes. I understand. I wrote *Nottakow* on the slate of your cell."

That's? Curious? She cocked her head. He noted in writing that she wasn't a cow, on her cell door? What would he have put there if she hadn't protested? *Fresh meat?*

"I am Brattoch. I brought you some food." He indicated two bowls with some sort of glistening violet fruit and a ball of cooked cereal. He started to rise, cautiously. Monitoring her reaction.

Food. Eating. Component of social ritual. Hunger growled impatiently in her belly, but responding with the right gesture in this ritual mattered. Anthro-class-blast from the past. Feeling other-worldly enough among the cacking aliens, Phoebe needed to push the civilized-being thing. The animal

194

thing, the cow thing, didn't bode well. Cows were grain-fed too.

"Thank you, Brattoch. I could use some water if you please. My name is Phoebe." Oh, the airs. Oh. *That's* why they called it *Gone with the Wind*. All that air. Great name for a ship. She attempted a vague floaty thing with her hand.

He stepped toward her and passed her a ceramic carafe of water. She tried to sip daintily. (Her Geiger clicked sullenly. Dainty: Item not found in Phoebe vocabulary.) She gave up and gulped the water down. Heavenly cool and sweet. Sat upright on the pallet with her feet stuck out in front of her, she wiggled her toes provocatively. He didn't nibble.

Spooning some of the soft cereal into her mouth she looked at him with partially closed eyes. Umm, yummy. A sly poke from her new men-urgies suggested that her mind wasn't yummy-ing over cereal. Men-urgies powered on, fouled up the old two-cycle. Phoebe didn't multi-yummy well.

"Oh Feebee is a very good name for me to remember. Much easier than Nottakow." He smiled at her with a lopsided lip curl seeming to acknowledge all the electric yummies between them. Men-urgies flared. Phoebe blushed.

Her brain, swamped by urgies, struggled to swim back to his words. She nearly rolled her eyes. "Not a cow isn't a name, Brattoch. You people kept calling me 'Long Hair'. That's a cow."

"What's a cow?"

"It's an animal from Earth."

"What's Earth?"

"It's the planet where everyone came from." She explained

patiently. How could he be ignorant? She'd seen the console. She'd seen the chickens. He shouldn't be ignorant. She had other plans for him.

But maybe she was the ignorant one. "At least that's what we thought." Peebletoad. She was speaking to an alien. Pause. Working overtime, like Betty Boop's cartoonist, she tugged the whole picture into the frame. Shitsky double spit. *She* was an alien. Whoa!

The male-lien takes a turn ...

"We come from here. The Longhairs come from the mountains. You don't come from the mountains? You come from the ship as Dern says?" Her words confused him so he focused on how he needed to change the letters on her slate. Feebee would be easy to spell. But in his plan, she wasn't staying long.

He felt unsettled by her words. 'Earth,' 'cow,' 'planet,' she might be crazy. Nothing about a partner or ship. He hoped she wasn't crazy. Because he wanted to reach for her so badly. A move he couldn't really countenance if she were crazy. He already held back because she was his prisoner. At least in her mind, she had to believe she was.

"Dern has told me of the rebel's plan to rescue you, to bring your partner. To return you to your ship." He watched her smooth brow pucker above her yellow Reaper eyes. Perhaps the news of her partner was not so welcome. Why did she have a smooth brow and Reaper eyes?

Quivering Goddess, Feebee. So beautiful even with the useless, silken sweep of soot-black hair. His people had no business capturing her. Their ignorance was no defense.

What difference did one Longhair make? The Shorn would soon battle the Longhairs so what did capture of one buy them? Why single her out for a kill separate from all the others on the battlefield? Disgusting. Another stupid move in the endless stupid game. The other guards didn't take her capture seriously either. Why had they washed her and cleansed her wounds? Why insure he fed her? Kertof would dispose of her. Feed her to the drones.

He was entranced by her, by her glide down a living wall of rock. But Brattoch also held to the rebel's creed. The wars with the Longhairs were a waste of people, energy and resources. Why did the little line they'd drawn in the territory justify systematic genocide? How had a 'we' become an 'us versus them'? How could his people advance when they were constantly torn apart by war? If the ship rumor were true, that signaled a real opportunity for change. Perhaps her similarity to his people suggested the ship had to be related to their ancestor ship. She had the Reaper yellow eyes.

Her rockfall dance spoke a new language. Mesmerizing. She was a magical being. If his people joined her kind, they could do anything. Walk on air above the rocks, above their Continent, in space among the moons and stars. They could reignite the craft of Reaper ships and bring new ones forth from the old Reaper scraps in the far valleys. Or maybe she came with the Reapers to bring them to their rightful home where there would be territory enough for all.

Feebee brought him to the brink. He didn't want to think. She had kindled something in him. He was overwhelmed with passion. He wanted to clasp her to his skin and absorb her essence, her difference, her fine, tall, form, her smooth brow. He wanted to thrust forward with her, far beyond this ugly cell and the tortured mundane politics of his troubled land.

Hmm, hold that thought ...

Phoebe finished her cereal. Her other appetite, the man-urgency from the rockface thrummed. Unsated.

New plan entitled, *Wet Desire Lubes Escape*. A well-tested theory from the ship vids from her childhood on the Third. But she'd use her updated version. Cuz right now she just wanted to fuck someone, preferably someone big and delicious and tender and muscular and creamy like a biscuit. And then fly out the cell door on her jet skates whetted like Lubey Lou.

Her mouth watered. Whet-wet too. She stood, and looked to the door.

"So alone. What will you do with me?" Man-urgies. Easy come since the rock. She slithered her hair across her shoulders and looked at him with a suggestive tilt from slatted eyes, her secret smile.

Udderly quackers. A sexaliciousness upcycled with men-urgies, more urgent than escape. Give a moose a muffin! Yay for living all fired up. Menergy. Full-bore. Ride the rock-it, Baby. Chalk up a new way of being for lusty-Lou.

Her drowning brain scrambled for purchase in a foaming lust lather. Kindly guard in the cell might mean an unlocked door. She cocked her head, listening. She stood and turned toward him, eyes cast down, letting her hair slink across her bare arms and spill around the rise of her breasts. Slowly, she stepped back toward the door as though seeking the support of the wall behind her. Bringing him to corner her, like prey.

That got him. Not so alien after all. He came forward ready to reach for her. His brain as easy to derail as hers. Ha-ha. Man-urge-ies. Gotcha.

"We are arranging to free you. You came from the ship, yes?" His voice all husky.

She nodded. Well, technically a boat, but since he said ship, she'd run with ship. VROOM-o-rama. A ship whet-upped the ante for sure. A slick new track of man-urgency. YUM.

"Yes," she said smile melting all the warm lies. Whoa, Phoebe speakeasy. She held out her hand. She hungered for the charge of their touch. Gimme a little jolt, Baby. Gimme some juice. Anticipation alone charged her parts. Swelling, puckering, wetting her. Molten. Pumping lust. Sheer heat smoldered in her smile.

"So calm now, as though we are alone," hint-hint, she said again, tugging him closer. Ignition on contact. Geiger off the charts.

"We are alone. They forget you because of the battle." He whispered burred. He pulled closer, his arm lifting, encircling her shoulder. And then his lips were on hers. And hers felt crushed like hot pillows. And he pressed her body to his own. Their tongues tasted and probed and suckled. Both of them panting. She pulled at the shift tearing it over her hair cascading across her hardened nipples like nets ripping across a heaving sea.

She helped him fumble to the pallet. He tripped over her ditched shift, stripping off his own in the race to connect skin to scalding skin. They torched each other. Instant sweat, heat, stupored brain, fog, need, man-urgency. He was hard, naked, hot, between her wet lips and then in her, rubbing, loving, pushing, thrusting. She grinding, rolling, rubbing her nipples across the rigid muscles of his chest.

A start, an eternity, and then they were done. They clung to each other mated. They had mated. Exalted. They had sexed and fucked. At rest she could feel herself quivering for more. More of every-fucking-thing and even all the unfucking things. Awake. This last just made her come. Just made her roar, alive. She wanted more.

He left; she might have napped. They murmured words without language. They hardly spoke. And then he was back again. In minutes? Hours? Seconds? She could feel the heat between her legs like hot iron as soon as he turned the key in her lock. She wondered whether she would forever feel herself open-open when a key turned in a lock.

Somehow she had her boots on. Her boots and her shift, and her legs spread and her shift up over her bottom as she pressed against the door wanting him inside her. Immediately. Man-ur-gently. Maybe not so gently. He kept trying to tell her something about help coming. Jesus, Toad. She didn't need any help.

And then Cai's face at the door squinting at her through the barred opening. Go-way, Cai. Primitive, lust-fogged, brain-squeak. She felt Brattoch's tumescence wither from her sex and she merely-only-please wanted to back up and rub wily-Willy hard all over again. Hell, she was just getting started. Vroom-vroom. Cai was here dammit. And she all alien, strobing topsy-urge-turvey with the rescue notion they were trying to squeeze at her through the bars. She stuck her tongue out at the muttered corridor protests. Outrage over 'Brattoch and Phoebe having sex.' Cai and the alien fools he rounded up, bent on rescue.

Phoebe pulled down her shift and greeted Cai sullenly through the door. "I'm going to swing from sex event to sex event." She announced, just in case he was wondering. "Wha'dja do with your eyebrows?"

"Earth called that swinging." Cai responded, calm, looking at the slate on her door. "Why'd you tell them your name is Nottakow?" He wouldn't remember her surname. Maybe she was a Nottakow.

"They kept saying I was a Longhair. That's a kind of cow from Earth. From that Texas place." She tapped her swollen lips with her finger, thinking. "Those eyebrows were my buddies, Cai. I hope you corralled them somewhere safe." She pictured his eyebrows all grey and hairy trotting around in a fenced paddock.

Cai looked tickled to see her. He chuckled low into his chest. "Longhorns, not Longhairs."

"Fine. Whatever. So, I'm not a cow, right?"

"Oh I don't think anyone believes you're a cow. What's with the sex with your captor though? He's on our side. I hope you knew that."

"Don't know. I just want to live like a man now. I have men-urge-ies. Like that rock face. Did you see me? Incrediballistic! Now I get it, I want it. I'm taking all that living. Skates-on, Scotty. 'Course that's what it feels like but maybe it's that whatchacallit, Stockton syndrome." She was proud of dredging that up.

Cai smugged his cheeks up like a froggie, like one of the fat mud chickens from 101.

"That's Stockholm syndrome I believe. Stockton is where the cows were."

"Oh. No wonder I got confused. A lot has happened to me while you were resting on my laurels. Your eyebrows could find a home here. They have Longhairs you know."

And just like that they were back to being grim-bear and Phoebe, Woomies, leaving her cell behind. Phoebe followed two men she didn't know down a hallway with Cai and lover-boy Brattoch bringing up the rear. Jesus Toad! She had to stop thinking rears. Already in arrears over rears.

☾ Cai's got Phoebe back

Cai was so glad to have Phoebe back his smile almost broke his face. At the same time, now that she'd entered her being-a-man-to-be-alive phase (coined *men-urgies*, he chuckled), he'd no doubt be suffering some pain. Bad enough when he had to live through *the men-urgies* for his own self. To witness Phoebe swing through the trees like Lusty Lola on a steroid stick promised real agony. Seriously awesome entertainment too. He smiled right down to his boots. Yes indeedy. These Shorn had certainly found themselves some aliens.

Cai poked her in the back to tell her about Taletha down below, hanging out ready to alert them, when Sig and Dern pulled up short. Sounded like a commotion heading their way.

202

Brattoch grabbed Phoebe and spun her around.

"Head that way, take the righthand corridors. Head down, toward the dark. Run!" Phoebe ran. Cai started to follow her. Brattoch blocked him.

"No. You look more like Shorn than she. We can head them off. Stay behind us. We will find her later. We can't let anyone follow her."

Sig and Dern tucked in behind Brattoch too. The four of them rushed toward the noise.

Cai saw a bunch of Shorn. Maybe a whole troop of guards charging their way. Beyond them, Taletha yelled, trying to redirect the troop toward her. The troop barely noticed. But she was providing the interference she promised, all the same. Giving plenty of warning about the troubles heading their way.

Brattoch turned to Cai. "These will know you are not Shorn." He pointed, "take that corridor and you will find a store room. Hide there and we will come back for you. We must run now. Go! Go!"

Cai turned down the new hall as instructed and within moments found a stores room brimful of cloth sacks, stacked furniture and very large woven baskets. He lifted the lids of several baskets in the darkened room until he found one big and empty enough to contain him. Climbing in, closing the lid on top, he heard nothing from the corridor anymore. He stifled a sneeze. Their coughing and sneezing in this dust-bearing air had already cost them plenty.

20

GEORGE KNOWS ERIC LONGHAIR MUST GO TO BATTLE

George watched Eric catch the relayed signal summoning him to battle. The leathery-skinned fungi near the shelter, thrumming like a drum. This was Eric's second battle. His first came just at the cusp of manhood. George remembered Eric's excitement. Young fool. Now Eric was older, wiser and bigger. A man with a lot more to lose. Much easier for war to rob a youngster of life, before they learned to cherish.

"I have to leave ya, George. Though I am not keen to war I cannot allow Kertof to kill my people." Eric lifted his marbled soil-red cloak from the wooden peg on the wall. Cloak slung over his shoulders, he looked like a giant velvet fungi hillock from the forest.

Gentleman giant, George thought. He nodded at Eric, knowing the secrets they shared would weigh heavily on him in battle. Would these ships interfere in the war that tore their peoples apart? Would Kertof gain an advantage with alien technology or Reaper ancestor technology that would allow him to wipe out Labbites and Longhairs entire?

"I will find a way to involve the best of the Labbites in this problem of the alien ships." George patted Eric's shoulder. "More than we two must somehow ensure that these unnerving arrivals don't threaten our peoples, and don't advantage Kertof. I wish I felt confident that lifeforms advanced enough to travel the star systems will be inclined to sally with the most technically advanced of our people. We have some minor home advantage. We know a little of Reaper technology. I will find a way to reach you if . . . ," George paused, unsure, "or when I discover more."

Eric nodded. He strode off visibly unsettled, silent. George turned off the feed to the stove and repacked his supplies. The closest Labbites weren't his own settlement. Labbites established small lab-centered colonies of one to two hundred individuals. Their marginalized population barely at a thousand across the entire Continent. The labs distributed throughout mountain caverns. George knew every single one.

George recalled Eric's anxious clasp on his forearm. The turns of the glass during their deep discussion and their sleep had allowed the pink snows to nearly fully recede. The melt on the ground glimmered in the dimming sun.

"It would be nice if Kertof dropped from the sky," George whispered to himself, smiling, watching Eric disappear. Kertof aloft in his balloon supervising battles posed such a tempting target.

The red soil splashed bloody with Eric's heavy tread. Inside, the lights dimmed and the warmth left the stove. A sobered George shouldered his pack and stepped out into the sodden forest letting the door close behind him.

His people were a small, stupid, speck of sentient life, surely only a trillionth of a fraction in the galaxy. A bug to crush under the heel in an accidental landing, certainly. But what untold resources had they worth two alien penetrations of their atmosphere? And why now?

☾ Kertof's war

War is chaotic at the best of times. Kertof had left Beezee behind in the palace yard, organizing troops to follow Kertof's transport out to the battle field. The men had reeled the pulleys from the anchor to his balloon transport. Holding the transport with difficulty, they waited for Kertof to mount up. A simple hard half shell enclosing a reclining couch, and room for Kertof to stand if necessary, the transport hung airborne by web-netted gas bubbles. The transport was anchored and steered from the ground with pulleys and large stone wheels on wooden axles. Two men poled the axle of the wheel steering the transport as Kertof directed from above. Kertof preferred a bird's-eye view to monitor his troops and the enemy in battle.

Once he boarded, the men released the reel and let the transport float above the city, headed for the killing fields. Their choice of battleground simple: Longhairs encroached on their farm territory. And so, a declaration of war. Permission for skirmishes in grassy plains, forests, mountainsides, along the rivers, lakes and streams. And then as anger and offenses mounted, they clashed in the thousands upon the open fields to kill.

With their hardened pikes and their knives, Shorn versus Longhairs thrust and stabbed until exhaustion forced a retreat. And so, peace ensued until the next transgression.

Such was their way since the calamity roughly eight generations before. During the calamity, for the first time in their history on the Continent, the seasons cycled twice without sun. All food sources withered to dust. The crops, the animals, the people, shriveled by the score. When sun and life returned, the fight of survivors over scarce remains was fierce. Their society's tether to the technology of their Reaper forebearers, already stretched before the calamity, frayed to threads. Many species both wild and domestic, were rendered extinct.

The struggle for survival bred aggression not thought, not careful governance, moderate consumption, or conservation of resources. Survival bred greed, hoarding, and the will to dominate. The scientists, the Labbites, those most akin to

Reapers, were marginalized—physically distinct and resented for their talents and proclivities.

Ancient labs in mountain caverns built under the direction of the original Reaper ancestors became the remote retreats of the most-marked descendants, the Labbites. Scientists all.

The Shorn, enraged by the moderating tendencies and feared advantages of the Labbites, rejected those with Reaper markings. Shunning progeny with antennae, with yellow or multi-lensed eyes. The long hair that disguised the antennae of the Reaper ancestors forty generations past, when they lived among humans on Earth, became a much-resented badge of dishonor. The Shorn displayed their scorn of Reaper attributes by being shorn.

In opposition, the Longhairs celebrated their links to Reapers. Even if they lacked antennae, sensate whiskers, or vision enhancements, they wore with pride the whiskers and long hair of their Reaper ancestors. But long hair alone did not make them Reaper-enhanced, or capable in the Labs. So they formed a nomadic society buffering the Labbites from the city-centered, antagonistic, aggressive Shorn.

The Labbites never entered the fray. They stayed neutral. They were the science, medicine and education leaders of the Continent. And their numbers, with the genes that marked them, receded with every generation.

Yes, Kertof, ruminating, annoyed, suspected that the Labbits were essential to the survival of the species. But he resented the easy relationship the Labbits maintained with the Longhairs. Sure that the Longhairs' education was just a little better, their medical care just a little more careful, and their introduction to the latest and greatest technology advances just a little more rapid than that afforded the Shorn.

But medical care meant more mouths to feed, and ultimately, more bodies to kill, to sustain existence on this small island. Education, science, and Reaper technology had not aided recovery from the calamity much at all, in Kertof's estimation. The wars were all that allowed a life sustainable within their Continent's resources.

True, the calamity cost them an entire Reaper-imported, domestic ungulate animal species that had once furnished meat, blood, milk, cheese and butter, gleaned from grasses the Shorn could not digest. True, the Labbites engineered a replacement, a nutritious fermented fungal product generated in large quantities from wasted grains, seeds and nuts. True, the cables and the netting capturing the gas bubbles that ballooned above his head were borne of a culture manipulation by the Labbites upon organisms that otherwise fouled their lives.

But Kertof wasn't inclined to pay Labbites either dues or respect. The services rendered by Labbits, as he preferred to name them, were simply not enough of an advantage to warrant concession from him or the Shorn.

"Blast you!" Kertof shouted as the transport shifted side-ways and knocked Kertof into the lounging couch. The reeling cable often snagged an extra loop or two when hauled, resulting in a jolting ascent. He was at the full extension of the cable, his view encompassing the marvelous violets, blushes and scarlets of his land. His domain entirely, soon. Especially with that ship.

Kertof braced himself to stand. His foot slid out from underneath him. His hands yanked violently on the cushions for balance. An angry hen flew from the nest she'd made underneath.

Feathers flying and squawking into his face, she scratched him with sharp claws. Kertof screamed in disdain and pain, pushing the vile, flapping creature through the pulley traces. Overboard. Furious, she flew directly back in his face. He fell back away from her shredding claws and slipped again in the muck she'd left on his transport floor. If he could wrap his arms around her vicious wings, he would wring her neck.

His hand dripped from scratches and broken egg. His cloak and shift smeared with chicken scum and mucous. He wiped the mess away with the underside of his robe and then attempted to settle himself. Raging. Indignant. Flooded with a passion to hail down the mighty chicken-spit scorn of the Shorn.

But there were other matters to attend to. Still irate, he scanned the horizon for evidence of ship maneuvers or signals from the invaders. Who sent them? Why now? Where had they hidden themselves? In the mountains, yes, of course. Had they trafficked with the Longhairs or the Labbits? Why hadn't Kertof heard more news of them?

A ship landing on this Continent the heraldic event of their civilization. He himself saw the entry through atmosphere months ago. Before the Winter snows. Yet he heard nothing of them. As though a ship and all it contained could and would cloak itself in fear of their primitive society. No word from spies, no notice from Labbits, no rumors from prisoners. Why?

Had the invaders infiltrated his people as did his Reaper ancestors among the life forms they harvested? Kertof felt a lonely urgency. Obsessing, Kertof struggled over how little he knew about a potentially catastrophic event. Something this threatening demanded containment and control. With so little information, how could he ever hope to grasp the puppet strings?

☾ Brattoch protects his Goddess

Brattoch led Sig and Dern headlong toward the other guards. "The prisoner! The Longhair! She is gone!" He shouted. He and the rebels were almost immediately engulfed by the troop. "Perhaps she has found the way to the yards, or the wall." Brattoch, breathless, leaned against the wall and gestured toward the nearest window overlooking the parade grounds. "I thought I saw that blue shift she wears up on the wall when I was headed up to check on her."

"Well why didn't you raise the alarm, Brat? And what are these two doing here?" Jared looked incensed. He glared at Sig and Dern. Brattoch knew Kertof would take Jared's head over this.

"If we don't waste time, we might be able to catch her, Jared," Brattoch interjected. "When I saw the blue shift, I was on my way to her cell. I didn't realize she'd escaped. These men say they knew her Longhair family. I was taking them to establish her identity. We will try to head her off this way. You should take the troop to the wall and see if you can surround her. Oh, and tell Beezee that she is gone."

Brattoch turned and trotted back toward the cell wing. He was certain he'd seen Uncle behind the troop past where Taletha harrowed them. Brattoch saw Uncle heading off in the direction of the tunnel entrances when Brattoch raised the alarm with Jared's troop. Fading footfalls assured Brattoch that Jared led his troop toward the wall. Being authoritative with Jared always paid off.

Brattoch stopped to instruct Sig and Dern. "You two must go back to her cell and break the dishes and such. Find some blood. Make it look like she has injured someone in her escape. I will get her partner from the stores room and then we'll join you and go to the caves. I saw Uncle. He heard me tell the troop she has escaped. He will know to head her off and help her through the caves. We'll catch up with him there. Go do it now."

Getting to the troop, raising the alarm, discussing with Jared and running back to the stores corridor took maybe half a glass. Brattoch activated the stores room lighting and softly called, "Hey Longhair? Hey, come out, you are safe. We can go after Feebee now." Brat lifted sacks and looked in baskets. Nothing. He checked the entire room. Feebee's partner was gone.

☾ Uncle's mission

Uncle clung to the shaded walls on his passage through the palace yard well ahead of Taletha and the others. Groups of noisy soldiers with pikes and spears chanted and gossiped, banging the dusty ground with their weapons in emphasis. Discarded frames for balloon platforms, handcarts, and assorted other implements made monstrous specters. They haunted the parade grounds in towering skeletal piles. The aquamarine sky pierced with flickering gas-lit bubbles embraced the human drama in shimmering oblivion. Like a hungry wolf, Uncle stalked alone.

The palace walls an unrelieved flesh-toned stucco, just like every other hive wall in the city, backed the mustering troops. There were none inclined to pay Uncle any mind as he skirted his way into a side hall that led to the prison cell wing.

Once he entered, everything changed. "Uncle," he was greeted, with a nod and salute. Inside these palace corridors he was well known. Here he exchanged tokens for information. His allegiances carefully ill-defined. He gave. He took. Direction in his pattern made indiscernible. Uncle, twisting, bending, slithering, tainted, sour, sundered—though few would, or could, define precisely in what way. Such was his pride, his mission, his mastery, and his disguise.

Some of the elder guards had gathered in a barracks mess for food. He timed his journey well. He joined them at table as the clay-baked birds were broken open. Hot and succulent, running with drippings and fat, the guards snagged meat-laden bones by hand or scooped flesh, lustily filling plates and gullets.

He grabbed a large crust of bread as a trencher and used the spoon he always carried to snag a meal for himself. Plenty. Especially before and after a battle with the Longhairs. The kind of inspiration troops needed. Uncle approved. Now to eat and listen.

"I'll fight all night and then spend the day sleeping in the forest," claimed one, probably too burley to fight in full light.

"Is that a short sleep or the long one you're planning?" This from Dyke, a fellow known for sharp wit. "I was thinking of finding entertainment with the spy before we leave."

Uncle watched, attuned to the reactions this bold claim inspired. Interrupting a dalliance did not suit his plan.

"Ah Brattoch's up there now taking his fill. She'll be no good for the rest of us. Did you see her dance on that rock?"

"Aye, she's yellow-eyed. None of us need any of that. You heard Kertof. We're to leave her and get on with the real fight." An elder with his shining silver pate, spat his denunciation of her breed.

Uncle wiped his mouth with the last of his bread and rose. Now certain Brattoch was in place. All was coming together as planned. Giving him a one-time chance to kill two birds with a single, well-aimed, stone.

The hallways spiraled away from the mess hall up, down, and lateral. Testament to eons of hatching larvae. Unnerving, this use of bug-leavings. Uncle found the insects repulsive.

He'd once glimpsed Shorn guards operated like soulless zombies in the deep cave tunnels. They'd been off on some foul errand, mute and stilted. Faces he once knew, never seen again. He raised the matter with Kertof. Kertof suggested they'd been envenomed by wasps, Queen or drone. Why? For whom? Uncle asked. A smirk in response. No answer. Uncle left profoundly disinclined to raise the topic again.

There were many ways in and out of the upper corridor near the cell block. Uncle hurried along a main route expecting to meet Brattoch near the spy's cell. But Uncle instead came up behind the back end of Jared's troop confronting Brattoch. An interfering Taletha nearby did not notice Uncle arrive. Uncle caught Brattoch's eye and tilted his head to indicate the cave tunnels. Then he sprinted away. He'd gotten the gist.

The spy was free. Brat would direct her to the tunnels. Uncle should be able to take care of his business with her and could expect the others to follow later. A development which eased the setting of his trap.

He'd head to the tunnel entrances first. The corridors should be nearly vacant as troops mustered outward for the coming assault.

Most of the halls were lit with reflective ports or with nets of small gas bubbles. Uncle needed to find a portable light tube for the caves. He had his knives. He had some venom-coated barbs. He should be able to disarm the woman, dispose of her and lie in wait to snare the others. None knew the caves as well as he.

Grabbing a light tube from a niche, he scurried away. He exuded confidence. Authoritative and sure-footed. The tunnels twisted and turned. He always took the darker branches leading down.

He wracked his brain as he trotted. Were there any offshoot corridors that might inspire her in a new direction? Might she stop and take refuge in an empty room? Would she wait for Brattoch and the others? If she made it all the way to the tunnel caves ahead of Uncle, she might escape his grasp.

Uncle could still claim he'd fulfilled Kertof's wishes. Kertof could hardly hope to recognize her in the unlikely event he encountered her again. He never patrolled the killing fields himself. But Uncle must fulfill his second promise to Kertof. To wipe out Taletha's rebel cell. A lack of success there would be noticed by Kertof.

His plan was sound. Uncle was certain he could trap and kill them all.

The corridor dove down sharply. Uncle ran his hand along the rough walls to steady himself so he didn't slide when the floor was slick and polished. He cautioned himself. He could not permit his light tube to break. He did not wish to find himself alone, without light, at the mercy of myriad, venomous cave-dwellers. Zombie makers.

☾ Brattoch's charge

Brattoch slogged his way through the corridors and tunnels chasing Feebee. He left Sig and Dern to catch up with Taletha and follow as they may. They would regroup at their first opportunity. Once in the caves beyond the hearing of palace guards, they could safely call out for one another.

How had Feebee moved so fast? How had her partner evaded him? And why? Brattoch wasn't entirely confident in his own directions to the caves. Why would a stranger take such a risk?

Brattoch ran down, always down. Every time he skidded around a corner or into a crossway he headed down, toward the dark, but not without casting a look every which way for some clue Feebee had actually followed his instructions. She didn't act like the type to obey.

He risked being seen running the corridors. No one ran the corridors here. Alarms would sound. If they saw Feebee running, or any Longhair running, the palace guards would chase and kill her in a heartbeat. His only hope, their only hope, was the battle muster. The corridors should be empty. At the same time, aroused battle lust guaranteed any encounters with Feebee would be violent and deadly.

Brattoch tried to anticipate her moves. She was brave and foolhardy. The rock dance told him that. Not timid. She wouldn't cower or freeze. His people should be more like her. They were violent. She was decisive, passionate. And that joyous rock dance? No taint of the mean and shallow marred her performance. Unlike his people crushing her triumph at the end.

Brattoch hated racing through the corridors. He barely knew his way and he doubted he could find a proper exit from the caves. The cave tunnels he avoided at all cost. Poisonous slime molds, huge venomous insects, man-trapping webs, impossible to escape. The caves themselves weapons, dark and slippery. A fall could cripple, render any traveler prey.

Brattoch had no light. He had no weapon on him. He had no water. And since he and Feebee frolicked, he'd had no sleep. If she hid somewhere under old furnishings or garbage or in a room full of stores, or in the rock fissures once she'd reached the caves, she would be lost to him.

Ever down, Brattoch followed the walls. Creeping, more tentative as the darkness spread. He rapidly scanned every opening in case she'd sought cover. He could hear nothing anymore. He had moved beyond even the range of the battle prep noise escalating in the palace grounds.

21

PHOEBE RUNS

Phoebe slunk as fast as she could down corridors, hallways and tunnels. Away and away from Cai, the guard Brattoch, the aliens. Her feet slapped the floor and her hands were sanded raw as she clung to the walls for balance. She'd passed rooms filled with junk, furniture, stores, dusty debris. Easy cover. She had left one cell. She wasn't about to trade up. As long as she could move, she would move out, hoping Cai and the others would catch up soon.

The emptiness of the corridors surprised her. She turned corners and, as instructed, took darkened branches on the right. After at least one forever passed, she could no longer hear sounds of any other being. Not guard, nor alien, nor bird or insect. Now for the fun of running in the dark unknown. All-in-all, she preferred waltzing down a cliff of living rock.

She could see well at night, her gift. But that meant every flash of new light blinded her. Temporary, for sure. But potentially catastrophic if an enemy wielded the light.

Darkness. The steadier the better. Leading her deep. Sometimes she trotted, sometimes, when she thought she heard something ahead of her, she minced. Abrading her hand on the side of the walls, silent. Sneakily coming up on muffled disturbances, or wan light glows, trying to anticipate how to pass, or whether to retreat.

Ahead, she saw the soft edges of a cone of light. She crept silently forward, listening, the hairs on her body stiffened like whiskers. Forward now, as softly as she could move. Laying each muscle of her foot down. She heard a scuff. Was a foot stepping toward her? Would the shadows hide her? Her guts chewed. Acid washed the cereal. Could she defend herself? Each step she took into her future recalled the tug of those cold, pale hands. She felt Future's finger trace a hold on her ankle. The same finger teased her forward. Now etched deathly white and cruel thanks to Cai's vision. Dammit, where was Cai?

Emboldened Phoebe let herself peek into a lit foyer collecting all the scary noises. A bag of light on the ceiling. Fine. A weaselly alien with a light and a knife just entering. Not so much.

Several dark hallways gathered here. Hers among them. Weasel man scanned his light at the entrance of each. Even with her head tucked back she could see his light trace the room's perimeter. Armed and looking for someone. He held the knife forward as though he'd knife her with the same ease he cast his light.

Phoebe held her breath, and tried to still her drumming heart. Her nerves alert, her muscles tensed. She willed him to turn away. Sadly, her will wasn't up to the mark. He entered the foyer. She shrunk back trying to melt into the rough, rippled walls soundlessly. She held her head down protecting her eyes from the blinding flash of his light. Watching the ground for his feet, hoping to see the glint of his knife before he saw her. Willing him, with bonus Toad prayers, to choose any other avenue. Not hers.

Her nostrils flared as she took in a breath. Retaking the one she'd gasped out seeing the knife. The knife coming toward her now, weasel's light illuminating the opposite wall. She could see the knife enter her hall. Less than a yard away from her body. Ugly, gleaming, sharp. His hand steady, rigid, wire-muscled, veins raised with a tense, sure grip.

Whew! The light backed out tracing the foyer perimeter, heading toward the next passageway. She smelled him now. She saw from behind, his greasy shorn head. He smelled of rancid sweat. Drips of grease stained his shift and his sash. His face corrupt with bristles. His nose hooked. The biscuit skin so smooth on lover-boy looked rough and swarthy on the weasel. He was shorter than she. The light tube occupied one of his hands, the knife another. Both of her hands were free. Geiger counting. Alert.

His light scanned two other exits. He didn't advance toward them. He instead chose the darkest corridor, the one she would have chosen.

She knew he was looking for her. Could she follow him? Could she use his steady light and his knowledge to find her way? She would be safer behind him.

She silently darted across the foyer and tucked herself into the corridor in his wake. She'd let him progress further. She could use his light for advance warning of his every move.

Weaseling along

Uncle spun his light around the perimeter of the foyer. Which way would she go? Darkest tunnel, like him, that's the one she'd seek. He caught a glimpse of a blue shift, prison gear, in the corridor next to him. Aha, he smiled to himself. He started to walk toward her corridor slowly, blade forward at the ready, thinking through his plan. If he took her here, he'd have to drag and dispose of her body before the rest of them caught up. He'd prefer to lure her into the caves.

Would she follow him if he took the dark corridor? Was she smart enough, daring enough, to try to use his light to guide her way? Ideal. The best way to draw her into the depths for quick dispatch. He felt squeamish considering the allies he might attract to his mission down there. Worth the risk. He had all the advantages. The superior knowledge, strength, weapon and light.

He light-scanned the other two exits. Informing her by gesture of his search mission. Then, decisively, he took off down the darkest corridor slowing only after giving her just enough room to feel secure, while allowing him to hear whether she'd taken the lure.

Yes! He heard her move; she was behind him now. He moved forward slowly, letting his light tube bob naturally, as though he was moving unconcerned. He kept his own breath slow and quiet to better discern hers. Once he felt certain she was securely hooked, he stepped confidently forward. There would be no reason to worry about her until he was ready to make the kill. He was giving her exactly what she needed now. A way out, light, and advance warning of her enemy.

Uncle chuckled to himself. Canny. The reason he became Kertof's man. Brattoch would soon follow. Uncle needed to move fast before Brattoch and the others caught up.

Brattoch distraught ...

Brattoch looked down the shaft of hallway. He saw the light at the end where it opened up again. That would be a hard call. Too many directions. Which one would she take? Would she try to go up and out now or would she follow his instructions and head deeper into the ground. At least he was fairly certain he was the only one chasing her. He hadn't heard any further warnings sounded. And perhaps Uncle had her in tow.

Then he saw a flash of moving light up far ahead. Someone had a light tube in that foyer. She couldn't have found a light tube. There was someone else in the tunnels. Why? No one came down here. He saw a flash of blue in the foyer. Shite! She was there, and so was someone with the light tube. Had she been caught?

He started to run, keeping his hand on the walls to stay steady. If they were fighting, he'd have a chance to catch up. He had no weapons, but what did it matter? He could defend her with his hands alone. He'd already made his choice.

His feet pounded the floor. No reason for caution now. "Hey! Wait!" he yelled, knowing she'd ignore him. He ran faster, getting breathless, he was sure his fear was tensing his diaphragm. He could hardly catch his breath. He skidded into the corridor.

Phoebe ...

Phoebe heard someone yelling behind her. She could hear the pounding feet. She wanted to move faster but she was caught between these two. If Weasel heard a yell, he might turn back to enlist the help of another guard. She'd be thoroughly screwed. Not in a good way. But just as she almost had to halt for fear of bumping into the Weasel in front, his bobbing light took off. As though weasel guy was escaping someone too.

Could he be an ally? No chance. That knife didn't describe someone looking for a friend. Maybe these tunnels were criminal haunts. She'd seen a ton of criminals on the vids. Lots of sewers and tunnels on those vids too. So maybe they were kinda on the same side. Aliens, criminals? What's the diff?

She bolted to keep up with his light. Maybe she could duck out. Let the one behind pursue the one in front. Maybe she could get away somewhere. So far, the light revealed nothing useful for cover or redirection.

The floor roughened under her feet. Not the same polished flooring anymore. Harder to keep up. The ceiling opened. Weasel's light cone much wider now and she saw only darkness above. But she had to concentrate on placing her feet. Breathless, and afraid of flashing knives that edged the closing jaws of a trap.

Uncle strikes one canny too ...

Uncle had just glimpsed his ultimate goal. The entrance to the caves. He heard Brattoch yell behind them. Kertof's Balls! He had to find a way to accelerate his plan before Brattoch caught up. He barely remembered these tunnels. He knew them better than most but he loathed to use them. He tried to remember locations of pools and chasms. Could he shove her into a web and gag her? Leave her to the bugs? His light bobbed in front of him. Tricky to move fast now, with rubble underfoot.

Then he saw his chance. There were a large pair of boulders ahead. He knew there was space between them and a deep depression. He'd hid there from cave menaces once before.

Uncle tore ahead risking everything to place his light on a waist high rock. Then he crept silently back to the cleft between the boulders. She would follow the light, safe in the delusion he was well ahead. But he'd grab her when she passed. This was his best chance.

"Wait!" he heard Brattoch yell from far back in the corridors above. Uncle stilled. The girl should be here soon. He imagined he could hear her breathing. No! Balls! She was here! He saw her vague shadow. He knew this was his moment. He flew out behind her, thrusting his arm around her neck. She was much taller than he realized. He struck at her with his knife. She pushed back into him unexpectedly. Levering herself against the boulder she smashed his head into the rock.

Kill Phoebe, Kill ...

Phoebe surged, adrenaline spiking when she felt the arm encircle her neck. Instinctively she turtled her neck into her collar bones. He was neither strong enough nor tall enough to choke her life away. But the knife was coming. She felt him tense for the thrust as he tried to pull her body back by the neck. She yanked her hips forward and arched back smashing his head into the rock. Then she turned and her hands were grabbing at him. He managed to slice her hand with the knife. Even with slippery fingers, she got hold of his knife hand and pushed it back at him. He screeched, "Witch!" Attempting to pull her onto the knife with the arm he had still crooked over her throat. He fought her. She ducked right out of his grip and down onto the rubble floor, turning around and pushing his knife, in his hands, under his arm. She felt the knife slice.

He hollered some more. She needed to get him dead before the chaser found her. Pushing hard and steady she felt the knife enter his flesh again. She pushed using the knife now in his gut as he slumped, to prop her to standing. She added her height and weight and legs to her thrust. He was going down. He grabbed her hair and pulled hard, tearing her hair out with all of his strength.

Phoebe wanted to scream, but kept pressing the knife. Her hand on the hilt met his flesh. Warm, wet blood. His hands grabbing her hair and her head yanked her head into the rock. His knee rode up under her chin. She felt her skull crack on the rock. Her teeth punched through her tongue. Her eyes ran with tears and she cried thickly in her throat.

She pushed up with her legs. She pulled the knife free of his gut and stabbed him again, thrusting between his knees into his groin. Oh, now she had him. Near, or in the groin, the knife sliding in hot through soft flesh. Blood-lust raged for the hot sharp knife plunging a flaccid dick. She brought up her knee ramming into his knife-skewered balls. She spit the blood and saliva from her ragged tongue into his face. She was breathing thick, gagging on the swelling and gore.

Blood-lust-spent, hot, and angry, Phoebe pulled the knife out of Weasel and lunged. But it was Brattoch who came running into the dark cavern. She didn't lower the knife. Her black killing moment cast every shadow as threat.

The Goddess takes a life ...

Brattoch yelled in utter shock at the violence he heard ahead, "NO! NO! Don't kill her!" He skidded into the cavern blinded by the sudden dark. The light was frozen twenty strides ahead. He heard moans nearby. Then he saw a crumpled body on the ground between two tall boulders just off to the side. Not Feebee. Feebee was standing knife out, in front of the boulder. She stood above the scarcely moving body on the ground.

Brattoch approached warily. She stared at him holding the flesh-wet knife in front of her. Fierce. A stride away he saw her streaked face. Her hair matted in wet clumps. Her arm shook as she faced him.

Brattoch held up his arms, "No, I won't hurt you, I won't hurt you." She didn't need saving from whoever bled below her. Looked like a man. She backed away, still holding the knife forward. Shaking, her arms, her legs, her head, "Stalphth, stalphth," she grunted as though her sounds would mean anything to him. When she mouthed at him runnels of bloody saliva dripped from her chin.

He let her back away. He bent to the body on the floor. But it was simply too dim in the deep shadows to recognize the man. Brattoch wasn't certain the man was a palace guard. Brattoch stood again, and pointed to the stationary light tube, "Can I get the light? I won't hurt you. I helped you. Remember? Your partner is coming. But I need to identify this man. Will you let me get the light?"

She nodded and slumped against the rock. He passed her, careful to lean away so their bodies wouldn't touch. He'd felt post-battle trauma himself. He knew she could dangerously startle. She held the knife ready but not in his path. With the light in hand, he bent again to the body, turning the buggered wet face into the light.

"Oh Kertof's Balls, it's Uncle." He felt the smeary throat for a pulse. Uncle groaned. Brattoch knew Uncle was critically wounded. Bleeding freely at the chest, the gut, and down between his legs. The back of his head was wet with blood too. Uncle's skull seemed spongy to Brattoch as he cupped the head with his palm. What to do? He should fetch help for Uncle. But Feebee? She needed to get away. Brattoch needed his rebel allies and Feebee's partner to aid her while he got help for Uncle.

He didn't care much about Uncle, none of them did. But leaving him here to die? While Brattoch aided a prisoner? That could become extremely complicated.

Uncle moaned. Where could Brattoch find help? How would he explain Uncle's injuries? He had to let Feebee get far from this battle scene. "I have to get help for Uncle. He is one of us."

Almost lost, almost alone, and almost free ...

Phoebe looked at Brattoch dully. Watching his mouth move, waiting for whatever sense he thought he was making, to penetrate her thickened head.

"We are resistors. We would help you. We don't believe in this war."

She blinked. Nope, still nonsense. What war? Hmm, was that ship he'd told her about part of the war? This all seemed too primitive for a ship's war. Lover-boy wasn't moving on her though. Smart man. Alien.

"Here, you take the light. I think if you go that way you might come to a cavern. The cavern leads out into daylight. You'll see. You should be able to find cover out of the cavern. Be careful. There is a battle out there. Follow the river. The river leads away from the killing fields. After I get help for Uncle, I will try to find your partner and the others to help you. Please follow the river."

Brattoch bent to the floor as though there were some final boon he wished to give to Weasel. Uncle, Brattoch called him.

Brattoch turned back to her and rose. "We will find you and bring you help for your injuries. There are bad things in here. Don't wait. Go as fast as you can. When you get out you can rest. Go! Go save yourself." He gestured forward as he handed her the light.

She barely registered his words. She needed to move. She needed to get away from the aliens. In the same breath she was hungry to stab a few more. Quite the violent indoctrination to man-ur-gies. She hoped Uncle Weasel was dead. She wanted Cai.

22

ERIC'S MARCH

For nearly ten turns of the glass Eric marched the forest, heading for the next mountain refuge to rest and recover before his final steps into battle. The killing fields 20,000-plus, strides from the shelter he shared with George. Such a distance promised at least two cycles of sleep. His journey would lengthen further with interruptions he expected from skirmishers along his forest path. Small groups of Shorn typically forayed in search of easy kills amongst forest-dispersed Longhairs.

Eric didn't envy George. George actually heard the alien ship land. George knew where the alien threat lay. And George had to manage that threat single-handedly. He might be able to rally some help from his Labbite fellows. But Labbites weren't fighters. They weren't strategists. They were good at argument, science and technology. They weren't much good at politics or decisions or wars. Bogged down by self-imposed complications. George had an intelligence challenge in front of him that might presage the wholesale demise of their entire civilization. Such as it was.

Too much dark and too much rain dogged Eric's many steps to the fields. Roots slicked with treachery. His face slapped raw and wet with dripping branches still strung with old, dead, leaves. Oh the killing fields, he sang, where he looked forward to plenty of death and stabbing not a whit. The arrival of these ships exposed the shame in the priorities of his people. Ridiculous. What in Kertof's Balls were they doing fighting this stupid war?

Unbothered by Shorn skirmishers, Eric instead measured his journey by cycles of hunger and sleep. The changes in light contributed little to the rhythm of his life. He'd had two sleep cycles since meeting George. At the next shelter he would wake beside the killing fields. The promise of death whimpering near enough to jostle him from his dreams.

George had proposed engineering some draconian deviltry. Something he and the Labbites would undertake to end the battle. Eric and George agreed the arrival of ships unraveled their collective future. The Shorn-Longhair regimented mutual assault, would shock an alien intelligence. The scheduled killings a patent offense to sentience. The aliens likely planned to annihilate them all. Eric was convinced the warring of his people prompted the ships to land. Spoils and easy prey for circling predators. But small prey even easy was hardly worth a dual incursion.

George was clever. Eric gave him that. But what in Kertof's Balls could George do to reset the entire battle regime?

Eric found his last shelter and let dreams draw his mind from worry. In the morning, not much rested, he stepped out to gather eggs to break his fast. There were eggs. He knew, because the damn rooster spent the whole of Eric's last sleep cycle crowing about them. How many soldiers had gone to their deaths raging at cocks? Count Eric among them. Sure enough, a set of three, still-warm, blue eggs were nestled in the ruddy grasses at the base of an old stump. Even here, within the forest, the nearby killing fields harkened their waking. Screams and rough yells, the clash of arms. More cocks crowed.

Eric patiently added some of George's cheese to melt atop the eggs. The hammered metal pan held grease, bubbling eggs and cheese. A hind of bread, also courtesy of George, functioned as spoon for the hot mess. All washed down with tea and honey. Food and toilette finished, Eric mustered forward, determined, pike in hand. His last day perhaps. Well begun.

The path of killing stood before him, long and oppressive. He walked a body-laden field. Some of the dying moaned, or cursed. Blood, sweat, piss and shite, wended wet pathways in the soil. All around him, life departed in little stinking streams and pools. Eric stepped on a hand buried in the muck. He felt the bones crunch, his tread crushing them against a hidden rock. He saw his own people strewn like straw across the ground. Dying. Their long hair braided, tied, or hanging, clumped with sweat and sticky ichor. Faces whiskered, sometimes seeming alive with movement, though eyes were sightless or closed. Gasps and fading cries hung in the gorgeous, glassy-green sky, like live paint drips from a canvas. As though awaiting a chance to dissipate. As though they wouldn't forever rot this welkin air.

The Shorn no longer so alien-seeming to Eric, despite their shaved faces, smooth scalps, and streaks of blue to mark their brows. Since he'd heard of the ships, they looked like his people too. The same people suffering the same battle deaths. Their blood, the same. The same exhaustion, remorse and loss. Eric hadn't yet killed. This day.

Angry, but resolved, he set to. Two Shorn were hammering a Longhair. His brother, or sister, kneeling, nearly felled by the dual force of the blows. No whiskers. A sister.

Eric strode up unseen, piking one of her Shorn attackers hard from the side. The metal-reinforced pike-tip easily penetrated flesh. The wound opened like a wet red mouth, squelching with gurgling red serum. The Shorn man turned soundless toward Eric, holding Eric's pike into his own wound. As though the pike would staunch his departing life force. Eric, merciless, twisted the pike and thrust the man aside. Just as he would at table, spearing a sausage with a pick. Not this piece. Not to my taste. The man fell back grunting.

His Shorn partner, alerted to Eric, backed from the sister on the ground. But sister saw her chance. She rose and stabbed into the distracted Shorn's gut dead-on with her pike.

The man fell backwards. She pressed him to the soil, lunging into his body with all her weight and might.

Eric pulled his bloody pike free, stiffening his resolve, ready for his next encounter. Thrust, duck, swing, smash, dance. The sweat poured from his skin, causing his shift to cling uncomfortably. He grunted on. His toll at this juncture, two turns of the glass in, perhaps three on the ground, dead or nearly so. He could barely lift his pike, so heavy with disdain for this work. He felt the pinch and wetness on his side. Sucked a sharp breath. Wounds.

His muscles felt stained, his soul too, with exhaustion, resentment, disgust. Only three, out of thousands, to spike through on his way. In the distance Kertof hung aloft, screaming as usual. Eric stopped at a spring to drink. There in the fields of death, a simple sign of life. Clean. Unsullied. Smooth, leathery fungi, a cushioning cleavage for sun-sparkled water jewels. A glittering crystal spray across a heaving breast.

Refreshed, Eric stood. And turned, his spirit washed, hitting the next Shorn butt-end with his pike. The man fell, barely injured, merely bruised. Stupidly, he rose, using his pike to lever himself toward Eric. Eric butt-ended him again. "Stay down."

The man still strove to rise, and again Eric butted him. "Stay down, dammit, I dinna wish to kill ye."

The Shorn's blue brow, an aged custard of wrinkled skin, furrowed with confusion. Yet he tried to rise. Eric flipped his pike, threatened him with the pointy, stained, metal end. "If ye rise, I have to kill ya. Just stay down."

Oddly, the Shorn understood. He lay back on the ground exhausted. Eric fell to his knees beside him, wheezing. Surrendering, Eric let himself fall forward on his stomach flailing his pike arm out to the side. And giggled.

His Shorn enemy, next to him began to snicker. Eric answered with laughter. Raised the bar. The Shorn laughed in concert.

"Mebbe we two can just lay this one out," Eric said. He rolled to his back, still guffawing against his will. The soil warm against his back, soft and comfy. He shut his eyes to the strobing sun.

The pair fighting next to them stopped in their struggle and looked at Eric and his Shorn enemy giggling on the ground.

"If ya just go down, ya don't have to kill any others." Eric tried a wan shout. Eric didn't recognize the Longhair who looked at him askance. "Tis Kertof's war, why should we kill each other?" Eric said. The Longhair nodded, looking intently at his Shorn enemy as he stood his pike to the side. Then he fell to his knees.

That Shorn smiled. He crumpled to his butt, and then gave it up and laid back, knees bared and splayed, ungainly. Both started to laugh. "It's Kertof's war, not mine," they chimed, chortling together. They whispered, heads rubbing, giggling. The Shorn threw back his head and started to laugh, his Longhair counterpart chuckled, hiding his own mouth with his hand.

Eric and his new Shorn friend began to make giant chicken wing patterns in the dusty soil under them. Turfed up to sun-dry with all the action and not yet wetted with bloody deaths.

"My wings are bigger than yours," confided the Shorn friend.

"Hah! Mine have special whorls," Eric replied, knowing his wings were infinitely superior. Around them the fields were filling with dropping bodies, giggling, clucking, laying down their arms. Eric could hear the refrain "it's Kertof's war," travel across the field. Admittedly, he hardly noticed because the fairies tweaked his nose as though they would lift it off his face. Shite, the aliens are fairies, Eric concluded with a weak chuckle, leaning back to burrow further into the great feathery wings he'd carved in warm soil.

Oh dudder-brains, Eric thought, realization blooming as he looked sideways at all the wings blossoming across the field. George put fairies in the water. He giggled. The devil.

☾ Maria takes the bait and runs

Linda dead. Across a whole Winter with real snow, soft as feathers, though Maria had yet to witness Linda join Joseph, a new haunt on the ghostly stage. Could she remember Linda's touch? When she was a small child, she felt their touches, The Three. But she knew them through the voice of CLEO. In Maria's mind, Linda's arms were CLEO's arms. CLEO, always there with just the right song, the right story, the best comfort. And sometimes CLEO held her with Linda's arms, or comforted her in the bony lap of Kendak or Davis. CLEO scolded her and Joseph using Kendak's finger to point emphasis. CLEO woke her in the morning singing, and tucked her in at night with borrowed hands. CLEO wasn't buried in that mound.

Maria knew real feathers, and snow feathers too. Before Winter's snow she'd discovered a chicken's nest filled with eggs. NEW CLEO had chickens. But on CLEO the nests weren't feathered with down and grass. No bright blue eggs, double-fist-sized, promising fluffy chicks bigger than Maria's head. CLEO's chicken clones a poor facsimile to these, these fat and full, with ruffled feathers, clucking and squawking. Linda's death, Spring, the almost-man on the side of the mountain, or the fat chickens, full of life: what tempted her out into this red world far from the safe plastic hallways and worn upholstery of her home with CLEO?

Maria had run away again. They, The Three Minus One, didn't know. When they first landed, she'd taken off a few times. Running after Josie. Climbing trees. Crawling up the ship to see. But not to see. She'd shut her eyes. To taste. To breathe, to smell, to feel. To run. She ran away to run.

Over Winter, in the snow, she bided her time, quiet, pondering life with CLEO. Maria didn't like the cold, the wet, the dead crushed everywhere, submerged under the innocent feathery pink blanket. Before the ground froze, Maria had dug Linda's grave with CLEO's robotic help. The Three Minus One said their goodbyes. Stilted, troubled. Worrying at death's hind leg like dogs at an old bone. Maria stood, numb to the stony pelt of their words. Odd, this Linda body resting beneath the red soil. All the other bodies had drifted away among the

238

stars. She saw Joseph look around at Maria's new world, his glance skipping past Linda's sorry hump of dirt. Happy. Ready to play. His presence pierced her even so.

Kendak and Davis stayed in over Winter too. They hadn't felt the feathery snow. Nor did they know as she now knew, that cold burnt worse than hot. They hadn't seen the art drawn in freezing ice by a blistering unbridled sentience. A stroke of nature's brush so powerful Maria fell to her knees. NEW CLEO didn't create like this. NEW CLEO only formed recycled colonies of used words and pixels. Never inspiring these feelings, this profundity. Old Earth vids, culture, art, just not resonant here. Not alive.

When the snow melted, not many Earth days past the Spring day she saw the bipedal alien man turn his head in question toward a cloaked NEW CLEO, Maria ran away. This time Josie didn't lead the chase. She followed.

The thunk-resist-spike of a body lent an odd sort of realism to the game these alien beings played. And the ichor that trailed as the weapon pulled back, thickened, dyeing the bodies red, then brown and uninteresting. In her tree perch, among the scratchy twigs and soft red leaves, Maria enjoyed the liveliness of the deadly spectacle. The actors were so preoccupied with their killing and wounding and dying, Maria was perfectly safe.

She couldn't adjust the volume. The deaths and violence didn't swell to background music. Screaming, shouting, moaning, crying, slapping, thunking, puking, spitting, the air was as messy and as fluid-laced as the heaving flesh, the ground, the rocks and the piles of bodies.

Teams distinguished by simple differences. One side had long hair and the others were shorn, with blue paint marking their lumpy brows. Maria's long hair instantly accorded her a team to root for. Picking sides was always the hardest part of watching vid games or wars. Vested interest the only attraction of competition. Across all their competing eons, what did the human teams on Earth finally win?

Action vids didn't draw her attention much these days. She focused instead on deepening her knowledge of CLEO's systems. The time was coming when CLEO would be hers.

Maria looked down at the real action beyond her perch. Her fists gripped the branch as a being with long white hair smashed his stick across a blued brow. A flash of memory bringing back her fraught terror watching action vids with Joseph. But video action dramas moved fast. The beings on the field beside her killed slowly, like farmers planting death.

She wanted a single brave or heroic move to entice her to root for the other side. She listened hard to decipher the yells. Anything to make her care. She wasn't close enough to make out words. They at least had words to yell with and spikes to kill with. As CLEO said, they were human enough. Like humans, they made work of war.

Not caring enough to feel afraid, Maria watched Josie shrinking into the brush, starting at every sound. The blows and screams steady and predictable, like rain. NEW CLEO entering atmosphere scared Maria. Warring beings posed a greater threat. Maria observed the war with clinical detachment. As though she were invisible. Cloaked, like CLEO. Untouched. Untouchable.

240

Tempted to follow a forest trail the alien had hiked a week or so ago. That alien-human pondering a cloaked NEW CLEO in the snowmelt. Maria traced his path marking the depressions his feet recorded in the soft ground. Here, a day's journey from the ship, Maria came upon these people. The alien-humans. Killing.

The pondering alien was on her team. He had her long hair. Possibly fighting out there now. With their robes and shifts, their war uniforms, they all looked the same. They laid the same in death. No wonder one side sheared their hair and dyed their brows.

Personal violence was not something Maria had faced. While CLEO's Old Earth vids were filled with violence Maria couldn't countenance. Totally unreal. Each side mustered around some stupid aim. Just an excuse to go to battle. War on vids indistinguishable from any other game. Except the players died.

Linda's broken leg was the ugliest reality Maria ever witnessed. Until this moment, clinging to a tree watching almost human beings in real clothes hack and spike each other to death. Making hard heavy work of it.

Maria looked down at Josie. Her heart fluttered. Warm need, spilt down her body like sap and ghosted gooey trails to Josie. Alive. A coal kindled in her breast. Maria shouldn't torment Josie by staying to watch. Josie guarding Maria despite obvious fear. She should have put Josie first. She should have resisted curiosity, temptation. She should have left these repulsive violent beings to themselves.

When Kendak and Davis were mounded with dirt just like Linda, CLEO would be Maria's only home, Josie her only family. Aliens, these others, these killing creatures. Hope she'd barely let surface as she watched the whiskered man, evaporated. Stillborn. Her kinship with Josie cemented. She felt alone.

Even she knew her life hung so thin. Overwhelmed by gravity, swamped by an excess of oxygen. Flattened in spirit. Her runaway adventure dead-ended. Ground underfoot was exciting. Running such breathless fun. Climbing a tree both cleanly innocent and dramatic mastery, electrifying.

But the dull deaths and loud violence of war abraded her yearning spirit. Incomprehensible. Foreign. Inhuman. These deaths too near. Noisy, ugly, stinking. Not remote like the breathless, silent deaths in Space. How could CLEO-born Maria hope to reach through this violence, these torn limbs and stacked bodies to make a first-time connection with another soul?

Uninvested, bored, completely alienated, Maria watched the war pause for breath. A living thing. A cadence. Run, push, and stab, then a killing phase. Mass movements shattered into duets. Quieted screams. All the energy conserved to pile a kill upon a kill. Intimate, final spikes with blades, or with a thrust to the ground to skewer the fallen like meat on a stick.

Bloody, fetid meat. Up in Maria's tree, stinky dust obscured her view. Maria molded a surgical mask to her face. A smell reminiscent of CLEO's waste locker when the filter clogged. CLEO's rare manual tasks fell to Maria, so the smell was far too familiar. Robots, and The Three, encumbered with hands too stiff, too inflexible, too old, not manually dexterous. Maybe twin incubator babies were saved for their hands.

The mass of heaving violence had shifted well past her tree. Death's meadow a broad valley stretching beyond the visible horizon. Maria must have drifted to sleep in the tree crotch, curled against the smooth, warm bark. With the violence moving on, she was safe to climb down to Josie's perch. She should return to the ship. A little faint, hunger perhaps. She felt intangible. She needed some substance to her. Like Joseph's ghost, except she alone stroked Josie's fur.

Maria would need to pick her way through bodies to reach the forest trail. The wounded and dying moaned. Cluttering her path, they crawled the battlefield mewing. Brown serums shone sticky or dulled, flaked, and crusted dry. Maria walked among them, invisible, intangible and unafraid. Sometimes an almost-human arm would snake up toward her. She thought she heard cries, 'help me, help me.' Her imagination gave them tongues. How else could she understand their words? They bled just like Linda, and Maria's hungry mind brought back Linda's words.

Josie moseyed along trailing Maria to collect buckles, buttons and other spoils from bodies that no longer moved. Josie stuffed the treasure into her pouch. When her pouch was full did she bury her collection? What had happened to Josie's treasure trove? All the little items Maria provided her from CLEO's own dead soldiers? Josie hoarded like a dragon, apparently. Kept her secret stash safe.

23

ERIC SEES A SILVER FAIRY

At least one sleep cycle had passed as Eric lay burrowed in his wings. The agony of his festering wound woke him. No fairies. He looked around, his Shorn, winged, friends had left. Others still battled far off, headed to the far forest fringe. If he could only turn, only roll in the dirt, grinding into the wet that had spilled when he lifted his shoulders to watch the silver fairy drift by. Somehow, he maneuvered his pike underneath himself and levered himself up.

He must've groaned. The silver lady looked at him across the litter of bodies with startled eyes. A sister? Too pale, too thin, her hair long and yellow. Too oddly suited, in silver metal, glinting pink in the sun. No draped cloak or shift. Her mouth was veiled in white. Eric thought he saw an adough standing up beside her, chittering at him, defensive. Forgetting about holding his wound closed, he snatched at his only chance of aid. A sister would help.

He poled himself to her in five strides on his pike, afraid she would evaporate like all the other fairies. But she stayed. Frozen, shocked and wide-eyed, like an animal. He leapt, despite his wound, and caught her arm in the fingers of his free hand. He saw he clutched a thin fragile twig. His own fingers, massive flesh, engulfed her silver-clothed, skeletal limb.

She cried out. "No! Josie help!" The adough skittered away.

Eric eased his grip, surprised she would fear him. "Be still sister," he gasped, "I'm not gonna hurt ya. I'm thirsty for water. Please can ya fetch some water for me."

Her fright and resistance added to his confusion. She should help. Any who followed the battle should help. Perhaps he was delirious. Eric looked at his hand. He felt the silver cloth. He saw her breathe. Her blue eyes shone. Their color rare among his people.

Not delirious, but addled with thirst and pain. The adough fearless now, bared its teeth. "Whoa," he smiled, adding the blue eyes to the stick body, silver-clad. "Just water for me please." He released his grip and fumbled under his cloak for his flask, letting his other arm and pike prop him steady. "Please, just go to that stream and get water for me in this." Why was she dressed in silver? Uncloaked, too thin, blue-eyed, and booted in silver too. The mask across her mouth dimpling with her breath.

The silver woman didn't respond. But the adough was not timid. She snatched the flask from his hand and ran off. Was she stealing? A chitin flask made for awkward booty. Far too big for her pouch.

"Lemme go. She steals." The woman spoke.

The animal was an easy mark weighed down with his flask. But it didn't run far. It led the silver woman to the stream. There the adough released the flask to the woman who knelt to the stream and let it fill. Rarer than the woman's blue eyes, an adough, tamed. His people slaughtered them after the calamity. Ate every adough they could find.

Eric dry-swallowed. As the woman and adough returned, he felt uneasy. She handed him the flask and moved out of his reach. Timid.

The water cleansed his mind. She had their speech. Though somehow she was alien to their Longhair comradery. Eric drank his fill. Near drowning in his thoughts. She made him think about George's ships.

☾ Josie expected her to help this man

She, who had never spoken to one before. The Three Minus One didn't count. Nor did Joseph count as a man, with his wide ears and fluffy hair. The stream had several deep, clear pools. Maria filled the flask and returned to the man who gripped his open wound. Her arm burned where he had grasped her. He moved too fast for her. He was too strong. She wasn't accustomed to touch.

She gave him his flask and returned to the stream, bending her head to drink. She was thirsty. Josie busily washed her face at the stream while Maria returned to the man. He spoke like a man. Not so alien. How could he speak a language she knew? He must be related to other Earth refugees. How had they ended up here, warring? And they had bred with alien beings. CLEO said their DNA wasn't human. His words penetrated her invisibility. He touched her. How had they come to war?

The man drank thirstily and splashed the water over his mouth, eyes and cheeks. "Thank ye," he gasped. He sounded breathless, maybe the pain, like Linda with her shattered leg. He tried to lever himself forward, but fell back groaning to his knee. The flask dropped from his hand as he gripped the wound and his weapon.

His weakness forced Maria to assist him. He was descended from Earth refugees. Like her. He needed her help. Josie watched her, holding paws across her pouch. And judged.

There were others moaning near them. This one could still stand, could grab, could chase her and had words. Josie took his side.

Maria braced her foot against the base of his weapon to help him.

"I'm afraid I need your help to get up. Please."

"Okay." She felt like a straw lifting a broken tree. She picked up his flask and tucked it in her harness. She, skeletal against this massive flesh. Her arm still burned from his first grip. Though she moved close enough for him to use her, in the end, her proximity alone gave him the strength he needed to stand. He held his weight propped by both hands on the pole weapon. His wound bled freely.

"Could ya help me belt me shift around the wound?" He untied his cloak and let it drop. "Just cut the neck of me shift and roll it down." He had a knife on his belt, and a holster for his flask.

Maria had to reach high to tear at the shift. The material thin, stained, wet with sweat and ick. She felt a vee at the back of his neck under his hair. His flesh was too warm and too moist, his hair damp at the neck. Maria gripped the fabric points of the vee and tore with all her strength. The cloth held.

"Ya need to use me knife."

Maria took the knife from his belt, surprised that he would give her a weapon. She snagged the knife tip in the fabric and ripped the opening. The shift slumped down his bare shoulders. He pulled his arms free of the cloth one at a time, still leaning on his weapon. His chest and abdomen bared, his gingerbread skin streaked and stained, his chest hairy. Not like Joseph's, pimpled with chill, bare and ghostly white.

Maria rolled the fabric with her quivering hands and pressed it into his wound. She heard him draw a sharp breath but she couldn't bear to look at his face. Human, but for the lumpy ridge at his hairline.

"Could ya tie me cloak around my shoulders again?"

His polite, patient, voice sounded strained, tense against the pain. She replaced his knife in his belt, using the hilt to

248

brace the roll of cloth against his wound. With difficulty, Maria hefted his cloak over his shoulders and tied it at his neck. She stepped back and looked for Josie. Josie chittered at her and nudged Maria affectionately.

"I am Eric. I thank ye silver woman."

Maria looked down at her stretchsuit, realization dawning. How strange she must look to him. "I am not like you. My name is Maria, and this is Josie, my marsupial."

"Ah, aye, the adough who got you to help me. Ya dinna seem to be like any others, true. And I have just spoken with George, a Labbite friend, about the ships from the stars. Have ya come from our ancestors on a ship?"

He rocked dizzily in front of her. Maria thought his wound smelled bad, festered. The dirty shift wouldn't help. But even fevered he painstakingly found his way to an utterly flummoxing question. He was right. These alien-humans must be related to her humanity. How could she otherwise explain their familiar appearance, the human genes CLEO noted, and the common language? But NEW CLEO gleaned no evidence of advanced Earth technology, and this warring people seemed far too primitive to be descendants of an Earth refugee ship. CLEO had determined they were not wholly human genetically.

Maria struggled to answer. "We are from a ship, well I am. Not Josie. But are you from Earth, descending from the refugees? How do we share a language?"

The man, Eric, shut his eyes as though in terrible pain. "A story beyond my ken, I fear." He gasped. "Maria, ancestor-cousin, we must get off these fields. The stink of the blood will draw the drones soon. I can take you to the Labbites who will answer your questions and who will help me with this wound."

"I should go back to our ship. Can you make it to your people by yourself?" Maria knew he would drop within a few steps. But she wanted to run away with every cell of her being. The touch, the warm, moist skin, the gentle voice, the massive power of this man, the kind patient words, his incisive question, the whole nasty ball of complicating feelings, terrified her. She felt cornered, herded. Not by him, but by all her holes and missing pieces.

Eric shut his eyes again, and leaned his forehead against his staff. "No Maria, neither me, nor you and Josie, are safe alone right now. I'm afraid, Cousin, we need each other. Please, lift a weapon from the dead, and help me to the shelter of the forest. I can already hear the drones."

She heard the drones too. She lurched to heed him. A body nearby clutched a blade in its fingers. Past rigor? She slipped it free and tucked it into her harness.

"Move sharp," he said looking up and indicating the sky with his head. "The drones are coming. They smell the blood."

It was true the droning buzz had gotten louder. She could see black specks dotting the sky. Josie had become agitated and was running back and forth between them. Eric hobbled toward the trees. Maria and Josie followed. The buzzing loud.

"They aren't machines," Maria cried, watching as insect creatures circled to land. Massive bugs. The size of Eric, winged. With great celled eyes and long black antennae. None were very near. But she could see them spin a sort of rope of fiber between mandibles and forelegs. She could see them wrapping the bodies like they were spinning cocoons.

"Get back," he whispered, intense. She realized Josie had been tugging at her ankle. "They will take me if they smell me. And ye, stained with my blood."

Stunned, Maria struggled to watch as Eric drew her deeper into cover. Sure enough, some of the bodies they cocooned still moved. "They cocoon them alive?" Her whisper revealing her shock. She felt almost compelled to stay and watch. Simultaneously repulsed and fascinated.

"They eat 'em dead or alive, or their queen does. We think. We never see the bodies again." He didn't look back. Both he and Josie were moving rapidly into the forest. Maria shivered, following. The truth smacked her in the face. She was grateful for him. His massive strength, and his insight into the horror of this predation, overcame her other worries. For all his size, he was kind, warm and patient. And unexpectedly wise.

Should she lead him to CLEO? Maria looked around her. Somehow he had conspired to draw her deep into unfamiliar forest. Her bearings lost. CLEO no longer an option for either of them.

24

BLOODY FREE

Phoebe followed the water streaming through the cave barely noticing her red-slicked hands and the rest of her wet wounds. Empty, drained by her spendings: lust, violence, adrenaline. The knife and light in her hands. Both weapons. Marked by first blood. She fought for her life and won. Like freaking Hercules. Every trial liberated something so deep in her, revealed an unknown quest. She thought she only wanted to fly. Turns out, she wanted to live. Living. Whiskey. Tango. Foxtrot. To live meant to claim. To win. To seize and to blaze, to thrive. Self-De-Terminator. Scorch the fuckers who get in her way.

She stalked like an animal, looking for an opportunity to shelter and clean herself. She needed water. She needed rest, but first she needed distance from the body of the filth who tried to steal her life. She won. That gutter weasel dead. Even though lover-boy left to fetch him aid. Good luck with that. Talk about a river in bleeping Egypt. Bye-bye, lover boy. Right now, she just wanted grim-bear. Where was Cai?

The mineral drippings hung the cave like statuary. Some name for that she was too dull to remember. For much of the way she clung to the water's edge. A path water found or made. At times she detoured to climb small slopes of broken rock or work her way around boulder dams. Distancing herself from the corpse.

Thousands of pounding steps later, she knelt and bent her face to the stream of water, the rocky path piercing her knees. She didn't care, desperate with thirst. After drinking, she stood breathing in some calm. The light stick let her examine the passage. Low ceiling. Narrow passage. The sides steep and littered with piles of rock. No handy cavity for sleep. She moved on. Dragging her feet, her legs rubbery, feeling exhausted, depleted, and alone.

The only sound her footfalls, a ticking record of her endless escape. So exhausted she could barely lift one foot in front of the other. Eventually something snagged her awareness. The stream had broadened into a large pool. A scan with her light showed a ceiling arched like a cupola above her. Suddenly so high. The path was smooth rock, now scored free of litter, glazed, almost slippery. She was freaking tired of caves.

She'd walked long enough to be desperately thirsty again. Remote from the corpse and all the hangers-on. The pool drew her. She could wash. She, a blood-crusted hotsicle. Her hair felt greasy, reedy, scabbed with filth. She laid her knife and light stick carefully in a generous cleft between some large boulders. Before she let the light down, she cast it deep in the fissure to see if there was room to sleep, to reveal any others who might have dibs.

All nice and clean and suspiciously free of other inhabitants. No dragons.

She lifted off her shift, made thick and stiff like meat jerky with all the pounded drippings. Pity she couldn't wash it. She'd need the remaining clean bits to dry herself after her bath. The rock temperate, ambient with the cave. Dry, she'd be comfortable even naked.

She pulled off her boots and walked barefoot to the pool, sitting, moving her legs into the cool water. Jesus Toad. A tall drink of water for her skin. She slid her whole self in, slithering sensuously, buoyant. Her hair floated out behind her. The crusts, the scabs, the clumps and lumps falling, drifting, sinking. All the nightmares cleansed away. She swished and wiggled and bobbed, a nymph, a fairy creature. A new self. Clean, fresh, softened. Reborn.

Tired, drooping, Phoebe emerged, dried her body, wincing over every bruise. She laid in the cradle of rock poorly wrapped in her wrecked shift. Dead asleep. When she woke she entered the water again. Desperate to feel refreshed. Not over-burdened, just beaten. Dull to this world.

She let all of her tension go, relaxing in the water's cool embrace. Her eyelids drooped. Was there such a thing as too much? She had felt so full of life. Charged. And now she had nothing. No will. If only the water were warm enough to rock her away to another less taxing universe.

Her guard so low, she barely registered the pink fleshy finger emerge between her legs. By the time she flew upright reaching with her toes for the bottom, a large pink worm had enveloped her. Coiling around her like a snake. Slinking ribbed skin up between her breasts, her legs, a probing pointy head nosing behind her neck, pulling her in, down.

She splashed violently, wresting for purchase. Her screams echoed in the arched chamber. The worm seized, pulling at her body despite her fighting limbs and buoyancy. Jesus Toad. Murdered in vulva land by a great pink worm. Her head went under. She pushed back, up and out. She choked. Fuck that. De-fucking-Terminator. She rides again.

☾ Cai gets lost

He would make it to Phoebe, with Phoebe he would be of use. Besides, he had to warn her about his little ship subterfuge with the rebels. He'd hid in the basket for less than five minutes. Aged ten years. He was outta there. Phoebe needed him. She'd called for him. Damned if he'd take orders from her alien boy toy.

Cai threw off the lid of the basket and headed down the corridors in Phoebe's wake. Fear spiked his every step. The path twisted and turned. Ever descending. Skipping heavily as fast as possible through the complex warren, he avoided dead end passages and empty rooms. But he had to look. He had to check to make sure she hadn't found refuge.

Then running with every chance. He felt the ceilings of the corridors close in above. Hallways and corridors became tunnels, or sewers. The darkness swallowed light and sound. He must be nearly upon her now. Even with a head start she couldn't have fled faster than he. Yet he found no trace of her and the light abandoned him.

So he walked, stumbling, feeling his way with his right hand on the rock wall. Not the cement from the quarters above. He was certain he'd followed the only route Phoebe could have taken if she followed the orders from boy toy. But with the dark, he was no longer sure.

The damp air staled. He began to doubt. He had no confidence in his path. His sweat felt cold on his face and body. He shivered. Alone in the dark. He stumbled but recovered before he fell. He had lost track of time. And something was wrong. With him.

He felt like he had gone back. He was there, like before, when their cleft opened upon the red world, and he saw light at the end of his tunnel. But he was alone this time. Traversing alongside a black, shining subterranean pool in a cavern opening onto light.

He remembered their fear. He didn't want the world outside the cave. Only Phoebe safe, mattered to him now. He touched his brow, clammy with sweat. A fever.

His wound filthy, festering again. He needed to clean it and rest. He couldn't go on. He had to trust Phoebe's Great Toad. If he stayed in one place, she would find her way to him.

He was no longer sure he knew where he was. He was sick. His head throbbed; his wound was hot. He was exhausted. By the time he fell alongside the pool, Cai was undone by fever. He splashed water on his torched face and then laid among boulders, dull to the grit beneath him. He knew he should cut open his wound and clean it, let it bleed free. And many other unimportant things. None followed him into his away. Astral protection. He dreamed. Oh Jesus Toad. He was turning into Phoebe.

When he remembered to think again, the fingers stroking his brow were mercifully cool. His eyelids fluttered as he drifted and wandered in his mind. He was blissfully numb to the leg that had flamed him all those years ago. Grateful for the icy fingers and the sweet softness that cradled him. He burrowed deeper into sleep.

For a dream, the fingers were oddly insistent. Annoying. "What? Whaddaya want?" he slurred. The fingers probed his mouth and his nostrils. "Whoa!" He spit out the fingers. He tried to open his eyes. He struggled to rise. But the fingers muscled him like clammy tentacles, pulling him back in a cushioned, firm, embrace. Panicked, he freed his hands and tried to push away whatever the hell covered his eyes. He felt like he was crawling with giant worms.

"Smudge?" How could Smudge have found him here? Finally he freed his eyes to see dull grey mottled skin, arms, more than twice the length of Smudge. He felt the familiar rubbery suckers fondling him.

Was he food? He surely couldn't be prey. He trusted octopuses after all his research on Smudge. Not Smudge. This one was enormous. When he relaxed his struggle, the octopus released him enough to sit up. She held him dangerously close to her beak. Her enormous yellow eye inches from his own. She blinked flirtatiously. Now that was a thought. Remembering Phoebe's protests over Smudge copping a feel. Research never told the full story. Jesus Toad. She'd eat Smudge alive.

He could see his wounded leg. Neatly wrapped with something gauzy like spider silk. Brilliantly white and clean. The wound no longer throbbed. No smelly festering. No fever. A mottled arm near his wound was carefully pushing away ugly white worms. He cringed. Remembering the crawling feeling. But then he realized they were large maggots. She'd been smart enough to let them feed on the decay in his wound.

He gently lifted her heavy arms from his body. "Thank you," he gave her a warm squeeze. "I need some water." He stood, feeling surprisingly strong. No longer enfeebled by the wound.

She slithered into the water alongside him and ducked under. Another freshwater, genetically-altered octopus. He hoped Smudge would be safe amongst them. He wondered how the aliens had programmed the cephalopods to seek interspecies social relationships. Now that he was recovering, this one was off to her midden he expected.

Cai bent his face to the pool and drank. He was hungry. He needed to find Phoebe. He sat back and ran through some scenarios. But he was shocked off his agenda by a glowing light emerging deep within the pool. Was his leggy nurse fluorescing at him? Her arm thrust out of the water splashing him. Holding up a glowing light tube in offer.

He grinned, delighted. "Wow, you are amazing. Are you giving this to me?" She answered by placing it with care on the path beside him. "I don't want to take your treasures. Will you stay with me so I can give it back when I no longer need it?"

As if in answer, another arm set a green metal platter filled with items on the bank. He sat back hard on his haunches. Shocked to his core. These were human things. Ancient human things. There were thick glass lenses with delicate, tarnished gold-wire frames, a finely worked tarnished earring, an hourglass, the glass dulled, which her arm picked up and placed carefully, allowing its sand to stream downward. She was showing him its function.

"Ahh, you have many treasures." Cai finally gathered his voice. "I have a friend like you. His name is Smudge. I'd like you to meet him. Maybe I should name you too. 'Ozzie' would work. For the wacko reality I'm living." The light tube would allow him to head back into the dark caves. He hoped she'd travel with him.

What weird genetic recoding allowed human things to become coveted octopus treasures, to be shared down generations, through centuries of middens? The octopus recoded to comprehend the use of the things made by human or other advanced technology. As Smudge did with his sTuffy. Like this one with the hourglass and light tubes.

The light tube's casing felt like plastic, the tube light worked underwater, and was cool to the touch. How? Weird. Like the friction lights at their base camp and the tech he'd seen at Taletha's.

He handled each of her treasures reverently. Deeply engrossed, he hardly noticed the faint sounds echoing across the surface of the pool. When the sound finally penetrated his consciousness, he stood abruptly and swung the light tube along the pool banks looking for the trail.

"That's Phoebe." He ran back deeper in the cavern, toward her screams.

"I'm coming Phoebe. I'm coming!" He saw the pulse of a siphon in the water beside him. And far ahead the grey-mottled skin disappeared.

☾ Another big, pink, worm

Cai watched Phoebe's bare white legs kick above the water, thrashing away the remains of a great pink worm.

"How come every time I rescue you, you're wrestling a big pink worm?" Cai couldn't stop the tears shooting from his eyes as he knelt at the side of the deep pool and offered Phoebe a hand.

"He was an alien," Phoebe gripped his hands like she'd never let go. Her eyes streamed too, but she'd nearly been drowned by a worm. "How do you know what color it was?"

She let him help her hoist her hip up on the rocky edge. Water poured down her goose-skinned, white flesh. Her black hair veining her face and neck. "I see you found another lecherous octopus." She shuddered.

"What makes you think she's lecherous?" Cai passed her his over-robe, fearing shock from the trauma of the cold water, the fight to the death.

"She's sucking down that great pink worm like there's no tomorrow." Phoebe let Cai wrap her in the robe and draw her against him. His throat spasmed on a sob.

The octopus was stuffing ribbons of pink worm into its beak.

"I may never eat spaghetti again." Phoebe was shivering uncontrollably, pressed into Cai's chest. He gathered her into the cloth, ensuring no wet, bare skin was exposed to the air. He gulped back another sob. An arm snaked itself from the water and curled around his back. Cai freed his hand from Phoebe and stroked the arm. Warm. Touched. Grateful.

"At least you don't have a pink worm to worry about anymore."

"Neither will you, if you don't move away from your new girlfriend." Phoebe shivered and started to push herself to her feet. "Not that I'm not grateful. What's her name anyway? Swallow?"

A strange feminine voice rang out across the cavern, "Her name is Lucid. You are lucky she found you. Water bear larvae can be very aggressive."

Cai stood abruptly and turned towards the voice. He held Phoebe behind him protectively. "Is that Taletha?"

The octopus, Lucid, he assumed, removed her arm and siphoned back the way they had come. Back toward the voice.

"I am called Mercy. I am a partner with Lucid. Bring your friend to the cavern entrance into the light. I will help with her injuries."

Cai and Phoebe slowly gathered the light sticks, knives and Phoebe's filthy shift, and headed back toward the warm light of the cavern entrance. Cai concluded that Mercy, not Lucid, must have bandaged and cleaned his wound. He was relieved to feel Phoebe move with an easy stride. She fared better than he feared.

When he and Phoebe came into the light, where the cavern opened out onto a reedy river plain, the woman in a dark, hooded cloak was comforting Lucid, the over six-foot octopus wrapped around her. Lucid, who had so dramatically rescued Phoebe from the worm. Cai squeezed Phoebe's shoulder and strode forward to thank them properly. The woman rose. She turned to him and shook her hood from her head. He heard Phoebe startle behind him as the woman's antennae leapt from the confines of both hood and her long salt and pepper hair.

"You are from the ship I assume. We must rush as soon as you are able. There is much danger afoot on our Continent. We Labbites have organized a network to aid you."

25

FLY, FLY, FLY!

Guided by two trusted men, the large rolling anchor below Kertof's floata tracked his indecision. How could he be certain? Even were he certain, he noted, irritated, the path they sought was well beyond the battle field. How would he justify leaving the battle? Still, his floata wandered, nearing the mountains and Labbit confines. A ship had landed there, Kertof silently asserted once again.

Not many floatas remained anymore. Though they were terrific for supervising troop movements and war. Clumsy but worthy. A battle-dogging vantage point with a panoramic view.

The floatas were downed by arrows in the regular wars of the last several generations. His father was murdered by an arrow to a floata. Kertof glanced sideways. To explode one of the gas bubbles with a well-aimed arrow, so simple. One explosion lit off all the other bubbles. A fiery end for occupants and transport alike. Their wars had become simpler. More organized. Like a sport of killing on a dedicated field.

Kertof's exile of the inventive Labbits reduced the Shorn's access to stores of lightweight materials. But they still had enough to maintain this old thing. He nested, finally sans chicken, on the couch. Aloft, he saw further than anyone else in his world.

"Trade off," he yelled down. "I want to reconnoiter with our advance guard in the Knoll Tain mountain range." He'd spent a full sleep cycle aloft, and another cycle harassing his troops in battle. With a few breaks for those below and a change or two in his guard, the floata would achieve the mountain valley where he was convinced the ship came to rest. Of course there was no advance guard or sortie. The words were just another sop for his flustered men. His men knew nothing of the ship.

Possibly the ship had departed. Any ship capable of landing would soon discover the Continent offered nothing to those with the wherewithal to fly among the stars. But Kertof needed to visit the site himself. To ascertain no advantage or threat remained. He needed to ensure his plans would not be undone by a surprise attack, or worse, derailed by yet another calamity.

For the many turns of the glass required to get his floata and guard to the valley of the ship, he would be aloft. He trusted his guard to cycle in fresh men to move along as rapidly as possible. He would have to devise another story to manage them once they encountered the alien ship. Their fear would stun them, make them malleable. He would need to hold them firmly in his grip.

Kertof leapt to the side of the floata and grabbed the ring of wood that rimmed the basket surrounding his couch. Some silly scuts below chanced a skirmish with the men driving his floata anchor along the mountain road. But the brief delay posed little threat. He cheered to see at least one Longhair brave gutted by one of his able guard.

A sensible order of things. If Shorn and Longhairs hadn't differences, they wouldn't have defined allegiances. Without allegiances, they would control their population in a joint endeavor. They, their society and civilization, would advance without the distraction of war. But once they took sides, neither trusted the other to impose limits in population growth equably. Hence war, where the better side gained the edge, improved their stock, and both sides contributed to a reduced population through deaths in battle. A strategic victory in every sense.

A tacit win for the drones too. The bugs were a remnant of the Reapers, in Kertof's estimation. They devoured the carcasses littering the fields after battles, and the remaining living population didn't become their prey. A shame the wasps didn't define carcasses quite accurately. Nevertheless, their failure to do so saved his people from facing some of the uglier aspects of war—like the festering wounds and the interminable march of slow death.

In the boring transit, Kertof made intimate acquaintance with every turding treetop. His impatience barely veiled. But at last his transport came to a halt. An unwelcome hold-up. The snowmelt swamped the anchor wheel path. His floata vantage must be sacrificed. They'd make the remainder of the journey on foot. Toxic walking. Inevitable labor with no assured outcome, made more torturous by the unwelcome embrace of his troops.

The damn ship entered atmosphere, he told himself firmly. Others, especially his enemies, will not be permitted to claim it first. Kertof cast one last scan aloft, focused on any disturbance along the base of the mountain, any evidence of aliens or a ship. He saw nothing. A big round shiny thing with layered lights: how in the Sun's name did such a vessel hide?

Ready to disembark he bolted upright, positive he'd glimpsed something at the base of the hills. Reaching for the rail in desperate excitement, he tripped on his supply stash. His guards averted their attention from his fumble.

"Sky-seared damnation!" He waved at them, furious. "Reel me in."

The scant handful of men attempted to pull the buoyant transport down through the latticed tree branches. He resented having to trust these men to back him in a stealthy approach on foot. The alien quarry he now knew was in his sights would unsettle them. He could barely contain himself.

266

They had a mile or two to traverse before he could be sure of what he thought he glimpsed.

"Jason, Brisa, come help reel Kertof. He wants down now. Move sharp!" Some member of his team shouted loudly and then whispered with the others as they regarded him in the treetops.

They skittered about like frightened animals. For an instant he wallowed in the pride he felt at their fear of his legendary rage.

Then he was down, on the ground, hiking in the lead, with half a dozen guards staying well back. In the thrall of the hunt, Kertof hurriedly sidled around the boulders and trees that separated him from the two silver beings mincing like prey at the base of the mountain. Exactly where he expected to see something. It wouldn't be long now. At last he saw them. He hung back in the cover, gesturing his men to stealth.

How little these beings conformed to his expectations. Like himself, they were men. How odd that beings from the sky should be so familiar. Even more confounding, they were bent sticks, frail and old. One had a long white mane of hair. A Longhair. Both were very old, skeletal. They were not Reapers. They had no visible antennae, no rumple on their brow. It occurred to him that he alone could simply overwhelm them. They moved stiffly. Weak and timid. They bore no weapons. What an extraordinary development!

But where was their ship? Why had old men, bred much like his people, arrived on this Continent? Was the ship ridding itself of the aged? Had the ship left them behind to die? Why break atmosphere and land? Why not just push the elders out among the stars? No, the ship must be somewhere nearby. Without a ship, these two frail beings wouldn't last an hour in the forests, let alone survive Winter.

No matter. His plan formed in the instant he saw them. He would snatch them, secure their ship and assets and deny the Longhairs and the Labbits any of their proffered boon. The fear Beezee had kindled in his breast over the advanced weaponry such a ship might wield evaporated. Kertof sighed. Rather, *he* would wield these two, as hostages to his will. As a result of his strategic arrangements with Beezee, these elder aliens would release their resources. Thus bolstered, he and Beezee could rally the loyal Shorn to overcome any further resistance from the elders' hidden shipmates. The alien ship and all it might provide would soon be secured exclusively in Shorn hands.

☾ NEW CLEO warns

"Indigenous bipedal human approaching. Intent hostile. Weapons primitive. Youthful and vigorous. Manifest physical advantages over you. Should we target him in weapons range?"

Kendak raised his eyebrows at Davis as they listened to CLEO assess the threat. The ship was cloaked. An approaching hostile, primitively-equipped alien shouldn't be able to detect NEW CLEO, and even her limited weapons would quite simply disable an assault. Neither of them had devised a strategy for

268

interacting with alien hostiles. Both so desperate for society, Kendak must be as flummoxed as Davis was himself, now faced with human-aliens poised in threat.

"Target him with the stun weapons only. Let's see if we can get some information about Maria from him." Davis whispered into the mic, linking Kendak into his transmission.

He and Kendak slowly moved so they were back to back. They opened their arms in welcome. "We know you are out there. We don't mean you any harm." Davis toggled his mic volume up so his voice would carry.

Kertof considers ...

Kertof snatched his head back behind the tree, stunned. How could they see him? Was there someone else watching him? He looked around the forest. Were the Knoll Tain Labbits already spying on him? Communicating with these shipmen? Surely not the Longhairs. The Longhairs were too stupid to even fathom a ship, let alone track and access the landing site. Kertof saw nothing. He heard nothing other than his winded troops. He gestured caution. Without the presence of the ship, his men wouldn't see these elders as threat or alien at all.

More than their resemblance to his people, he was shocked to understand their speech. They weren't Reapers, but they looked just like the Shorn and Longhair inhabitants of the Continent. He expected to encounter advanced technology. To hear instead a greeting voiced by old men unnerved him. He gripped his chitin knife. A great weapon. Tipped with venom. So easily he would slay them. An adept at knife play, he had weighted the hilt for throwing. But really for these, he could simply bash their heads together like ripe fruits.

He moved toward them, sticking close to the cover of boulders and trees but no longer bothering to duck or hide himself. He muscled his frame into a fighting stance, and held the knife out. They watched him approach. They were clothed in silver. Each had a shiny chitin shield on their breasts. He wouldn't stab them in their chests then. Their necks were bare. He saw wrinkled white skin, plucked like chickens. Disgusting. His mouth wore his revulsion and he swung forward into the open.

"What do you want? Why did your ship discard you? What do you have for us?" Kertof waved his knife with menace.

Kendak responds ..

"Are you from Earth?" Kendak croaked. He was distraught hearing a human voice on this planet, unexpectedly speaking hostile words he understood without translation. "Are you descendants from the exodus ships?" Why would refugee descendants from an exodus ship approach other obvious Earth refugees with such hostility? Kendak was utterly undone. He didn't have an inkling of how to proceed. NEW CLEO detected no signs of advanced Earth ship technology on this foul-water-wrapped continent. So how had humans, speaking English, found their way here? Unfathomable.

The hostile human looked disoriented, and lowered his weapon. "I am a Reaper grandson over forty removes. I am the Leader of the Shorn. We have wrested this place from hostiles.

270

They will attempt to steal you and your assets. You must let me help you."

Kendak got the gist of the politics in play from that assertion. The fellow wanted to secure the ship for his own agenda. NEW CLEO transmitted a similar assessment.

"The hostile leader of these Shorn wants to secure ship assets. There is a tribal battle taking place within five miles of this location. Combatants are bipedal, partial humans. Maria is among them." NEW CLEO's drone must have a bead on Maria.

Davis chimed in, "No one can get to our ship. Our Captain is missing. That is why we have entered your forests. We are searching for her. She is the only one who can access the ship." Davis held his hands out in front of him.

Quick thinking Davis. Kendak was impressed. Davis came up with a way to avoid revealing CLEO and at the same time, enlist this fellow's help in safeguarding the runaway Maria.

Exit Kertof...

Kertof was horrified by those words. He knew at once his forces had captured the Captain of the ship. The very Longhair spy he had arranged for Uncle to dispose of. He must immediately return to the palace and stop Uncle. But these men had to be convinced to hide so the Labbits or Longhairs or worse, his own troops, didn't discover them. Without his guidance his battle troops would surely slay them. They were too similar to the Longhair enemy, and none of his people knew of the ship's landing. Of course, the only one that really mattered was the Captain. Kertof had to ensure she remained his hostage.

"I believe I can find your Captain. You should hide in the forest from the hostile tribes. I will return with her before the next moon rises. You will be safe enough." Kertof turned and ran to harry his guard back to the palace. How would he get there in time? There was no way he could cover ground fast enough afoot. Even the floata wouldn't get him there rapidly. He could only hope that Uncle performed at his usual level of incompetence. At least Kertof had kept the Captain out of the hands of the Longhairs. He ran through the brush unhinged. His confused and weary guard tagging along behind.

26

MARIA, FIND A LARGE EGG

"I can use your aid, to get to shelter, to cover my wound. I can lead ya to folk who will understand about your ship. They will help you and your people to understand this world. I am Eric of the Longhairs. But I can lead you to Labbites."

Maria felt like she could barely stand under the weight of him. "Could we rest here for a few minutes?" They were deep enough in the forest that she no longer heard the buzz of the drones or the faint cries of those in their clutches, who were near death.

"Aye. We can rest." Eric nearly fell to his knees. And then he sat back on his butt, resting his body against the trunk of a tree. He indicated the forest litter with a nod of his head. "Could ya look among the brush and grasses for an egg?" He held his hand to his wet wound. And then dragged out his flask for a drink of water. He watched as Maria searched the forest fodder with Josie.

"Look. Look here, there is a large white thing. Partly buried. Would this be an egg?"

"Ahh! That's very good. Now, be careful. If ya touch the shell of the white thing does it feel soft like skin?"

"Yes. Should I dig it out of the soil?"

"This be exactly the egg that we need. Aye. Be careful not to tear the skin. Dig it clear and bring it to me. We will open it together."

Maria teased the white egg free. A soft thing roughly the size of a human skull. She brought it to Eric and laid it on the ground where he could reach.

"I must hold my wound closed." He spoke breathlessly. "Use your fingers to make a small tear in the skin of the egg. We can see if it be ready." She made a small tear in the membrane and they both saw clear mucous encasing an inner white lobe. Eric nodded at her. "Aye, it is ready. Ye must with care tear off the membrane, but don't let the lobes touch the ground. Keep em within the membrane."

Maria opened the skin and brought it down as cleanly as possible, revealing a tri-lobed globe sectioned by three orange stripes.

The mucous ran out over the edges of the peeled membrane, slicking the ground.

"Please, with care separate the lobes and unfold the orange pith. S'long as the mucous protects the lobes from the ground, they will stay clean."

Maria tugged at the orange material, lowering each of the three white lobes to the ground as the material came free between them. Then she unfolded the orange pith. It formed a large square flat sponge, perhaps twice the size of the pillow on her ship bunk. Eric reached for it.

"Help me press this into my wound. It is filled with healing."

With obvious reluctance Maria knelt upright and pressed the unfolded soft, moist sponge into Eric's uncovered wound. He had pushed his shift down to his waist. The sponge stuck to the wet wound instantly. Eric moaned in relief. He wiped his tarry, dirty hands on the free edges of his rolled shift. Then he covered himself with his cloak again.

"Thank ye. That was the right egg to find." Eric bent forward and lifted a white lobe, broke a chunk off and passed it to Josie. "We can eat this cheese. Tis very nourishing and very good. Ya see?" He nodded at Josie stuffing her cheeks. Eric passed Maria a small sample and put a large chunk into his mouth.

Eric watched, chewing, as Maria timidly sampled the cheese. He chuckled when she smiled at him. She broke off a larger piece for herself. They chewed contentedly. Passing the flask of water between them. They had rested and eaten two lobes taking perhaps a full turn of the glass when Eric began to push himself to standing.

Maria gave him a hand and stood patiently beside him as he leaned an arm on her shoulder. "We can find shelter and then we will rest some more. Bring the cheese. And I'll not need ya to lean on. My pike will be sufficient. My wound is much better."

Maria looked up at him shyly. "When you rose from the ground out there, there were marks in the soil like angel wings. Under you and some of the others."

"What be an angel?"

"On Earth, they said that angels were winged beings sent from God."

"Like the drones what take our dead and dying?"

"Oh no. The angels have feathered wings, like chickens. Their great father sends them, God, they believed on Earth."

"So the great chicken sends them down to gather the dead? Have ye ever seen an angel?"

"No. It is only a belief. They are not real."

"Well now you have seen winged beings carry the dead. So ye have seen real angels. And those are not the wings that we carved in the soil. I think we made chicken wings in the soil. Or the wings of fairies."

"Do you have fairies here too?"

"Well, like your angels, our fairies are beliefs, not real. More beautiful than real, like your angels. As ye see, real is nay so pretty."

"On Earth they had fairies in their fantasies too. I wonder how you have a language from Earth, and how you have some ideas from Earth, but you are not Earth refugees."

"We be going to see the Labbites. They may have some answers. But if not, they'll still be able to help ya find your ship and they can take care of my wound."

"Why Labbites?" Maria followed him closely now. Not so timid—curious and trusting.

"Because they are our Lab people. They live and work at the Labs the Reapers, our ancestors, built for us."

"Labs? Like for science? And yet you fight with knives and pikes?"

"Why would Labs have any business with our weapons? In our Continent, the science is against war and deaths. Ye imply that our knives and our pikes are basic, stupid or primitive. But your people believe in the giant chicken what sends winged beings to gather your dead? And ye never see this chicken? There is no need to use science to kill. Killing is easy. We use science to advance life. Not to waste life. For example, the Labbites developed the cheese egg that we just ate."

Maria stood stock-still, taken fully aback. Eric continued to walk. He said they had another 5,000 strides or so, until they would be at the shelter. He glanced over his shoulder and saw her running to catch up. At first he had seemed intimidated by her, afraid of the beings who brought the ship. But he asserted himself now.

They each had something to learn from the other. He sounded perfectly aware his people had their faults. But having faults didn't mean they were inferior beings. There were so many ways to suffer for stupidity. He did not deserve her judgement when he had shown her such kindness and intelligence.

☾ A Ship? Asks Phoebe

Phoebe scooted out in front. Following in the wake of the antennaed alien.

"Ship?" Phoebe looked back over her shoulder and bugged her eyes at Cai. Doing her best *'you better be filling me in fast Woomie,'* glare. "What do you know about our ship?"

In the bright sunlight outside of the cavern, the alien woman sat and gestured Phoebe to a flat-topped rock. "Please sit. I would like to examine your wounds."

Phoebe hunched her shoulders, curling inward. Shy, at facing the weird, thin, erect antennae. Talk about a pair of hard-ons. Phoebe remembered the rough bumps on her hump-boy-Brattoch's brow. Did his people cut them off? Finally she sat. Her quest for a ship quelled the feral fight within. Future fucking never let up.

Cai's cloak barely covered her naked body. Mercy brought a hefty pack out from underneath her cloak. Cai left them some privacy and turned to interact with Lucid, who was following them like she had a mission. Mercy held up a clean shift.

"You can put this on after I look at your injuries. Please drop the cloak."

Phoebe dropped the cloak and tried to ignore the long brow hard-ons. Fine. Quivering antennae. Light fingers probed the wounds on her scalp under her wet hair. The woman passed her a wooden comb. "Pull this through your hair gently and tie it with this rag. Your scalp wound is clean. The knife wounds are superficial. You seem very pale. Are you much shaken? Have you lost much blood?"

278

Phoebe stood and tied her combed hair. She took the shift and pulled it on over her body. She sat on the rock again and tugged on her boots. Even though the sun was warm, she wrapped herself in Cai's cloak.

"I feel chilled. Blood loss and shock. I need food. Thank you for helping me. And I am grateful for Lucid's rescue from that worm." Jesus Toad. Phoebe sounded so civilized. Her feral, killer-self shrunk like a vampire in the sun.

The antennae danced as Mercy rifled through the pack and brought up a chunk of bread and a sodden, cloth-wrapped cheese. "Take these. Share them with your friend. We may sit in the sun safely here for a time until you are ready to walk again. Let me check your friend's wound."

Mercy and Phoebe joined Cai on the banks of the narrow river winding out of the cavern. Lucid was playing with a buoyant ball in the water.

"Lucid, give me the ball. Here, you can take this to your midden." Mercy handed the octopus an embellished blue eggshell she pulled from her pack. Phoebe only captured a brief glimpse of the ornate design, studded with metal circles and spirals. Cai passed the ball Lucid left floating behind her to Mercy.

"Do you use these for sport?" He asked as Mercy accepted it from him with tender care.

"Oh no. These are food. We farm these with help from the water bears and from Lucid and her kin. They contain a rich milk. We use it to make our cheeses and butter."

Mercy laid the milk ball in the grass and then bent to Cai's leg, touching the bandage on his wound. "This is staying clean.

No more festering or fever, I think. You were in a bad way when I saw you before the last moons.

Please, sit and enjoy the cheese and bread. I must take this ball to our stores cave out of the sun. I will return soon and take you to my people and safety. You will be safe enough here for a turn of the glass or so. Drink the water from the stream." She passed them an earthenware cup. "It is sweet and good." Mercy lifted the ball and carried it away following the perimeter of the rocky hill that contained the cavern and pool.

"Great. More octopee." Phoebe broke the bread and smeared half with cheese for Cai. She smeared a half for herself too. "Here. Grow some antennae. Your brows are way too empty these days." She was so happy to see him she couldn't talk straight. "You better tell me about that ship of ours while she's gone."

Cai chewed the bread and cheese. He smiled at her. Phoebe knew. The food was awesome. The ship a great tickle. But being back on the far side of reality with him would twist a smile out of a rock.

"They think we came in on a ship. They've seen a ship land."

"Oh goody. More aliens. Was it something to do with that console Smudge activated?"

"I don't think so. Apparently, they saw the ship enter atmosphere before the Winter snows. They don't find ships familiar. Some of them barely believe in the ship. But they know we aren't from here. Our looks, our clothes and the things we refer to make us stand out. Your yellow eyes are here too though. My blue eyes are rare. And everyone wears dresses here." Cai sipped some water and then refilled the cup and passed it to her.

"Hey Cai." Phoebe thumped the ground. "What if it's another ship from the Third? Makes sense, right? I know they're out there looking for Earth settlements. Maybe they dropped in here."

"Doesn't fit the data. A ship from the Third would be able to detect Earth tech before breaking atmosphere. Remember? That's what you guys went looking for."

Cai chewed his cheese and bread. "But you and I have proof Earth refugee ships aren't the only ones out there. In fact, Earth ships look like they've come late to the game. The brass platter and hourglass Lucid showed me from her midden isn't advanced Earth tech. Definitely came from Earth, but not from any recent refugees. The beings who crashed here were navigating space while Earth barely sailed ships on the oceans. Plus, any Earth refugee would investigate the locals, not hide away for Winter without attempting contact.

For all we know the alien beings from that ship could be right beside us, too small to see, or cloaking themselves while they scope out the planet. I like the ship notion as well as you do, but whoever landed here is not acting like humans from Earth. Hell, even these aliens act more like us. Antennae and all."

"How do ya like them antennae, Cai? Weird to wear flex-tube hard-ons on your head eh?" Phoebe's brow mobilized.

Cai rolled his eyes. "She's pretty. She cleaned my wound. I like her. The antennae don't bother me. You and your pink worm should talk. You'd like the women here. Competent, no womb-bear pressure on women that I've detected. She has the first antennae I've seen. You get they're all at war?"

"Yeah. Yay, human genes complete with testosterone poisoning. Looks like selfish-determination still rears its ugly head. Their War premise is really stupid too. Something about long-hair ones against the shaved ones. But then my guard said he was going to save me and he and some other shaved guys came with you to help me, a supposed Longhair, so I don't really get who's fighting whom. At least we've got shaved people and long-haired people like Mercy, helping us. Wherever this ship's from, it's better if we work together to check it out. I say we fake that it's our ship until we see what we're up against."

"Agreed. Mercy and the other antenna people might be the separate science group. I don't know how they figure in with the war. They seem more linked to the aliens that brought genetically manipulated organisms here from Earth. Mercy is more certain of the ship than the Shorn rebel group was. So we should stick with her. Not that we have much choice. We have food, water, allies, good atmosphere, another octopus, and the possibility of a ship. We're better off now than we were on 101."

"Truth. When was 101 anyway?"

"I dunno. I don't trust much of anything anymore. You and Smudge. That's it. All my other assumptions keep getting reshuffled into a Tarot deck. I'm still coming to grips with chicken eggs."

"Scudder-budder Cai. Now I'm wondering where that cheese came from. I don't see any cows here."

"There aren't cows on 101 either. You've never eaten cheese from cows."

"Yeah, but I saw people make it from nuts and stuff. S'not like snot."

"Same as drinking octopee. Or eating a big, flabby frog because it's all you know as chicken. That cheese we just ate on the bread was near to the best meal I've ever tasted. You're a space traveler now. You can't appreciate new stuff if you keep lining it up against the old. It's like my Grampa said about when they landed on 101. Everyone was talking about what happened to the billionaires."

"What are billionaires?"

"Exactly. Irrelevant. That's what happened to the billionaires. They belonged to a reality that didn't transfer. A meaning fixed in space and time. The only things that matter for us are the heres and nows that transfer to a soon-will-be future."

"Looks like Mercy's coming back."

"Good. The sun is nice and warm after that cave, but I feel a little exposed out here."

"Hey Cai."

"Yeah." He tipped his head down and she knew he tucked his smile back into his heart.

"You were right about Future and her jet skates. Once you strap 'em on, you're pretty much stuck flying."

"Never seen anyone take to the skies on those jet skates like you do, Phoebe. Future's got you in her sights. Me? I'm riding your wake for dear life." Cai wiped Mercy's cup dry and stuck it in her pack. Her antennae seemed all agitated when she got up close. Maybe she was happy to see them. The mouse in the pocket thing.

He hoisted the pack. Without a word, he and Phoebe stepped in behind Mercy as she led off along the trail beside the river. If this was the same river that broke off from the cavern way back when he and Phoebe entered the red world, they should link up with Smudge eventually. Then Cai'd know for sure her jet skate wake took the right turn. Just because you had men-urgies didn't mean you weren't a womb-bear.

27

ONE SPY DEAD. ONE SPY GONE.

Beezee swung his feet off Kertof's table as he saw the floata bob toward the city. Kertof racing back wasn't a good omen. But as far as Beezee was concerned, all was well.

The Longhair spy had escaped into Uncle's clutches as planned. When he checked with Jared, none of the known rebels had been sighted in the city since the last moons. Uncle hadn't reported back either, but all the loose ends might draw Uncle's continued attention for a while yet.

By the time Kertof thundered into his quarters, Beezee had finished gathering all the latest intel, and he'd cleared all evidence of his restful pleasures from Kertof's suite.

"Beezee! Beezee! What's this I hear about the Longhair spy escape?"

Kertof was infuriated. Good pose for sure. But the realism of his fury confused Beezee. "It is as we thought Kertof. The rebels aided her we believe. Of course Uncle is attending to it as we agreed." Beezee tried to query Kertof with facial gestures.

"She isn't a Longhair Beezee. She captains the ship. We need her to access the ship. IMMEDIATELY."

Ah, now Kertof's panic was clear. "Our best hope is in the caverns Kertof. If they've gone to ground, that's where they'd take her from here. We'll get all the men we trust and scour the caverns. That's where Uncle will have traced them. Take your floata to the North rockface and have your troops clear that end back in the cave toward the palace. Then your floata will already be in place if we find they've managed to get her out."

The need to limit searchers to trusted guards befouled a rapid muster. Two small troops, ten with Beezee for the caves, and seven with Kertof and the floata, evacuated the palace within a turn of the glass. By the setting of the moons, just short of the new sun, Beezee had discovered the slaughtered corpse of Uncle deep within the caves. No sign at all of rebels or the Longhair spy.

Jared's tale ...

Jared wanted to be out on the killing fields with Kertof and all the other troops. Instead he was here in the palace funneling spirits and sumptuous feasts to Beezee, ensconced in Kertof's suite. Jared was depressed over his guards' failure to prevent

286

the escape of the Longhair spy. He was surprised that Beezee seemed so calm about the loss. True, the spy was of little value, a distraction to the battle now well underway. But the failure and the utter pointlessness of the whole exercise from the start had given Jared the excuse he needed to overindulge in the spirits he sampled when he carted Beezee's tray.

Now Kertof was thundering back. And Beezee was demanding he muster a guard to undertake a search. Jared tried to rouse a sullen Brattoch. A Brattoch who told Jared he was leaving the guard. He claimed he would seek solace with the Labbits in the mountains. He no longer had the stomach for the palace guard work.

"But Brattoch, if you come and help us succeed in recovering the Longhair, Beezee will reward you. Also, I need you. My head is sick. Too much spirit. I'm in no shape to endure the caves with a screaming Beezee." Jared slumped aware of the resentful stares of the guards at Kertof's floata.

"Besides, Brattoch," Jared whispered furtive, so no other would hear, "Kertof says the spy is a captain of a ship from the stars. Only we trusted are allowed to search for her. She will take us to her ship, Kertof says. That is why they are readying his floata. We will go through the caves to ensure she is not sheltering there, and then we'll join Kertof in flushing her from the forest. She is not to be permitted to reach the Labbits."

Brattoch's charge ...

Taletha, Sig and Dern were lying low. Hiding in a hovel at the outskirts of the city. They had joined him in his return to bring aid to Uncle. Not much aided a corpse though. Feebee was long gone. Her partner never located. He and Taletha's boys were worried about the discovery of Uncle's dead body. The rebels would suffer great scrutiny now, as would the guard associated with Feebee. A prisoner gone, one of the Shorn butchered under the palace. The rebels had much to fear if Kertof linked them to these events. Kertof would manufacture a link anyway. He would need a scapegoat to vent his fury.

But Brattoch felt new life rouse him with Jared's pitch. He had to get to Taletha. He had to try and help Feebee flee. She needed to know that Kertof would chase her with the floata.

"I wish you luck, Jared. I don't believe the Longhair is an alien with a ship. Such a silly fantasy. Beezee is not the only one indulging in spirits. No," he patted Jared's shoulder kindly, "I am tired of all this. I will make a home with the Labbites. Goodbye Jared."

Jared crumpled even further as Brattoch wheeled away.

Brattoch was in a hurry now. He'd round up the rebel troop and they'd sneak to the river's egress from the caverns. Hopefully they'd find a sign of Feebee. Since the muster was far from complete, he and the rebels would get there well before the floata arrived with Kertof and whatever trusted troops he managed to gather.

There was a chance Feebee had found her way clear of the caverns. The river offered the easiest pathway to the mountain forests, the Labbites, and her ship. In other words, allies, cover and her people. Not the most direct path, but the one that was easiest for a foreigner on the run. Surely she would head toward her ship. Sig and Dern had seen it land in the mountains. They had some inkling of which peak was near. If she made it out of the caverns she would see the river led to the mountains. She must be warned of her danger from Kertof. If he brought Sig and Dern to the river mouth at the caves, they might pick up her trail. Brattoch could bring her allies with a clue to lead her to her ship. If he could only help Feebee, he would restore his life's purpose again.

28

MARIA'S LESSON

When Eric stood, he looked much better. He handed Maria his cloak, unrolled his shift and pulled it up over his arms. Underneath, the orange sponge was still stuck to his flesh. The crust on his shift must have been uncomfortable. But he didn't seem feverish. Their rest and their meal had refreshed both of them.

"We'll go now to the shelter and take a proper rest. By the next sun we'll be much nearer to the Labbites. Are ya cold?"

Maria was not cold. "No. I am sorry, Eric. I did judge you. I was wrong. I have much to learn about being with others in a community."

Eric simply nodded at her. Accepting her apology, she supposed. When he strode down the trail, she and Josie followed. She was grateful to be free of his body weight but she felt weighed down by her own shame. Still, something about shame felt good. As though for the first time, another's opinion mattered. Inside she could feel a deep well of loneliness for shame. For the care.

The striding was rhythmic. Easy. She stepped along pensive, but fully committed. Leaving an old, mean world behind her. Following a straightforward path to the new.

More than half a day must have passed. Eric occasionally bent along a stream to fill his flask. Always he would pass it to her. Sometimes with a word or two. She barely noted the change in light. A shift along the gleaming edge of a leaf, from rose to silver. The shadows deepened. The earthy floor was springy, spongey. Warm, ripe, sweet, dark notes of decay released with nearly every stride. Maria quivered at the drone of insects. Sickened to recollect those struggling white corpses borne into the sky.

The night of silver moonlight had come when Eric finally strode without concern through a door in a large round mound. He rubbed the walls with his hands and light flooded the room. Maria felt another blush of shame tinge her cheeks. No light on her ship responded that well.

He placed his cloak, laden with a knife, a flask and cheese, onto a bunk. He waved Maria toward the other. He rubbed a square stone box on the floor and even from several steps away, Maria felt the warmth. He took a metal kettle and pumped a lever on the wall. Water spilled from a short spigot.

The kettle filled. From a shelf he pinched some grassy material and dropped it in the kettle, and placed the kettle on the little stone stove.

"Here," he said, opening another door to another room. "A seat to empty your waste." He rubbed the sides as he sat on it. "Heat and this lever will remove the waste." He pedaled a lever on the floor. Then he stood and showed her another lever at waist height. "This is for warm water to wash . . ." he paused, uncertain. "Everything." He waved at her from top to bottom. He pointed to the back of the door. "Hang your things. And use the cloth to dry. And I'll go find us an egg to eat. Perhaps some rounds from a good root to cook with the egg."

Maria understood he was giving her privacy. Josie rooted around in the other room, probably seeking food remains or treasure. Maria nodded at Eric. Still staggered by the comforts of his alien hovel. She followed him to the door and then turned back and closed herself in the inner bathing room. Stripping off her suit and boots with little hesitation, she pumped water from the wall. Even the seat on the toilet was warm. When he returned, she was much cleaner. Inside and out.

He had two blue eggs. He washed the knife she had taken from the dead soldier and peeled and sliced a long white pod. He extracted large seeds from the slices and passed a couple to Josie who consumed them enthusiastically. He smashed a remaining seed with the flat of the knife and put it in the pan on the little stove. Almost instantly fat slicked the pan. Eric added the four slices from the white pod. Maria could see their edges brown. The fragrance was sweet, like a cookie or caramel.

When the slices were translucent in the middle, Eric broke in the two eggs. He grabbed a chunk of their cheese and added that on top. Now all was white and bubbling with bright orange yolks and melted cheese. Maria had never known such hunger. He salted the surface of the food with a pinch from a small clay jar. Then he slid the hot pan to the little wooden table, and offered Maria a wooden spoon.

She scooped egg and cheese onto her spoon and blew on it before she touched it to her lips. Eric used the knife to lift a browned pod-slice free. He drew back his fingers stung by the hot fat. He drank from his water flask and passed it to her while he poured hot tea from the kettle into earthenware cups. Maria chewed her cooled mouthful contentedly.

"This is the best egg I have ever eaten. Your chickens are so big."

"Do you have chickens on your earthen world? Are there chickens everywhere?"

"I don't have a world. We have chickens on the ship. But they are small. They have thin shells that are white, not blue." Maria wanted to emphasize the inferiority of the chickens on CLEO.

"How do ya have things that grow and yet ya have no world?"

"We took the growing things from the world and put them on our ship. We left that world, Earth, because it ended. Oh Eric, we lost so much. Like the lives of everything that could ever be beautiful, gone forever. Our planet broke apart. I was born on the ship with the only growing things we took. Yours

293

is the first world I have seen where things can grow from the ground."

"How do ya know war and weapons on a ship if ya have only hard floors and no ground? Why would ya war over space? There is plenty of room up there for everyone." Eric had finished eating. He sat back on the bunk with his cup of tea and considered Maria.

"We have pictures of our history on Earth. Ground war is part of our history there. Our ship is to take us to a new ground, a new planet for a new home. Our ship doesn't war." Maria already thinking ahead about how to explain pictures. "You have many things here that are like the things we see in our history pictures of Earth. But not from the recent world of Earth before it was broken. Do you have letters and reading and writing?

"Aye, our History Keepers gave us words from our past. We teach our children to make letters and to use numbers. But there is little use for letters and reading words. Since our calamity we have lost our interest in letters because we have to save our people, grow enough food to feed all and fight wars when the Shorn get too many people and steal our food and our places from us. But what are pictures?"

Maria used her spoon to draw a stick figure in the eggy remains in the metal pan. She showed it to Eric. "Do you draw pictures in the sand, or with colors on paper?"

"Ah aye." He laughed. "Some will make pictures in metal and in the clothes they wear. But not often. Mostly children make 'em. We have too much to do to make our world safe. I believe the Labbites use pictures in their science work. They use reading and numbers much more too. Among our people such things are complications. Feared cuz they distract from our simple, urgent, aims." Eric stood and took the metal pan and spoon away. He washed the cooking things in the stone sink and moved the table from between the bunks.

"And I'll sleep now. There is a cloak on the door if ya need warmth." He pointed to a blanket hanging on a hook on the back of the door. He took off his soft boots and pulled his legs upon his bunk. After Maria grabbed the cloak and wrapped herself with Josie on her bunk, Eric stroked the wall and the lights dimmed. Maria slept. Unafraid.

☾ On the river

Phoebe, Cai, and Lucid followed Mercy along a path through the tall striped grasses shielding the river that ran beside them. Every hour or so, Phoebe cast her eyes toward the mountains. She'd been convinced for some time the mountains, the ship they sheltered, and the beings who would lead her to it, were moving further away. She poked Cai and whispered, "Are we there yet?"

Cai refused to acknowledge poke or question. Phoebe struggled on, happy to be clean in Mercy's fresh shift. Acclimating to the first walk free of dried gore she'd enjoyed in more than a week. Not in a damn cave either. She hoped they'd catch up with Smudge soon.

Cai used his machete to slash the soft grass. Mercy, the resident expert leading the way, didn't display a similar need to violently thread her path through grass. Phoebe, following Cai, had to stay clear of his energetic strikes. He was working out some aggro.

Phoebe didn't hold out hope for much help from these primitive people in deciphering how best to face the advanced technology of an alien spaceship. At least they shared a language. Apart from pikes and knives, she'd seen no weapons. Though Cai assured her they used bows and arrows too. Weapons of comic value in a prospective encounter with an advanced, space-traveling, sentient.

Mercy provided her first exposure to the antennaed, science tribe of alien beings. The human attributes, some human culture, and their yellow eyes, were testament to a very sophisticated manipulation of organic material. Plus, they interacted with their octopodes. Boded well for Smudge. But why did they war? And why hadn't the sophistication of their sciences spread to other areas of their culture? Like communications, or transportation. Why were their most advantaged people relegated to the fringe?

"Hey Cai." Phoebe risked getting close enough to poke his back again. "They can move mountains here."

"Are you going on about your pink worm again?" Cai let his machete arm fall to the side while he turned and regarded her.

"Nuh-uh. I moved that mountain all by myself with my men-urgies." Phoebe did her little woombah dance. "I mean those mountains. The ones that have the ship." She pointed ahead. "We've been walking all day and those mountains are further away."

Cai rolled his eyes and went back to slicing and striding. Phoebe took to counting her steps. She'd hit a thousand a few hundred times when Mercy brought them to a halt at the side of the turquoise river.

"We'll be in silver light soon. We should drink here. And take a small rest. I have bread and cheese for us again. And some fruit." Mercy sat on some grass she folded across the sandy soil. She passed a cup to Cai, who filled it in the river and gave it back to Mercy to drink. Cai repeated his filling for both Phoebe and himself. Phoebe saw Lucid in the water teasing some bug out of a small rocky fissure. Cai bent back to the river and pounded a couple of stones together attempting to connect with Smudge.

Cai hears echoes ...

Cai turned from the river bed alarmed, as Mercy jumped up and looked around. Her antennae quivering. Mercy passed her pack to Lucid in the water.

"Take this under water Lucid. Hide. Someone is coming behind us on the path. Quick-sharp now. Cai and Phoebe, into the water. Pull your clothing under and keep your bodies hidden with me in that grass." Mercy pointed to reedy shallows in the river. Cai and Phoebe did as she bid without quarrel.

Peering through the reeds Cai saw nothing but he could hear approaching voices. Footfalls echoed across the surface of the water. He could barely see Phoebe's eyes. Her hair floated around her head and melded with the shadows of the reeds. Mercy's antennae stood tall but unremarkable with the other thin blades standing above the water. Cai felt the soft mud beneath his knees. He gripped at submerged roots to hold himself under and still. Long arms wrapped around him. Why didn't Lucid cling to Mercy? He almost jolted airborne when Smudge zapped him with his sTuffy. Every single muscle he controlled worked to keep the water surface unruffled. He stroked Smudge's familiar skin. Cai's heart thrummed. Finally. The full family reunion.

"Feebee, Feebee," came the call. Cai looked at her in consternation. Who knew her name? The voices neared. Heavy breaths and shouts. "I see their prints by the river!" A woman shouted.

Cai watched the tall heads of grass move, mirroring the traverse of people among the stems. Cai tensed ready to duck or stand depending whether friend or foe emerged on the trampled sandy bank.

Yes! He stood. Taletha, Sig, Dern and Phoebe's big guy, chests-heaving, stepped onto the beach. "Taletha! We are here." Cai called. Her smile broke wide when she caught his face. Then she tilted her head in confusion at the distortion of Smudge on Cai's chest.

"Phoebe, Mercy, come on. We're safe. These are friends." Cai and Smudge helped Phoebe stand in the soft riverbed first, then Cai reached toward Mercy. All of their sodden clothing sunk them into the sucking muck.

"Hiya Smudge. We've been looking everywhere for you. Didja meet Lucid?" Phoebe reached over to hug Smudge against Cai.

Smudge flashed a couple of kissy emojis. But when Cai turned to show him Lucid in the water, Smudge pulsed the gagging emoji a few times. Cai hid the flashes from Mercy and the others.

"Oh, you know a seffie too? Lucid will be glad of company. But if yours is male we should keep them separate. Lucid will eat the male if they mate." Mercy approached but Smudge collapsed more deeply into Cai's chest. He sketched a little graphic with a human woman, a man and a stork holding an eight-legged baby in a nappie.

"I don't think keeping Smudge from Lucid will be a problem, Mercy." Phoebe tugged Cai and Smudge off to one side.

"You having twins Cai? Why is Smudge flashing a twin baby delivery?"

"Not twins. He modded that emoji. He's saying he's our eight-limbed baby. I don't think he considers himself an octopus. He flashed that before Mercy told us Lucid would eat him."

"Like I told you, Cai. If they have a voice, animals show us they're just as self-determined as we are. 'Cept we're more like selfish-determined. We wiped 'em out on Earth just like everyone else who didn't have a voice. He is our baby Woomie. No way Lucid gets near him. Cool that he can mod the emojis. We wuv you Smudgie-woo-woo."

"We must hurry away, Feebee." Brattoch bent over double, braced his hands to his knees as he forced the words from his mouth. All four of them were soaked with sweat.

Cai's friendly family reunion feeling tanked. A sense of urgency stiffened him. "This is Mercy. She is taking us to our ship. What happened to you guys?" Cai carried Smudge to the others. Mercy and Phoebe tucked in beside him. Mercy leaned back and reclaimed her pack from Lucid's long arm.

"Kertof discovered that Feebee is the captain of the ship. He has been to the alien's ship. He also knows Feebee escaped his prison. His troops are checking the caverns. He will fly here in his floata as soon as they find Feebee is not in the caverns. He wants to capture Feebee. Did you clear your footprints?" Sig had caught his breath and addressed Cai.

Mercy, Cai and Phoebe looked at each other, questioning. "No," said Mercy, summing up their leave-taking from the cavern. "There is much sign of our passage out of the cavern and up the river. As you must have seen on your way."

"Yes. He, too, will track you with ease. We must hurry to the forest. Will the forest cover us the whole way, until we reach the ship?" Taletha spoke to Mercy, as one who would take charge to another. Cai found he enjoyed watching these two competent women handle strategy. They knew more about everything in the whole damn world than he did.

"I believe the ship is in the forest at the base of the mountain near Knoll Tain Lab. We have another several turns of the glass out here. As many as five before we will be under heavy forest cover. Will Kertof get to this grassy plain as soon as that?"

"Possibly." Brattoch had his breath back. "He hadn't moved his floata when we left the city. He will wait to ensure Feebee has not found shelter within the caverns. We should leave now. You are burdened with your wet clothes. But there is nothing else we can do. They will dry. We will carry your wet cloaks. Let us move as fast as we can."

Brattoch approached Phoebe with a shy smile. He reached for her cloak. Cai rolled his eyes. Romance and his new baby woomie were gonna make this some kind of journey. Smudge flashed his leering emoji. Oh this would be fun. Plenty of women, too many pink worms and their weapons expert was running commentary.

☾ Eric rushes Maria to the Labs

Eric looked over at Maria with concern. She looked weak. Wan, pale, bloodless. He had slept well despite the wound. The orange sponge had adsorbed into the wet, smelly parts of his wound and he could see his flesh knitting together cleanly.

Maria claimed to have wandered the forest before she met him. She said she'd slept and had seen the suns and the moons rise since she had left her ship. She didn't seem very aware of her need for food and water. Maybe she was dehydrated. Maybe she wasn't eating enough. His only hope was to get her as fast as possible to the Labbites. With their help, she would mend. With George's help, she could return to her ship.

Eric nodded to Maria as she wiped her eyes on waking. "And I'll see what I can get for us to eat. We have some roots. And I'll surely find us some more eggs. You can make us tea. There is honey in the jar."

301

When he returned with two more large blue eggs, she sat clean and dressed on the side of her bunk, holding a steaming cup of tea. He deftly fried them a breakfast matching the meal they'd eaten the night before. He made sure that Maria drank healthily from his flask. She still seemed far too weak.

"We must make our way to the Labs. I can touch the network fungus. Others maybe are gathering there. I dunno for sure." Eric tapped his forehead to indicate his uncertain receptivity. "Are ya ready?" He stood and took their things to the sink to wash and leave for the next traveler.

"Yes. Josie is already outside. She slept with me all night."

Eric chuckled. Of course the adough would love to stay the night inside the dwelling cuddling a warm body, fed, safe and content. Her little pouch had been full of treasure. There was no way she could add anything more. He wondered if she would start trading things out. Eric dried the dishes and picked up his knife, flask, cloak and pike. And then put them down. The belly of his cloak had clanked against his shin when he started to shoulder it. He spread it on the bed and found his pouches were filled with buttons and buckles and metal tabs.

"Josie has picked me to carry her treasures I ken." Eric spread out the things so Maria could understand. "Did she sleep with 'em?"

"I think so. I felt her pouch poke me. It feels different, less pointed than her claws. I can carry her things if they are a bother."

"Nay, nay. Her treasures don't be trouble for me. We won't need to forage much on the way. We will be there in time to eat with them all. Would you like to use my pike to walk? Twill

302

be a long walk." He picked up his cloak and tied it on and then held out his pike in offer.

"I think your pike is too heavy for me. Maybe we can find a stick for me as we walk."

She already sounded breathless. They hadn't even opened the door. They'd not yet taken a single stride. How would she manage several thousand through the woods?

Compared to her, Eric was a giant. As he held the door for her, the top of her head merely reached his breast. So thin and skeletal, if it came to a question, he could wrap her in his cloak and carry her like a pack. He would notice the burden, certainly. Especially since his wound had weakened him and still gave him some pain. But he would get her to help. She was his to care for, just as any one of his people.

Eric stepped onto the path. Maria followed closely behind him. He could hear the chittering adough bringing up the rear. Within a turn of the glass, Maria was wrapped in his cloak and tied across his shoulder. She had laid herself in the path behind him. Silent. Only the noisy, attention-seeking Josie warned him in time. Maria hadn't the strength to protest when he wrapped and lifted her. He strode as smartly as he could despite her weight, the pain, and the wound sapping his strength.

Maria and her ship were a bridge to a better future for all of the people of the Continent. She was kind, intelligent, and good spirited. He couldn't fail her. When he saw a velvet swath of fungi, a part of their communications network though now basically defunct so few were capable in its use, he bent his wrinkled brow to its surface. He tried to thrum as though he had antennae. He tried to thrum the urgency he was bringing to the Labbites. The drums of change. The importance of the dying alien he brought to his people's healers. And then he swung out on his way. Hurt, burdened and determined. But powerful. A giant.

He didn't know how many strides he had taken; how many turns of the glass had passed. Many times he had filled his flask with water, shared with Maria whenever she woke. She slept now.

Like the adough skittering noisily beside him, he was certain they were approaching a Labbite settlement. The signs were everywhere. He saw the defensive marks, the alerts and alarms, and felt the watching eyes.

No one could approach Labbites these days without permission. Even those that had permission weren't sure they were actually admitted into the settlement but rather into some clever artifice. None outside Labbites themselves ever walked the halls of the Labs anymore. For surgeries and medicine, outsiders were made unconscious, or treated in situ, far from the Labs. With the warring between the Shorn and the Longhairs, the Labbites were too vulnerable. They were too few.

Eric spoke aloud to Josie, "Let's lay her on the ground."

Eric knelt beside Maria. She hadn't stirred. The Labbites were near. They must be aware he brought Maria. They befriended adoughs too, so they would be relieved to see Josie. He needed their aid for his own wound. If George had notified them, they would be ready to receive the shocking news of Maria, an alien from a starship. He trusted they'd assist Maria.

He hoped they could. But he feared his Continent had sickened her, and if so, none of them could help.

As soon as he looked up again, he saw he was surrounded. One black-clad arm thrust out with a crutch to trade him for his pike.

"I am Herald. George has been to us. He will be back to the Lab this day. This woman?" Herald gestured at Maria, as he knelt beside Eric and helped to unwrap the enveloping cloak.

"From one of the ships I know George told ye of. She be very weak. Fading like. All at once. I dinna know why. Can ye help her? I be wounded also, but she be in danger I fear."

Herald's antennae steepled. He touched them to Maria's skin. He looked toward the nearby mountainside and stood, patient. Several Labbites emerged from a profusion of foliage on the side of the mountain. In dark cloaks, unhooded, they approached carrying a stretcher and poles. Only for one. Eric assumed he was expected to walk.

"You have a woman from the alien ship. Much in common with us, but not Reaper. One of the sentients in the Reaper joining, I suspect. Of course we will help you both." Herald let the Labbite assistants lay Maria on a stretcher. He helped Eric rise. Then he nodded for Eric to follow with him behind Maria's entourage. They walked toward the mountain without haste.

"I'm Eric. The woman is Maria. The adough she named Josie." Eric watched as efficient hands swept loose branches aside, and opened a large double door carved into the face of the mountain. "Maria is very weak. I'm merely wounded. I dinno what happened to her."

The translucent mineral-walled corridors of the Lab they entered lit up as they walked. Soon the stretcher crew turned into a treatment room and laid Maria's stretcher on a high open bunk. Maria's eyelids fluttered open.

"Maria you are not dying. Your systems cannot adapt so fast to a sudden expenditure of energy in this atmosphere, with this gravity. You are completely drained, and likely dehydrated. We will set you up to rest and we will administer liquids and nutrition." Herald stood aside as two other Labbites entered.

"I am named Herald, Maria. We have much to learn from each other but your recovery comes first. This is Richard," he indicated one of the new arrivals, "and the woman healer is Stellar. They will handle your care and protect you. Let them provide anything you need. I will take Eric to another healing room, but you may keep your adough with you while you recover."

Josie jumped up on Maria's bunk and snuggled beside her. Eric and the others left Maria alone with Stellar and Richard. Eric saw Maria's eyes close as he walked away.

Maria wakes ...

She woke in a palace of crystal. The walls, ceiling and floor were shiny and translucent, seamless. There were lights everywhere like lit gas bubbling behind the walls, under the floor and in the ceiling. Maria blinked, startled. Then she slumped back. For a second, she felt nearly at home in the bright, slick, sophisticated environment.

The healer Richard had antennae. He turned to Eric as though just recalling him. "Lacy," he nodded to a young similarly antennaed woman who'd been standing at the door to Maria's room, "please take this young man, Eric, to Nell and the others, and send wound management supplies with them." Then Richard spoke to Eric, "We'll be preoccupied with Maria for some time, Nell will see to your wounds and comfort. Please be patient."

Josie cuddled contentedly against Maria's side, as Eric and his attendants left the room. They all had antennae. Maria clutched at Josie, trying to process her mixed emotions, her weakness, shame and shock. She had no fight left.

Eric at ease ...

The Labbites knew about the ship and they knew about Maria. They accepted without question her ability to interact with them in a shared language. Having dispensed with that anxiety, Eric sat back and wallowed in the pain of his wound.

He was astonished by this facility. Staggered by the relaxed efficiency of Herald and his Labbite company. Perhaps for the first time, Eric began to appreciate how the prejudices of each tribe burdened their whole people. Dull and weary, he let Lacy lead him away. She stowed him in a room where his wound would be evaluated. While he waited for Nell and her supplies, he laid on the single bunk. He must have drifted into sleep. He forgot the last thing he remembered.

29

GEORGE

George left Herald behind at Knoll Tain Labs. He, Justice and Moriah had taken charge of informing the Labbite leaders of the ships' arrival. They were especially concerned about notifying the leaders of the two other Labs in the vicinity of the landed ship. They also wanted to consult with the Labbite leadership. They wanted accord over handling the threats and risks posed by alien ships arriving while their Continent population warred.

The fungi communications network, part of their Reaper legacy, at best conveyed urgent summons and alarms amongst Labbites. Since the calamity, there were few with sensate whiskers and antennae, and few Labbites. With limited use, the network atrophied.

But George, with the help of Moriah and some younger Labbites at Knoll Tain, had managed to distribute hallucinogenic spores through the fungi to those battling on the killing fields. Their strategy was not a long-term solution, but it provided a distraction and served to reduce the killing. George hoped the disruption would allow some, whether Shorn, Longhair or Rebels, to join the Labbites in attending to the greater problem of the alien ship incursion.

Moriah and George appreciated the side benefit of activating the fungal network. They obtained confirmation of the network's restored viability. But even so, the network was rudimentary, crude. The tale of the alien ship incursions demanded in-depth, in-person meetings, and a painstaking organization of the facts to set strategy.

So George, Moriah and Justice were on the move. They'd had meetings with each leadership at three Labs. These had no further intelligence to contribute, beyond reports of activated Reaper ship consoles. As far as George could ascertain, none had noted the descent of the ship in the mountains before Winter, nor had any discovered an alien presence or witnessed other anomalies. The activated consoles only activated once. Just as Eric described to George eight or so moonrises past.

Now on their return leg, George and his compatriots were skirting the killing fields on their way back toward the cloaked ship. The only ship of the two whose whereabouts they knew. George told them the ship still hummed in the mountain valley near Knoll Tain Lab. By transiting near the battlefield, he hoped to enlist Eric's help. He also wanted to connect with some rebel leaders so that the three Labbite scientists didn't approach an alien intelligence without at least some backup. If anything happened, he wanted someone who knew the whole story to carry the news back to their families and communities.

George trusted all Labbites had now heard of the alien ships. He believed all those who were out foraging far from their home labs, managing their animals and collecting their specimens, were on the lookout for an alien presence or signal. Any who had news would be instructed to head back to Knoll Tain Lab to report. George's party would pass near the Lab on their way from the killing fields to the cloaked ship. They would check in.

"The drones are busy." Moriah watched the laden insects with her mouth curled.

"For now at least, the killing is done. There aren't as many bodies as I feared. Our little spore delivery must've helped." George forgave the carrion hunters. The killing that invited their attention however, was not so simple to forgive.

"If the drones are gathering, we can't expect to find any walking-wounded nearby. Anyone at risk and mobile would clear out." Justice sat on a fallen tree near the stream, looking out at the fields as the drones picked them clean. "We are near the river; we can follow the river trail back to the Lab. If we can't find Eric and some other aid in the forest, we can muster some assistance from the younger Labbites."

The Labbites were few in number. Their children were fewer. Marginalization had thinned their numbers, and reduced the diversity and health of their people. But the ships would change the equation one way or another. No risk now was too great.

Moriah passed some wrapped food to George and Justice. "We'll fill our flasks here in the stream. Do you see Kertof and his floata?"

"Thank you. I thought I saw the floata heading toward the city when we broke the edge of the forest. Far off, but not too far off for these eyes." George pointed at his yellow eyes. A gift exclusive to just some Labbites. "Some chance I mistook the floata for a gas bubble, but I think not. If Kertof has returned to the palace, that might promise a break in the fighting. Or he could be going back to muster more warriors. The behavior of those we put 'under the influence,' would distress him grievously."

The three completed their brief repast and set out toward the river. George limp with worry. Eric might be one of those being drained and carted off by the insect drones. He couldn't think on it. He had to believe Eric was saved. All that power and promise. Wars wasted their young. When next he saw a velvet fungus, he stopped Moriah and Justice. He bent his antennae to link in. Would the network bring any intelligence?

George threw back his head. Seized in torment. Moriah and Justice clung to each other.

"To the river. We must go as fast as we can to the river. There is news of the aliens. And an alarm." George was ready to swing out at a run but he regarded Moriah and Justice, assessing them thoughtfully. "Moriah, would you come with me at speed? Justice, can you make your way back to Knoll Tain without us? I fear I must make a pace which would be too much for you."

Justice nodded assent. "Go George, Moriah. I hope the news is bearable. Come to us at the Lab as soon as you are able. I will prepare Herald and the others. Perhaps there are others with news already there. Go."

Moriah clasped Justice's arm in farewell and then strode off matching George's pace. Perhaps a turn or two later, when the river was in sight, George saw the tall heads of grass thrashing with movement. He put on a great push despite his heaving lungs. Whether friend or alien foe ahead, he was determined to meet the emergency and fight to protect his people and their home. Moriah also responded in kind. She joined him, leaping forest debris and pushing branches from their path. They ran pell-mell, all caution abandoned.

☾ Mercy

Lucid's great arm swung out of the water and whipped around Mercy's ankle. Forcing Mercy to fall in the river shallows and bringing the others with their broken breathing, sweat, and hoarse voices to a sudden halt.

"Kertof's Balls, Lucy! Why have you stopped us?" Mercy rose in the water and glared at the great seff languid in the water beside her. Just then they all turned at the noisy entrance of two Labbites who pelted in toward them on the other side of the water at the river trail. Mercy recognized Moriah.

"Have you trouble, Moriah?" Mercy called, breathless from her run and fall. She thought the man with Moriah was George. He walked the mountains. A Labbite from a remote Lab community. He might've been the one who told them of the ships. Both Moriah and George looked as exhausted as her own crew. They splashed across the river and knelt on the banks to catch their voices.

"George heard an alarm about the aliens on the river. Did you send the alarm? What news have you? Or is the alarm from Lucid?" Moriah asked her questions calmly while swallowing breaths.

Mercy turned toward her companions. "We are close enough to the forest here. We can rest on this bank and then reassume the trail. But these are Labbites. We must tell them of Cai and Feebee's ship and of Kertof's chase. They will help us."

George and Moriah looked curiously at the six people traveling with Mercy. Mercy felt a smile tug at their blatant curiosity. They were clearly trying to establish whether aliens were among her companions. She recognized their shy surprise that the aliens fit among their people. Phoebe, their Captain, even had the Reaper yellow eyes. Cai was ducking into the water with his seff.

George strode forward. "I am George. I am from Deep Mountain Lab. I am the one who saw your ship and I know where your ship is located in our land." George scanned the faces obviously hoping for a reaction.

Cai pulled himself out of the river. He and his small seff had found some edibles. His seff, Smudge, clung to Cai's chest. Cai patted the creature affectionately. Nestling Smudge against his body, Cai reached out for George, as though to make a forearm greeting. "I am Cai. Phoebe and I are not from your planet. Nor is Smudge," Cai nodded his head, grinning toward Phoebe. The creature flashed a light at them. A child's picture of a face smiling.

George startled away from Cai and the creature. "How does this seff creature make light?"

Phoebe was laughing and stroked the seff. "Smudge has a whole vocabulary of light pictures for you."

"Do you know this kin to Lucid the alien ship brings?" Moriah asked, hurrying over to try and make sense of their interaction.

"Smudge is not a kin to Lucid, Moriah. We brought him to your planet. He is able to speak with light on his skin. He doesn't recognize Lucid. Smudge says he is my child. I believe he activates a device that is something your ancestors might know." Cai shifted to allow Smudge to display his sTuffy.

George came forward again and firmly grasped Cai's forearm. "You speak as we do. You look as we do. But you have come in a ship? Yet you are not Reaper. But your Smudge seff has Reaper technology. Perhaps the ship I have seen is your ship, and the Reaper device your Smudge seff has, alerted our reaper consoles. Maybe there is only one ship."

The creature called Smudge manifested many colored lights making word arrangements. These flashed too briefly for Moriah to read their message.

Sig, Dern, and Taletha came forward. Each clasping first Moriah, and then George by the forearm. "I am Taletha. These, Sig and Dern, are my nephews. We are rebels who have left the Shorn. And that," Taletha said, pointing at Brattoch, "is Brattoch, a Shorn palace guard, who is our friend and brings us news of Kertof."

Brattoch greeted Moriah and George in turn. "Kertof returned to the palace in his floata. He had traveled far from the battlefield way up into the Knoll Tain mountain valley. He brought news from the aliens at the ship. When he returned to the palace, he told a select group of his guard of a woman Captain from the alien ship, lost on our Continent. He concluded that the woman must be the strange Longhair spy his guard had captured. Feebee," Brattoch motioned toward Phoebe.

"I, and the rebels, arranged to free Feebee before Kertof brought this news. But I was there when he came back with the news. I know when he was told of Feebee's escape. I saw his muster of two groups of troops to search the caverns and to follow the route of her escape, guiding his floata. If he can capture her, he means to use Feebee as a hostage to access her ship and control the ship's troops, weapons and technology."

Mercy watched Cai and Feebee exchanging looks of wonder. "Very helpful Brattoch. I know all of us have much to discuss with each other. But Brattoch's news is urgent. If everyone has caught their breath and had some water, we should push on to Knoll Tain. There we can devise interference for Kertof and his minions. And then we can go to the ship with Phoebe and Cai. I hope they will help us understand what their ship's arrival means for our peoples. And if George is correct that your Smudge seff has activated our Reaper consoles, then we only have one ship to be concerned about."

Many turns of the glass passed by the time they arrived at the Lab, thoroughly exhausted. They moved so rapidly, none exchanged more than a few words. As they came up to the mountain Lab entrance, Justice emerged from the double doors in the cliff. Swinging the doors wide in welcome.

"Well met, well met, all. We have wonderful news for you. We have saved an alien from the ship. She is sleeping now. But let me tell you we should rejoice in the ship's arrival. We now have it on her authority they mean us no harm. What news have you? Come, eat, rest. We have time." Justice held his arms open wide, a smile splayed broadly across his face. His antennae pulsed excitedly.

George and Moriah embraced him. Mercy grasped his arm. "Good news, Justice. I also bring exciting news with me. These two, Cai and Phoebe, are from the ship. Phoebe is the ship Captain. Brattoch, here with the other Shorn rebels, deserves a special welcome from us. He has rescued Phoebe from Kertof's prison. He has brought us notice that Kertof is on his way up the river behind us, giving chase to Phoebe. Kertof, too, knows of the ship. We are grateful to be here with you where we can all smartly and safely plan our defense."

Mercy stepped aside to gesture Cai and Phoebe forward. "What welcome news you have given us of Cai and Phoebe's shipmate finding safe refuge with you!" Mercy turned to Cai and Phoebe. "As you know from their shipmate, Justice, these aliens speak our tongue. Though not Reapers. And not so alien, are they?" Many in the group tittered with delight.

Cai and Phoebe moved forward to meet Justice and to introduce their rebel friends.

"Let us get everyone food and beds. Our journey has been fraught and long. We have much to discuss. But let us not require further explanations at this time. Should Cai and Feebee bunk with their shipmate?"

"Forgive me, Mercy. Yes, all will be given rooms and beds and food and some privacy to recover. We would prefer to keep Maria asleep on her own. She is recovering from too much activity in our atmosphere and gravity we fear. She is drugged now and resting well with Josie, her adough. I assume you know?" Justice looked toward Cai and Phoebe for confirmation. Both nodded their heads sagely, lips parting in wonder at Justice's happy news.

"Yes, I fear we share the same problem. Could you put Phoebe and me together in a room? We are comforted by each other's presence and I have not had a chance to be with her since her capture by Kertof's troops." Cai looked between Justice and Phoebe. Phoebe nodded affirmation at his words and leaned against his shoulder.

"Oh the miracle of your words Cai. We have been so frightened over your ship's arrival. We are much relieved. But yes, you will have a room together, food, and privacy to recover. Medicine too, for your wounds. In fact, we will put you in a room by Maria. You will be the first people she sees when she awakes. What a surprise for her!" Justice clapped his hands with joy and led the group off to rooms and food.

Brattoch ...

Brattoch followed Justice and watched with despair as Cai and Feebee were led to privacy. He hadn't had much time with Feebee either in recent days. He wanted the closeness she had with Cai. But he also wanted more.

However, unlike the two aliens who were still recovering from wounds and their anxious escape, he was full of energy. He was done with Kertof's threats. Now with the Labbites and this alien ship at his back, he would cut Kertof clear out of the picture. He had an idea too. It came to him as he watched Cai strop his large knife, a machete he called it, on a rock while they discussed their options at the river. Brattoch had touched the sharp edge and felt the burn. The friction of stropping had not only sharpened the edge, it heated it to burning.

As Mercy and some of her fellow Labbites led Brattoch, Sig, and Dern to rooms, Brattoch broached his idea.

"Mercy, Sig, Dern, I am too filled with anger over Kertof to rest here and await his pleasure. I want to go back and head him off. Could I have some help from the Lab?"

Mercy turned to him and stopped him, placing her palms flat against his chest. "Brattoch, I understand. But anger alone is not a strategy. Kertof in a floata with troops is a formidable opponent. You will only risk yourself to no end."

"I know what you are saying, Mercy. But give me credit. I have seen something in Cai's weapon that gives me an idea. Will you hear me out?"

Sig also stopped in the corridor, tugging at Dern's shift. "I will come with you Brat. Dern too, I suspect. We aren't tired. Or should I say, we are only tired of Kertof. Whatever idea you have that has a chance to end him, I will join you." Dern nodded enthusiastically.

"Mercy show me to Cai and Feebee. I will ask Cai to loan me his weapon. And then I need some help from the Lab."

Mercy and Brattoch rejoined Sig and Dern seconds later, now with Cai's 'machete' in hand. "Mercy, who among your people has that salve that heats the metal? I would take enough with me to heat this blade of Cai's."

One full turn of the glass later, Sig, Dern and Brattoch headed back toward the river plain in the silver light of the moons. Just at the cusp of the forest, the banks of the river formed a large flat beach, grassless because of shade cast by an enormous, heavily branched, leafy tree. Shorn troops, in fact anyone who traveled the path up the river, often took their ease on that beach. The soft sand a fine bed. The water clean and refreshing. The last, best place to take refuge before broaching the forests.

Brattoch climbed the tree and secured himself for sleep amongst the dark branches. Sig, Dern, and a cluster of young Labbite helpers, made their own bed in the nearby brush.

☾ Kertof

Outside the caverns, at the base of the rock where the palace caves drained their swollen pools into the river, Kertof waited, kicking sand. His troops had gone a short way into the cavern from this end. They claimed they could hear Beezee and his men approach. Two of Kertof's guard stood near him at his anchored floata.

Half a glass had turned before the combined parties emerged, blinking in the dimming light of the sun. They jogged toward Kertof. Beezee heavy, pulling up the rear.

"Found Uncle's corpse. Found the Longhair spy's tracks. Other tracks too. Some remains of larvae. Two light tubes. Two conclusions. She survived and she exited here with help. You find anything here?"

Kertof was nearly ashamed to admit he hadn't looked. He tipped his head at Jared, who had enough sense to begin to scour the area. Kertof kicked the sand with more impatience. By another half glass, Jared returned, holding out a stained, crusted blue shift.

Kertof took it and shook it out. "Wounded. Not badly. This was discarded after the wound was dry. Unless she's running naked, someone has given her clothing and thus likely otherwise supplied her. Which way did she go?"

He wanted to head straight up the river. The ship was in that direction. But her shipmates said she was lost. He himself had ensured she was captured and held in his territory far from her ship. She may well not know how to locate her ship. They would find sign of her direction. Soon he would find her and kill those who had given her aid.

His troops fanned out at Beezee's command. They soon tracked signs of passage. Broken stems. Drops of effluvia. Disturbed soil. Piss, dung. Spit. Kertof stopped fouling the soil he stood in, and cast a few glances toward the river. Too much to hope for. At least Uncle hadn't succeeded in killing her. But Uncle had managed to involve the rebels in her rescue, and now these same were aiding her still. Kertof was certain. He could always be certain of a poor result from Uncle. Conveniently dead. Saved Kertof killing him.

Another quarter turn and three men returned. "We have her tracks. At least three travel. Perhaps six or seven total. Two groups. One more recent following the first. One group may have obscured the trail of the other. To begin with, both trails follow the river."

Jared caught Kertof's eye and nodded at him. He waved the men to pull the floata down for Kertof to mount.

"Go back and get the palace guard ready, Beezee. I will be away for several moon rises, I fear. But I will send men back. You must provide me with fresh troops to help us proceed rapidly and to aid in the capture. The chase up the river will be wearying." But only for the men, Kertof added silently, waving Beezee off and mounting his floata. Soon he was high above the river, lying in comfort on his couch.

The men would run now he was up above, able to pick out any hint of their quarry in the moving grass of the river plain. After a few turns of the glass they could rest at the cusp of the forest to cycle in fresh troops and make haste again at the rise of the new sun.

Kertof felt his spirits soar. They were almost on her. The rebels and even the Labbits could not protect her from his skilled troops and their weapons. She would have to give him her ship. A new day was indeed upon them. He could almost feel himself in flight. Lifting off beyond the painful limitations of his useless people and this empty land.

30

CAI

"Jesus Cai. A ship. I'm a Captain. Of a ship. And they speak English. It's an Earth ship, Cai. I know it."

"Maybe Maria wants to be Captain."

"Fine. Make her Captain. Let's go."

Phoebe flung herself on the bunk. There were two in the room as promised. Plus, a translucent tank for Smudge. A small womb, they called it. Cai was itching to explore the whole facility. Their door opened and aliens with antennae brought in trays of food and pitchers of water.

"Thank you. I am Cai." He found the twitching antennae entrancing. He didn't know how to ask about them without sounding pervy. These two, one man and one woman, might have been part of the crowd when they entered the Lab.

This Lab was far slicker than the shipboard ones he worked in on 101. His Lab had whirring devices, electricity and electronics. Advanced microscopes, test tubes, slides, scalpels, pipettes and all sorts of other equipment they'd brought from Earth. This Lab had crystal walls that glowed with light. He noticed that when Phoebe laid on the bunk, the light on her side began to dim. When someone entered the door, the light near the door grew. Justice even spoke of atmosphere and gravity when he described Maria. Cai could hardly contain his excitement.

The woman filled a cup with water and passed it to Phoebe. "I am Radiance. We will speak another time. Meeting so many is taxing for you all at once."

The man who had entered with her, nodded agreement. They left their laden trays on the table and bowed as they exited.

"Wow. These are like those emphatic people on the vids."

"Emphatics?"

"Yeah. You know. The ones that thought feelings were really important. You coulda been one. Cuz you're a womb-bear, y'know. Especially back when you had hairy eyebrows. I miss your eyebrows. They really knew when you were saying something important. Brows like that, you never have to say anything twice."

"Yes." Cai nodded, and added sotto voice, "what would be the point?" He gestured to the food, "besides, I think you're emphatic enough for both of us. At least until my eyebrows grow back. Let's eat and sleep. See if this place shuts down. Hey Phoebe?" Cai swallowed a mouthful of food and waved his spoon. "I think this is roasted chicken. You'll never eat a mud chicken again after you taste this."

"Oh Jesus Toad. You're right." Phoebe directed the orchestra with a half-chewed chicken bone. "Course I'm not sure we'd find 101 out there even if we have a ship. Eff a Great Toad, Cai. A ship. And chickens. Plus that rock wall was sexsational!" She munched happily then lowered her eyes when she swallowed. She took a walloping glug of water and licked her lips. Laser eyes on high beam, she burned a look at Cai.

"I killed that guy, Cai. I'm not sorry. I almost wanna go back there and kill him again." A reluctant hiccup punctuated her statement.

"I'd go back there and do it again with you if you like. You did a clear-headed thing, Phoebe. Of course you'll taste some backwash for a while. But if someone is out there, ready to take a life, even if they only want to feed on it like a predator? They're forfeit. You gotta get in their way and end them. No ifs, ands, or buts. I am so grateful you did it. So grateful you had the guts to kill, to face facts and do it. Because if you wavered, you wouldn't be here with me and Smudge now." Smudge flashed a sad face emoji and reached an arm out trying to snag Phoebe's chicken bone.

Cai felt the stopper in his throat. His eyes stung. He took a sip of water. The chicken tasted awesome but he was too choked up to swallow. He stood up behind her letting her lean back into his belly. He clasped her head to his diaphragm, bent down and kissed the hair on top of her head. "I'm going to sleep now. Wake me up so we can consult with Maria about our little problem." Cai took his boots off and laid on his bunk.

"Night Cai. Love you."

For a while he just laid still, listening to her chew her chicken, splashing the bones into Smudge's tank.

"Cai? I think I used up all my men-urgies."

"Don't worry. They'll come back."

"That's what I'm afraid of."

"Me too." Cai whispered.

"Hey, did I sound like an emphatic just then?"

Cai squeezed his eyes tighter and muscled the lump aside. "Yeah Phoebe. You've got their perplexicon down."

"So I'm like a perp too, right?"

His shoulders spasmed. "You're a perp alrighty. Shhh. Gotta sleep." Cai was happy when the lights on his side dimmed to nothing. Phoebe wouldn't see the tears streaming out onto his pillow.

Phoebe ...

Phoebe listened to Cai snore. Sleep wasn't consuming her. Maybe she'd napped off and on. She flung her knees from side to side. Whatever. Time to wake up that Maria and have a heart-to-heart about her new ship. Cai needed to be done with the snoring already.

Phoebe stood above him and tried to wake him with her laser eyes. Oh screw the toadswallop. She wandered back to their dining detritus not entirely sure of what she was looking for. Old grim-bear needed his sleep, but they had some

325

galaxies to conquer. Nothing on the table. Frustrated, Phoebe teased a few threads free from her cloth shift. She let them loft down onto grim-bear's face. Nothing. Stupid gravity. She wandered back to the table and picked up some thin stems from the fruit they'd consumed. Last call Cai. You don't wake up now I'm bombing you with chicken bones.

Only one of her precious stems hit his face, but one was enough. He flew upright batting his arms at her.

"What? What? Trouble?"

Phoebe giggled into her shoulder. His eyes were so crusty even the normal-sighted would have seen the tracks.

"Jesus Cai. It's just me. C'mon, we need to meet Maria."

"Lemme put on my boots. Wait a minute. Any sound out there?" He was putting on his boots as Phoebe peeked out their door.

"Nuh-uh. All clear." Phoebe couldn't stand still any longer. She was tapping lightly on the door. "Maria? Maria? You awake?" If she wasn't, it wasn't for lack of Phoebe's effort. Phoebe touched her head to the door. Aha. Movement. Then, yes! A soft voice.

"What is it? I am awake now."

"Ask her to open her door. We shouldn't do this in the corridor." Cai stood beside her. Great, mingeing Toad, he looked bad. His scalp was all pink, shiny, and hairless. His forehead was bare of eyebrows. His whiskers were growing in rough silver all over his face. He was wearing a rumpled gown and his boots were coated with crap.

"You don't want her to open the door. She sees you and I'm not getting my ship." Phoebe whispered at him.

"Maria, I'm Phoebe. We're Earth refugee descendants. We suspect you are too. We need to talk before the aliens wake up and bring us breakfast." The door unlatched and began to open. Phoebe pushed Cai behind her and looked into the crack. A timid, feminine voice squeaked out at chest level.

"You're from another Earth refugee ship? Did you settle here?" The tiny blonde woman standing barefoot in front of her was drowning in a crinkled blue shift. She opened her door fully and gestured Phoebe and Cai into a room now flooding with light. Cai shut the door.

"No. Just the two of us. No ship, er, well, that is, a crash-landing of a small, little, um, ship. A smidge of a ship. And an octopus. Named Smudge." Phoebe blustered. Weirdly ashamed of MIDGE and not wanting to lie, exactly. They came in on the Great Toad's tongue. So maybe not. A rogue space bubble. Even she-who-lived-it had trouble believing their experience.

"A shuttle? Is your ship still out there then? We didn't see anything. Did you just come in?"

Cai shouldered himself in front of Phoebe and held out his hand. "Hi Maria. I'm Cai. All our Earth ships landed on the Third, another planet. We got away on MIDGE, a smidge of a transport, as Phoebe says, when the Third busted up like Earth. But where did your ship settle? Why'd you come here?"

"Yeah, and I'm Phoebe. Let's not get into all that yet, Cai. The point is Maria, the aliens here think we are from your ship too. And since we don't have a ship anymore, we'd actually like to be with you guys. I mean, a full ship contingent, maybe a thousand Earth-refs, hell that's like going home. More than we ever dreamed of."

"Okay, sure, I guess. I mean, we have plenty of room on NEW CLEO. Everyone's dead. Just me, Davis and Kendak are left. And they're really old. They actually lived on Earth." A furry creature wound its way around Maria's ankles. "This is Josie. She's from here. They call her an adough. She's friendly. You can touch her. Is your shuttle some kind of octopus drone transport?"

Cai held out his hand and let Josie sniff. "Hoo-boy. Umm, we have way too much to tell you about and I hear activity in the hall. We are getting company. So let's table this until we can get some more time alone together. There's going to be a big mission to your ship cuz some local nutcase wants to try and appropriate it. For everyone's safety, we should all act as NEW CLEO's ship's company. Phoebe and I, but especially Phoebe, are familiar with Old Earth ship tech. We can help you to set up the ship for defense until we get through this trouble. But for now, we should act as a unit. That work for you Maria? There's no reason to confuse the aliens with our different stories. The important thing is to get the ship protected and keep it in human hands."

"I get it. I think. I'll be grateful for your help with CLEO. NEW CLEO is our ship. So I pretend you are from NEW CLEO too? The aliens have to lead us back to her. I got turned around here. I don't know how to find my way back. And she's cloaked. I don't think the aliens can capture her while she's cloaked."

"Well that's the thing," Phoebe tried to structure her message clearly. "Apparently this alien leader-nutcase found someone from your ship who said the woman Captain was lost and needed to be found to access the ship. The nutcase, Kertof is his name, assumed that woman was me. He'd imprisoned me." Phoebe held up her hand when Maria startled, "long story. But I escaped and he's trying to track me down. He doesn't know about you. The aliens here think I'm the woman Captain that's missing from your ship."

"Oh my god, Davis or Kendak must've tried to go after me. That's pretty clever though. Leaving CLEO cloaked and getting that other guy to find me for them. Keeps all of us safer. I'm surprised they came up with that. I don't have any problem letting everyone continue to think you are the missing Captain, Phoebe. You look like you can handle the risk better than me anyway. I'm not coping that well with gravity and atmosphere. Are you okay with that? We have to give Davis and Kendak the heads-up when we get there. NEW CLEO won't be a problem. She adapts well to strategic agendas."

Phoebe closed her eyes almost in prayer. "Oh I am definitely okay with that idea. I am more than ready to cut this Kertof guy out of the playbook. And with a ship at my back, no threat here stands a chance. But I'm also looking forward to getting to know you, Maria. I haven't been with a woman my age since I was a Space Cadet on the Third." Phoebe's eyes watered.

Maria cast her own eyes down. "It sounds like we all have some stories to share. I am so happy you are here. I've been very alone for a long time. Just me and Josie, really. The aliens are really nice, and really smart. But . . ." She bent and picked up the creature. She buried her wet cheeks in Josie's fur.

Gulping, she turned her sad face to Phoebe again, "as Cai said, we'll have to wait until we have more time. I've never had anyone to talk things over with, though. It's a hard story for me to tell."

Cai opened the door. A crowd of Labbites stood outside. Eavesdropping? Cai wondered if their antennae allowed them to decipher minor vibrations, enhance hearing.

A large man without antennae moved up to the door. He seemed concerned to see Cai in Maria's room. He wove his way forward.

"Maria. Are ya well? Ya look so much better. I was afraid for ye."

"Eric, yes, thank you for bringing me here. I am much better now. I guess it has been hard for me to be on your planet and moving so much. This is Cai and Phoebe. They are from the ship."

Phoebe noted the careful wording. She clasped her arm around Maria's shoulder and gave her a small squeeze. The beady black eyes of the creature stared up at her. She let Josie sniff her finger. Was Cai worried about Smudge? Lucid was so enormous. Surely Smudge would like the adough way more. Poor Smudge should've seen Lucid regurgitate her old chewed pink worm. Talk about a femme fatale. Phoebe flexed down on her shudders.

Justice, one of the head Lab guys, stepped out in front of Maria's Longhair buddy. "Brattoch and the rebels left in the silver light many turns ago to head off Kertof. We should eat and make our way to your ship. There must be something we can do with your people to stop Kertof. Will your ship be able to defend us if we come with you now? We Labbites are very few, but even so, I am reluctant to add our need for protection to the defensive burden your ship may face." Justice spoke to Phoebe, ignoring Cai and Maria. In a subtle gesture of support, Cai and Maria both slid in behind her.

"Absolutely, Justice. If you can help direct us back to NEW CLEO, she will easily deliver the space and resources to protect your people and to keep Kertof out of our hair. I think we all need to eat and ready ourselves for this long hike. We've got to get a move on. We can't expect Brattoch to hold an entire troop back for long." Phoebe felt herself swell with the assumption of command. Command. Make the world safe. If she actually ended up in command of NEW CLEO, she would have to consider her lust with Brattoch, or anything else muddying the waters. Deep waters.

Pack up Smudge. Get the puck outta Dodge. Oh yay. Devices. She could look shit up. Not the muddy waters though. Not how to lift the weight of the leaden mantle on her shoulders. More rocks on the cliff. She'd find her way. She closed her eyes and bowed her head. Some kinda Toad.

Someone had to do it. Something had switched on in her when she flew down that mountain slope. Reverberating when she stabbed that man to death. Not dimmed a whit by capture. Ya turn that kind of spirit lamp on and nuthin' can dim it. Brought her to the truth of herself. And now she was Wombier. Carrying the whole of a crew, fostering all the new lights. Sheltering all the tiny flames of life from the storms.

Not everyone had the will. Not everyone had the way. She had both. If you had both, even when you didn't seek it, even

331

when command was too heavy or scary, you still had to take the lead. She had to take command. She knew she'd give it up in a heartbeat to someone better. But so far as she could tell, there was no one better. She could already feel herself shoulder the weight. For now, she was the best on offer. Phoebe gave Maria a final squeeze. Gratitude and acceptance. Maria was one of her people. A tiny light struggling with so many heavy burdens. But they had each other, and Cai, Smudge, little furry Josie and NEW CLEO.

The Labbites, joined by Taletha and Eric led the way down the corridor. Phoebe assumed they'd eat and gear up. And then, Jesus-fracking-thank-you Toad. A ship.

☾ Brattoch in the branches

Brattoch saw the warm light of the new sun begin to spill across the river plain. He knew what woke him. He heard the loud shouts of Kertof pushing his tired troops forward up the river. He could practically smell the stench of his evil, hanging up there in the sky. Brattoch hated him. Hated his vacant leadership, a blind, self-indulgent masquerade. An unleader. A will to power, but no vision, bearing no care for his people. No acceptance of responsibility. No generosity of spirit. No wisdom. A mean, limited, vain, unimaginative, arrogant man.

Even now. Up there in his floata. Enjoying his leisure, while tired men pushed his anchor through the grasses over the soft ground. How did the floata buy him anything? Even if he saw the escapee and her rebel companions from his perch, he'd still need to be down among his men for the capture. Nor was ascertaining their direction any excuse. They'd leave a trail, just as easy to follow from the ground. Every pleasure he stole for himself, every relief he gave himself from the pain and suffering caused by his war, his aims? Each distanced him. Each reduced him. Each revealed the emptiness, the worthlessness of his leadership claim.

Soon. Soon the anchor for the floata and the accompanying troop would be underneath Brattoch's tree. Everyone to take a rest before Kertof climbed down and joined them to advance on foot through the forest. Brattoch heard Sig and Dern in low-voiced discussion with the Labbite youngsters. Good, they were also roused.

Brattoch untied his sleep anchor from the tree. He had slept surprisingly well. He left his cloak in the crook of the branch and sidled deeper, closer to the trunk. There he carefully pulled out Cai's machete. He liberated the cloth-wrapped whetstone and the ointment the Labbites prepared for him before he left. Kertof's shouts so near they sounded in his ear. He even heard the heavy breathing of the troops. They'd sling their packs down on the beach soon. Brattoch began to strop.

"Anchor here. Unpack sharply now. Take some food and water. Pull me down, blast you. Pull me down!" Kertof shouted. Whining. Angry.

Brattoch poised himself. Ready now.

And there it was. Kertof's men bent over, breathless, dropping their packs and filling their flasks in the stream. A muddle of bodies. Murmuring, coughing, gasping and then a

333

victory yell. Sig and Dern crashing through the water just beyond the beachhead.

"You'll never get us Kertof! We have her! She leads us to the ship. You'll never catch us now." A cluster of hooded Labbites swarmed behind Sig and Dern. The whole bunch of them disappearing, thrashing into the deep forest cover, well beyond the worn trail.

Brattoch saw the floata dip as Kertof moved aggressively, throwing his weight around. "After them men! Don't let them get away!" Kertof clung to the edges of the floata. Stuck up there, his men fleeing as fast as they could from the clearing, chasing after Sig and Dern. "Get them!" Kertof screamed.

And then the clearing was empty of men, strewn with packs, littered with dropped flasks and cloaks. The floata anchor tipped on its side. The floata bobbing silent but for Kertof's agitation.

Brattoch dropped to the ground. He took two rapid strides to the anchor and then he heaved Cai's machete and swung it down against the stiff strand of webbing that swayed with the movement of the floata above. The blade edge of the machete glowed with molten heat. And sliced cleanly through the heavy strand. The machete hadn't even bumped the strand. Just sliced clean through.

Up the freed end flew, silently reeling away as the tension holding the captured gas bubbles released. The netting-encased bubbles lifted the floata up, up and away. Quiet smooth, silent. Until Kertof, perhaps finally appreciating the meaning of this slow, soundless, remove from land, began to scream. In this wan light of the new sun, ever fading words wafted, rising with the river mists, "Help me. Come back, help me."

Brattoch barely heard him. The pounding of his own beating heart so loud in his ears. But Kertof's plaintive cries were loud enough. His breathless men, bedraggled and sweating, filtered slowly back to the beach. They looked skyward, confused.

Brattoch recognized Jared. He held Cai's machete firm in challenge as he turned to them. "He is gone. I am done with the Shorn. I am going with the alien ship and the Labbites. Give it up Jared. Kertof is gone."

Brattoch watched stiff and alert as Jared dropped his pike to the ground, and stared at him wordlessly. Then Brattoch swung on his heel and left, his machete arm at ease along his side. His path opened in front of him like a metaphor. He began to trot, anxious to return to Feebee. Sig and Dern waited for him. They were holding each other, leaning against a tree, not too far from the clearing. Close enough to see the faint smear of Kertof disappear in the brilliance of the early sun. Sig and Dern pointed and laughed. They didn't bother to wipe at the tears that shot from their eyes. Their young Labbite helpers milled around the path, faces wreathed with smiles. Their hoods down, antennae aquiver.

"Kertof's Balls, Brattoch! You did it. He's gone. I can't believe he's gone. It's over isn't it? There's no one else. You did it." Dern grabbed Brattoch by the arm, squeezing him. Tears welled in his eyes.

"You're a hero, Brattoch. You saved us all. You saved your Captain and her ship." Sig joined them. The three of them embraced, congratulating each other. As one, they and their Labbite companions picked up the trail heading back to Knoll Tain's Lab. To Feebee. To the Ship. To a new beginning.

☾ Davis

He could ask CLEO how long they had waited for some news of Maria. How many Earth days had passed since she left and how many days since the alien had scuttled away to find her. He and Kendak had devised a strategy to separate the alien and any of his minions from Maria when they brought her back. With CLEO's help, they would ensure Maria wasn't made hostage. Threat assessment and containment. An old drill, but they brought it back feeling more alive than they had in decades. They were ready for whatever threat the alien presented. Whether to Maria, to them, or to NEW CLEO.

Davis still struggled to understand how someone with an obvious connection to Earth's humanity could act like a hostile primitive. He and Kendak had reluctantly tabled their hope Maria would enjoy a society here, a people, a fertile new world. This was not to be. They and NEW CLEO could keep her safe and give her some company for as long as they lived. He and Kendak were at their end though. In only weeks, perhaps before the Winter returned, NEW CLEO and Josie, her little furry marsupial, would be all the society Maria had.

Maybe, someday, another Earth refugee ship would find their way here. Davis recognized vain hopes when he saw them. No ship would come here. Nothing would draw anyone here. Hostiles, limited natural resources, a chemically suspect sea, the total lack of any advanced technology, put this planet on a reject list even if the surrounding galaxy was probed. NEW CLEO could emit a regular star signal if Maria chose. He and Kendak had no business messing with her future anymore. They had failed. And they would leave her with no one.

Kendak joined him on the bridge. Both waiting. They hoped Maria came back. Davis wanted to officially bequeath her NEW CLEO.

He watched Kendak startle at a red flash accompanied by the patient beeping of CLEO's drone proximity alarms.

"There are beings in the forest coming this way." CLEO sounded excited but Davis understood that was his own emotion projected on her.

"Are they armed and hostile, CLEO? Is Maria in their company?" Davis croaked, his voice underused in the silent vigil they held these past days.

"Maria is with them. She walks at ease with her marsupial. She is talking with the others. The alien human that walked the mountain trails when we arrived is leading them. I will advance the drones. The hostile alien is not among her party."

CLEO generated a camera feed to their monitors in short order. They saw Maria look up at the drone and wave happily at the camera. She pointed at the drone, catching the attention of a very tall bald man and a young, dark-haired woman who walked beside Maria. Those two waved, smiling as well. Davis wrinkled his brow, puzzled. This was not the reaction to a drone camera he expected from primitives.

The camera flitted across the walking assemblage. Most of the aliens had a headdress on. No. Hmm, not a headdress. Antennae. Yet Maria reached for their arms and patted them with affection on the shoulder.

The group was roughly half a mile away. They headed directly for the ship. Maria seemed happy and at ease. Some of their number carried staffs, but they didn't show weapons. The seedy, hostile man who claimed he would bring Maria to them was definitely not there.

"Oh my dear God, Kendak, I think we should uncloak CLEO. I think Maria is bringing her new friends to her home. We can keep our traps ready. But I think Maria has found the society we wanted for her." Davis looked at Kendak. He knew his own eyes watered too. Kendak nodded. Their desperate search for a home in these last few pages of their lives had indeed delivered to Maria the chance for a new beginning.

"CLEO uncloak. Let's welcome Maria home."

31

CAI

River mist clung to their ankles. Cai gripped Phoebe's elbow too hard, barely felt the weight of Josie in his cloak. Smudge clung to his chest. Great friends already. Josie romped, thieving her way through the Lab before they left. The spoils she couldn't fit in her pouch gifted to Smudge. 'Hairy-baby-in-a-nappie,' was her personal, Smudge-crafted, emoji-name.

"Dr. Doo-Doo," Phoebe whispered. His cloak billowing with all the activity underneath. They floated alongside Maria on the trail leading to her ship.

All Cai saw sparkled bubbles. Maria and Phoebe talking. Soil glimmered; sun pinked the shining faces. He didn't even groan when Phoebe claimed to Maria that his one emerging brow hair was a baby antenna. Gravity abandoned them again.

Outwardly placid faces can't scream excitement. But theirs did. Squeezes, jabs, pokes and secret smiles popped like hot wires between the three. Maria, still frail according to his inner womb-bear, rode their effervescence like a cushion of air.

Out welling joy near burst his heart when Maria rave-waved NEW CLEO's welcoming drone. Cai appreciated CLEO's caution. Her shipmates checked. They needed to know Maria wasn't hostage to Kertof and his troops.

Beaming like a bobble with his family, he was taken unawares. Stepping down into an open mountain valley, Cai looked up just as NEW CLEO uncloaked. And there twinkling monstrously ahead of them, striped insanely pink along her reflective coating, was the largest intact Earth ship he had ever seen.

The Labbites with Taletha and Eric in tow, swooned and dropped to their knees. Justice, Mercy and Herald crossed their arms above their foreheads as though the blaze of NEW CLEO would blind them.

Maria trotted forward in excitement, pulling Phoebe ahead of the others and gesturing to Cai. As the three moved well out in front of their companions, symphony orchestra music bellowed from the ship and Cai looked back to see their alien friends fall prostrate to the ground.

Cai teared, holding his chest where his heart pounded. Maria called the drone close. Telling NEW CLEO she needed to direct-message the ship.

"Kendak, Davis and CLEO, meet Phoebe and Cai. They are descendants of refugees from Earth. Briefly, I need you to ready yourselves. I have an urgent request. Please feign to the aliens that Phoebe is NEW CLEO's captain. That she and Cai are our crew. I will explain when we see you. We are safe. All is well. But we need your help in this simple subterfuge for now." Maria gestured the drone away and then turned back to the Labbites, waving them up and forward.

"This is our ship NEW CLEO," Maria called. "She is singing a welcome to you with music we brought from Earth. Please don't be afraid. She is your friend and protector too. You will be safe with her. Come and see. My shipmates will want to thank you for finding me." Eric, George and Moriah stood and came forward with tiny steps. Maria turned to Eric, "For helping me. For befriending me. Please accept my thanks, and our welcome to you all. See? Even Josie is not afraid." Josie scampered from Cai's cloak, ran ahead and waited for Maria to board.

The remainder stood, slowly. They gathered in a fold like someone pulled a thread through them. Taletha took Moriah's hand. George grasped Eric at the shoulder. Tiny ants facing an elephant, they filed forward to the ship. Like Cai, the aliens held hands to their breast or cheeks. Completely stunned, as much as he, by the apparition. Bent timid by the background swell of an orchestral symphony. He, Maria and Phoebe, pierced through by similar threads, stepped bravely forward, hand-in-hand.

The drone swooped back down toward Maria. "Recalculating. Captain Phoebe, Maria, recalculating. Shipmates, CLEO has detected another group running up behind you," voiced the drone.

"Run that camera feed on the exterior monitor CLEO, so we all can see."

On the face of the ship a large video transmission immediately illuminated aliens thrashing through the forest. As the camera zeroed in on the face in the lead, their friendly native companions collectively gasped. They clearly couldn't understand Brattoch made so large and so near. The camera followed Brattoch running hell-bent along the trail. Sig, Dern and the Labbite youngsters chasing in his wake.

"It's okay," Phoebe muttered into Maria's ear. "Those are our friends who went to waylay that Kertof nutcase."

"These are friends too, CLEO. They were stalling our enemy. They wouldn't lead the enemy here on our trail, so they must have succeeded in their mission. Keep the monitor going. And the music too CLEO. You are providing quite a vision for them." Maria took Phoebe's hand and motioned toward the drone. "Do you agree, Captain?"

"Yes, of course. Thank you, Maria. Thank you, CLEO. Kendak and Davis, Cai and I will be very happy to meet you. Er, to meet up with you again and tell you of all our tales." Phoebe grinned at the camera. Her eyebrows stretched in question above her widened eyes.

"NEW CLEO has missed you Captain. Entirely. See you soon. Davis out." The drone buzzed away.

Phoebe ...

Phoebe shook from head to toe, as she placed a foot upon the old, broken grass and fresh-striped shoots that lined a path to a woven metal step, cutting a perfect cookie in the red ground. She bent forward to shake huge tears from her lashes.

Her eyes swamped. With careful patience, she scraped her jet skates off on the stiff, machine-crafted platform. Maria, excitedly leading her aboard, tugged at her hand.

"Captain on board," announced CLEO.

A ship. Phoebe. An accident that happened? Or selected for her will and for her way by steadfast crew? So she would fly. A nice life, this. Claimed. Future a friend again.

Epilogue

Phoebe sat at the head of NEW CLEO's officer table

"Has everyone said their goodbyes?" All the bright-eyed faces looked at her and nodded. There was Eric, still gulping sadly, after taking leave of George and his family. George chose to stay behind. A lonely Labbite leading the Continent's people. He charged himself with holding the Shorn and Longhairs together in joint community with a shared mission to live sustainably on the Continent. George had help from NEW CLEO. Months of videos played, telling the Continent of better ways, with the hard-won wisdom from Earth. All Earth had left to offer them represented in her demise, her refugees, her video testament to her accomplishments and profound losses, too infinite to count. The word of those who'd been forced to abandon the planet their people destroyed.

Phoebe had already learned much from her new friends here. Like George's thoughts when she told him of her home planet, the Third, desperately seeking other refugees from Earth. As though to rekindle their Earth past, to claim their history as a culture, a future they might still foster in the galaxy.

Instead of looking to reclaim your past, why not define a better future? Perhaps our blending, Reaper with Human, shows one such path. While we evidence the pitfalls of the false politics of biological distinctions, we also prove species integrity is not defined by biology alone. There is integrity in the will to join, to create a common destiny, an unselfish determination. With NEW CLEO's painful wisdom, and our Continent's successful blending of human and Reaper integrity, we look upon a new way to map the destiny of all species whether separate or combined.

Phoebe recalled indulging in some eye-rolling at this point in George's sermon. NEW CLEO was carting off most of the physically distinctive Labbites, so the successful 'blending' was a question.

This message of blended futures constrained by cautions from the bitter lessons of the past, maybe this is the treasure you have found here, Phoebe. You have a new testament and a

345

*blended ship's company to carry it throughout
the stars. You bring this wisdom to those who
might, with selfish-determination, propose to
shape any planet's future. You can prove will
shapes science. Will determines whether we
find harmony or make harmonious all the
voices of the Universe. Biology is destiny only
for the voiceless. I would hope our new species
integrity ensures we seek a voice from all.*

Brave words, Phoebe thought, looking at their sober faces. Earth history proved that common sense and new testaments couldn't hold a candle to the sheer destructive power of competitive human will. But while preaching new testament to the unconverted was a vain enterprise, giving voice to the voiceless seemed a very worthwhile mission to Phoebe and her company. They'd already started that mission. Smudge, Eric, Maria, the aliens in their ship's company, Josie, and even she and Cai, all had a voice in their future now. And George had a new voice too. One of leadership over the Shorn, Labbites and Longhairs, left behind in the fresh pink light of this Red Sun.

NEW CLEO would return to this Continent one day. Hopefully bearing welcome connections to other worlds that might aid the tiny population.

Phoebe was proud of her ship's company. Almost all the Continent's Labbites had joined with enthusiasm. Cai, now chief science officer, led their contingent. His mission to bridge human and Reaper technology put him back in the lead scientist saddle again.

Taletha, Brattoch, Sig and Dern took their places at the officer's table. Like Eric, Mercy, Moriah, and Herald, Richard and Lacy, ship officers taking roles in engineering, logistics, communications, medbay, operations, security and systems management. In these past few months everyone settled into the command structure. Phoebe herself as Captain, and Maria choosing a place as first officer. Each crew member at home with their roles and with NEW CLEO's Old Earth technology.

Her crew so entranced with simple things like the comms devices, the computers and the library of vids, Phoebe could hardly wait to see their faces when NEW CLEO broke free of atmosphere today. Smudge was safely tucked away in his tank. Josie had the run of the ship. For Phoebe their voices too meant family. Smudge was even linked to comms because Cai configured an easy device hook-up for him. He studded everyone's scroll feed with copious embarrassing emojis. Fair enough. They'd taken his sTuffy. It was one of the key pieces of Reaper technology Cai and the Labbites were trying to understand with help from CLEO's libraries.

Phoebe looked at Maria. Maria smiled broadly and clutched Eric's hand. Maria's goodbyes had been unexpectedly easy. She trusted Phoebe, Cai and Eric in ways she'd never experienced with The Three. Her history with Kendak and Davis was clouded by the death of her twin and the bizarre accident that killed most of the ship's company.

Kendak and Davis gave her NEW CLEO in a formal ceremony. But Maria discovered that all along she merely craved a voice in NEW CLEO's direction. She was grateful to have Phoebe take command. She had come alive with her untainted relationships with people like Eric and Cai, Taletha and Mercy. She told Phoebe she finally felt like she had a family she wanted to embrace in every way.

Kendak and Davis on their part, elected to spend their dying days upon the Red Continent fishing contentedly in the rivers. They were safe within George's capable hands. Both looked more spry than when Phoebe first met them. She often saw them totter off to the river together to fish. Lucid kept them company, driving the fish toward their baited lines. Maria was happy to leave them and her past behind her. With Eric, Phoebe, Smudge, Cai and Josie as her new adopted family aboard CLEO, she was finally free to claim a fresh future, a clean slate.

Josie sat in the center of the officer's table. No doubt hoping to score a treat from one of the many officers who spoiled her. Phoebe saw her cradle her bulging pouch. Josie and Smudge traded trinkets these days. Everyone knew to keep tabs on loose valuables. Like a Dickens cutpurse, Smudge and Josie worked in concert to rob their marks. Lost gear was only recovered when Smudge used it to decorate the midden in his tank. They had yet to find Josie's stash, but at least she'd mostly stopped stealing critical ship's parts. CLEO was now rigged with a special theft alarm.

Today was lift-off.

Phoebe nodded as she looked around at their eager faces, not bothering to conceal her own glee. "Batten down CLEO. Start the engines. Come on people. Let's get up to the bridge and strap on our jet skates."

Acknowledgments

My journey as a writer started very early and followed strange pathways. I remember watching my English-lit prof mother squirrel away handwritten notes: *I am trying to write a novel,* she'd say.

I have many people to thank. And most of those would prefer to be anonymous. But my husband Sandy comes first. After 25 years of wild adventures he still continues to support my dreams and inspire my fantasies. I can't believe our luck in finding our together story.

A chance real estate encounter with best-selling author Meghan March pushed me from my mother's *trying to write,* to actually writing and publishing this first book of mine. Meghan is my hero and always an inspiration.

Courtney, Bobby M., Neil, Arlie H., adopted me and nurtured me at some of my most critical moments. I feel gratitude for them every single day of my life.

Can I be grateful to institutions? Because my Ph.D. work at UC Berkeley was utterly transformational. Like it kinda gave me religion. Even now when I walk the campus I feel I walk hallowed halls.

I have so many truly wonderful friends all over the world, Madtoo, Pauline, Penny, Lucy, and new friends in my writer's group: Jani, Eldon, Loye. So many who gifted me with their thoughts and company. Every single one contributed to the joy you find in *Say Hi 4 me*.

Pranada, Bhaktirasa, Raghu and Rachel helped this book come to life and they did so with humor and kindness. Paige Mitchell was so profoundly encouraging as the only one among my family who knew the book was in gestation. Chelsey Mitchell gave me many examples of courage and they both provided frequent hilarious distractions.

No other family or friends knew the book was *trying* to be. But I feel their hope, goodwill and kindness. As Colet always says: *it takes a village*.

About the Author

Amy Tychell is the fictional name of a real person (Dr. A. Mitchell), whose real life rivals Amy's fiction.

She started early. Ambitious to put herself through 15 years of University. A forester, the only female on an all-male crew. Earlier still, a model. A loping Amazon live on radio at 16 boldly challenging broadcasters on their skewed, limiting, sexist views of women.

Addicted to science, to ways of thinking that break the mold. An adventuress, she recounts the enduring hallucinations from being too long on watch in a small sailboat in Force 11 seas. A perfect storm.

Chasing black bears over morning coffee, polar dips in ice-rimmed lakes, a junior member of the Alpine Club at 11 years of age.

A love, Sandy, 25 years and counting. An endless stream of war-torn cats to rescue. They learn English and prove they know by precisely defying every single word.

Fire-fighting. Waving bikini-clad from the Rodeo Float in the Calgary Stampede Parade. Fiction. Not. But fiction, drawing out the irony, the comedy, the sense and power of place and being, is the truest way to share. She is still waiting for maturity to kick in.

If you enjoyed this book, please take a few moments to write a review of it.

Even 3 words profoundly gift life to an Indie author's book

POST A REVIEW NOW

search for "Say Hi 4 Me" at <u>*https://Goodreads.com*</u>

or your favorite Online Retailer

Thank you!